#BOOKTOK AN

KRISTEN CALLIHAN'S

GAME ON SERIES

"Pulse pounding sex and stomach twisting emotion."

—TESSA BAILEY, #1 *NEW YORK TIMES* BESTSELLING AUTHOR, ON *THE GAME PLAN*

"Gray is delicious—sweet and sexy and a more than worthy book boyfriend. Did I mention sexy? *The Friend Zone* is a must read!"

—MONICA MURPHY, *NEW YORK TIMES* BESTSELLING AUTHOR

"I honestly had NO IDEA how much I would end up loving *The Hook Up*! WOW. Wow wow wow!"

—LACEY @LACEYBOOKLOVERS

"I LOOOOOOVE THAT BOOK, the whole series."

—KRISTIE @READ_BETWEEN.THE_WINES

"WOW, this one crept up on me and blew me away."

—S.M. WEST, *USA TODAY* BESTSELLING AUTHOR

"Guaranteed to make you swoon, make you sweat, and make you smile."

—LANA @DIRTYGIRLROMANCE

"In a word, THEHOLYCRAPBOMBYESMOREYES."

—LIA RILEY, *USA TODAY* BESTSELLING AUTHOR

"AN EXQUISITE, DELICIOUS CUPCAKE OF A BOOK." **—SARINA BOWEN**, *USA TODAY* BESTSELLING AUTHOR

THE FRIEND ZONE

Also by Kristen Callihan

Game On series

The Hook Up
The Friend Zone
The Game Plan
The Hot Shot
Only On Gameday

VIP series

Idol
Managed
Fall
Exposed

For additional books by Kristen Callihan,
visit her website, kristencallihan.com.

KRISTEN CALLIHAN

THE FRIEND ZONE

CANARY STREET PRESS

Recycling programs for this product may not exist in your area.

ISBN-13: 978-1-335-01588-4

The Friend Zone

First published in 2015 by Kristen Callihan. This edition published in 2025.

For questions and comments about the quality of this book, please contact us at CustomerService@Harlequin.com.

TM is a trademark of Harlequin Enterprises ULC.

Canary Street Press
22 Adelaide St. West, 41st Floor
Toronto, Ontario M5H 4E3, Canada
CanaryStPress.com

Printed in U.S.A.

This one is dedicated to you, dear reader.

A Note from the Author

The Friend Zone deals with a number of themes, including discussion of cancer, the death of a parent from cancer (off page) and miscarriage.

PROLOGUE

4:13 a.m. Text to Gray Grayson from unknown source.

Unknown: Mr. Grayson, my father tells me he lent you my car. I don't really care if he's going to sign you or not. As said agent's daughter, I know football players and their ways. So let me be clear. There will be no shenanigans taking place in it or you'll answer to me. You want to hook up with one of your women, do it in a bed and not in my car.

Sincerely, Ivy Mackenzie.

GrayG: Hey, Miss Mac. You do realize your car is a bubblegum-pink Fiat 500, right? Even if I could get it up surrounded by all that heinous pink, the car is better suited for Lilliputians. So don't worry, there will be no shenanigans (Shenanigans? Srsly? What are we, 80?) anywhere near the car. I'm not about to pull a hamstring in the pursuit of pleasure.

—Btw, beds are overrated. Branch out a little.

IvyMac: You're schooling me on my use of shenanigans? Really, Mr. Lilliputian? I don't know whether to choke on the hypocrisy or be impressed that you know what a Lilliputian is.

I won't make mention of your pink phobia, and I don't care where you do your business. Just so long as it isn't in my car.

GrayG: Yes, I read. Contain your shock. Or maybe chill. I think you're developing a fascination with my bzness.

IvyMac: Ok. Fine. I was an ass. Of course you read. Read this: one scratch on that car and you bought it.

GrayG: It's a tempting offer. I mean, who wouldn't want this car? I'm assuming you take gumdrops as currency?

IvyMac: Sure do, Cupcake. But the car's not for sale.

GrayG: I see you've discovered my inherently sweet and tasty nature. Wait until you taste my frosting.

IvyMac: Eww… Keep your frosting to yourself!

GrayG: Heh. So why are we having this conversation at 4 in the morning? Don't you sleep?

IvyMac: Sorry. I'm in London. It isn't four in the morning here. Hey, shouldn't you be sleeping? Why are you answering my texts anyway? 😉

GrayG: I don't know. Some previously unknown masochistic need to argue over a powder-puff car?

IvyMac: I always thought tight ends loved pain.

GrayG: Naw, we bring on the pain, Mac. And have awesome asses. Obviously.

IvyMac: Okay, I'm going now.

GrayG: K. Bye.

IvyMac: Bye.

GrayG: See you.

GrayG: Or not. Because you're in London.

IvyMac: Gray?

GrayG: Yep.

IvyMac: Go to sleep.

GrayG: K. Night. Or morning. Or whatever.

GrayG: Mac? Hello? Right. You're gone.

A few hours later…

GrayG: Mac? How do you feel about 18″ chrome rims? Pretty sure when you see the result, you'll love them.

IvyMac: What? You're shitting me, right?!?

GrayG: Foul language, Miss Mac? I am appalled. Keep that up and I'm going to have to call shenanigans.

IvyMac: Gray! What the fuck did you do to my car?!?

GrayG: Ha! Gotcha. You freaked. Admit it.

IvyMac: I admit nothing!! Are you waking me up to terrorize me as payback for waking you up the other morning?

GrayG: Mac, it's 8 p.m. in London. Why are you asleep?

IvyMac: Gotta get up at 3:30 a.m. I'm an apprentice at my mom's bakery.

GrayG: Pastries and shit? Oh, God, I'm having a moment.

IvyMac: Like the sweets, big guy?

GrayG: Are you talking dirty to me, Mac?

IvyMac: *eye roll* Is there a real reason for this text?

GrayG: Guess not. Sorry to bug you. Night, Mac.

IvyMac: You aren't bugging me. I'm just grumpy because I hate getting up early. People say I'm…prickly. I don't mean to be.

GrayG: Prickly? Naw. You're…saucy. Like that sauce on a Big Mac.

IvyMac: If you call me special sauce, you lose a nut.

GrayG: I knew it. You're talking dirty to me! Shenanigans!!

IvyMac: lol. Dork.

GrayG: That's Cupcake to you, Special Sauce. Go to sleep, Mac. I'll get to work on the rims.

IvyMac: 😛

And the next morning…

IvyMac: I was walking down Jermyn Street today. Saw a guy in a bright pink suit, very flash. Thinking of buying you one to match the car. You could make a whole pink power statement.

GrayG: Great! But I'm pretty sure that'd have to be custom-made. Extra-long too. I dress left, btw.

IvyMac: Is it just me, or do you mention one of your body parts in every convo we have?

GrayG: You're the one who brought up my nuts last time.

IvyMac: Only in regard to kicking them.

GrayG: But you're thinking of my nuts. That's the important part. ☺

IvyMac: Sure I am, Cupcake. *pats cheek* Keep dreaming the dream.

GrayG: I knew it!!! You want me bad. It's okay, all women do.

IvyMac: Right.

A bit later…

IvyMac: Why are you borrowing my car, anyway? I find it hard to believe you don't have your own. Is it in the shop? For-like-ever?

GrayG: My best bud Drew (he's our QB) broke his leg. His car has a stick shift. My truck is auto. So I lent him mine and borrowed… The Pink Nightmare.

IvyMac: Gray. That's really nice of you.

GrayG: Told you I was sweet.

IvyMac: You actually are. Totally sweet.

GrayG: Now you're just embarrassing me. I lied. I'm a hardened thug. For realz.

IvyMac: Aw, Cupcake.

IvyMac: Gray?

IvyMac: Hello?

IvyMac: Fine, you're a stone-cold killa. Happy?

GrayG: Yes. Although I'd prefer lady killa.

IvyMac: How about Sir Fucksalot?

GrayG: Hi-larious! Really. Night, Special Sauce.

IvyMac: Night, G-Man. ☺

Several text exchanges after that…

GrayG: I'm bored. Talk to me. Again. Heh. Heh.

IvyMac: Soup has got to be the best thing ever. It's an entire meal in a bowl! But in hot liquid form.

GrayG: Hot liquid form…? Unh. I'm pretty sure you're my dream girl, Ivy Mac. Or did someone tell you that soup was my favorite meal?

IvyMac: You love soup too?!? Soup-lovers' fist bump! Booyah!

GrayG: Booyah! And, baby, I make the best soup you'll ever taste.

IvyMac: Oooh, talk to me, Grayson. Just. Like. That.

GrayG: Marry me, Mac.

IvyMac: Okay, but only for the soup.

A few minutes later…

GrayG: Why is six scared of seven?

IvyMac: Why?

GrayG: Because seven "ate" nine.

IvyMac: Hur! How do you count cows?

GrayG: How?

IvyMac: With a cowculator.

GrayG: So awesomely bad. I think you have to marry me now. No one else likes my jokes.

IvyMac: Good to know my bad taste in jokes is a selling point.

GrayG: It's fucking sexy. I'm actually sporting wood.

GrayG: Mac?

GrayG: Hey, I was kidding. I'm not trying to hit on you, I swear.

GrayG: Mac?!?

IvyMac: I'm here. Sorry! I'm on the tube. Lost you in a tunnel.

GrayG: Okay. Cool. Got worried.

IvyMac: Naw. I know you were just being you.

GrayG: That's me, always joking. Gotta head out to practice. Txt U when I'm done.

Later that day…

IvyMac: I spent the entire morning baking bread and thinking about your name.

GrayG: My name? Honey, if you're going to think about me, concentrate on my gigantic…hands. Magic hands, baby. The things I can do with these hands are mind-boggling.

IvyMac: Like palm balls all day long?

GrayG: 😕

IvyMac: Heh. Heh. Your name is way more interesting than your penchant for ball handling.

GrayG: Har. Gray Grayson is a special kind of torture to inflict on a kid. What can I say? My mom was reading The Pelican Brief right before I was born. Decided to name me after the hero Gray

Grantham. No one could change her mind. I used to hate it. But now I love it because she picked a name she loved.

IvyMac: It's a cool name. Bounces in my head: Gray-Grayson. Gray-Grayson!

GrayG: Hands, Mac. Think about the hands.

IvyMac: Gray-Grayson, grabbing balls with his big, strong hands...!

IvyMac: Helio?

IvyMac: Hello?

IvyMac: Spoilsport.

And a few hours after that...

IvyMac: I can't sleep. Talk to me.

GrayG: Why can't you sleep?

IvyMac: Because it's nine-fucking-thirty. I have to go to sleep early because I have to get up early. Have I mentioned how much I hate getting up early?

GrayG: Aside from the three times in that text? Yeah, a bit. ☺ I run plays through my head when I can't sleep.

IvyMac: Yep. That should do it. I'm glazing over just thinking about it. Thanks, Cupcake.

GrayG: Glad to be of service, honey. You can always count on me.

IvyMac: You're starting to be the first person I turn to. If that freaks you out, tell me. I'll dial it down.

GrayG: What? No. Don't take this wrong, but I've kind of become addicted to your texts.

IvyMac: Me too. Talking to you is like talking to myself. Only better.

GrayG: It's scary that I get that.

GrayG: I feel like I can tell you anything.

IvyMac: You can. That's what friends do.

GrayG: I've never been friends with a girl before.

IvyMac: I'm honored to be your first.

The next morning…

GrayG: So as friends, can I still say inappropriate, sex-related things?

IvyMac: Sure. Think of me as just another guy. With a vagina.

GrayG: A. Impossible. You'd never be "just another guy."

B. Don't bring your V into this.

C. I had this dream that you were sucking my 8==> But when I looked down, I discovered it was actually a goat…you know. Then I really woke up because I yelled so hard, I fell out of bed. And now I live in mortal terror of goats.

IvyMac: LMFAO! Gray got it from a goat!

GrayG: 😠

IvyMac: Goat-on-Gray action! Heeeee! *falls down ded*

GrayG: You suck, you know that?

IvyMac: No, the goat does! *dies again* My sides. My sides!

GrayG: Laugh it up, Chuckles.

IvyMac: Okay. I'm good now. Aw, Cupcake, I'm so glad we're friends. It means a lot to me. I feel safe with you. Like I can be me without worrying about sex getting in the way of things. Or something.

IvyMac: I'm rambling. Ignore me.

GrayG: Honey, your friendship is a fucking gift. Don't ever doubt it.

After a few more texts, and a few hours of going without…

GrayG: So I got into it with Drew. He accused me of trying to fuck his girl. I would NEVER fckn do that. Whatever people think about me, I would die before I did that shit.

IvyMac: I'd never believe that of you, Gray. I'm sorry you're hurt. ☹

GrayG: I'm not hurt. You wouldn't? How do you know for sure? I'm kind of known as a player. Shit, maybe I should call myself Sir Fucksalot.

IvyMac: Stop it. Any guy who crams into a tiny pink car and willingly drives it around town as a favor to his friend wouldn't turn around and stab that friend in the back. Player or not, you're a good guy. And I'm the only one who can call you Sir Fucksalot! 😠

IvyMac: It's okay to be hurt, btw. I'd be hurt if my friend accused me of that. Do you want me to come home and kick his ass? 'Cuz I got skillz. Mad ass-kicking skillz.

GrayG: lol. Not necessary. I know Drew doesn't really mean it. He's going through some stuff with his leg being broken. Just. Okay, yeah, it hurt that he took it out on me.

IvyMac: ☹ {{{{hugs}}}}

GrayG: Ivy, is it weird that I kind of wish you were home? That I kind of miss you?

IvyMac: No. I wish I were there right now. I miss you too.

IvyMac: Okay. About to go into another tunnel. Txt me later, Cupcake.

GrayG: Will do. Thanks for listening, Mac.

Next day…

GrayG: Everything is cool with Drew. He apologized for being a dick. We tossed around the football today. He hadn't touched one in a while, so that was good.

IvyMac: Good. I'm so glad. I know how much he means to you.

GrayG: I'm going over to hang out with him and his girl, Anna. You'd like her. She's saucy too. But, you know, not *special* saucy.

IvyMac: You're risking your nuts, calling me special sauce. Don't think I won't make good on my threat whenever we meet.

GrayG: There you go, talking about my nuts again. One day, we gotta address this fascination you have with them.

IvyMac: Sure, we can address it. And then you can limp away.

GrayG: Empty threats, Mac. You know you couldn't hurt me. You love me too much.

IvyMac: Whatever, Cupcake. Have fun tonight. Helpful party tip: don't mention your nuts <— basic rules of polite society 101.

GrayG: Damn, you're telling me this now? The topic of my nuts has always been my go-to conversational opening. O.o

IvyMac: The more you know, Gray.

GrayG: What would I do without you to guide me?

IvyMac: Best not to think about that, Cupcake.

GrayG: Yeah, the idea is too terrible to contemplate. Stay safe, Ivy. I'll txt later. You gonna be up?

IvyMac: Yes. Don't think I can fall asleep anymore without your nightly text.

GrayG: Miss you.

IvyMac: Miss you too.

A few days and several texts later…

GRAY

IF LIFE HAS taught me anything it's to appreciate what you've got. Take something for granted and it could be gone before you even realized what you had. I learned that lesson from my mom, though I wish every day that I hadn't. One day she was baking me apple cake and reminding me to study after football practice, and the next day she was pulling me into the den to tell me she had cancer.

I remember every word of the conversation. Every fucking word punched into my flesh as if they were nails. But particularly I remember how she ended it: *Live every day to the fullest, Gray. Appreciate* life *to the fullest, promise me that.*

And I have. I still do. Enjoy the moment. Revel in it. Soak up life and fuck the rest.

It's simple, really. I party because it's fun. Enjoy women because I love them. Love their sweet scent, their musical laughter, and their soft curves. Play football because it's the greatest fucking game on earth.

And it's worked for the most part. I've had fun. Only now, living in the moment is getting harder to do. I find my attention wandering to the future. I find myself wanting that distant future now. Because of Ivy Mackenzie.

It's strange. I have friends. Some guys on my team I'm so tight with, I'd throw down for them no matter what the cost. Drew? He's like a brother to me. So why do I feel this intensity in my newfound friendship with Ivy? I'm not sure.

It's only been a little over a week of nonstop texting, but already she's become essential—a bright spot in my life.

Maybe *too* bright: I miss her and want to see her. That's the truth, as weak as it sounds. I don't want to be lying on this bench doing endless reps until my pecs burn and my arms feel like thick, wiggling slabs of raw beef. I want to be face-to-face with Mac, actually have a real conversation with her, take her out for a beer and shoot the shit.

Mac would love it; she's like one of the guys, only better. More fun, maybe? I don't know. I just know I like her. A lot.

I grunt, sweat trickling down my brow and into the corner of my eye, and try to concentrate. But it's hard. The tile ceiling overhead blurs, and I think of my phone in my pocket. The urge to pull it out and text Mac is strong. But I'm supposed to be training, not goofing off. So I push the weight-laden bars up once again and blow out a breath.

Shit. I've lost count. Doesn't matter. I know my limit. And when I'm done, I can text Mac.

As if my thoughts activated it, my phone buzzes against my thigh. I hesitate, weights overhead, my arms quivering. The phone buzzes again. Mac.

I let the weights settle into place with a clank and then heave upward, digging in my pocket for the phone. It isn't a text but an incoming call.

"Yeah?"

"Remind me to work on your social skills, Grayson," says a gruff voice. "Can't be answering like that when scouts are actively checking you out."

It's Sean Mackenzie, Ivy's dad and the man I've decided to sign as my agent as soon as I'm done with my season.

I run a hand through my hair, pushing the sweat-slicked strands off my forehead. "Pretty sure they'll want me regardless of my phone manners, Big Mac."

I reach for a water and guzzle it down.

"Don't be too sure of that, kid. Image is everything."

He's right, of course. Which is why I know I'm making a good decision in choosing him.

"What's up?" I ask, wiping my mouth with my forearm. Big

mistake—I'm sweaty as fuck. Grimacing, I reach for a towel. "Or is this part of some random buff-and-polish-the-client initiative you're testing out on me?"

Mackenzie chuckles. "Smart-ass." Silence and then, "I have a favor to ask."

Surprised, I pause in taking another drink of water. "Shoot."

"It's about Ivy."

Instantly, he has my full attention. I sit up, my heart beating oddly fast. "What about Ivy?"

"I know you two have been *corresponding*—" the word comes out as a sneer "—and we'll be discussing that in detail later, Grayson." He doesn't hide his irritation.

"Uh…"

Yeah, witty reply, but I can't blame Mackenzie for being pissed. Ordinarily, a father has every right to want his daughter far away from me.

"Look, Mackenzie, Ivy and I are friends. She's like a…" I trail off, the cliché stuck in my throat because what I was about to utter isn't the truth.

But Mackenzie finishes it for me anyway. "Like a sister to you. Yeah, yeah, I've heard the same from Ivy."

He has? I guess that's good that she thinks of me as a brother. I dig my fingers into the tense muscles at the back of my neck. "Right, so we're good? Because I got—"

"I'm stuck in New York. A ball player got arrested for a DUI, damn idiot." He sighs. "Anyway, Ivy is coming home from London and is due to arrive at the airport in… Hell. She's probably there already. Her sister has the flu, or I'd send her."

I jump up, knocking the water bottle down with my knee.

"You mean Ivy is sitting at the airport and no one's there to greet her? After a fucking year away from home?" Okay, I'm shouting. But fucking hell, Ivy deserves a better homecoming than that.

And what the fuck? I just texted her last night. She said nothing about leaving London. Why?

Ignoring the weird hurt in my chest, I jog toward the locker room.

"All right, kid," Mackenzie grumbles. "You don't have to rub it in. Could you—"

"I'm already on it. What airline and gate? Do you know that much?"

It's low of me to keep rubbing it in, but fuck. What was Mackenzie thinking? How could he forget his own daughter? And then I'm not thinking of Mackenzie at all. Ivy is home. *Home.*

I'm about to meet her, and I'm totally unprepared.

My heart is racing like it does before a game, that same adrenaline rushing through my veins. I'm no longer thinking about the future, but of Ivy. Getting to her is all that matters now.

ONE

IVY

MOST PEOPLE HATE the airport. I get that. Everyone is in a hurry, hauling around luggage, some afraid to fly, some annoyed by the heinous TSA lines.

And yet, for me, there's an air of excitement to an airport. At least as a traveler. Because either you're going somewhere or you've arrived. For that alone, I love the airport. But my absolute favorite spot? The arrivals gate.

I love those gates. Love watching the people who wait with an almost nervous anticipation for their loved ones to arrive. Love seeing faces light up, people cry out with joy and laughter or even tears when they spot that special person. Mothers, fathers, sisters, brothers, friends, lovers... An endless stream of reunions.

In the years after my parents got divorced, I used to go to the airport and simply sit on one of the cracked pleather chairs and soak it all in. Here, at least, I would see the good side of love.

I'm here again, at the arrivals gate. Only this time, I'm the one arriving. And there's no one here to greet me. No sister. No dad.

After being in a plane for nearly eight hours, my eyes are gritty, my knees ache from being crammed into a too-small space, and I probably stink. It's hard to tell; my fellow travelers kind of stink too, making us one big moving, bleary-eyed unit of airplane funk. Or we were. Now people are picked off one by one as open arms embrace them. I scan the crowd for a familiar face, trying hard not to be disappointed when I don't see one.

Too soon it becomes obvious that I've been forgotten. The crowd thins, and what remains are the people waiting for the next wave of passengers to be cleared through customs.

Clutching the handles of my massive rolling suitcases, I lumber over to an empty seat and make myself comfortable. My phone is out of juice and is a useless black screen.

"Fuck," I mumble, blinking hard before running a hand over my face. I want to speculate why my dad or sister isn't here, but if I do, I might cry. And I'm not crying *here.*

I shouldn't be surprised. Being Sean Mackenzie's daughter means waiting until clients are appeased, crises are averted, and deals are hammered out in ironclad contracts. Given that my dad is one of the top sports agents in the country, there's almost never an empty moment left for me. But you'd think the infamous Big Mac, as the sports world dubbed him, would remember to pick me up. Or, at the very least, ask my sister, Fiona, to get me.

They're just late. They were tied up in traffic. You've been gone for a year. They wouldn't miss your homecoming.

In a minute, I'll get up and search for an outlet to charge the phone and then call Dad. Right now, I don't want to move. I've sat for hours, and I'm suddenly too weak to do anything but slump in a chair.

Worse, without the phone, I cannot appear busy, as if I'm intentionally sitting on my own. I can't scroll through my screen and watch TikTok while pretending it's important business. I can't text Gray, which is ironic since I didn't tell him I was coming home, wanting to surprise him instead. I can only sit in perfect silence as the world moves past me.

Travelers walk in several distinct paces: brisk, trudging, and harried—the last usually reserved for families. Viewed as a whole, these paces set a rhythm that's almost hypnotic. Maybe that's why I notice the lone person bobbing along at top speed from far down the massive corridor. A guy. And he's running.

Idly, I watch him. He's easily a head taller than anyone in the airport, which is something in and of itself. Even from this distance, his face hovers above the moving sea of people. Though I can't distinguish his features, it's clear that he's anxious. And he's fast, weaving around slower-moving passengers with an ease that's impressive for someone so tall.

He's closer now, close enough that I can see his broad shoulders and wide chest. Close enough to see the gold glints in his dark blond hair as he runs past a thick block of sunlight shafting in through the plate-glass windows.

All at once, my breath grows fast and my heart trips. A smile pulls at my face as I rise to my feet. I want to hope, want to believe.

His gaze, hard and determined, is on the arrivals gate.

God, but the way he moves—fast water over smooth stones. People stop and stare as he goes by. How could they not? Massive, muscled, yet perfectly proportioned and at ease within his skin, he's clearly an athlete. And he's gorgeous. Strong jaw, chiseled features, golden skin, and sun-kissed hair.

He blows right past me, only to stop on a dime at the edge of the cordoned-off area of the arrivals gate. For a minute, he scans left and right, his gaze never going far enough to meet mine. Then he bends over, bracing his hands on his knees, and curses under his breath. He isn't winded, but upset. It's clear.

He curses again, pushes himself straight, and then starts to pace, as if standing still is too much for him.

Muttering and scowling, he stalks a wide circle, bringing his hands behind his neck in aggravation. The move does crazy things to his biceps, bunching them up, making them even bigger. I doubt I could get my hands around them. Though I imagine trying.

And all the while, I grin like a fool. I can't help myself; he's just so cute. I'm still grinning when his gaze finally collides with mine.

Distracted as he is, his eyes almost scan past me, but he sort of stutters and then freezes. For a moment we stare at each other. His soft mouth parts and his arms slowly lower. Recognition clears the haziness from his blue eyes, and a flush of color rises up his neck.

A current crackles between us, lifting the tiny hairs along my arms. My breath catches then turns swift.

This is joy, unfiltered and pure. And so heady I almost don't know how to handle it.

As if he feels some strong emotion too, his cheek twitches. He takes one step toward me, then pauses, tilting his head to peer at me as though trying to make sure.

I smile wider. Seeing me smile has his lips curling, a slow, tentative move.

"Mac?"

Although he's at least twenty feet away, I read my name on his lips with ease. And then I'm laughing, a total goofball snort.

"Gray."

Even from a distance, he hears me. And then he's moving, so fast he's almost a blur. On the next breath, I'm enveloped by a wall of hot skin and hard muscles.

He gathers me in his arms and swings me around like it's effortless. For the first time in a year, I feel delicate and small. He smells of sunlight and sweat and, strangely, of home. I press my nose into the warm crook of his neck, as he laughs and squeezes me tight.

We've never touched before now, never even seen each other in person. Yet there is nothing awkward about wrapping myself around him. It feels perfect.

Gray's hand engulfs the back of my head as he holds me close. "Holy shit," he says in a voice that's resonant and yet light with happiness.

We've been texting back and forth so much I had to pay extra on my phone plan, and I've never heard his voice until now.

"It's you, Mac. It's really you."

And it's really Gray. The person I've communicated with almost nonstop since that first text. So quickly, he became a friend, a necessary part of my day. My strange addiction. The thought leaves me shy. Yet I don't want to let go.

GRAY

I can't believe I'm holding her in my arms. Ivy Mackenzie. Aside from Drew, I've never clicked with someone so quickly. Now she's here.

And, God, she feels good. Solid, real. Soft, warm. She smells of airplane food, stale coffee, and travel. Not the best scent. But beneath that, there's a hint of something sweetly feminine, like sugar and vanilla. I draw it into my lungs and feel a stab of alarm because it's going to my head—the smaller, greedy one. Not the way I want to think of my best girl. And if she notices my reaction, I'll feel like a dirty perv.

I should let her go. Take a step back. But a sudden and not-altogether-unexpected shyness hits me. What if it isn't like before? What if now that we're face-to-face everything turns awkward? I've never had a close female friend. Never really wanted one.

Part of me doesn't want to let her go because then we'll have to talk, to look each other in the eye. Another part of me just wants to hold her because it feels so damn good—perfect. But I can't stand here forever. Eventually, she'll want to be let down. Only she's clinging to me too. Her long limbs wrapped up around mine. Maybe she's just as nervous.

The realization gives me the courage to ease my grip and let her slide down my length.

She doesn't go far. She's tall. Amazonian tall. I didn't expect that. But I like it. I'm six foot six and two hundred and fifty pounds of muscle, which means girls are usually dwarfed by my size. I'm constantly having to bend down to so much as wrap an arm around them, let alone get a kiss. And fucking them? I worry about crushing some girls. Literally.

But Mac? She's got to be around six feet tall. The top of her head fits nicely under my chin. And she's not a twig either. Just a perfect run of long limbs and soft, sweet curves.

Shit. I'm ogling her. I take another step back and meet her eyes. I can't help but smile. I'm so fucking happy to see her, it's a little scary.

"I'm sorry I didn't recognize you," I tell her, still nervous. "You look…different from the picture your dad has on his desk."

It's the only one I'd seen of her.

Mac's blunt little nose wrinkles in disgust. "God, not that one of me at fifteen?"

"Pretty sure that's the one." I'm trying not to laugh, but it's hard.

Her scowl grows. "That's a horrible picture. I'm going to kill Dad for leaving it out in the open."

I don't blame her. She was a round-faced, braces-wearing teen in that picture. In my mind, I'd still viewed her that way: chubby cheeks, button nose, big brown eyes.

The reality is different. Her eyes are still big and brown beneath almost straight brows, but the baby fat is gone. Her cheeks are high and defined, her jaw a smooth curve. And, no, I didn't think she'd still have straggly hair pulled back tight in a barrette. Or maybe I did—but it's not straggly or pulled back.

Her glossy dark brown hair comes to rest just above her shoulders, with a strong sweep of bangs over those eyes of hers.

I gravitate toward women who wear their hair long and flowing, but Mac's cut is kind of sixties retro.

My girl, I realize, is hot. Not obvious, sex-kitten hot, but girl-next-door, I-gotta-know-what-she's-hiding-under-that-shirt kind of hot.

No. Not going there. I'm just proud, is all. Mac won't lack for attention.

Frowning, I bend down to take hold of her luggage. "Let's get you home."

We fall into an easy pace, her long legs keeping time with mine, which is so novel to me that I find myself relaxing into my natural stride, not the shortened steps I usually take around women.

I can't seem to stop looking at her. It's weird: every line and curve of her is utterly new to me and yet familiar in some bone-deep way. It makes me think of amicable numbers. Each one is capable of summing up the other.

Fuck, this girl is already turning me into an emotional sap. But it doesn't make me any less happy.

"Your dad sends his apologies."

"I just bet," she mutters, hurt and anger simmering beneath the surface.

I feel like shit for her, and more than a little pissed at Big Mac for putting that hurt in her eyes.

"He was stuck—"

"Taking care of a client," she finishes for me with a wave of her hand. "I know." A small sigh leaves her. "I'm used to it, believe me."

I do. Doesn't make it any better, though. It makes me even more pissed off at her dad.

"I'd have been here on time, but ah..."

Hell, I don't want to tell her that I'd only just gotten the call to pick her up. But she figures this out on her own, and her mouth tilts in a smirk.

"So I'm guessing he hit up Fiona. Only Fi was out, so he begged you." Her brows draw together. "What's Fi's excuse, do you know?"

"Puking her guts out, apparently. He said she has the flu."

"Oh." Mac's annoyance visibly deflates. "Poor Fi."

She pronounces it "fee" instead of "f-eye."

I haven't met Mac's younger sister. I know she goes to a local all-girls college, where I'd trolled for chicks during my freshman and sophomore years. But I'm not telling Mac that. She already gives me grief for being a "manslut."

Stupid term. Personally, I prefer "equal-opportunity fuck master." Again, not telling Mac that.

"You don't mind, do you?" I ask as we make our way out into the bright sunshine. Fresh air mixing with jet and bus fumes assaults my lungs. "Me picking you up?"

"No," she says quickly, maybe too quickly. "Why would I mind?"

I shrug, sidestepping a businesswoman booking it into the terminal. "You didn't tell me you were coming home."

Until the words are out of my mouth, I don't think I'd realized how much that stings.

It's worse when she grimaces. "Yeah, I know..." She stares down at her red Chucks as she walks. "I should have told you. I just..."

"Ivy," I warn.

Saying her real name for the first time is intimate in some strange way, and I don't know how I feel about that.

"Okay, okay," she hurries on. "It was shitty. I just. Fuck it."

She glances at me and there's steel in that look, as if she's bracing herself. "I wanted to, of course I did. I planned to surprise you tomorrow. But, I dunno, I was afraid too. What if it got all—"

"Awkward." I start to smile, and my step grows lighter.

Especially when she smiles back at me, her apple cheeks going rosy. "You worried too?"

"Well, yeah. I mean, what if you didn't like me in person? We've been so close..." I trail off, strangled by my own discomfort. And *now* it's fucking awkward. *Brilliant.*

She solves this by slinging an arm around my waist and giving me a hug. The action sends warmth straight through my veins, and I find myself leaning into her embrace.

"I'm glad you're here, Gray." Her fingers press into my side. "Really glad."

I've just officially met Ivy Mackenzie, and I realize I've missed her for what seems like years.

"Me too."

TWO

IVY

EVEN THOUGH IT'S my car, I ask Gray to drive. And, shockingly, he doesn't simply accept that as his manly due.

"You sure?" He dangles the keys off the tip of his long finger as if waiting for me to snatch them up.

"I'm liable to drive us off the road right now. Chauffeur me, sir."

"Well, then." He unlocks the door for me and opens it with a sweeping gesture. "Your pink chariot awaits, madam."

Ah, my little pink Fiat. I've missed her. Gray hates the car, and I get that. He's way too big for it. Proven by the way he's got the seat rolled back as far as it can go, and yet he still has to cram himself behind the wheel while muttering curses.

For weeks I've tried to envision Gray driving this car. Nothing does the reality justice. His hard-packed muscles bunch and twitch, his wide shoulders hunch, and his long legs bend awkwardly. The steering wheel looks delicate under his big hands.

"Oh, this is so awesome," I say, barely holding in my snickering.

Gray turns to glare at me, but his eyes are smiling. "This is why you wanted me to drive, isn't it?"

"Partially. You just look so cute." I give his cheek a tweak.

He bats my hand away with a short laugh. "Little punk. I swear to God, I'm gonna find a way to get you back."

"I'm terrified. Truly."

We're soon driving down the highway. Despite Gray's cramped position, he maneuvers the car with ease. I can imagine him on the field, those quick reflexes of his working in perfect tandem with his body. It must be a beautiful sight.

I've wanted to view footage of his games, but just as I've feared seeing his picture, so have I feared watching him play. Some part of me understood that, if I knew those things, I might have become too shy, too enamored of his talent.

I roll the window down a bit, and cold, asphalt-tinged air blows in. "I've missed the scent of America."

He glances at me. "America has a scent?"

"Yeah. Don't ask me to describe it, but it does. England has a scent too."

I lean my head against the headrest and watch the world pass by. "Cars feel different when they're driving on the other side. Do you know how long it took me just to figure out which way to look for traffic when crossing the street?"

The feeling of homecoming sinks further into my bones. "I loved being in England. But now that I'm here, I realize how much I missed home."

Gray's forearm brushes my knee as he reaches for his iPhone dock. He fiddles with his song selection before sitting back. Tom Petty's "American Girl" floods the space. Gray gives me a cheeky grin, and I return it.

"Only half-American," I say. "My mom's a Brit."

He chuckles. "Noted."

For the entire song, we don't speak but simply drive. It's both odd and entirely normal. I have so much that I want to say to Gray now that we aren't limited by texting. But it can wait. Something about him puts me at ease enough to just enjoy the moment.

"Can I ask you something?" he says when the song ends.

"When someone says that it's usually because they're about to insult you."

The corners of his eyes crinkle in good humor. "Fair enough. And my question will probably be construed as insulting."

"Mmm." I fight a smile. I can't help it; driving down the highway with Gray just makes me happy. "Go ahead then. But beware, I bite when provoked."

"Promises, promises." He grips the steering wheel, the ropey muscles in his thick forearms bunching. "Why did your dad get you this car? Don't get me wrong, it's got great styling for what it is and handles well. But I mean, you've got to be what?" Pink races up his cheeks as his gaze travels over my legs. "Six feet tall?"

He had to bring it up. Of course he did. I don't think I've met a guy who hasn't remarked on my height. But I act unaffected.

"Hey, I'll have you know I'm a petite five foot twelve."

Gray grins wide at my joke. It's a good look for him. Lines bracket his mouth. They're kind of like dimples but longer. Just as irresistible, though.

"Cute," he says, changing lanes with confidence. "So, Little Miss Five-Twelve, why the clown car?"

I sigh and lean back against the seat, trying to find room for my legs. "I think my dad still sees me as his baby girl. And compared to him, I am small."

"Shit, I'm small compared to your dad," Gray says easily.

He's exaggerating, but not by much. Dad has a few inches on him. Before my dad was an agent, he played center in the NBA. He might have gone into coaching, but Dad always liked the kill of the deal better than the stress of the game.

"Okay, but pink? It really doesn't seem like your color," Gray says with a pointed look at my clothes.

I'm wearing black skinny jeans, a white vintage The Cure concert tee, and red Chucks.

No, I'm not much for pink.

"There's also the problem that he often confuses me with Fiona. As in, one Christmas I got Fi's coveted Barbie Dream Townhouse, and she got my much-desired make-your-own-alien kit." I shrug. "Now it's cars. I'm stuck with a pink Fiat that I can barely squeeze into and little five-foot-three Fi's swimming around in a black Acura MDX."

"Shit." Gray shakes his head. "That sucks, Mac."

"The only consolation is that Fi is equally miffed."

"Why don't you guys just exchange cars?"

The million-dollar question.

I thrum my fingers against the windowpane. "First off, he bought us cars. How many kids can say that? We knew how lucky we were in that regard. And we didn't want to hurt Dad's feelings. Despite his faults, he'd be mortified if he realized his blunder. Dad tries, you know? He's just…kind of clueless when it comes to us."

Gray nods, but there's a sadness in his expression that says he's got no idea what it means to deal with a caring-yet-misguided parent.

Until now, we haven't talked about family. I refrained because Gray plans to sign my dad as his agent.

Not wanting to bring down our happy mood, I lighten my tone. "Besides, I'm used to my little powder puff now. And just think—" I give his hard side a nudge with my elbow. "I'd never have seen you crammed into it if Dad had gotten it right."

Gray laughs before ducking his head a bit. "Oh yeah, sure, that's worth all the pain."

"You know it, baby."

His blue eyes flash with humor and slide over me before returning to the road. "And we might not have met."

Something swells between us, warm and tender. It gets me all sentimental, the very thought of not knowing Gray making me weepy. Or maybe I'm overtired.

Gray clears his throat. "Where am I taking you?"

"City Diner."

When he raises a brow in surprise, I give him a look that must be bordering on feral. "I'm craving a heaping bucket of crispy fried chicken with a side of biscuits like you wouldn't believe."

"And she eats," he says to the car. "A girl after my own heart."

"Just drive, Cupcake."

"Easy now, Special Sauce, I'll get you your chicken."

He's grinning as he rolls down the window and turns up the radio once more. Wind whips through my hair and music pumps through the speakers. Happiness floods my veins, as light and fizzy as champagne. It's good to be home.

When I graduated high school I knew exactly where I was going: off to Sarah Lawrence to soak up college life. The prospect excited me so much I was packing my trunks while still wearing my graduation cap and gown.

All through college, I kept my head down, nose to the grindstone, and finished a year early for my efforts.

Now college is over, and I feel adrift. The friends I made have been flung to the four winds, all of them taking that next step in their lives. It's a lonely business graduating. So lonely that I understand why many people automatically enroll in grad school to feel that sense of camaraderie once more.

But I need an academic break for now. And I'm no longer lonely. I'm here with Gray, who seems to fill up the space around him—literally, because he's freaking huge, but also with his energy, like he's his own solar system, a swirling vortex of planets and stars and suns.

He's comfortably slouched in the booth where we're sitting, his long arm draped over the back of the seat. Sunlight glints in his dark blond hair, and there's a small smile playing on his lips.

"What?" I ask before taking another bite of fried chicken. A moan *may* have slipped free. I've been craving real fried chicken for ages, crispy, golden, juicy, tasty. In short, heaven.

Gray full-on grins. "Just like watching you enjoy the hell out of that chicken."

"You make that sound illicit."

"You're making it look illicit."

I'm about to tell him to piss off, in the nicest possible way of course, when he pushes his sleeves up to his elbows and something on his inner forearm catches my eye.

"Hey, what's this?" I grab his wrist and gently turn it to fully see the tattoos gracing his skin from wrist to inner elbow. They're mathematic symbols done in indigo ink.

Gray stiffens a bit, taking a sharp breath. But he lets it out easily and answers with a light voice.

"That one there—" he gestures with his chin to the bit I'm tracing with my fingertips at his wrist "—is called Euler's identity." His blue eyes meet mine. "How well do you know mathematics?"

I grimace. "I got up to calculus because it was a major requirement. But I passed thanks to sheer will and short-term memory devices. You might as well be speaking in tongues with this stuff."

Gray gives me a quick, understanding nod. "Okay, then in the shortest sense, mathematicians often refer to Euler's identity as the most beautiful mathematical equation in the world because of its elegant simplicity and because it links what we call the five fundamental constants, or fields, of mathematics."

"I'll take your word for it." I stroke a finger along the equation, then trail up to another tattoo—a long number sequence full of fractions and letters and a bunch of things that look like gobbledygook to me. "And this?"

"Ah, that's a basic proof for Euler's formula." He eyes me with amusement. "I could explain it but—"

"That's okay," I say quickly, and he chuckles.

Slowly I stroke the tattoos. They're beautifully done, the script elegant, almost feminine in some way. And though the proofs and equations are thrown down in a haphazard fashion, there's a surety to them, as if the whole thing was written free-flow without pause.

"I didn't know you were into math."

Gray's skin prickles, the fine golden hairs on his forearm lifting as I reach his inner elbow.

"It's just something that comes easily to me," he says with a shrug. "For my mom too. She could have gone into any field—physics, engineering. But she loved history and theoretical study so she ended up being a math historian. Euler was an eighteenth-century mathematician and physicist, a genius. Mom kind of had a thing for him."

I grin. "That's cute."

Gray leans closer to me. Our heads nearly touch as both of us look at his tattoos.

His voice is almost a whisper it's so soft. "She, uh… She died."

My breath hitches. "When?" The idea of him hurting over the loss of his mom, and me not being there for him, makes my stomach hollow out.

"When I was sixteen. Breast cancer." His throat works on a swallow. "She was in a lot of pain toward the end. I'd sit with her, hold her hand."

His thick lashes lower, hiding his eyes from me. "She needed that physical contact. But she was in so much pain. She needed more of a distraction than holding my hand."

Gray's broad chest lifts and falls as he regains control. He swallows hard, and I rest my hand on his arm, holding steady.

"One day, I took a pen and told her to give me a lecture. She used to do that with me, expound on the beauty of mathematical theory through proofs, functions, and equations." He laughs, unsteady but fond. "My bedtime stories."

Gray's hand curls into a fist, and the muscles in his arm bunch. "She drew on my arm. Every time. I'd clean it off, and she'd start all over again. These tattoos. They were her last… I had someone ink over her writing. To keep it."

"It's beautiful." I don't think, just lift his arm and press a gentle kiss to his soft skin.

His forearm tenses, and I find him staring at me with wide eyes. Pain resides there, and a sort of longing too. I recognize it in myself—that need to have someone understand how empty life can feel, as if you're the only one in your universe.

Gray holds my gaze for another second then clears his throat. "Shit, Mac, you're going to have me bawling like a baby soon." He gives me a lopsided smile.

Returning his smile, I let him go and lean back in my seat. "So, incredibly complex math is easy for you, huh? You never told me your major."

I'm thinking it's not what I was expecting.

Gray's gaze slides away and he takes an extra-big bite of chicken. "Mechanical engineering and nanotechnology," he mutters around a mouthful.

I choke on my drink.

"Holy shit," I say when I can breathe again. "How the hell did you have time to double major in those fields and still excel at football?"

He shrugs then slouches down further in his seat. "Added nano to keep things interesting."

"Because you were breezing through mechanical engineering?" I squeak.

He fiddles with his napkin. "Yeah, well… Like I said, it's kind of easy for me. And I really wanted to learn more about nanotechnology. Do you know the cool shit that's coming out of that field? When you get into the hierarchical architectures of nanostructures—"

He stops abruptly, his face a little flushed as if he's afraid he's rambling. He is, but I love it.

"You could have gone to any Ivy League school, couldn't you?" I ask.

"This university has the best football program in the country and a very decent physics department," he says with a small shrug. "No big deal."

Stumped by the way he obviously wants to hide his intelligence, I stare.

He scowls, his big hands curling into fists on the table. "Aren't you going to ask why I risk playing a dumb jock's game when I could be more?"

"I wouldn't ask that. I know there are highly intelligent men who play football."

He relaxes a little, then runs a hand through his bright hair. "I'm sorry. I am touchy. I don't like the extra attention. I mean, I'm freaking six-six. I'm a star player on a championship-winning team. I get enough as it is without questions about my IQ." He laughs, but it isn't amused. "Anyway, I love football. I love mathematics and science. This way, I get both. And if football doesn't pan out, I know I'll have a good future lined up in nanotechnology."

"Understatement of the year, Cupcake." I give his foot a nudge with my own, and he relaxes further.

"So what you up to now that you're home, Ivy Mac?"

We've talked about so many things, but for some reason not our plans for the future. Somehow Gray and I have a relationship focused on the present. I think it was easier for us to simply enjoy each other. But when faced with having to tell him my plans, unease bloats in my belly. I've mapped out my life, but right here and now I don't want to look at the paths that I've drawn.

I wipe my hands on a napkin before taking a long drink of

lemonade. "Technically, I'm not home. You know how for the last year I've been with my mom, learning how to run one of her bakeries?"

Mom is a first-class baker. She owns and runs three highly successful bakeries around London. Her specialty is breads and cakes.

Gray nods, and I flex my hand, my fingers suddenly shaky and cold.

"In the spring, I'll return to London and take over her bakery in Notting Hill."

Aside from her Chelsea location, it is her most lucrative store. Letting me run the place is a huge responsibility, and a huge display of trust.

Absolute silence greets me. Gray frowns as if he hasn't heard me, but then he clears his throat. "You're leaving again? To live in London?"

"Yeah."

Sunlight hits the side of his face, highlighting the strong lines of his nose and jaw as he turns to look out the window. The curve of his lower lip plumps before he presses his mouth into a line. And then he's looking at me. "When are you going back?"

"March." My fingers curl around the greasy napkin in my lap. "I majored in business. I've always liked baking. It all fits. And this way, I can spend more time with my mom. She was so happy to have me with her this past year."

He nods, not looking at me but at the ruin of chicken bones scattered in the red plastic basket before him.

"That's good, Mac. Really…good." He gives himself a little shake, then lifts his head.

His smile is wide, carefree. It might be forced. I don't know. I only feel this weird sense of loss and guilt. But he doesn't let me wallow.

"So we have a few good months before you take the baking world by storm. What are you going to do here?"

I let myself relax against the booth seat. "I'm going to hang with Fiona. Dad is living here too for the time being. He has an apartment in New York City and a house in LA, but Dad has always been overprotective of Fi and doesn't trust her to be on her own."

Gray frowns, pausing before taking another bite of chicken. "But he doesn't worry about you?"

"Naw, I'm like rubber, always bouncing back. Fi's the fragile one." I shrug. "It's always been that way. 'Don't worry about Ivy; she's the steady one.' 'Protect Fi's feelings at all costs; she'll break if you don't.' Frankly, it's bullshit. Fi and I are more alike than not. But that's how our parents see us."

"I get that," Gray says. "It's what parents do. 'You see us as you want to see us. In the simplest terms, in the most convenient definitions.'"

"Did you just quote *The Breakfast Club* to me?" I ask, amused.

"Good catch." He grins, which draws my attention back to his mouth. It's lush, sweetly curved yet still masculine. Even when relaxed, his lips hold a smile. "So you're going to live with Fiona?"

"Yep. Fi's living in the guesthouse behind my dad's house. I'll stay with her."

Gray sputters on his drink. "Wait. Your dad has a house big enough to include a guesthouse, but you two won't live with him?"

"Fi refuses to live with Dad. But she loves the guesthouse so..." I shake my head. "I know. We're odd ducks."

"You're a cute duck." Gray reaches out to muss my hair. His touch is warm, familiar in attitude, yet a completely new thing for me. I can't help but stare at him, much as I've done since he picked me up.

He catches my look and simply grins. "I know."

"What do you know?" My voice has gone oddly soft, warmth and happiness spreading through me.

Pink washes over his cheeks as he leans forward, bracing his forearms on the table. And I notice another thing about him—his body is always moving in some fashion.

"Okay, this is probably going to sound insulting," he says. "But it isn't meant to be."

"Already, I'm totally reassured," I deadpan.

He grimaces, but doesn't hold back. "When I was sixteen, I bought my first car. My truck. It was a piece of shit 1983 Ford F-100."

"Not liking the sound of this, but go on."

A smile grows on his face. "It was a junker, but I could imagine what she'd look like someday."

"She?"

"Yeah, she. Would you pay attention to the story, Mac?"

"Sorry." I'm grinning. "Go on."

"So I spent the summer at Drew's house, fixing it up with the help of Drew and his dad. John Baylor was awesome that way. He'd oversee, teach me and Drew what we needed to do, but left it up to us to learn.

"We rebuilt the engine, fixed the body, found a new interior for her. Day came that the truck was done."

Gray's expression turns inward. "God, she was perfect, shiny black with a cream interior. I sat in my truck all day, just looking at her lines, running my hands over the leather bench seat. I couldn't stop staring." His eyes meet mine. "Because the dream was finally real."

My throat constricts, and I swallow hard. "Cupcake..."

Gray flushes deeper pink, and he picks at the edge of our chicken basket. "It's corny, I know. But I thought of that." His gaze flicks up to mine. "You're finally here, and I can't seem to stop staring."

Suddenly it's too much. The squiggly red lines of the retro Formica table blur as I blink down at it.

"Shit," Gray mutters. "I shouldn't have said that. It was a compliment, I swear. I'll take it back if—"

"Don't you dare," I snap, lifting my head to give him a fierce look. "It was the nicest thing anyone has ever said to me."

His smile is lopsided and a bit unsure. "Then we're going to have to work on improving that record."

I know he's trying to lighten things up, and he probably regrets telling me that story. I kind of regret it too, because he's turned me into a ball of mush.

Staring back at this insanely gorgeous, sweetly thoughtful man who is now my friend, I feel a twinge of loss. From early on, I'd put him firmly in the friend zone, not wanting to develop deeper feelings for a guy I know is a player and treats me like his best pal. And that was okay, because I want Gray's friendship. I cherish it.

Only now I wonder if I've made a mistake. Would we have been more than friends if I hadn't drawn that line in the sand?

But what-ifs don't matter; we're friends now, and there is no way I'd risk ruining that by dreaming of more. Besides, in a few months I'll be back in London with a whole ocean between us.

Smiling back at Gray, I discreetly put a hand to my aching chest and try to press that sense of loss away.

THREE

IVY

WHEN GRAY PULLS into the circular drive of my dad's home, he lets out a slow whistle. "That's some house."

It's a monstrosity. One of the new Southern mansions that attempts to look like a chateau but uses sandstone brick and terracotta tiles and has an obvious newness about it that will never fade into gentility.

I know it pisses my dad off that we refuse to live in it, but he's rarely home and the place literally echoes when you walk inside. Fi and I are holding out hope that he'll take the L and find himself a nice townhome more suitable to our small family.

I stare up at the house. "Sometimes, when I look at this place, I feel like the biggest asshole."

Gray's laugh is startled. "Why?"

"I know how many people would kill to live here. And I don't want it. I hate the place. And I don't know… I feel like an ingrate."

He tilts his head to get a better view of the house. "I don't know, Mac. There's a house, and there's a home. That doesn't look particularly homey to me."

"But I shouldn't complain. I've lived my life completely cosseted. I take the money my parents give me and have never needed to support myself. What kind of person does that make me?"

"My friend." He crosses his big arms over his chest and gives me a hard look. "So don't go beating up on her. Hell, Mac, you worked your butt off and graduated a year early. It isn't as if you're going around partying and blowing through money. You want to know what pisses me off?"

"What?" I ask with a small smile, because he's cute when he's irate and his brows are inching toward his hairline.

"All our lives, we're told work hard, strive for more, do all you can to live that life less ordinary. Money, power, fame, everyone wants it. But you get there, and suddenly you're supposed to be ashamed, be humble?" He shakes his head. "Fuck that noise. I say live your life on your terms. If someone judges you about material things, that's their problem."

I set my hand on his arm where the muscles are thick and bulging beneath his warm skin. "Then that's what I'll do."

"Damn straight," he mutters, still worked up. "And no more feeling shitty for things given to you by people who love you."

"Okay."

He huffs, not looking at me but drumming his fingers on the pink steering wheel. "Where am I taking you, then?"

"Head toward the portico next to the garage. We're back there."

Gray drives to the rear of the property and the little guesthouse appears.

"This is home," I say. "Or as close to it as we have in the area."

It looks like a gamekeeper's cottage, with mullioned windows and a peaked roof.

The house is raised from the ground, and a set of stairs leads up to the front door.

"Now, that looks like a home," Gray says, sounding pleased.

As soon as we step out of the car, Fi opens the front door. Her skin has a greenish tinge but she's smiling wide. "Well, well, well. Look at what the cat dragged in."

Petite and lithe, with short pale blond hair and big green eyes, my sister is like a big-mouthed Tinker Bell.

I've missed the hell out of her.

"Hey there, Fi-Fi," I call up with a grin.

"Ivy Weed." She shifts from foot to foot, as if she wants to race down the stairs and launch herself at me. Which would be our customary greeting, complete with hugs and kisses. But clearly, she's too ill to do that now.

Her gaze leaves me and settles on Gray. I almost laugh at the way her mouth falls open and she stands straighter.

"Fiona, this is Gray Grayson."

Gray, who has been hauling my luggage out of the trunk, turns and gives her a smile. "Hey. I've heard a lot about you."

Fi clears her throat. "Likewise. Although it looks like my sister left out some pertinent parts. I'd come say hello properly, but you should probably stay well away from me at the moment."

She grimaces as if she's just realized that she's standing in the doorway wearing her fuzzy pink robe and slippers that look like SpongeBob's head.

"In fact," she says faintly, "I'm going to lie down now. I'll see you in a few, Ivy."

I get a nice, hard glare before Fi practically runs away.

"She's mortified," I tell Gray as we head toward the house. "Fi never wants any guy to see her in anything other than full-on makeup."

"She's cute as a button," Gray says happily.

I'd be worried, but he doesn't look interested in Fi, which is a relief. I've been friends with guys who have panted over Fi. It never ends well.

The house is open concept with a living room in the center and a dining nook and an L-shaped kitchen to one side. Fi's redecorated since I'd last been here. Now the walls are chocolate brown, the couches big and covered in cream-colored fabric. A distressed-wood coffee table sits between them, and sepia photographs of cityscapes hang in a grid pattern along one wall.

"Fi's majoring in interior design," I tell Gray as I set my purse on the hall console that looks like it was once a pharmacist's cabinet. "I'm thinking she charmed my dad out of a few dollars."

"It's nice." His eyes scan the room. "Kind of reminds me of Drew's place. But, you know, more professionally done."

"I'd give you a tour," I tell him. "But I want to scrub down the area first."

Gray sets my bags to the side. "Yeah, I'm not going to stress your sister any more than I've already done. I'll just leave you here."

For a moment, we stare at each other. I don't want him to leave. Maybe he doesn't want to go. It's a strange feeling, as though I'll lose him if he walks out the door. Which is ridiculous. Perhaps that's why I launch myself at him and wrap my arms around his neck in a fierce hug.

"Sorry," I tell his shoulder, because I don't want to let go. "I'm just so happy to finally be with you."

And then I realize that he's hugging me back. His arms are tight bands around my waist, his body pressed to mine.

He kisses the top of my head. "Me too, Ivy Mac."

I make a production out of smoothing his rumpled shirt before stepping back entirely. "I better go and see to Fi."

The corners of his eyes crinkle as he brushes my chin with his knuckle. "Call you later, okay?"

He hesitates for just a moment more. And then he's gone, leaving the house in utter silence.

That is, until Fi lets out a pitiful moan. "Can I come out now?"

I laugh. "No. Stay put. I'll come find you."

"I'm in your room. Puking on your bed because you didn't warn me that you were bringing a hot guy home, you fuckface."

Our rooms flank each side of the living space, mine closer to the kitchen. I head that way with a grin. "I'm sorry! Really, I am."

"Sure, sure." Fi's voice grows clearer as I enter my room.

I stop and take it in with shocked awe. Because she's redecorated in here too. "Fi… Wow."

"Surprise," she says feebly from her sprawl on my bed.

The entire room is done in shades of cream—the walls, the simple-lined but elegant furniture, the plush carpet over pine floorboards. I never would have thought of it, but it's so restful and serene that I'm in instant love.

The bed is the showstopper, with an enormous white canopy. Because Fi knows my style, she didn't go for girly but chose a classic, wood frame so that the bed resembles a structured cube. White linens and a mass of plump pillows make it soft and inviting.

"It's beautiful," I tell her.

"Well, I figured we could add some splashes of color here and there, if you'd like."

I kick off my shoes and plop down on the bed beside her. The cool feather duvet swallows me up with a sigh. "It's perfect. I feel like I've walked into a cloud."

Fi gives a weak laugh and closes her eyes. "Good. Cloud is what I was going for."

"How are you doing?" I touch her forehead and find it clammy.

"I feel like shit on a shoe. Not the welcome home I was planning."

"We'll make up for it when you're better." Because she's sick, I kiss her shoulder instead of her cheek. "Missed you, Fi-Fi."

At this, she turns and grins. "Missed you too, Ivy Weed."

Her grin fades and her pale brows knit. "And what the fuck? Why didn't you tell me that Grayson was gorgeous? Hell, I might have to reconsider my ban on football players."

Fi has channeled her resentment of my dad's job into a dislike of all things Sports.

"Honestly? I didn't know. We hadn't exchanged pictures or anything."

She snorts. "Only you would befriend a guy and have no clue what he looks like."

"I didn't want to know," I admit. "I can't really explain, but if I knew what he looked like, it would make our separation more real, make it harder on me that we were three thousand miles apart."

The confession has me feeling oddly exposed, and I curl up tighter on the bed.

"I'm pretty sure finding out he was a babe would make it worse," Fi agrees with a leer. "I mean, tell me you didn't see him for the first time and think, 'Holy hotness, Batman!'"

"I was…surprised." *I'd been floored.* "But it's not like I expected him to be ugly or anything."

Even if Gray had ended up being less than attractive, it wouldn't have mattered. He has charisma in spades.

"I nearly wet myself when I saw him," Fi prattles on. "Jaysus, he's hot. And freaking huge. A veritable mountain of sexy."

She fans her face with exaggerated movements. "Seriously, Iv…you could climb him like Everest, make base camp at his cock, and tackle the rest in the morning."

"Fi! Would you stop?" My cheeks burn at the image she put in my head.

"Why? It's true. And I bet you agree." She narrows her bloodshot eyes. "Don't you."

It isn't a question.

I hug a fuzzy white throw pillow to my chest. "He's my friend. I'm not thinking about him in that way."

"Friend I'd like to fuck."

I lurch up and turn to glare at her. "Don't you even think about it."

Fi's expression is placid. "I was kidding. But it looks like someone's already territorial."

"Of course I am. He's awesome. One of the few people I've instantly clicked with. And I'm not going to have that mucked up with…with…*emotions*." I wave my hand in irritation, nearly bopping Fi in the head in the process.

She ducks and snuggles further down into my bed. "Something tells me emotions are going to be involved regardless. But you don't have to worry about me. I have a boyfriend. Jake. He's a senior and he's beautiful."

"Does he wear plaid shirts and drive a red Porsche?"

"Har. Although he does bear a passing resemblance to Jake Ryan. Hmm… I wonder if I could get him to rent a Porsche and wait for me in front of a church."

Fi nibbles her bottom lip as if picturing this *Sixteen Candles* reenactment.

"You'd actually have to attend church," I say. "Which would put you at risk of being struck by lightning."

"As if you can talk." She pins me with her stare. "I give it one month before you jump Gray's bones. And that long only because I know you're stubborn."

"Shouldn't you be napping?"

"I've napped enough. I may puke sometime in the near future, but I'll be sure to let you know when."

Making a gagging face, I swing my legs over the side of the bed. "Brilliant. I'm going to shower this airplane funk off me."

Fi's voice follows me as I escape to the sanctity of my bathroom. "Glad you're home, Iv!"

"Glad to be home, Fi," I call back.

"I dare you not to think of that sexy mountain of man while you wash your lady bits!"

I slam the door on her evil cackle.

GRAY

"So." Drew's voice comes at me from beyond the sound of blood rushing in my ears. "Tell me about this Ivy."

I glance at my best friend. I'm at his house because I'm finally getting my truck back. Anna borrowed her mom's car, which is automatic, and he no longer needs mine. I made a half-hearted protest that he could keep the truck longer, but the truth is I've missed the old girl. Drew, on the other hand…

The fucker is kicking back on a sun chair, drinking some fruity drink Anna made for him while I bust my ass sprinting back and forth between two cones set ten yards apart. Fucking shuttle drills.

My thighs burn, my lungs are on fire, and still I go faster. I grunt as I crouch down to touch a cone before launching back up to book it to the next.

"She's not…'this' Ivy," I pant out. *Dip, touch, turn, sprint.* "And what's to tell? She's…" I touch the next cone. "My friend."

"Hmmm…" Drew takes a pull on his straw—Jesus, the drink has an umbrella. I swear he put one in it to fuck with me. It's forty degrees out here, and he's acting like he's on a beach somewhere. "And yet you're attached to your phone like it's become your second dick."

"Don't see a problem with that." I grunt. "Two dicks, twice the fun."

One. More. Set. *Fuck.*

Drew watches me with that stare of his that always sees more than it should.

There's an evil light in his eyes that looks way too pleased for comfort. "Yeah, as much as I'd love to discuss your disturbing multi-dick fantasies—and believe me, we really ought to discuss that issue—I'd rather talk about your new girlfriend."

I race through my final drill, panting as I grab my bottle of

Gatorade then guzzle it with enough zeal that sticky rivulets of drink run down my chin and drip onto my bare chest.

Sweat stings my eyes and I ache all over, a hum of sensation that causes me to shake. Is it sick that I love the feeling, love pushing my body to the brink? It's as close as I can get to the aftermath of hot sex without the awkwardness of "thanks, babe, see ya" getting in the way.

Drew tosses me a towel while the bottle is still at my lips. I pluck the towel from the air without looking then use it to wipe my face. When I chuck the damp towel back at him, Drew lurches to his feet, the long cast encasing his left leg making the move awkward.

Though I'd never admit to it, the sight hurts me. Until a brutal sack broke his leg, Drew was our starting quarterback and the team's undisputed commander. The injury ended his season. And as much as I hate to think it, I'm afraid our team will be lost without him. We were a well-oiled machine, a fucking brilliant team. Now what? The conference championship game is next, and our mojo is off.

Worse, I hate seeing Drew hobbled because I know how much it tortures him. But Drew seems to be getting on all right lately. Much of it having to do with his girlfriend, Anna. According to Drew, being in love does that for some guys. Personally, I think it's the steady diet of sex with a hot girl. But what do I know?

Which reminds me…

I toss away my empty bottle and give him a look. "Ivy is my friend, who happens to be a girl. Not my girlfriend. Big difference, sweet cheeks."

"Ha." He grabs a football from the ground beside his chair. "You do realize that when a guy has to define that difference, he's usually lying to himself."

"You just want me to be all cow-eyed in love like you are. Then you won't look like such a sap in comparison."

He grins. "Nice try, Gray-Gray. Now spill it."

Jogging to the back of Drew's yard, I get in place for him to throw me the ball. I might have gone to practice at the school's stadium, but I want to keep Drew company, and the more I can get the football in his hands, the better it is for him.

"She's fun, easy. I like talking to her." I take off running, halt, turn, and catch the pass Drew drills into my hands.

Tucking the ball tight against my side, I turn again, run back to my starting place, then toss it back to him. "And, no, I don't want to fuck her."

This is mostly true. Mac has a natural sexiness that I'd have to be dead not to notice. But I'm not going to even entertain thoughts of sex and Mac. No. Way. That would make me a dirty, low bastard, and I don't want to be that with Mac.

Drew palms the ball. "I didn't ask that."

I catch another pass, this one launched far over my head, forcing me to leap high. "You were thinking it."

Drew laughs a little. "Yeah, okay, I was. But only because you usually want to fuck any girl who comes into your orbit."

"Okay, fine," I admit, starting another route. "You got me, I am a sex god."

I talk over Drew's obnoxious snort. "Truth? Had we met before the texts, I'd have tried something. She's funny and smart and hot. Who wouldn't want her? Shit, I don't know, man. I just like her. I really like her. She's the first person I want to talk to. Every day."

Drew cocks his head, his mouth twitching as if he's fighting a smile. Annoying.

"Uh, bud," he says with a barely repressed chuckle. "That's how I felt about Anna. From the very start."

I frown, gripping the ball tight in my hands. "Ivy and I are just friends, though."

His silence is deafening. And I resist the urge to shift my stance.

"This relationship is important to me. Hell, she flat-out said she feels safe with me because we're just friends. I'm not going to fuck up that trust by hitting on her." I want to be better than that. For her.

My oldest friend in the world looks at me like I've grown horns, then slowly blinks.

"You're not tucking the ball in fast enough when you catch on the right," he says. "Take better control."

Asshole. But he's right, so I can't complain.

"That's it?" I ask him instead. "No more ribbing?"

"Naw." Drew spins the football on the tip of his finger before he palms it. "I was just curious."

Right. Sure. I continue to run short routes, catching each ball Drew sends my way, practicing quick hands, tight ball tucks, and balance. He waits until I'm done and dead on my feet, a fresh batch of sweat coating my skin and soaking the waistband of my shorts, to attack.

"I want to meet her."

Why that idea has me breaking into a cold sweat, I don't know.

FOUR

IVY

GRAY SENDS ME a pass to view his practice. Due to the intensity of prepping for the postseason, the coach has put the stadium on lockdown, not wanting a bunch of fans watching his team as they prepare. So only a few people are allowed inside.

Since I now have my car, I head over, parking in the student lot. Being on a campus brings back memories of my own school. And as much as I loved college, I'm not sorry to leave it behind.

The team is already in the thick of it when I arrive. It's a cold, crisp day, the winter sun weak yet shining onto the field and my section of the stadium. Snuggling down further into my puffy coat, I cup the cocoa I brought with me and watch.

Even though he has his helmet on, Gray is easy to spot, tall and lean in comparison to the stocky linemen he's standing next to. They're sporting full pads and jerseys today but wearing running shorts on the bottom. I track Gray's number eighty-eight as they huddle then break to get into formation.

I love sports. It's always been a part of my life. Football is no exception. I grew up with Hall of Fame winners coming over for Sunday dinner. I have numerous Super Bowl–winning "uncles" and standing tickets to all major sporting championships.

I might easily have turned jaded. But I haven't. I still get a thrill watching athletes perform at top level.

But it is abundantly clear that Gray's team is off their game. Missed passes, bad timing, sloppy defense, uncoordinated offense. Squabbles break out, players' tempers on edge. Oddly, when viewed as individuals, it's also clear that the players are excellent.

Their talent is evident. It's when they must play as a team that the weakness is exposed.

The head coach seems to agree. He nearly has a fit after yet another bad play. I say *nearly* because he's one cool customer. Most would be shouting. The offensive coordinator is: his face is purple as he bellows at his players to get their "damn heads out of their asses and fucking get it together."

The defensive coach has been reduced to ribald cursing that's basically one long spew of "Fuck!" But the head coach merely whips off his hat and slaps it against his thigh before pacing along the sideline.

Whistles are blown and the players go to their respective coaches. The rest of practice consists of endless and brutal drills.

When they're finally set free, the guys trudge off the field with their heads hanging low. It's too silent, and I ache for them.

Slowly, I make my way down to the field. One lone player has remained. Gray pulls off his pads and jersey with a single tug, sliding the entire kit over his head and tossing it next to his helmet on the ground with a look of self-disgust.

"Hey, Cupcake," I say softly as he plops onto a bench seat.

"That was some shit, eh?" His usual smiling mouth is a flat line. "Fuck it, we're so fucking off now."

"Is it because of Drew?" Losing the starting quarterback can often mess with a team. From talks with Gray, I know Drew was their leader and their friend.

Gray runs a hand through his hair. He's cut it, the thick mass shorter on the sides and sticking up along his crown in a messy faux-hawk. With his current scowl and fine features, he reminds me of young David Beckham. Well, if Becks was giant and had a smooth, sexy voice.

"I think we're spooked. And something's going on with Rolondo. Fuck if I know what, though."

"What position does he play?"

"Wide receiver. Jersey number four."

"Ah." I'd watched the wiry guy with long dreads.

Rolondo had dropped catches and got in two scuffles with the defensive backs who'd been covering him.

"Yeah," says Gray with a sigh. "'Ah.'"

His unhappy expression sends a pang through me. But while his team might be faltering, Gray played to perfection. I now know why my dad wants to rep him.

Gray's what most would call a freak of nature, though I prefer the term gifted. He's quick, coordinated, and huge. Incredibly strong, and once he gets hold of the ball, he does not drop it, no matter who knocks into him. His blocking abilities are killer. A triple threat, because he's also excellent at plucking the ball out of the air with deft precision.

Whatever happens during this season, Gray will be a big contender come draft time. But I know that won't make him feel better now.

"You guys will get it back," I tell him. "Anyone can see that you are a first-rate team. You just need time to reorganize."

"Time we don't have." With another curse, Gray grabs his water bottle and takes deep pulls on it, his throat working.

The silence draws my attention elsewhere, to how he's now half reclined and nearly all on display. Dressed in nothing but a pair of silky red basketball shorts over tight workout shorts, his long, toned body glistens with sweat. And sweet baby Jesus, he's a specimen.

Muscular bodies shouldn't faze me. I've seen dozens. Gray, however, is on another plane. He's so perfectly sculpted he could be an anatomy lesson. He doesn't just have a sexy V-cut; his lower abdomen is so defined it lays like a plate of armor over his narrow hips.

And while some guys get too bulky with muscles and others too ropey, Gray is like my own personal Goldilocks story come to life because he is just right, lean yet strong, cut yet smooth.

And all that honey-gold skin shining in the afternoon sun.

"Look your fill?" Gray's tone is amused. "Or should I just send you a picture of my rockin' bod?"

Horrified, my gaze shoots to his face to find him wearing a smug grin. He wags his brows while slowly rocking one leg from side to side, the movement overtly sexual, if not for the fact that he's obviously teasing me.

It's a struggle to keep my expression neutral. Hopefully I do.

"You have no body hair." It's the only thing I can think to say.

Gray's cheeks pink a bit. "I'm not a particularly hairy guy, no. Though I can assure you I have hair in some key places."

I should drop the topic. But better to tease than admit I can't take my eyes off him.

"Your legs look as smooth as mine." Hairless though they might be, there's nothing feminine about Gray's thick, strong thighs.

The pink on his cheeks deepens to red. "Yeah, well, my legs can cramp up a lot and the PT has to massage them." Gray clears his throat and scratches his jaw. "It hurt like a bitch when he'd pull on the hairs so..."

"You shaved your legs for better massages," I supply with a wide grin. Lots of athletes do, but it's kind of cute that he's embarrassed.

Gray scowls but then nods. "Did it one time. Then tried to grow the hair back, you know? Fucking itched like the devil."

I laugh. "Oh, I know. Fiona once talked me into getting a full Brazilian—"

Gray chokes on the water he'd been drinking, spitting it out and sputtering. Blue eyes glare up at me as he wipes his mouth with his forearm. "Jesus, Mac. Don't tell me these things. I cannot be imagining you all…" He waves a hand in my general direction. "Bare down there."

I snort at his indignant look. "Oh, please. I'm not bare down there anymore—"

"Not helping the situation," he says darkly.

"I'm trying to commiserate, you noodle. Because the itching was torture when it grew back. And do *not* get me started on the pain of waxing. I was certain that evil woman had ripped my lady lips off."

"Lady lips? Oh, Christ." His gleeful laughter echoes through the stadium.

"This is so not funny," I protest, my hands on my hips as his abs clench—which, *unf*—and he cracks up. "It was the worst pain of my life. And I've broken my arm in two places."

Wheezing with laughter, Gray wipes a tear from his eye and tries to control his humor. With one last snort, he grabs hold of my wrist and tugs me onto his lap. I land with a yelp as he wraps an arm around me and gives my cheek a big, smacking kiss.

"You always make me feel better, Mac."

Ignoring his happy look and the way the spot on my cheek tingles with awareness, I lean away from him, wrinkling my nose. "Great. So glad my traumatic past could help."

"I think I might be traumatized by 'lady lips,'" Gray retorts with a snicker, but his expression is content and his gaze is on me, as if just looking at me makes him happy. Which is vain to think, but hard to interpret any other way. Not when his eyes travel over my face and his lips curl into a soft smile.

I'm in his lap, sitting on his thick thighs that bunch and flex against my butt. My palm cups the hard curve of his shoulder, and his skin is smooth and warm and slick. All I want to do is stroke it, run my finger down the valley of his chest, maybe circle the little indent of his belly button.

I let my hand fall to my lap and clear my throat. "'Lady lips' will soon be a faint memory."

"Nope," he says, wrapping his arm around my hips. "It's burned into my brain."

"My work here is done then. Now go and take a shower, Stinky, before you freeze to death."

The truth is that Gray's sweat-slicked body doesn't smell bad to me. No, it's the opposite. I have the mad urge to burrow my face into the crook of his neck and breathe him in. Which *is* bad.

He laughs again, not letting me go, but pulling me against his tight chest. Jesus, his body is gorgeous up close. So solid and steady that I want to press into all that strength, ease this sudden ache in my breasts.

His voice is a luscious rumble in my ear. "I'm in no danger of freezing right now, Special Sauce. Believe me."

I don't know how to interpret that. Or what is going on with me.

"Boundaries, Gray." I edge back, because I'm in danger of doing something embarrassing, like drooling. "Sweaty, gross boundaries."

"Yeah, yeah. I'm going. Only one thing first." His eyes gleam, shining lapis blue in the winter light.

"What?" I ask, slightly weary of that glint.

"Is this overstepping boundaries?" he asks with mock innocence, right before the shithead crams my head into his sweaty armpit.

GRAY

I'm still smiling as I make my way into the locker room after my shower. Mac's squeals of horror were adorable. She fought the good fight, but still ended up with a face full of my sweat. Which is disgusting but oddly satisfying to me, in a caveman kind of way. I would feel bad about it, if it weren't for the fact that Mac had been laughing her ass off the whole time we wrestled. That, and she'd gotten a few good hits in.

"What's with that smug look, Gray-Gray?" Dex asks me as I pull out my boxers.

The big center is far too perceptive and I'm not about to go under the microscope. "Nothing."

Johnson glances at me too. "Uh-huh. Got anything to do with that hickey on your chest?" He shakes his head, sending his long yellow hair flying around his shoulders. "Damn, boy, only you could fuck around with a girl five minutes after practice."

I look down at my chest where a small bruise is forming near my nipple. My grin grows and I rub the spot.

"Not what you think, man. Mac pinched me." Hurt like a bitch but totally worth it. "We were just messing around."

The guys all stop to look at me with varying expressions of disbelief.

"Is that what you kids are calling it these days?" Dex asks.

"Yeah, well, she was kind of pissed that I gave her a noogie." I button my jeans.

"Mac?" Diaz, the big—usually silent—Puerto Rican lineman is putting on his shoes. "That the tall dark-haired honey watching our practice? The one who looks like Strawberry Fields from *Quantum of Solace*?"

"Gemma Arterton," Johnson supplies. "Nice."

I suppose Mac does kind of look like her. Especially with that hairstyle. Only Mac is more appealing.

"Yep. Oh hey." I look around at all of them. "Palmers is doing Eighties Night. I told Mac we'd go."

I text Drew about it. He wants to meet Mac. Now's his chance.

Silence greets me, and I lift my head to find my guys playing a game of Let's Not Acknowledge Gray.

"We're going out," I tell them emphatically. "So stop pouting about practice and fucking get with the program."

The guys need to relax and, frankly, we need to bond or whatever. We need this.

"Fine," Dex mutters. "But only because I have to meet this girl who is your 'bud.' I'm pretty sure this might be one of the seven signs of the apocalypse."

"True dat," Diaz agrees with a snort.

"She's awesome." I tug on my shirt, then look at Rolondo, who's rubbing lotion on his elbow like he's auditioning for *Silence of the Lambs*. "You're coming, 'Lo."

It wasn't a question, but he treats it as one. "Naw. I'm not up for it tonight."

"Bullshit. You're going."

He doesn't answer.

"Rolondo Jamal Smith, don't make me drag you out by your ass."

His eyes narrow but he's obviously trying not to laugh. "You imitating my mama, G?"

"Hell no." *I totally am.* "I've no desire to piss her off. That woman is a sweet potato pie–making goddess."

'Londo smirks. "Damn straight she is."

"Speaking of, when is she sending another shipment? Tell her I love her, okay?"

"Little suck-up." He tosses his lotion into his bag with a sigh. "All right. I'll go."

Grinning, I give his head a nudge, and get a slap on my arm for my efforts.

Rolondo saunters off, still grumbling about punk-ass, shit-talking white boys, but his step is lighter.

It's only when all the guys head out, leaving me to finish dressing, that I notice Cal Alder, our new starting QB, coming in from the showers. He'd been in there for a while and now moves with a reluctant slowness that I know far too well. I've had shit games after which I've sat under the spray of the shower like a zombie, hoping the water would wash away the shame of defeat. Never works, though.

The poor bastard has some big shoes to fill. He's a sophomore, forced to play the big game with a team that loved their former quarterback. Oftentimes, Drew barely had to communicate with us during a play; he just knew where to throw or pass, and we just knew where to catch it. Fucking strange, but true. We were in sync. We're not in sync with Cal.

"Hey, Cal."

He flinches as if he hadn't noticed my presence. Despite the stiffness in his shoulders, he turns to face me.

Cal is nothing like Drew. He's not a pretty boy. He doesn't laugh much or talk like an English professor. Truth be told, he looks more like a bruiser. Blunt features, a nose that might have been broken at one point. And his eyes are eerie as fuck. Frosty green, surrounded by dark lashes, when he points them at you it's like you're expecting lasers to shoot out or something.

"Hey." His expression drawn and tight, he looks like he's expecting me to give him shit. "We're going out to Palmers tonight. Come along." Again, not a question.

Cal blinks in surprise before weariness pulls at his mouth. "Thanks, but I don't—"

"Look, man, I don't envy you your position right now. It's gotta be stressful as shit. But I do know that a QB who bonds with his men has an advantage."

"And you think having some drinks with a few teammates is gonna make everything all right? Yeah. Sure."

"I think we need you," I answer truthfully. "And you need us. So, yeah, you do what you can to help get the win. Suck it up and get your ass over to Palmers tonight."

The tension goes out of his shoulders on a sigh. "All right, I'll go."

"Your enthusiasm overwhelms me." I grab my bag. But then

I pause and give him a good glare. "You bail, and I will hunt you down, newbie."

He rolls his eyes but almost smiles. "I'm terrified."

"I know. My tackle is a thing of fearsome beauty."

Cal snorts as I leave. I'm almost out the door when he calls out, "Grayson."

When I stop and glance back, he gives me a nod of his chin. "Thanks."

It's not like I've done anything but be decent. But I nod back. "Buy me a beer and we'll call it even."

As soon as I'm out the door, my thoughts turn back to Mac, and I rub the small sore spot on my chest where she pinched. Tonight can't come too soon.

FIVE

IVY

"WHERE ARE YOU going tonight, sugar pie?"

Fi's voice, garbled by her cold, cuts through the music that fills my room. I lower the bronze eyeliner I'd been smudging along my lids and glance at her. "Palmers."

Her red-tipped nose wrinkles. "That meat market? No fair."

Laughing, I pick up where I left off with the eyeliner, giving myself a soft cat-eye line. "Go there much?"

"Not recently. I hate being sick." With that whine, she plops down on my bed, lying with dramatic flair among the many pillows.

Her puffy eyes narrow onto my docking station, where I'm playing songs on my phone.

"'SexyBack'? Really?" A huge grin cracks her face. "It's like that, is it?"

Shit. It is a deep, dark secret of mine that, when wanting to get my sexy mojo going, I'll play "SexyBack."

I suppose my preteen lust for Justin Timberlake never died.

Flushed, I make a production out of selecting a red lip tint to blot on before my gloss. "Whatever. It's set on random."

But Fi knows me too well. She eyes my outfit, and her smirk returns. "Uh-huh. Nice top."

I'm wearing a red silk halter top. It has a high, gathered neckline, but it's cut so that my shoulders and back are exposed. A strapless, low-backed bra assures that my breasts aren't swaying out of control, but the top is definitely sexy. Paired with black jeans and high-heeled boots, the outfit is also fairly comfortable. And because Gray is as tall as a tree, I can wear heels and not dwarf him. Always a bonus in my world.

"I'm not going to a bar looking like a schlub," I mutter, dabbing on the red lip tint.

"Speaking of sexy," Fiona drawls. "Is that mountain of man hotness coming to get you?"

I snort at her nickname for Gray. "No. I'm meeting him there. This isn't a date, Fi."

I don't mention that I'm taking a cab. Gray got his truck back from Drew and promised to not only be the designated driver for tonight but bring me back home as well. He would have picked me up, but he's driving a few of his friends, and I refused to cramp their ride. I hadn't wanted Gray to drive me home for that same reason, but he insisted.

"Trust me, Mac," he'd said. "They'll find their own rides home."

Hooking up. I'd looked at Gray when he'd said that and thought of him finding a girl to hook up with tonight. Taking her home and…

Even now a shudder of distaste runs through me. Damn it. I have no right to be upset. Hell, the fact that I am upset is upsetting.

I'd pulled up my big-girl panties and suggested to Gray that I might be a third wheel.

He'd reacted as though I was insulting him, insisting that tonight was our night to hang out. So I let the matter drop. But eventually I'll have to deal with seeing Gray pick up women.

Frowning, I detach my phone from the dock and slip it into my little clutch purse.

"You going to be all right?" I ask Fiona before I go.

She shoos me away with a weak hand. "I'm almost better. Now go and have fun with the entire freaking football team of hotness, you hussy."

"It's not the entire team," I say with a smile. "Maybe like half. Three-quarters at the most."

Fi tosses a pillow at me, but it falls with a sad little thump far short of me. "So jealous. Go then, get your sexy on. And you'd better send me snaps of their arms!"

Fi is an admitted lover of big biceps.

"Will do." I wave and head out.

The bar where I meet Gray is filled with people, and apparently doing a retro night. Eighties hip-hop pounds from the speakers as I weave through the crush. My height has an advantage here, as does Gray's; I easily spot him above the crowd, his dark gold hair shining like a beacon as he strides forward to meet me. I love that I can wear heels and he still has inches on me.

"Hey," he says when we get to each other. "We've got a booth in the..." He trails off as he truly looks at me, and his lips part as if he's taking a quick breath.

"What?" My voice is too loud, the music making it hard to hear anything, and I lean closer. Enough that I feel the heat of his body and catch his clean scent. Soap and man has never smelled better.

For a moment, we kind of just sway around each other. Like magnets in too-close proximity deciding whether to slam together or split apart. A strange little dance that has us both flustered.

Gray clears his throat and edges back as if my nearness is too much for him. Well, okay then. I don't smell, do I? I scowl, but his mouth quirks on a smile.

"You look…nice, Mac."

"High praise there, Cupcake." My scowl grows, and he laughs.

"Okay, you look *really* nice. Hot, even." Again, he looks me over, this time lingering on my top. "Totally, smokin' hot."

A flush of heat rushes over my body, settling between my legs, and I'm the one doing the throat clearing. It doesn't stop the slow tide of unexpected lust that makes my steps unsteady. What the hell? It's just Gray.

"I like to dress up now and then. Don't look so shocked."

"I'm not shocked." Gray takes hold of my elbow gently, and guides me toward the back of the club. "I'm grateful."

"Grateful?"

He's still giving me sidelong glances as if he's convinced the scenery will change and doesn't want it to.

Gray just shakes his head and leans in until his lips brush my ear. His warm breath and deep voice caress my skin.

"Mac, I'm a healthy heterosexual male. Anytime a girl looks hot, I'm fucking grateful."

Lips pursed, I make no further comment. It's ridiculous how much his admiration pleases me. And disconcerting, as if I've taken a shot of hard liquor that's gone straight to my head.

I am still a bit dizzy when we reach the large circular booth that holds Gray's friends.

They all smile at me with varying degrees of interest, as if they've been waiting to get a good look.

"Ivy," Gray says, giving a nod in my direction by way of introduction. "Diaz, Rolondo, Dex, Marshall, Johnson, Cal, Drew, and Anna."

Anna, the curvy redhead and the lone girl at the table, has the widest smile.

She gives me a little wave. "Hey, Ivy. We've heard a lot about you."

Clearly. I'm like the new exhibit at the zoo.

"Hey. I've heard a lot about you guys too." I slide into the space left open next to Anna as the guys say hello.

They're all huge and probably intimidating to anyone not used to being around football players. To me, though, it's a bit like coming home. My whole life I've been around male athletes, strong guys who use their bodies as a musician would an instrument. Oftentimes they behave like overgrown boys, no matter what age they are.

Gray takes the seat opposite me, his muscular forearms resting against the table.

For a second we just smile at each other, and happiness floods my veins like pink champagne.

Then Drew leans in. "I've been meaning to thank you, Ivy, for letting Gray borrow your car." His tone is sincere, but there's a gleam in his light brown eyes.

"I didn't let Gray drive my car," I clarify, even though I know I don't have to. But I'm willing to mess with Gray just a bit. "In truth, it pissed me off. I kind of wanted to kick his ass."

"She talks a good talk but she loves me," Gray assures everyone.

"You didn't hurt the car," I say. "So I'm feeling more charitable toward you, yes."

Gray winks at me, and I laugh.

The gleam in Drew's eyes grows. "Gray would never damage that car. I mean, he looks so good driving it."

The guys all chuckle. And Gray coughs out, "Asshole."

Drew ignores this and leans back with a laugh. The guy is ridiculously good-looking in a chiseled, clean-cut way, with light brown hair and eyes. Gray and Drew sitting side by side, with their muscled physiques taking up a good portion of the booth, look like a comic book come to life.

They catch me staring and both say, "What?" at the same time.

Smiling, I shake my head. "Nothing. I just had this image of Thor and Captain America having a beer."

They both color at the same time. Which is kind of cute.

"Ha!" cries Anna at my side. Her cheeks plump with a wide grin. "I had that Captain America thought about Drew too."

Drew perks up. "You did, huh?"

Gray snorts. "Dude, I've just been compared to Thor. I totally win."

"What the hell does Thor have? A little hammer?" Drew waves a hand as if to say, *Please.*

But Gray smirks. "At least he isn't hiding behind a wussy shield. Thor is a *god.* Enough said."

"A boring god with the personality of a post," Drew volleys.

"And you're saying Captain America isn't boring? Bruh. He doesn't even understand modern culture. He's like a 1940s Boy Scout."

Drew and Gray eyeball each other for a second. Then Drew relents with a laugh. "Touché."

"And Thor reigns victorious in battle!" Gray throws up his arms in a touchdown gesture.

All the guys groan. Someone lobs a balled-up bar napkin at Gray, who neatly bats it away.

"Are they always like this?" I ask the table.

"Always," Anna mutters, but she's laughing.

Dex, who is massive and wears a full beard, shrugs. "Sometimes they slap each other's heads around too."

"Quiet down there, Bruce Banner."

Dex rolls his eyes at Gray.

"You disagreeing with that assessment, Cupcake?" I ask, grinning.

Instantly Gray groans loud and long, and his friends start to choke on their shock. And then my mistake hits me. Oh, shit. I should know better. Give a bunch of football players a new nickname to play with and they'll eat it up.

"Ivy," Gray chides. But it's too late—all his friends are on him now.

"Cupcake?" says Rolondo, the hot, lean guy with the dreads sitting in the middle of the round booth. His smile is blinding. "Oh, hell no, I'm not letting that one go."

With another groan, Gray presses his face into his massive hands.

"Glamour Cupcake. Sounds about right."

"'Cuz he's sweet, pink, and oh, so pretty."

Between his fingers, Gray's blue-eyed glare promises retribution. I grimace, giving him what I hope is my best sorry-I-ruined-your-life look.

"I distinctly recall Gray claiming to have a gooey center," Drew remarks with an evil grin.

"Now, now, pudding cup," Anna drawls at Drew. "You shouldn't throw stones. You're all sorts of gooey inside."

She gives me a conspiratorial wink as Drew sits up in his seat with an irate scowl, and the guys laugh.

"Low blow, Jones."

"Ah, but you love me anyway, Baylor," she answers with cheek. Drew's expression says she's right.

Gray, however, is far from free.

Rolondo sits back in the booth. "So, Ivy, aside from hanging with Cupcake, here, you go to school in the area?"

"No, I graduated last spring from Sarah Lawrence. I spent the summer and fall with my mother in London. I'm returning in March to manage one of her bakeries."

Rolondo's brows lift a little and it seems he's struggling not to look at Gray. "That's cool. I don't know how you bakers do it, getting up so early. That would kill me."

"Actually, it kills me too." I hate that part of the life. Going to sleep before nine p.m. and missing a regular social life in the name of baked goods kind of sucks. I've been reveling in staying up late and sleeping in late.

"Better get used to that hell schedule, Mac," Gray says lightly. "It's gonna be your life."

I shrug the comment off, not liking the way my insides do a little uncomfortable dip. "Could be worse, I guess."

"And now you're here with your dad?" Drew asks me.

"The super agent," Johnson supplies.

"Well, I think so." I grin. "But I'm biased."

They all chuckle. Then Marshall leans in, his big body making the table creak. "Hey, if he brings in the dollars come signing, I'm all over that."

I shake my head. "Good agenting isn't about negotiating professional contracts. Salary caps take care of most of that. It's about life planning."

"You sound like the money manager my parents had come to our house when my dad had a heart attack," Dex says with a laugh.

"But that's what it is, really. None of you will play forever. That's a fact. Prepare for the future, pad your bank account as much as possible, find a way to live after your first career is over."

None of them look particularly pleased at that. Athletes like to think of the now, when they feel invincible. It keeps them sharp. But that's not how an agent thinks.

"It's an agent's job to protect you so that, one day, you don't end your career penniless. Because you all know that happens."

"She's right," Drew says.

"How would you protect your client, Mac?" Gray looks genuinely curious.

"What? Me? I'm not an agent."

"If you were," he prompts.

"Well, let's take Drew here as an example. I'd get him voice coaching, for one thing, because the camera loves him. If he wanted it, one day he could be on ESPN, wearing a chunky purple tie and bringing home a nice salary."

They all laugh, but Drew nods. "Yeah, that'd be pretty cool."

"As for you." I look Gray over and begin to chuckle. "You're not gonna give me shit, are you?"

Gray's smile is lopsided as he braces his forearms on the table. "Hit me with it, Mac."

"Jockey, Under Armour, anything to show off that body in action."

He turns bright red, as the guys roar.

"That goes for all of you, really," I say to them.

"Hell yes, it does. The world needs to see these abs." Rolondo pulls up his T-shirt to reveal tight abdominals.

"Nice," I tell him honestly.

Rolondo winks. "You know it."

"Why does Drew get an anchor position, and I get underwear?" Gray protests over his friends' laughter.

"Honestly? I don't think you would like sitting still for that long." I give him a soft smile. "Would you really like to be an anchor, having to follow a script? Because they totally do."

Gray tilts his head and regards me. A pleased expression softens his features. "No, I don't think I would." His voice lowers, yet I hear it loud and clear over the music. "You should be an agent, Ivy."

"What? No." An uncomfortable knot forms in my chest. "That's… They're…" I shake my head. "That's my dad's thing, not mine."

I can't tell these guys that I've always resented Dad's job and how it took him away, broke my family. In truth, how deeply that anger runs in me is a shock. I hadn't realized until just now, and it chokes me.

My hand shakes as I reach for my beer and take a deep drink.

"I'd sign with you," Drew says, making me sit back with a thud.

"Yeah," Dex says. "I would too. You give a shit. That makes all the difference."

"Experience and clout in the industry matter as well," I say faintly.

But the idea of helping them is seductive because I know how satisfying it would be to ensure their safety.

Twitchy, I get to my feet. "I love this song," I say to no one in particular. "Who's going to dance with me?"

The guys look like deer in headlights. It takes me a second to even concentrate on what the song actually is. And I bite my lip hard. Madonna's "Material Girl" is playing. It's a struggle to keep a straight face. Gotta love Eighties Night.

"Uh-uh," Johnson says with a rampant shake of his head. "This is a girls' song."

Drew points to his leg. "I need to rest it. Doctor's orders."

Anna rolls her eyes before popping out of the booth. "Let's dance, Ivy."

"Looks like we're on our own," I say to her.

"Yeah." Gray leans far back into his seat as though he's in danger of being pulled out. "Maybe the next song."

Anna shrugs and grabs my hand. I follow, perfectly happy to lose myself on the dance floor.

SIX

GRAY

"I LIKE HER," Dex says as the girls leave.

"She's great, isn't she?" I watch Mac's long legs stride toward the dance floor. The top she's wearing dips down nearly to her waist, revealing the satiny expanse of her narrow back.

I've never been one for noticing backs, but I have the urge to follow her, run my palm down that smooth curve, down to her...

I take a breath and get a grip on my wayward thoughts.

Johnson turns to me. "You gonna sign with her dad, for serious?"

"He's cool. And clearly knows what he's doing if Ivy thinks that way about agenting."

She'd lit up when she talked about the business. But I don't like the way Mac fled the table. My suggestion that she should be an agent clearly made her upset, and I have no idea why.

I can't ask her now, so I turn my attention elsewhere, raising my voice so it can be heard over the pounding music.

"Hey, newbie," I say to Cal, who has been quiet all night.

"Drew and I are going to practice some drills tomorrow morning. Join us."

Drew nods. I've talked to him about it, and he's agreed to help Cal. The trick is getting Cal to accept the help.

My new quarterback glances between us and a frown pulls at his face. But before he can protest, Drew attacks.

"I'd like to keep myself in condition. I'd rather have another QB to work with."

Cal isn't stupid—thank God—but he shrugs, obviously unwilling to argue right now. "Sure."

He's about to say something else, but a strangled sound leaves Rolondo. It's as if he's stuck between laughter and horror.

"Uh, G-Man." He makes the sound again, his eyes on the dance floor. "Your girl…"

The guys all turn, and their expressions mirror 'Londo's.

Drew winces and mutters, "Damn," as if he's witnessing an atrocity.

I wrench around, my fists clenched and ready to pound the shit out of anyone who might be bothering Ivy. And freeze. Good God Almighty. My mouth falls open.

"What is she…?" Dex shakes his head as if poleaxed.

I can only stare, numb with shock. Because Ivy is dancing. At least I *think* she is. Her long limbs are flailing around without any apparent rhythm, her hips all over the place. It's like a full-body convulsion. And people are backing up. Probably fearful of being clobbered on the head, which is a very real possibility.

My lips twitch.

Behind me, Rolondo leans close. "Man… That's some impressively bad dancing."

I glare at him over my shoulder, then grab Ivy's beer and take a long drink.

Slamming the glass down, I stand. "Gentlemen, a man has to do what a man has to do."

With a deep breath, I brace myself and head out to the dance floor to save my girl.

IVY

Gray is a horrible dancer. I wouldn't believe it if I wasn't seeing it with my own eyes. When he'd joined me on the dance floor, I'd given a happy shout. But then he started to move. And it isn't good.

He's flopping around as if he's having some sort of toddler tantrum. It's so bad that the small circle of people around Anna and me gives us an even wider berth.

With good reason—Gray has a long reach. Anna, who had been sort of smiling when I was dancing with her, looks at Gray with shocked eyes. Her gaze slides from me to the spectacle he's making, and then her face breaks into a full-blown grin, as though his antics make her happy.

Then again, he's really going at it, and I can't help but smile at his enthusiasm.

Given his excellent coordination on the field, I'd expected him to be better at this, but we can't be perfect at everything.

We dance for another song. The beat pulses around us, and soon his guys are all there too. Even Drew, who draws Anna close, and they kind of just cling and sway together. The rest of the guys join Gray and me, forming a wall around us. They're better at dancing, but they don't seem to find anything wrong with Gray's performance. As good friends do, they simply nod at him with varying degrees of amusement, respect even, and then dance.

It's fun. Rolondo attempts to teach me some of his moves, setting his hands on my hips and guiding me, but it's hard to keep up with him. Gray slides closer, getting in front of me, and his uncoordinated motions calm to something more like Rolondo's.

Together, they sandwich me, taking control of the dance. Not so close that I'm pressed in or overwhelmed, but enough that I'm laughing and breathless.

All of the guys dance with me, each of them taking turns to

show me different moves. But I always end up back with Gray, who gets better at dancing but never quite manages to perfect his technique. I think he might be trying too hard, because I see glimpses of greatness.

When the song ends, Gray leans close, the clean scent of sweat coming off his skin. "You want to sit down now?"

"No way," I shout back, because another song has started. "I love dancing!"

He grimaces—the poor guy probably hates dancing since he does it so badly—but then pulls me close. "Then that's what we'll do."

So we dance, stopping every so often for me to drink more beers and then go back out again. The night becomes a blur, with Gray in its center, laughing with me, dancing with me. And it's brilliant.

SEVEN

GRAY

MY LIFE RUNS on patterns. Always has, probably always will. Now there's a new pattern: football, coursework, Mac, sleep. And I don't really want it any other way.

When I'm not studying or at practice, I'm searching out Mac, heading to her place. It feels like home to me now. I like the quiet and the fact that I don't have to yell at some dickhead to flush the fucking toilet or not leave his underwear on the couch. But mainly it's just hanging out with Mac, where the only interruption is the occasional arrival of Fiona, who always grins at me like she knows something I don't and calls me a "mountain of hot man-flesh."

Mac blushed bright red the first time Fiona called me that. It was cute.

But now we're alone and curled up on the couch, eating pizza and watching college hockey. My bloodthirsty Mac is shouting her approval at the TV as some guy smashes another player against the boards.

A twinge of envy hits me. It must be sweet to fly across the ice. But I have to chuckle when Mac yells, “Good deke!” as she grips her pizza crust like a hockey stick.

It occurs to me that, a month ago, I’d have laughed my ass off if someone had told me I’d prefer staying in, without the possibility of sex, to going out and hooking up with some girl.

What I really want to do is put my arm over Mac’s slim shoulders and draw her close to my side. I have the constant urge to run my finger down her blunt nose, then trace the heart-shaped curve of her upper lip. Rosebud lips.

I’d heard the expression before but didn’t know what it meant until now. Mac’s lips are a perfect rosy pink, and plump, like she’s in the process of blowing a kiss even when relaxed. They kind of drive me crazy.

So does the way her nose wrinkles every time she laughs. Which is often.

It makes me disgruntled. What the hell is wrong with me? Am I so oversexed that I can’t just be friends with a girl without having the desire to try something? I want this friendship to work, want to be more than a guy driven by the urges of his dick.

Annoyed with myself, I sit back and cross my arms over my chest. “You got any video games?”

Mac tosses her crust onto the pizza box—and I grab it, not willing to waste perfectly good crust.

She smirks at this but answers me. “Nope. Video games aren’t really my thing.”

“Figures. You probably avoid them because you suck at them.” I don’t think that, but it’s fun to egg her on.

Predictably Mac sits up straight and glares. “I rock at video games. When I so choose to play them.”

“When you ‘so choose’?” I snicker. “The formality of your speech reveals the falsehood behind your claims, young Padawan.”

She turns in her seat, her knee knocking into my thigh. "You're calling me a liar?"

Pink washes over her cheeks and her dark eyes shine.

God, she's pretty. So pretty it hurts my heart. I want to haul her onto my lap, settle down, and kiss her sexy little mouth until I can't move my lips anymore.

Since I can't do that, I give her my best patronizing look. "It's nothing to be ashamed of. You just don't have the reflexes necessary to compete."

"I have the reflexes of a cat."

I snort, totally enjoying myself now. "If you mean Garfield, then yeah."

A couch pillow hits me in the face. I sputter and find myself nose to nose with Ivy, whose eyes spark with challenge.

"You better run, Grayson, because in about five seconds I'm gonna have you pinned and begging for mercy."

Hell yes, please. Make me beg. Take my stiff cock out and ride it until I cry.

Because I'm in serious danger of tackling her, I jump up and back away as if it's all a joke to me. "Bring it, Mackenzie."

IVY

I know Gray is teasing me. I accept the bait. He's going down—hard. I get to my feet and raise my fists. "First hit wins bonus points."

"You're so cute when you're delusional, Mac." He gives me a little come-hither gesture with his hand.

That smug…

"Oh, it is on like Atari *Pong*!"

Gray halts midlunge, his mouth falling open as a laugh sputters out. "It's supposed to be 'on like Donkey Kong.'"

"You say what you want. I say what I want." I swing, but he ducks, and my fingertips catch air. Damn it.

His blue eyes crinkle at the corners. "Okay, but why 'Atari' *Pong*? Why not just 'it is on like *Pong*'?"

"I like my descriptors."

A full-bellied laugh erupts from him. Distraction enough that I bap the side of his big head.

"Point!"

That shuts him up. Narrowing his eyes, he circles closer. "Bring it, Special Sauce."

"Oh, Cupcake, you are so dead."

We dance around each other, lunging and feinting. When his hand throws a playful swat toward the crown of my head, I twist and duck.

"That's right," I say, doing my best Ali, feet moving in an intricate pattern. "Fear the wrath. Bob and weave. Bob and weave."

Gray is cracking up now, red-faced and teary-eyed. He's trying to concentrate but he's laughing too hard. Which leaves him wide open on his left.

Unfortunately, I'm laughing too, and the rat fink keeps getting in taps on my head.

"Take that," he says, tweaking my nose.

"You…argh!" I duck and barely evade.

He freaking cackles with evil glee. "Oh yeah, I own this like a *patronus*, baby."

The words kind of hover like a bad stink, as our gazes clash, and we both pause.

"You," I gasp through a laugh. "Are such a nerd."

"That was boss and you—" he snorts "—know it."

"Nee-rrd."

I don't even see Gray move, he's so fast. One moment I'm singing out my disdain, the next his beefy arms are around my waist, and he's bringing me down. He controls the fall, taking the impact and sheltering me from banging into the floor. But we still land in a tangle of limbs and laughter.

"Silly girl." His grin is wide. "You fell victim to one of the most classic blunders."

Weakened, I let my head rest against the hard swell of his biceps as I quote *The Princess Bride* back to him. "Never get involved in a land war in Asia?"

Slowly he shakes his head, and his golden hair falls over his brow. "Nope."

"Never go against a Sicilian when death is on the line?"

Gently, I flick the lock of hair back.

He watches me do it, but his smile doesn't falter. It grows as he leans in close.

He takes my air with his proximity. Suddenly I'm aware of Gray all around me: the massive wall of his chest pressing into mine; the thick swell of his thigh resting on my legs.

He's warm, strong, and alive. He doesn't move, just studies my lips as if he's never seen them before. The soft heat of his breath tickles my nose, his lips near enough to brush my own. For a moment we simply exchange air, and my head grows light, my body heavy and languid.

The heat within me surges. I want to close that distance. I want to know what he tastes like.

"Gray." Panic mixed with urgency has me breathless.

"Mmm?" he asks absently, his gaze somnolent.

And then I feel it: the length of his cock growing heavy and hard against my thigh.

"What…?" I take a short breath, and our lips almost brush.

Gray makes a sound deep in his throat. He's gone so tight that tension vibrates along his frame.

Think, damn it. Friendship good. Kissing bad.

"What is the most classic blunder?" I ask in a haze.

His long lashes sweep down on a slow, dazed blink. "I don't know," he whispers. "I forgot where I was going with that."

Our eyes meet, his such a deep, true blue that I can't think straight. I should stop this, lighten the mood, fucking get my head together. But he feels so good, the wall of his chest against my breasts making them sweetly ache.

He trembles, his eyes closing, as if he can't concentrate either. As if he might dip his head and brush those gorgeous lips of his over mine.

"What in the hell are you doing, Grayson?" snaps the distinct voice of my father.

It has the effect of a gunshot. Gray leaps up with such speed that it takes my breath in a sharp whoosh.

The next instant, he's got my wrist and pulls me up so quickly that I practically fly. Jesus, but his strength is impressive.

"Ow." I glare at him, rubbing my wrist.

Gray winces. "Sorry. Are you okay?"

"Yeah." But I'm not looking at my wrist.

My father is standing in the doorway, his dark brows forming a line over narrowed eyes. He's in a suit, though it's rumpled around the edges like he's come here straight from the airport. I'd forgotten he was coming home today.

"Hey, Dad." Shit. What he walked in on couldn't have looked good.

"Ivy." His tone is pissed. Pissed-Off Dad takes things slow and steady. Right before he blows.

Gray tucks his hands in his pockets, as if this will somehow convey innocence. I want to roll my eyes. We *are* innocent. But he's not looking at me.

"Mackenzie. Hi."

Dad raises one brow. "Want to tell me why you were on top of my daughter, Grayson?"

"Uh…"

Smooth, Gray. Really smooth.

"Dad, stop with the overprotective father act."

"It's not an act. I *am* an overprotective father, Ivy."

I shove past both of them and head to the kitchen. "Do you want a beer?"

Dad grunts. "I could take a beer."

Gray finally finds his voice. "So you just get back in town?"

"Yes. And not a moment too soon, it seems." Dad's glaring a hole into Gray's forehead. "We have things to talk about, Grayson."

"Yeah, sure." Gray doesn't recognize Dad's I'm-going-to-give-you-a-lecture-from-hell tone, but I do.

"For now," Dad says, "I need to discuss some things with Ivy."

Great. Cue the needless lecture to me as well.

"Right." Gray nods. "I'm headed out anyway."

I'm about to protest, but Gray edges toward his coat, keeping his gaze on my dad as if he'll attack when his back is turned. I almost roll my eyes again, only I'm not so sure my dad won't attack.

"See you tomorrow, Mac." Gray gives me a look that I read well. *Don't argue with him. Just get it over with.*

I'll be good, I answer with my own look. At least I will until Gray is well and gone.

EIGHT

IVY

I'M WAITING FOR the first strike. But Dad goes for my underbelly instead.

"You look good, kid." My dad gives me a ghost of a smile. He's pissed but trying to play nice. "Glad you're here."

He doesn't say *Glad you're home.* He never does. And I've never really noticed until now. It hits me; I have places to stay, but not a home. Our family is too transient for that.

Forcing a smile of my own, I give him my standard reply. "Glad to be here."

Dad tugs on his ear. "Listen, I'm sorry I missed your arrival—"

"It's okay." I don't want to hear him make excuses. And because I've missed him, I don't want to fight. Quickly I go to my toes and kiss his cheek. "You look good too."

Dad pats my shoulder and gives the top of my head a peck. There are few people who make me feel small in size. Dad is one of them. At nearly seven feet, with a wingspan of eighty-six inches, he was a formidable opponent on the court. His size makes him look a bit like an overgrown scarecrow, all long limbs and bony joints.

I step back from him. "Besides, Gray picked me up, and I was happy to see him."

Maybe I *do* want to fight.

Dad scowls. "Gray Grayson has the potential to be a superstar."

His voice is so low, I need to strain to hear it. Which is exactly what he intends—force your opponent to focus on you and you're in control.

Like that, our fragile bubble of keeping the peace bursts.

"He's a superstar now, Dad." I pop the top on a beer and hand it to him with a little more force than necessary.

Dad simply stares down at me from his great height. He's more silver-haired than brown now. But his brows are still dark, and this makes his glare more penetrating. I wonder briefly if he's coloring those damn brows just for that effect.

"You know what I mean, Ivy." Dad doesn't drink his beer. "I'm this close to signing him."

"He is my friend."

"That little show just now didn't look like friendship to me."

Chest tight, I flop into a chair. "We were goofing around, and I'm twenty-two years old. I really don't need a lecture."

Dad sits as well, only with much more decorum. Setting his untouched beer on the table, he steeples his hands together as he leans back. "No, sweetheart, I think you do. You're right. That young man is a superstar. With a reputation."

Heat prickles over my chest, and it's all I can do not to huff like a child. "I know all about his reputation. It doesn't matter to me."

"It ought to if you're going to fall for him." Before I can protest, he leans forward and pins me with a look. "Guys like that… Hell, Ivy, my career as an agent is built on them. You know what their lives are like. Women at every turn, offering to do anything—*anything*—they want. These guys will screw their way from game to game and enjoy themselves without a care for who they hurt."

"Guys like you," I snap without thought. Instantly, I'm horrified that I've spoken so crassly to my own father.

Dad freezes, but his gaze doesn't waver. "Yeah, Ivy. Guys like me. I loved your mother with all my heart. And I cheated on her constantly. Didn't even consider it cheating, to tell you the truth. Thought of it as my due for being a star."

Cringing, I look away, not willing to face him when he's talking about hurting my mother.

Maybe he knows, because his tone goes soft. "I regret the man I was. But it doesn't take away the reality of this life. Have you any idea how many wives and girlfriends I've had to handle because one of my guys has done something stupid with some young piece of ass? Too many, Ivy. I see that bone-deep hurt in those women's eyes, and their resolve to just ignore these indiscretions, and—"

"Okay, Dad," I all but wail. "I get it. I know." My jaw locks as I turn to him, and it takes effort to speak. "I've lived this life too. But I refuse to judge Gray by what others have done."

Dad gives an expansive sigh. "For Christ's sake, he already fools around so much there are TikTok accounts devoted to his castoffs. One search on him is a PR nightmare of party pictures and half-naked women."

Reason number one I have never googled Gray. I ignore the thick sludge of jealousy pushing through my veins.

"We're just friends," I insist, my tone rising. "How many times do I have to say this?"

His response is a level look full of skepticism. "For argument's sake, let's say this friendship grows into something more."

Dad raises a hand when I open my mouth to protest. "Hypothetical here, Ivy. What happens when it all goes south? You think he'll want to work with me anymore?"

Like that, I go utterly cold, then flush white-hot. For a moment, I can't make my mouth work. "This is about you." In a fog, I stand, my fists clenching. "You don't give a shit about me—"

"Watch your mouth."

"No. You sit here putting all sorts of unwarranted fears in my head, and it's all because you're afraid of losing Gray as a client!"

Dad stands as well, and the edges of his mouth go white. I brace myself for the explosion, knowing firsthand just how loud Dad can yell when he's pissed.

Bring it on. I'm pissed too. But it doesn't happen. No, his reaction is worse because he deflates. His wide shoulders wilt on a sigh as he sets his hands low on his hips and looks down.

"I need Grayson." It's almost a whisper. "There are things… Business isn't what it used to be. Guys…they're going to big-name firms. Salary caps, scandals, bad PR. It's all taking a toll."

A painful lump fills my throat. Dad has *never* talked to me like this. In all honesty, I don't want to hear it. I used to think of him as Batman—questionable tactics, but on the whole, unbeatable and enduring. I cannot think of him as less.

"We're just friends," I whisper, as if saying it enough will somehow protect me from messing things up.

Absently, Dad nods. "Whatever you want to tell yourself, kid."

His flippancy has me grinding my teeth. I kind of hate him right now for manipulating me. For putting Gray in the middle.

Dad sees it in my expression. He blanches, apparently shocked. "Ivy… It might not look like it, but I am always on your side. I don't want to see you hurt."

GRAY

My nerves are a twitchy mess. I keep thinking of the look in Mac's eyes when, in a completely ill-advised play, I sprawled on top of her.

What would have happened if I had kissed her? She'd been…

receptive. Hadn't she? I'd wanted to. I'd never wanted to do something so badly in my life.

God, her lips had been too close to mine, too pretty, too pink, looking so soft and inviting and just *fuck*. The temptation to simply touch them with my own, to lick a path across that cute little heart-shaped mouth of hers, had been so strong that I still ache deep in my bones.

But then I blink and remember Sean Mackenzie glaring at me as if he'd been contemplating good places to hide my body. It makes me queasy.

I get where he's coming from. Worse, I don't know what the hell I'm doing in regard to Ivy anymore. She means so much to me it freaks me out, and I'm suddenly on some tightrope where the wrong step will send me plummeting.

On that happy note, I turn my truck around and drive away from my house.

I head to Palmers, hoping that someone will be there to shoot the shit and get my mind off having to eventually talk to Mackenzie. That discussion should be fun. I shudder just thinking of it.

I find Dex in the booth at the back of the bar. It's a good spot, dark enough that the chances of being left alone on a busy night are decent but positioned at the right angle to watch the TV hanging over the defunct jukebox. Dex is sprawled along one side of the booth, his back against the wall, his legs hanging over the edge. He's watching TV, and the place is quiet enough to hear Morgan Freeman's deep voice roll on about the universe.

I slide into the opposite side of the booth. "Whatcha watching?"

Dex keeps his eyes on the TV, blue-and-purple light coming off it reflecting over his skin. "*Entering a Black Hole.*"

"Dude, you want to learn about anal, watch some porn like the rest of us."

As hoped, his mouth twists and his nose wrinkles. "Hot sick has just surged up my throat."

"'Hot sick'?" I laugh. "That's a new one."

Rubbing his chest as if he really might be sick, he keeps his gaze on the program. "Don't you have someone else to pester with really bad sex jokes?"

"Nah." I reach for his beer, taking a swig before he can grab it back. "It's your turn on the rotation."

A waitress ambles over, stopping beside me. "Hey there, gorgeous. You need anything?"

"Yep. Give me a Shiner Bock and put it on his tab." I grin at Dex, who sends me a sidelong glare but nods and goes back to his show.

The waitress stands there, not moving, and I shoot her a questioning look. She leans in until she's brushing against my shoulder. "Anything else?"

"Nope. Wait!"

She hasn't gone anywhere, so she grins. "Talk to me, handsome."

"Add a basket of wings. No, two. And some cheesy tots." I glance at Dex. "You hungry?"

Dex's mouth twitches. "I could eat."

"Two barn burgers with everything, as well. Food's on my tab, thanks."

Okay, I just ate pizza at Mac's, but it's either eat, work out, or fuck away this tension. As I'm at a bar, I go with the only feasible option.

I sit back and watch the show that's turned Dex into a social zombie. Well, *more* of a social zombie. Truth is, astrophysics isn't my sweet spot, not like quantum mechanics, but I still find it fascinating. Silence falls as we listen to scientists explain the mysteries of space on a simplified level.

At my side, the waitress is all but hovering. I'm about to ask her why she isn't moving when she finally stirs and then walks away.

Dex takes the moment to look over. And he smirks.

"What?" I ask.

"You totally ignored her."

"Who?" I watch TV. "Man… They're explaining a theory that's years out of date."

"Yeah, that's because this was produced in 2011," Dex drawls, still staring. "The waitress. You ignored her."

"No, I didn't. I placed my order."

Slowly he shakes his head. "She had her breasts thrust right under your nose. Not to mention that she was clearly expecting you to respond."

"So, I didn't notice. What's the big deal?"

"She's hot, available, and waiting?"

"You fuck her, then." Is it too much to ask to watch TV in peace?

Dex's feet hit the floor with a thud as he turns in his seat and leans his elbows on the table. "I've been your teammate and friend for four years, Gray-Gray, and I've never seen you turn down an opportunity like that."

"Maybe she's not my type."

"Bruh. If you'd even looked at her, I *might* buy that."

"Are we having a girl chat here? We gonna braid each other's hair next?" I reach forward and try to ruffle Dex's hair, but he swats me away.

"Here we go," says a chipper female voice. "One Shiner."

A frosty bottle is set on the table, and I look over.

Jay-sus. Okay, now I get what Dex is saying, because the waitress is smoking. And the tits she apparently thrust under my nose are so huge they're practically falling out of her low-cut top. How in the hell did I miss that?

She gives me a smile filled with promises I know will be delivered with much enthusiasm. And what do I want to do? Drink my beer, eat my food, talk to Dex, and then go home. In that order.

"Thanks," I tell her before taking a long pull of the beer and tuning her out.

Dex's eyebrow lifts in emphasis. Yeah, I know. I'm fucked.

The waitress huffs off.

"You know it isn't going to go away just because you won't acknowledge it," Dex says.

"What isn't going away?" Johnson asks, suddenly at my side.

Fuck. Me.

He, Thompson, and Diaz are here and they cram into the booth without ceremony. Diaz takes the seat next to Dex, while Johnson and Thompson shove me to make space for their massive bulk. Which means I'm squished into the corner. Though Johnson is pure Iowa farm boy, with straw-colored hair and pale blue eyes, and Thompson is an inner-city kid from Detroit with a retro fade, there's a similarity in their size and the way they move and talk in unison. Brothers from another mother, we call them.

"What we talking about?" Johnson tries to grab my beer but he's too slow. Linebacker speed is sad.

"Nothing."

"Gray's special needs," Dex says over me as the waitress comes back and proceeds to dole out the food. I take possession of my burger before it's gone. As it is, Thompson shouts, "Wings!" and claims a basket.

"You mean how he's hot for Ivy?" Johnson dives into the cheesy tots. Fucker. Those are my favorite.

"Man," Diaz drawls, shaking his head. "Don't do it."

"Why not?" Johnson asks around a mouthful of tots. "She's wicked hot. I'd hit that."

"Hey," I snap with a death glare. Johnson shrugs in apology but doesn't look too sorry.

"She's his potential agent's daughter, knucklehead," Thompson says to Johnson. "You do not fuck with the daughters."

Dex watches us between bites of his burger. "Every girl is

some guy's daughter. What if she wants to be with Gray? It's her life, not her dad's."

"True that," says Diaz.

"Whatever," I cut in. "She is my friend. Which means off-limits."

"But you want her." This from all of them. In unison. And they laugh at that.

Yeah, fucking hi-larious. The burger is starting to land hard in my gut. I've got to start eating better.

"Come on, Gray-Gray, you know you do."

"Kiss the girl, already," Johnson begins to sing. Badly. A cheesy tot hits his cheek, and he chucks a wing at Diaz in retaliation. It goes wide.

"Isn't that the song the little crab sings in *The Lion King*?" Dex asks.

"It's *The Little Mermaid*. And stop playing like you don't know."

"Says the dude who knows the lyrics."

"Please. My little sister watched it five million times when we were kids."

"Whatever you have to tell yourself, Johnson."

And then they're back to me.

"You really should admit to it. Probably make you feel better."

"You want her *baaad*."

"Fine," I snap. "I do. But it's not happening, so shut the fuck up and let a man eat."

Johnson gives me a once-over as he swipes Dex's beer. "Man, this is bad news. Soon you'll be so jacked up for it, you'll get distracted on the field."

"I'd like to think I'm a better player than that," I say, truly offended, because what the fuck? Football is my life's focus.

Johnson shrugs, unconvinced. "When's the last time you got any?"

"Why do you care?" Nope, I'm not going to squirm in my seat.

Diaz looks me over and rubs the fuzz he likes to think is a goatee as if he's contemplating. "Not since he's been driving that car."

They all stare in obvious shock. I can't blame them. Has it been that long? Shit, it has. My skin prickles, a sinking sensation tugging at my gut. I haven't touched a girl since I started texting Ivy. It wasn't even a conscious decision, because I can't remember making it. And the realization freaks me out. So much so, I take a bite of my burger to keep my shaking hands occupied.

Unfortunately, Johnson isn't through with me. "Why don't you just fuck her and get some relief?"

I roll my eyes. "That has got to be the dumbest idea in the history of sex."

"Explain."

"Okay, just for shits and giggles, let's assume that I make my move and Ivy agrees to let me into her bed. What happens afterward? She. Is. My. Friend. I don't want to lose that."

Hell no. A world without Ivy in it would be like a world without the sun—cold, dark, devoid of gravity. I'm pretty sure I'd drift aimlessly. A shudder hits me just thinking about it. Hell, it's bad enough that I have to face her leaving for London in a few short months.

"So no to the friends with benefits?" Dex asks in a subdued tone, as if he's truly curious.

"Oh, that's always a great idea." I snap my fingers. "It never works. And then I'll be out a friend just because I can't keep my dick in my pants."

"You never know unless you try," Dex says. "Maybe once will be enough for both of you."

I toss my half-eaten burger into its basket. "Why do you think alcoholics don't take another drink after they're sober? Drug addicts a hit? Because just once is never enough. Not when it's the only thing they crave."

And God help me, because the truth is Ivy has become a craving in my blood, racing through me hot and thick.

Around the table my friends look slightly horrified, and more than a little sorry for me. It burns, and I pick up my beer, avoiding their gazes.

"Can we please talk about something else now?"

"Yeah, all right," Thompson says. "You hear about Marshall's little stunt last night?" Already he's snickering.

"What did that fool do now?" Dex asks.

"Tried to perform a *Cool Hand Luke*." Thompson tears into another wing.

"What? With the eggs?" I ask.

"Yeah."

We groan as one.

Johnson leans in, taking up the tale, a gleeful grin lighting his face. "He got some sorority chick to boil him up a shit-ton of eggs. Swore he could down like sixty of them or something."

Diaz shakes his head as he listens. Hell, we all do. Marshall is a fuckwit of the first order.

"How far did he get?" I ask, knowing the outcome wouldn't have been pretty.

Johnson starts snickering. "Man, he eats around two dozen, turns white as chalk, and then bolts."

We're laughing now.

"He make it out of the house?" Diaz asks.

"Shit no. Got tangled up in a bunch of girls," Johnson says, still laughing. "Fucking hurled all over them. You should have heard them squeal."

I'm laughing so hard, I have to wipe my eyes. "He's never gonna get laid again."

"They're already calling him Big Barf."

Our conversation moves on from there. Until Dex catches my eye and leans across the table as the guys discuss their NFL fantasy leagues.

"I gotta ask. If you want Ivy, why not make it real?"

Heat rushes over my face. Real. As in girlfriend. The idea

makes my heart pound and my palms go clammy. I kind of hate Dex for asking. But he's like that, always finding your underbelly and poking at it.

I run a hand over my jaw. "Who says I want a girlfriend?" Just saying the word makes me cold. I'm not a look-forward guy. Live now. Play hard. Those things are safe. Fun.

The look Dex gives me says he reads me like a playbook.

I sigh, picking up my beer to mutter into the bottle before I gulp the rest down. "Thing is, Dex, this isn't football. That's easy. Friendship is easy. Relationships?" I push my empty bottle away. "It's not my game."

Slowly he nods, his fingers tight around his glass. "Yeah, except you want her. Which means your game is already in play. Only way to go is forward, man."

Sometimes, I really hate talking to Dex.

NINE

IVY

TONIGHT, I MEET Gray at Palmers again to hang out with his teammates. Because their coach has a strict no-excessive-drinking policy, the guys limit themselves to one beer each. Also in effect is a no-partying rule while they train for the postseason. So sitting around, talking smack, and telling jokes is as wild as they get for the moment.

I prefer this, actually. I like hearing their stories and seeing the obvious love they have for each other. They're now talking about Thompson's, Johnson's, and Marshall's sexcapades, which are varied and a bit disturbing.

"What about the time Thompson left us stranded in some seedy bar in Cancún because he took the car to drive some co-eds to a party?" Gray glares at Thompson. "Without telling us."

"So wrong," Marshall says with a shake of his head. "Bros before hos, man."

"You cut us deep," Gray adds.

"Don't let him fool you, Ivy," Thompson tells me as he rolls his eyes. "Gray is as crazy as any of us."

Gray shoots up straight in his seat. "Oh, no. Do not be putting me in your neighborhood of Crazy Town."

"Look at Mr. Nightly Hookup, trying to play like he's a saint. Boy, please."

Drew too makes a noise of disbelief. "Are you forgetting the stripper who went down on you in front of everybody at your birthday party?"

Anna elbows Drew's ribs, and he does a double take, his gaze shooting to Anna and then to me. Understanding sets in, and his eyes widen in obvious chagrin. He coughs and looks away.

Gray, however, waves a hand. "Please, that is nothing compared to these chuckleheads' antics." Despite his light tone, he resolutely doesn't look at me.

Marshall takes the moment to add, "Man, that chick had a mouth on her. Sucked me off that night too. Bless her heart."

Only then do all the guys pause and glance at me, wincing a bit as if they know they've gone too far. And what can I say? *Yay, I'm so glad Gray got a blow job from a stripper! I sure hope he gets checked on the regular!*

I take a hasty sip of my soda. Rolondo looks at me for a second, his dark eyes serious. Then he pulls a grin.

"Did your boys ever tell you about Cheerio?" he asks Anna and me.

Instantly all the guys groan. Drew ducks his head into the crook of Anna's neck, while Gray simply starts to laugh and shake his head as if to say, *No, no, don't do it.* But how are we supposed to resist that tease? Even more, I'm desperate to hear any story that doesn't involve Gray and sex.

Anna and I demand that Rolondo enlighten us. But it's Johnson who answers. His eyes gleam as he settles more comfortably in his seat. "This was back when most of us were freshmen. Dude was a senior. Defensive end."

"Defense. Crazy-ass motherfuckers," Diaz mutters, though he looks amused.

"You know it," Johnson says. "Anyway, Cheerio decided to have a party. You know, introduce us newbies to the team. It's all cool until the end."

"Some things cannot be unseen, man." Dex shoves his fries toward Thompson as if he's lost his appetite.

"Anyway." Johnson gives Dex a pointed look of annoyance. "As I was saying, Cheerio—"

"Who we used to call Marcus," Drew adds, his lips twitching. "Until that night."

"Marcus," Johnson stresses. "Goes to the kitchen, grabs a box of cereal and a jug of milk, and brings them back to the living room." Johnson starts to snicker, glee making his face turn red as he continues his story. "We think nothing of it. The fucker is hungry, and so what? Until he drops his pants."

"What?" Anna's red brows rise high. "Why?" They're all choking on their laughter now.

"Dude grabs hold of his nut sack, stretches it out, and fucking pours milk and cereal into it."

The guys roar with laughter, the deep sound of it bubbling over the room.

"Wha—?" Anna, horrified, glances at me and then back at Johnson, who is laughing so hard, he's crying.

"Why would he do that? I don't even understand how he could accomplish it. What do you mean 'into it'?"

"Like he made a little bowl out of his sack." Johnson seems to think this makes everything clear.

"He must have had an enormous ball sack," I mutter.

Which only makes the guys lose it entirely. Gray slaps a hand against the table as he doubles over.

Anna turns to me. "Can you even?"

"I can't. I really can't."

Drew coughs back a laugh. "Which is why he will be forever known as Cheerio."

I'm never looking at cereal the same way again. But I can't help laughing too. Even if it's the most disgusting thing I've ever heard. Which means I don't see them coming, though I should have expected it.

One second, we're all still chuckling, the next a swarm of girls descends on the table. I try to be charitable about my impression of them, but it isn't working. Not when they nudge both me and Anna out of the way and drape themselves over every male at the table.

Two of them head for Gray. They sit on his lap, wrapping their arms around him. I find it hard to breathe, my skin suddenly hot and uncomfortably tight over my bones.

"Hey there, sexy," Thing One says.

"We've missed seeing you around," Thing Two adds, running her fingers through his hair.

Okay, I need to calm down. I glance at Anna, who looks ready to flip the table.

Drew pulls a girl off him and sets her away. "I'm taken," he tells the girl. "Very."

She pouts but saunters off to join her friend on Diaz's lap. Drew pulls Anna close, murmuring something in her ear that makes her smile and rest her head on his shoulder. Envy hits me, not of their love, but of Anna's smile and obvious relief.

Across from me, Gray catches my eye, and I struggle to give him an amused look. As if I don't care. I shouldn't; I know this is part of his life, of who he is, and I need to see it, not live in denial. But maybe I fail at my charade because Gray winces, clearly embarrassed. And he edges back from their stroking hands.

"Ladies." He forces a smile. "We're kind of in the middle of a conversation."

Everyone at the table seems to freeze for a millisecond, as if

Gray's statement has sent a shock wave over them. Then it's back to the guys groping the women and looking far from interested in continuing any conversations.

As for his new friends, I have to give them credit; they've perfected the art of glaring with absolute disdain. A glare that's focused on me. Both of them quickly turn their attention back to Gray.

"But me and Angie have a bet," says the girl with a tattoo peeking out from her low-rise jeans. "We want to see which one of us you make come first."

"Mmm," Angie coos, pressing her breasts against Gray's arm. "You were so good at getting me off. Alyssa wants a try. And I know you'd be game."

And I'm done.

Beneath the table, a slim hand wraps around mine. I glance at Anna, both surprised and warmly comforted by her silent support. She gives my hand a squeeze but doesn't look my way. Instead, she stands.

"Drew and I are headed out." Drew immediately rises, pulling out his wallet and tossing a few bills on the table. Anna turns to me. "You want a ride, Ivy? Or—"

"A ride would be great, thanks." I force another smile and make to grab my purse.

But Gray stands, upending the girls from his lap. Like cats, however, they manage to land on their feet. He ignores their yelps of protest.

His blue gaze is serious and apologetic. "I said I'd take you home."

That he's being considerate has a small smile pulling at my lips, despite the growing tightness at the center of my chest. "That's okay. You don't need to leave."

The scrutiny of his friends burns; I know they're all watching, soaking in this little scene. It's awkward, and I just want to go.

Angie rubs her hand up and down Gray's arm. "Let her leave,

Gray." Her sly gaze travels slowly up my body, and her nose wrinkles. "She's obviously big enough to take care of herself."

Her friend snorts, making a false show of trying to hide it. "I think she's part of the team, Ang."

Nope, but I'm definitely big enough to squash you two like fucking bugs under my heel. I'm about to tell them as much when Gray glares at them. He catches hold of Angie's wrist and moves her away from him.

"Yeah, I don't think so. Not when you've insulted my friend." He gives her another assessing look. "Not ever, in fact."

Her mouth falls open, but he isn't paying attention. Gray grabs his coat from the hook behind him and brushes past the two girls.

Ignoring the looks of his friends, and the pouting protests of Things One and Two, Gray takes my hand in his. "Come on, Mac, let's get something to eat. I'm starving."

I don't point out that we're in a restaurant or that we devoured wings an hour ago, but let him lead me away.

As soon as we get home, I go to my room, put on my PJs, and scrub my face clean.

I might like to dress up now and then, but I'd rather be comfortable. And it's just Gray with me now.

He's heating up leftover white-bean soup when I return. Gray had brought the soup over earlier. It's no secret that he loves cooking, and he's really good at it. Apparently, his mom taught him, and he'd been the one to cook for his family when she was sick.

His big body moves with ease around the kitchen. He's taken off his sweater, and his thin, ratty T-shirt drapes over his tightly toned torso like a caress. For a moment, I envy that shirt, the way it slides over his skin when he reaches for the bowls.

My gaze moves to his firm ass encased in old jeans. I'm pretty sure his butt should be cast in bronze and immortalized for posterity. Or maybe all of him. It's like Thor's landed in my kitchen and taken over late-night supper. Suppressing a snicker, I join him.

Gray turns, and his gaze slides over me. "Wonder Woman PJs. Excellent."

"Just be glad I wore a bra." I grab the spoons.

Gray halts midstride and utters a small groan. "Is there any chance you'd take your bra off now?" The tip of his tongue flicks out to touch his bottom lip. "Because that would so make my night, Special Sauce."

His teasing shouldn't send a pulse of heat between my legs. But it does. And I'm thankful that I'm wearing a bra now. Otherwise, I'm fairly certain my nipples would be saluting him.

We're quiet as we eat. I don't want to talk about what happened, but it's all I can think about. Is this how my mom felt when she went out with Dad? Had other women been constantly rubbed in her face? But my mom and dad had been a couple. I'm just Gray's friend. His buddy.

It's a struggle to eat.

As for Gray, he looks equally downcast. I'm not sure why. He's never hidden the fact that he likes to hook up. A lot. Am I getting in his way? I don't want him to feel as though he has to babysit me. That would be too humiliating.

"You..." My hand clenches tight. "You didn't have to take me home, you know. You could have gone home with those girls. I wouldn't have been offended."

I shove a spoonful of soup into my mouth to stop myself from taking it all back. But it's too late. Gray's eyes narrow, and his soft lips become flat and hard. He eyes me for an uncomfortable minute, one in which I inwardly curse my big mouth.

When he speaks, it's low and deep. "Yeah, I know, Ivy." His chair creaks as he leans forward, the irritated glint still in his eyes. "I wanted to hang out with you."

Seems that's all both of us want to do lately. Gray has quickly become my world, and it scares me a little. Because it's becoming something I can't control. I stab at my soup.

"It's just...ah, well, the guys made it sound as though you

kind of used to hook up every night." And didn't that make my stomach turn to lead? Which is all kinds of messed up. I certainly don't own Gray.

He makes a noise of annoyance. "The guys were exaggerating. And what the hell? I didn't want to go home with those chicks. It's no big deal."

His expression is mulish as he tucks back into his soup. I don't know whether I want to smile or cringe. But I've upset him, which I don't like.

"I don't like how they talked about you," Gray grumbles.

Though my face flames, I shrug. "It's not like I don't hear similar comments. A lot."

"Doesn't make it right."

"No." I sigh. "But who are we kidding? I'm six feet tall. Growing up with my dad, or when I was around his clients, I never felt particularly tall. But there are days when I feel like a total oaf around other women."

Around guys too, but I've said enough. I'm too tender from tonight's humiliation.

Gray's brows lift in outrage. "You're perfect. And hell, Mac, have you seen me? I'm a fucking tree."

Perfect? Me?

Oblivious to my pleased shock, he snorts with self-deprecation. "I remember hitting my full height. Kept banging into everything. I really did feel like Gulliver around the Lilliputians. Sometimes I still do."

"Yeah, but you lumber so gracefully."

The corners of his eyes crinkle. "Never let them see you sweat, right? And I'm serious, Mac. You're perfect just the way you are. I love not having to throw my back out just trying to meet you at eye level. So no more crazy talk about letting me go home with a couple of jock riders who I didn't even want touching me, anyway. Okay?"

"Okay, okay. Sheesh."

We both kind of glare and nod in agreement, slightly smiling at each other but still a bit awkward. And then we're silent again.

"You should know," I say slowly, because I can never seem to let anything go. "I'm fairly crap at expressing gratitude. I'm always saying the wrong thing."

At this, Gray sets down his spoon and leans back in his chair before running a hand through his hair. The action has his biceps bunching. There's a slight smile playing about his lips. "I kind of like that about you, Mac."

I like everything about Gray.

"All I meant was that I'm happy you're here."

He grins wide. "Me too." But he pauses, his brows knitting. "And I don't hook up with someone every night. To clarify."

"Just every other night, then?" I tease.

He glances away. "Yeah, maybe." But then his deep blue eyes connect again. "And friends always come first."

"Bros before hos?" I say, remembering Marshall's line earlier.

Gray chuckles. "Something like that. Only my mom taught me never to call women whores." His gaze lingers on my breasts just long enough that I feel it, then he catches my eyes. "And you're definitely no bro."

"Glad you noticed."

"Hard not to notice, Mac." He says it in a dry tone, but all I can see is that assessing, *interested* glance he gave me earlier, and it's messing with my head, making my body too warm.

Frowning, I take a bite of soup to cover my disquiet.

Oblivious, Gray soldiers on. "I've never had a girlfriend before. So I'll probably act like a douche now and then." Color paints his cheeks pink. "I mean, a friend who's a girl."

"And a girlfriend?" I can't help but ask. "You ever have one of those?"

"Nah. I've never had the inclination."

"Never?" The word rings hollow in my chest. "That's a tragedy. You'd make someone a great boyfriend."

His cheeks darken, but he shakes his head as if I'm missing the point. "Pretty sure monogamy is a key factor in a relationship."

My spoon clatters to the table. "You'd cheat?"

Gray frowns. "No. Never. But that's kind of the point. I've never wanted to stay with just one girl, so why put myself in that situation?"

"I guess that makes sense." The hollowness grows. Which is ridiculous. Gray's an awesome friend, and that's all I need.

"What about you?" he asks far too casually, as if this conversation has grown uncomfortable for him too, but he can no more stop than I can. "I'm guessing you're pro-boyfriend."

"That such a bad thing? I'm not into hookups."

He flashes a quick, tight smile. "I can see you, Miss Monogamous, going through a string of boyfriends."

I roll my eyes. "I've had one boyfriend, smart-ass. Senior year of high school."

Gray's brows lift. "One boyfriend? That's it?"

"Yep." I steal his beer and take a long sip.

He watches me do it, amusement dancing in his eyes. It hits me anew, the way he makes me feel utterly at home, yet excited. Which is strange; we're just sitting here, talking and eating. And all I want to do is drink in the sight of him, the way the corners of his mouth curve upward in a perpetual little smile, the strong cords of his neck, or how his evening beard dusts his jaw like raw sugar glinting in the lamplight. My tongue can almost imagine how it would feel to lick that stubble—rough, delicious.

Wait. What? *No. There will be no licking of Gray's jaw.*

As if he notices my sudden flush, he peers at me, inspecting my face.

"What?" I ask in a sad attempt to escape my inappropriate thoughts.

"Nothing." Gray gives the back of his neck a scratch, and I ignore his flexing muscles. "I just find it hard to believe you've been single all this time. You're...well... You're great."

"Thanks, Cupcake," I say in the face of his blush. It's cute. And because it's Gray, I feel comfortable enough to tell him the truth. "I've had guys interested. But it soon becomes apparent that they were just as interested in my dad, or rather, who he knew. It would always come up. Could I get them tickets to such-and-such sporting event? Did I know Peyton Manning? Or Eli? Was that really my dad in a picture with LeBron James? Had I met him? And when I answer yes, it's all they can think about." I shrug. "I know, I know, hard problems to have."

"That's not what I'm thinking," Gray says softly, his expression somber. "I was thinking that those fuckers missed out."

Again I shrug and pick at my food, unable to face Gray just then.

"So," Gray says. "This high school boyfriend wasn't into sports?"

"He was. But his father was a record producer so he had his share of fame."

Gray's brows rise and I feel the need to explain further.

"We lived in Manhattan at the time. Life is kind of different there."

"I bet."

Not wanting to go on with my tired poor-little-rich-girl tale, I hurry to finish it. "My boyfriend was fine. We hung out. He took my virginity. The act sucked enough that I didn't ask for a repeat. I left for college. End of story."

"Sounds awesome," Gray deadpans.

I leave that one alone.

"No one in college or London, either?" Gray presses, looking shocked.

I resist the urge to toss my spoon. "I met guys, sure. But no one that I wanted to start a relationship with, okay?"

"Okay." He says it as though he's placating me. Which makes me want to snarl more. But I don't. Instead, we eat.

Until Gray starts shifting in his seat, getting antsy, his thumb tapping out an agitated rhythm on the table.

"What now?" I ask him.

Gray bites down on his lush bottom lip then blurts out, "If you're not into hookups, and you haven't had a boyfriend in five years..."

"Are you trying to ask about my sex life, Cupcake?"

It's cute the way his nose wrinkles. "Please tell me I'm wrong in thinking you haven't had sex in all this time."

"You're not wrong, Gray."

The room goes silent as he gapes at me.

Annoyance crawls along my skin. "God. Your expression. You look like I'm in danger of damaging my vagina."

"Not damaging it, but maybe depressing it. This revelation sure as hell is depressing my dick." He visibly shudders.

I throw a napkin at him, and it skims his head, making his hair stick up.

"For Pete's sake, Gray, it's no big deal. I'm not suffering. Or," I talk over him because his mouth opens to make another protest, "abstaining because of some greater purpose. I'm not waiting for a husband, or afraid of dick, or whatever. It just is what it is. I've been busy with school and—"

"No one is too busy for sex, Mac."

"Oh, please, I'm only twenty-two. I've fooled around with guys, done plenty of things to satisfy me just fine. I just haven't gotten to the point of having sex again. And, anyway, five years isn't that long..."

"It's long enough. What are you waiting for? Your kitty to go on strike and completely shut down? I've heard it happens."

His scoffing hurts. Everything hurts suddenly, as if he's ripped off a bandage and taken a good chunk of skin with it.

"So, you're saying I ought to go out there—" I wave a hand toward the door "—right now and find a guy to fuck before my *kitty* stops working? You know, you're right. That's a brilliant idea."

"What? No, I'm not telling you to go fuck someone *right now.*" He actually looks appalled. "Just that—"

"That what?" I snap. "You've made it abundantly clear that I'm a sorry sack for not having had endless sex all this time."

Gray's massive hands slap the table between us. "I'm just saying that sex is awesome, so excuse me if I'm shocked that you're going without it. If it were up to me, I'd do it ten times a day."

I picture it, Gray screwing an endless parade of girls. "Tell me something this entire town doesn't know, Gray."

As soon as the words lash out of my mouth, horror floods me. The feeling grows when Gray's head snaps back as if I've slapped him, his skin leaching of color.

"What the hell is that supposed to mean?" he whispers.

But we both know. A sick lurch goes through my stomach, and I stand, my chair scraping across the floor.

"I shouldn't have said that." I run my hand over my eyes as I back away. "I have to go."

Gray stands as well, his face a mask of outrage and hurt. "Go? It's your fucking house. Where the fuck are you going?"

I'm already halfway out of the kitchen, headed for the hall. "I've got to get some air, okay?"

I'm losing control, a rarity. And one I avoid because I usually say something I later regret.

"Ivy," Gray shouts.

"Just lock up behind you."

"Fuck this." Gray's snarl is the only warning I get before his hand wraps around my arm. He's angry. Clearly hurt too. Yet when he spins me around, his touch is careful, as if he absolutely knows his own strength and will never use it against me.

"What the fuck, Ivy?" His blue eyes are denim dark beneath the slashes of his brows. "You just say that shit and then walk out on me?"

"I'm sorry," I blurt out, the back of my throat prickling. "I have to… Shit. I'm judging you, Gray. And I don't want to do that."

His grip tightens. "So don't."

"I can't help it. And what the hell? You're judging too."

His lips purse but he doesn't let go. "Because it's stupid, you not having sex. Stupid to make it more than it needs to be."

"I can't be like you, like my dad. I can't treat sex like it's nothing—"

"Not nothing," he interjects. "Just not some holy event that you need to send out invitations to. It can be simple, you know. Dirty, hot fucking."

Hearing Gray's deep, creamy voice say those words is not what I need right now. Not when they lick along the back of my neck and cause a hot little shiver to break out over my skin. I ignore the sensation in favor of anger. It's easier than useless longing.

"It's always 'fucking' to you. A basic act, like getting a bite to eat or playing football—"

"Now, that I resent," he says with a bit of levity. "Football *is* a holy act."

"Right." I wrench out of his grip. "Football means more to you than being intimate with someone."

He snorts, his eyes rolling at the term *intimate* as if it's a joke, and I poke his rock-hard chest with my finger.

"Right there? That disdain. What's wrong with intimacy? What's wrong with treating the act as something more? You're taking all the beauty out of it. All the meaning."

"And right *there* is your problem," Gray snaps, his own long finger poking back at my shoulder. "You're building it up so high in your mind that any guy who dares try with you is doomed to fail under the weight of your expectations."

"Of all the asinine, ridiculous…" I lean in, my breath coming in hard pants as I struggle not to wring his thick neck. "You dare to lecture me on wanting more? Why should I listen to you, of all people?"

A dark flush works over his face, and I know I should stop, I know I'm being unfair, but I've snapped.

"You, who lets a skanky stripper suck you off while your friends watch, and then laughs about it afterward. Ever heard of VD? You can get that from oral, you know."

"Stop," he whispers, his eyes going glassy.

But I can't. Ugliness is a river pouring out of me. I think of my dad cheating on my mom, of how I felt tonight, watching those girls hang on Gray.

"Maybe you don't care who it is you fuck. But I'm not like that. I need more. And if you can't understand that, well…tough shit!"

He lashes out, grabbing my upper arms and hauling me into his chest. Strong arms wrap around me, as my nose crushes into the hard swell of his pecs. He squeezes me as if he needs to contain my words, my judgment.

"Stop it, Ivy," he says, loud, desperate. "Please. Please, I can't fight with you." His voice is broken now. "Not you."

The full impact of what I've said to him hits me. Horror, thick and dark, rushes up my throat on a strangled cry.

"Oh God, Gray." I wrap my arms around his waist and hold on to him. "I'm so sorry. I'm so fucking sorry."

He's stroking my head, as though I deserve comfort. I want to crawl into a hole and stay there.

"I didn't mean it, Gray." I shiver, burrowing closer, my fingers digging into the loose fall of his T-shirt. "I hate myself."

"Yeah, well, I'm not too happy with you, or me, right now either." Gray sighs, his hold becoming more secure. A soft touch on the top of my head, a gentle kiss. "But it's okay. It's okay."

"It's not." I breathe in the clean, comforting scent of Gray. "You're my friend, and I hurt you. I never want to do that."

Standing as we are, not an inch of space between us, I notice the warmth of his body, the utter strength of it. When he holds me, I'm safe, enveloped.

"It's over." His lips press into my temple. "And I'm sorry too. I was being an asshole, getting on you for stupid shit."

We're quiet then until Gray sighs, easing impossibly closer, his big hand slowly stroking up and down my spine. Comfort. That's what he's seeking.

But I'm no longer thinking of comfort because awareness has set in, of his tight abdomen against mine, the bulge of his cock nestled against my sex. He isn't hard, but it's there, obvious and substantial, causing me to think about things that should never enter my head.

Deep within my belly, I clench, heat whispering over my skin. I want to melt into him, stay there all day. I want to open my legs, have him fill that lonely space in between them. If I tilt my chin, my lips will brush the satiny curve where his neck meets his shoulder. I want to lick that spot, taste it and bite it. I don't want to think of other girls doing the same.

My breath hitches. All my anger—the vicious words I'd said—is fueled by jealousy. I am jealous of those faceless, nameless women.

Shame is a lump in my throat, the pricking burn behind my lids. I lashed out because of jealousy, and it was so wrong of me. I'm so fucking screwed, and I don't know what to say to make it right.

"Gray..."

"I don't want you to have sex like I've been doing it, Ivy," he says with sudden heat. "It *should* mean something. For you. It should be good like that."

My heart hurts at the hollowness in his voice, and I spread my hand against his lower ribs, holding him. "Why can't it be like that for you too? Why the endless hookups?"

Because we're so close, I feel the tension snake up his back.

"It just..." He swallows hard. "I guess I keep waiting for the one who will make me want to stop."

"Stop having sex?" I'm chilled to the bone. And a hypocrite

because the thought of him not wanting to have sex again is horrific.

My hair musses as he shakes his head. "Stop moving on to the next girl."

His chest expands on a breath. "Ivy, I love women, and I love sex. But you're right. It doesn't mean anything to me other than quick pleasure. I don't care who it is. I don't remember their names. Shit, I am as bad as you said."

He sounds so despondent that I clutch him tight. "No, Gray. Please don't say that. Can we just… I wish I could take back our fight."

Slowly, he eases away from me, though his arms remain loosely wrapped around my shoulders. It takes us both a moment to meet each other's eyes.

It's awkward, and his expression is twisted as though he's tasted something foul. My fault. But he forces a smile.

"Hey, we're good." He pats my hair with a clumsiness that's unlike him, his thumb hitting my cheekbone and nearly poking me in the eye. "It wouldn't be normal if we never fought."

Wincing a bit, I grasp his forearms and hold on. Because I can't keep my hands off him, apparently. "This is true."

Gray studies me, his blue gaze unnerving. The air between us is too thick, and I can't breathe properly. A crease grows between his brows, as if he can see my guilt and the fact that I am fighting not to rise on my toes and press my mouth to his soft lips.

Fuck. A. Duck.

God help me if he really knew what I was thinking. He'd probably run out the door.

But he doesn't move. Not yet. No, he presses his forehead to mine, cupping my cheeks in his massive palms. It warms me all over.

"I'm going to go now," he tells me after a moment. "Gotta get up early for a hell practice."

"Okay."

But he doesn't go. He seems closer, his breath mingling with mine, brushing over my parted lips. It's too quiet. His fingers twitch, gripping me harder.

And then he lets go so abruptly that I almost stumble. Gray's smile is wide, maybe too wide. He's backing up, maneuvering around a chair.

"'Night, Special Sauce."

I give him a smile back. False. Strained. Fucked-up. That's me, Fucked-Up Ivy. "'Night, Cupcake."

TEN

GRAY

FOR THE FIRST time in our relationship, I've outright lied to Ivy. Okay, it was a small lie, but a lie nonetheless. I don't have early practice. I just had to get away from her. Fast.

She hurt me. Not when she told me the truth of how she saw me. Hell, I know what I am. No, it was the pity in her expression, as if my inability to find any meaning in sex made me pathetic.

Now I'm vacillating between outrage and hurt. Sex is sex. Fuck if I should be ashamed of having as much of it as I want. But then there's this pain, right behind my sternum. Because she's brought up things that I don't ever like to think about. Such as why I can't find meaning in the act. But I know, don't I? And that knowledge is a scab that I don't want to pick at.

Only she's already picked it, and now I'm slowly bleeding. I know Ivy's sorry she hurt me. It doesn't change things. The cat's out of the bag. And I can't stop thinking: Am I really living for the moment, or am I running away from reality?

But even that isn't the real reason I escaped Ivy. It was because for one blind second, I'd been about to say the stupidest thing I could. *Make me stop, Ivy. Be the one who makes it all stop.*

I have the feeling that she could. I'd stood there, aching and hating that we were snapping at each other, and all I wanted to do was kiss her, explore the gentle curve of her lower lip before sucking on it.

And Ivy would have flipped out. Because friends do not maul other friends' mouths.

I'm in uncharted territory here. Usually, when attraction hits, I'd make a move. Or the lady in question would. But now? I'm not so sure it's a good idea.

"Shit." I pick up the pace and head into the team's gym. I could work out at home—and, God, I need to do something to ease this twitchy feeling—but I don't want to talk to anyone. It's late so I have a good chance of being alone here.

Gyms stink of bleach, lingering sweat, and funk, of steel weights and rubber matting, and I love that. It's familiar as home to me now.

I hustle past the locker rooms, ready to hit the treadmill, when I see them.

It's a small movement out of the corner of my eye, nothing I'd notice if I weren't alone at night in a supposedly abandoned gym. I know Rolondo so well by now that I recognize him almost instantly. He's leaning against one of the shower walls, a towel wrapped around his waist, his torso still wet.

But it's the guy next to him who catches my attention. Many scenarios could explain what I'm seeing, but the way the guy leans into 'Londo, half his body blocking my view, and the expression on my friend's face, tight and miserable, give me pause.

As if someone's snapped their fingers in front of my eyes, I suddenly get it.

Understanding hits me the exact moment Rolondo notices me. He stiffens, standing tall, his shoulders straightening as if bracing for a fight. The guy next to him, a big black dude who looks like he'd be at home on the field with us, turns and glances at me. Fear widens his eyes for a second before he narrows them and glares at me, then 'Londo.

Without a word, he pushes off from the wall with one hand and stalks past me, his shoulder almost brushing my own.

I'm left alone with Rolondo, who stares back at me. I suppose the knowledge is there in my eyes; I'm not really trying to hide it. That won't help anymore. But it breaks something between us. I see the moment he decides I'm now the enemy because I know his secret.

He makes a noise of defiance and strolls my way, heading for his locker. He doesn't look at me when he passes, but his muscles twitch and his walk is awkward. Hell. I can leave now, not say a word, but I don't.

"Whatever the fuck you think you saw," he says as he grabs his boxers, "you're wrong, G."

Weariness has me rubbing my face before I move to the bench and sit on it. "You think so?"

"Yeah," Rolondo snaps. "I know so." Already he's raging, ready to attack at the smallest provocation.

Bracing my forearms on my knees, I stare at the waffle-weave pattern on the rubber floor matting. "Is this going to become a problem for us?"

He pauses, one leg in his sweats, the other out, before he continues dressing. "You gonna make it one?"

"Look, I can pretend, and that would probably make things seem easier for you."

He snorts, shoving his feet into his shoes without tying them.

"But in the long run, it won't," I finish.

"I swear to God..." Rolondo holds up his hands, and his arms shake. "If you start in on some white-boy, let's-talk-about-our-feelings bullshit—"

"Sit down, 'Londo."

When he grabs his bag and makes a move to go, my voice, hard and loud, echoes in the room.

"Sit. Down." I snap my head up and catch his gaze. It's a game of chicken but I don't blink. 'Londo might be fast as fuck, but I'm bigger and a better tackle. I will take him down in a minute, and I let him know that with a look.

Scowling and muttering under his breath, Rolondo drops onto the bench next to me. "What, then?"

I almost smile at his petulant tone, only this night has officially gone to shit, and I just want it all to end.

My fingers lace as I sit there. "In high school, I had this friend. Jason. He played receiver. He…ah…" A lump fills my throat and I have to clear it. "Sophomore year he tried to hang himself."

Utter silence expands between us. Until I clear my throat again.

"He couldn't handle it. Couldn't face his dad, his team, thinking they'd reject him because he was gay." My hands clench. "I was his friend. I suspected. But I never asked. I didn't want to upset him. But I knew he was troubled about something."

Rolondo's voice cracks when he speaks. "Why are you telling me this?"

I risk a glance, find he's gone ashy gray. My eyes burn. It hurts thinking of Jason.

"I want to be clear. Do not think for a second that I'd turn my back on you, think of you any differently. And do not even imagine that I'd tell anyone. That's your business."

He glances away, then nods. Once. Sharp.

I don't say anything more, knowing that he'll talk when and if he wants. We sit together for a full two minutes before he finally decides.

"It's wearing on me. Hiding. Pretending to be something I'm not."

"I feel you."

Rolondo laughs low and without humor. "Not hardly, G. I'm

a Southern black man who plays football." He licks his lower lip in agitation. "Hell, my mama is already bugging me about *when is she gonna get some grandbabies?* What do you think she'd say about this?"

We both deflate a little and stare at the floor in silence.

"That guy..." I glance toward the showers where I'd found them. "You love him?"

'Londo nods, but it's abrupt, as if he's still fighting his feelings.

I want to help, but what can I tell him that won't sound trite? He's in a shitty position and we both know it. I pinch the bridge of my nose and think of Ivy. She'd know what to say to make it right.

"I get being afraid to take a stand, change things," I say. "I think... No, I *know* that I'm falling for my best friend."

"Tell me something we all don't know, G." For the first time tonight, Rolondo sounds like his old self.

I fight a smile. "Yeah, well, she pretty much thinks I'm a manslut so..."

"Again, tell me something we don't all know."

I glare at him, and he laughs. I deserve it, though. I have been hiding behind a party-guy persona for so long, everyone in my life thinks it's who I really am. It doesn't sit right with me anymore. Sure, that guy has gotten me laid countless times. But I am tired of being shallow.

Shaking my head, I lean forward and rest my arms on my knees. "It's probably for the best. What the fuck do I know of relationships anyway?"

Rolondo snorts. "You're asking me?"

"I'm saying we're both screwed."

"Yeah," he says slowly, almost smiling. "Yeah, I guess we are. I'll tell you this. You better figure out how to deal with her dad if you do make your move. Mackenzie will kick your ass, for sure."

It might be worth it. Sighing, I straighten and roll my tense shoulders. "I'm gonna head out. Just... You're my friend and my teammate. Whatever you do, I'm with you. One hundred percent."

"Thanks, man." It's barely a whisper. But I hear it.

My face feels hot from too much emotion flowing through me for one day. I stand, give him a brief tap on the shoulder, and walk away.

Despite what I said, my stomach is queasy with uncertainty. Everything is changing around me, so quickly it feels as if a rug has been pulled from under my feet.

IVY

Gray lives with a bunch of his teammates in a house near campus. Normally, I'd look forward to visiting his home. I've tried to picture it several times. Gray at his desk doing assignments, or in bed, doing… Yeah.

But now with our fight still fresh in my mind, I hesitate to get out of my car.

We haven't seen each other in days, not since that night. Gray has been practicing and then watching game footage like a fiend, learning his competition's strengths, weakness, and playing style.

A few texts are all we've exchanged. But now he's heading out of town for his conference championship game, the first stop on the road to the National Championship. I promised to come by before he goes.

With a deep breath, I leave the quiet confines of my little car that still carries Gray's scent.

The house is a white center-hall Colonial, the type which could be stately and welcoming, but with its peeling paint and barren lawn, just looks kind of forlorn. The four recycle bins, filled with empty soda, Gatorade, and beer bottles, fairly scream "group house."

The sounds of explosions and gunfire echo from behind the

door, and a bunch of guys shout and laugh. I bang on the door hard, hoping someone will hear me over the blasting video game.

Gray opens on the second knock. I don't think I'll ever truly get over how big he is. He dwarfs the doorway, his broad, defined shoulders visible beneath the threadbare team T-shirt he wears. Sweats hang low on his hips, and his toes peek out from a pair of sports flip-flops. I don't know why I fixate on his toes and the fact that they seem strangely vulnerable, all bare to the elements.

But I can't avoid looking him in the eye forever. Especially when he utters a husky "Hey."

He's giving me a small, hesitant smile. As always, when I meet Gray's eyes, I'm hit with warmth and a fuzzy happiness that pushes past any other thoughts.

"Hey. I'm here!"

God. Smooth. Real smooth.

Gray's face lights with a full grin. "Yes, you are. Come on." He gestures with a jerk of his head. "Get out of that cold."

Instantly, I'm greeted with the overwhelming scent of funk, like gym socks and men's deodorant and old house. The floorboards are scuffed and stained. And I have to smile because there's a broom in the corner of the hall with a sticky note that says, *Use me, dickwads, before I paddle your ass!*

Gray notices and rolls his eyes. "Dex's sad attempt to domesticate us."

We walk past a pyramid of duffel bags tucked against the hallway wall. To our left, the living room opens up. Two mismatched couches that look in danger of snapping under the weight of six massive guys are positioned around a giant TV. Some warzone video game is playing, but the guys all turn as one when I walk in.

"Ivy!" they shout in unison, their deep voices bouncing over me.

"Boys!"

I get a few head nods, a couple of smiles, then they're back to their game. The sounds of war blare throughout the room.

At my side, Gray takes my elbow. "Let's go to my room."

The stairs squeak beneath our feet. Gray's room is a welcome surprise. At the back of the house, it's simple but clean. Orderly. His desk is spotless, as is the floor. A king bed takes up most of the space. A chest of drawers by the door and a worn blue IKEA armchair in the corner make up the rest of his furniture.

I peer up at the only artwork in the room. "Wow. Where did you get that?"

Hanging on the wall opposite of the bed, the painting is massive. Done in tones of grays and blues, it's a close-up of a man's arm holding on to a battered football helmet.

"Dex did that," Gray says, looking up at it. "I loved it so much, I nagged him until he gave it to me."

"It's fantastic." The composition is simple, but the strength in the arm and the way the hand grips the helmet speak of suffering, perseverance, and love of the game.

"Yeah. He's ridiculously talented. Not that he lets anyone but us know about it."

I'm not surprised. A lot of athletes have hidden talents or hobbies they like to do in their downtime.

"There's a guy in the NBA who can play the violin like a master. But he only performs for his teammates."

"Who?" Gray's voice is curious but subdued. Our fight stands between us, and I hate myself for what I said to him in the heat of jealousy and defensive anger.

I give him a forced smile. "That's his secret to tell."

Gray shakes his head. "Tease."

He flops onto his bed, the frame screeching in protest, and promptly lies back, tucking his arm behind his head.

Okay then, maybe I'm the one overthinking things. Taking a breath, I sit next to him. Gray has other ideas and tugs me down next to him. I land with an "oof" and he grins.

"So."

"So," I repeat, rolling on my side to face him. "You ready

for the game?" While his team is favored to win, anything can happen on the field.

"Fuck yeah. We got this." His smile fades, replaced by a searching look. "The bus leaves in three hours, so we'll be heading out soon. I wish you were coming."

Guilt hits me anew. I want to be at his game more than anything. But I'm staying put and celebrating Fi's birthday, which happens to be the night before the game. "I wish I were too."

"You sure Fi wouldn't want to celebrate with us? My guys know how to party."

Sighing, I flip onto my back. "My dad has ditched Fi on her birthday for as long as I can remember. When we were little, it was for a ball game. Then for championship games. It's a big recruitment time for him."

"That's kind of shitty of him."

I don't know why I feel defensive of my dad; Gray's not saying anything I haven't thought, but nothing in life is straight black-and-white.

"It's his job. Follow the players. Score the deal. Take care of the client. Talk to sponsors." I glance at Gray. "When was the last time you weren't expected to play on or around a major holiday?"

"Fourth of July count?" He gives me a cheeky look but then sobers. "I said it was shitty, not that I don't understand. Which is another reason I haven't done relationships. I hate the idea of doing that to anyone."

Sadness sits heavy on my chest. Gray isn't the type of person who should walk alone through life. But it's not like I can protest his choices. A selfish part of me doesn't even want to encourage him to find a girlfriend, something I know would put even more distance between us. Which makes me all sorts of wrong.

I pick a piece of lint off his comforter. "Anyway, Fi's kind of touchy about her birthday and football. She doesn't want to be anywhere near a game during her time. I'm not going to ask her to change her plans. No matter how much I want to."

"I get that too." He sighs as well. "Fuck, how I get it. Aside from my mom, I came second—hell, more like fifth—to football."

"And yet you love it."

He's frowning up at the ceiling, but as if he feels my stare, he turns.

Joy fills his expression. "I do love it, Ivy. It gives me a high unlike anything else."

He says it with such reverence, I find it hard to swallow. I've never loved anything that way.

A strange sort of yearning fills me. To love something with that intensity. To be loved in turn, put first above all things. How would it be? If Gray's love of football is anything to go by, it would be the best thing in the world.

"I envy you," I say, my eyes focused forward so I don't have to see his face. But I feel him watching me.

"Why?"

"I want that out of life, that excitement."

"You don't have it with baking?" Gray sounds genuinely surprised, but his voice is gentle, almost hesitant. Does he pity me?

I shrug. "Not in the way you love football."

His shoulder moves against mine as he takes a breath. "What excites you, then?"

You.

"Sports. Interacting with others…" I shake my head. "Nothing concrete. Nothing flashing a big sign that says, 'Here is your passion!'"

He seems to soak this in before responding. "I don't know, Mac. I still think you'd make a kick-ass agent. Maybe not the sharky parts, but life planning. Marketing and coaching athletes through their social issues."

The comforter pulls as he rolls fully onto his side to face me, and I can't help but turn my head. A shock of dark gold hair flops over his forehead as he peers at me.

"You should have seen the way you lit up when you talked to the guys about that stuff." The corner of his lip curls upward. "It was beautiful."

My fingers dig into the worn comforter beneath me. "I don't know, Gray… I've grown up hating my dad's job half the time."

"What about the other half?"

"Fascinated, jealous that he got to do those things while I was left behind." My free hand lifts in a helpless gesture. "It's complicated."

"Family stuff usually is. Just remember, you're not your dad."

"Thank God for that," I quip, earning a snicker from Gray.

"Oh, hey…" Gray leans over me as he reaches for his bedside table, and his chest presses against mine. I suck in a breath so my breasts aren't touching him, but he moves away just as quickly, now holding his phone. He flops back down next to me.

A few swipes and he draws up his email, then hands me the phone. "Check it."

I scan the email, not understanding at first. Then I truly read it, and I feel a little sick.

"Gray…"

He talks over me. "See? Totally clear."

I click off the screen, not wanting to look at his sexual health report. He's healthy, and I feel like shit.

"Wh-why did you get a health check?"

His shoulder moves against mine as he shrugs. "You got me thinking. I mean, I've never done it without a condom, but like you said, oral…" He shrugs again. "Just thought it was a good idea."

"Jesus." I toss Gray his phone, and he catches it against his stomach, frowning as he turns.

"What's wrong?"

"Wrong?" I press the heels of my hands against my eyes. "Fuck."

"Mac." Annoyance and worry color his voice. "Why are you freaking out? I'm okay."

"Because I feel like a total asshole, that's why." I hold my palms to my hot face, blocking him out. "You got a checkup because I shamed you—"

"Oh, please," Gray says with a forced laugh. "I get checked out once yearly. Just moved it up on my things-to-do list, was all."

I don't lower my hands. "Uh-huh."

"Mac..." Gently, Gray pries my hands away from my face. A groove runs down either side of his mouth. "Come on. It's no big deal. In fact, it's pretty cool. I'm healthy, and believe me, I plan to stay that way. No more stupid shit for me."

"Gray." I lick my lips, and his gaze follows, his brow furrowing. And the uncomfortable tension that began with our fight grows even more.

Suddenly, I'm tired. Down to my bones. My hand feels heavy as it lifts and cups his cheek. "Win this game, and I'll make you any dessert you want."

I don't know what else to say. Or to do. Something broke between us when I let my jealousy get the better of me. Now our friendship has shifted. He's my favorite person in the world, but I no longer feel at complete ease with him. I don't know what the fuck I want, but it isn't this strange new *thing* that we have going.

I sit up as Gray grins wide, oblivious to my unease. "Anything, Mac?"

I keep my back to him, making a pretense of smoothing my hair. "You saying there's something I can't make?"

The bed dips as Gray sits up too. "I was gonna win the game regardless, but now? Icing on the cake, baby."

I roll my eyes and stand. "On the cupcake, you mean." Quickly, I bend over and give him a peck on his forehead. "Give 'em hell, Gray."

I pull back to go when a touch on my cheek stops me. Gray's calloused fingertips are gentle on my skin.

"Ivy," he says with hesitation.

"Yeah?" I whisper.

There's a look in his eyes, intent yet almost afraid, like he's struggling, and I'm not sure I want him to say whatever it is he's going to say. But then slowly his hand glides over my cheek. It's such a tender caress that my heart gives a little flip.

"Every inch, Ivy."

My brows knit as I search his face. "What does that mean?"

Gray shakes his head, his mouth tilting with a faint smile. "Nothing really. Just something I say before a game. For luck."

Swallowing hard, I touch his face. His jaw is warm and rough with stubble. "Well, then," I say. "Every inch."

The broad line of his shoulders sags on a sigh, and he nods as if I've given him a rare gift.

I leave him then, relief mixing with a strange sense of wrongness within me.

ELEVEN

IVY

WITH GRAY OUT of town, I find myself struggling with an excess of restless energy. I don't know what to do with myself. And, really, I should be figuring it out. I'm a college grad without a job. I know what I want to do, but I dread telling my dad, who's been footing my bills until now.

Skin twitching and gut clenching, I soothe myself the only way I know how.

Hours later, the house smells of golden, buttery-sweet goodness. I have enough donuts to feed Gray's entire team. Which sucks since they're not around to feed.

Fi arrives just as I finish glazing the last batch.

"Hermey, Rudolph, and Yukon Cornelius, what the hell smells so good?" Like a tracking dog, she stalks into the kitchen and nearly sticks her nose into a tray of donuts. "Is that bacon on the top?"

"Yup. Honey-chili bacon. I'm trying to break out from the standard maple bacon."

She picks up a donut and takes a bite, groaning as she does. "You done good, Iv."

I select a raspberry-filled with a toasted marshmallow topping. The flavor combination is reminiscent of peanut butter and jelly, but not as heavy and more creamy. Fi steals a bite of it and groans again.

"Hey," I say with a laugh. "Don't go getting me sick."

"Bah. I'm not sick any longer, and if you were going to get sick, it would have already happened. Ooh…what's that one?"

"Christmas donut. Eggnog flavor with a burnt rum-sugar crust like you'd get on a crème brûlée."

"Yum." Fi continues to munch on her bacon donut and speaks around a mouthful of food. "So what's with all the donuts? You channeling Mom?"

Hedging from answering Fiona, I reach for the bottle of red wine on the counter. "Want a glass?" I ask instead.

She eyes me for a moment then shrugs. "Red wine with donuts? Why not?"

I don't talk until we both have a full glass of wine. "It relaxes me."

"Of course it does. It's in our blood. I mean, I hate it, but…" She grins, her cheeks plumping, before becoming serious. "Seriously, Ivy, why are you cringing like a guilty convict over these donuts?"

I take a sip of wine and glance away. "I realized today that I bake—or fry in this case—best when I'm tense."

The kitchen wall clock ticks away as Fi watches me. "You fried a lot, Ivy Weed."

"I know." Before me is a sea of donuts, each perfectly frosted. "I've always thought that I should join Mom because I am good at baking. I like working with my hands, making pastries, and coming up with new flavors. I like feeding people. But lately, I've started to think about how I want to live. The thing is, Fi, I want to be excited."

"And baking doesn't excite you?" She glances at the donuts.

"It inspires me, makes me feel good. But running a bakery? I hated it."

Guilt grips me as I confess. Because I did hate that part. I'd hated getting up before dawn, always being on my feet, worrying about the store and customers. Before, I'd pushed that concern to the back of my mind. But now it's too close to ignore.

"So don't do it."

Setting my glass down, I start to wipe away a glop of honey glaze on the counter. Fi watches me do it.

"If you don't want to run one of Mom's stores," she asks carefully, "what is it that you want to do? Not that you have to know or anything."

My fingers curl around the damp rag, and I toss it aside. "I don't know."

But I do. I just can't seem to voice what I want because it sounds too crazy. And I'm not ready to face it. I take a large gulp of my wine, letting the mellow smoothness warm my blood. I feel foolish, frustrated. Doubt dances over me with sticky feet. Maybe this is just a silly flight of fancy.

"Mom and Dad are going to think I've lost it."

"Hey," Fi says softly. "I've changed my major about six times in two years."

"You're a sophomore. You have time. And you love decorating. Why not do that?"

Absently, she nods. "Yeah, maybe."

For a moment, we're silent. Then Fi sets her glass down and reaches for another donut.

"I'm gonna regret you," she says to the donut. "But I can't seem to care." Her gaze finds mine. "I'm calling a frat boy I know to pick the bulk of these up before we go into a sugar coma. Then we're going to celebrate my birthday in style, which will include drinking more wine and telling our deep dark secrets to each other."

"Fi." I'm trying not to laugh. "That basically sums up all our nights together."

"Does not! What we drink and eat always varies."

I grin and start packing up the donuts.

Much, much later, we find ourselves sprawled on my bed among the copious throw pillows. The wine has been ditched in favor of mojitos, and my head is swimming.

"Red wine makes me sleepy," I complain.

"It's my birthday. You can't fall asleep." Fi rolls over and glares at me.

"Mmm-hmmm." My lids grow heavy. I start to drift off, but that strange restless feeling returns as soon as my mind wanders. I think I might be coming down with a cold. But that's not what's bugging me now. "Fi?"

"What?" she mumbles, her face stuffed into a pillow.

"Can a person…I don't know…be oversexed when they aren't having any sex?"

The instant the words are out of my mouth my face flames and I want to call them back. As it is, they hang over our heads, dancing around like mocking pixies as Fi's mouth drops open.

Her stare drills into me, and I resist the urge to squirm. Before I break, she shrugs, all casual as if I haven't blurted out something ridiculous. "Explain."

I don't want to. My big mouth has gotten me in enough trouble. But mojitos have made me warm and loosened my tongue.

"God, Fi, where to begin? I think about sex. All the time now."

About cocks. Pushing into me. Filling me up. Sliding into my mouth. Hell.

"My breasts feel heavy, my nipples…let's not talk about those." It brings back the restlessness, makes them tingle, and I cuddle the throw pillow closer.

It doesn't shut me up, though.

"I ache. So much that my lower belly hurts. Hell, my freaking thighs feel hot." Annoyed now, I slap a hand against the mattress. "I find myself dreaming of running my thumbs along those grooves on a guy's abdomen. The ones formed by those muscles right over their hips. You know the ones? That form a V." My mouth actually waters thinking about them now.

"Oh," says Fi in an expansive voice, "I know them well." She grins, all cheeky, her brows waggling. "They bracket Victory Lane on the road to Cocksville."

"Yesterday," I tell her on a sigh, "I ended up staring at a nipple for ten minutes."

Fi chokes as a laugh breaks out. "A nipple?"

"Yeah," I say, despondent. "There was this picture of a shirtless guy in *Vogue*—"

"Oh, a *guy's* nipple."

I bite my lower lip. "I'd probably get turned on by the sight of a woman's nipple too. I mean, boobs are sexual and all that."

Fi mutters something under her breath before glancing at me. "Never figured you'd be the type to get enthralled by a dude's nipple."

"Apparently so." Frowning, I pick at the hem of my shirt. "You know, they're just so tiny and hard, like those rivets on jeans?"

I ignore her snort. "And I wonder how one would feel against my tongue. Would the guy like it if I licked him there? Would he make a little groan—"

"All right there, Little Miss Spanish Fly, I get the picture."

Sighing, I turn to my side to face her. "Fi, this is serious! It's a problem. I'm hurting here!"

Her cheeks plump on a grin. "Oh, I hear you, Iv. Though I'd say this is more an issue of being undersexed rather than oversexed."

"Under, over, the point is I'm horny."

"Then go out and have some sex, already."

"I can't." It's a pathetic wail. "I'm not made that way, Fiona. I can't screw just anyone. I need—"

Damn it all, I don't want to talk about this anymore. My stomach turns with the thought of nameless sex, even as my breath quickens with the thought of a hard, male body pressing against me.

"I need to like the guy," I mumble. That's the shittiest part about it. I want sex so badly my teeth ache. And yet I don't have the guts to go out and get it.

"Hmm..." Ice clinks as Fi swirls her glass. "You know who you should talk to about this? Gray."

"What?" Heat rushes my face. "Please. No." I wave, my hand nearly slapping my nose in the process. "No way, Fi. Do you want me to die of embarrassment?"

Gray would either smirk and give me the same shit as Fi, or he'd be horrified. Gray has a startling tendency to get prudish on me. God help me if Fi suggests what I think she will. I can't think about that. I *won't*.

"Why not? He knows all about sex. He's hot as fuck. Maybe he could help you out, give you a little friends-with-benefits relief."

She went there.

"Fi! How can you say that?"

"Ow! Volume, Ivy. My damn ears are ringing."

Grinding my teeth as my face bursts into flames, I manage to speak. "I cannot believe you said that."

Did the heat come on or something? I'm going to burn up from embarrassment. Maybe melt into the bed.

"Oh, please. He'd do it, you know he would. Everyone knows the guy will hump any hot girl that looks his way."

"Stop. Gray isn't some cheap manslut."

Never again will I let myself or anyone else belittle him.

"He's not?" She doesn't even try to hide her sarcasm.

"No. He's my friend, and I'll thank you not to talk about him that way." I hug my pillow tight. "Never mind that friends-with-bennies has got to be one of the stupidest ideas in history. It *never* works. Not," I add, "that I'd even consider it. I don't..." A breath puffs out of me. "I'm not going there with Gray."

Just the thought of sex with Gray... Nope, not going to even entertain the idea. Sex with him would only lead to trouble. I'm a relationship gal. And I know it would become too much for me, sharing that sort of intimacy and not having Gray as more than a friend. I cling to that fact like I would a life raft.

Her shrug is careless. "Well, then maybe he can hook you up with one of his hot friends."

"I'm not having sex with one of Gray's friends." Everything within me revolts at the idea. It would ruin what I have with Gray. Wouldn't it? And besides, I don't want one of his friends.

"So you don't want a hookup, or to ask Gray to help you out or set you up." Fi glares at me. "What do you want?"

An answer pops into my head before my booze-addled brain can squash it down. I bite my lips together and refuse to say it. Again, the horrible, squirmy, we-need-some-lovin' heat flares between my legs.

"I just want to feel like myself again."

"Good luck with that. Horny doesn't just up and go because you ask it nicely."

"Great." I lift my hands in irritation. "So I what...?"

Fi laughs at me, the jerk. "Become real familiar with your hand."

"Pillow," I correct without thinking.

"What?" Her eyes are wide, her smile scandalized.

"Nothing. I said nothing." Fucking booze. I'm never drinking again.

"Sure you didn't, Miss Hump-and-Pump."

The throw pillow flies out of my hand and whacks her face.

"Eew," Fi shouts. "This had better not be *the* pillow!"

"Better smell it and see."

Fi's answer is to smother me with the pillow, and the night devolves from there.

GRAY

For the first time before a game, I'm nervous. Usually I'm pumped up, anticipation and adrenaline surging through my body. I get off on it, like good sex, only with a fine edge of aggression to sharpen the feeling.

Out on the field, I can let myself go. Let out all the anger, hurt, frustration of life. And yet it never really feels like rage. It's a battle, sure, but there's love too. I fucking love this game. The intensity. The pain. The mind games. Nowhere else do I feel more alive than when I'm playing, my body and mind working at full tilt to obtain my goals.

I'm not gonna lie; I have a hard-on for football. I get totally jacked on game day.

Which is why I'm pissed now. Because I'm not jacked. Excitement does not run through my veins. Instead, there's a boulder in my stomach and invisible hands clutching my neck.

Though the crowd is roaring their excitement, and the air almost vibrates with their enthusiasm, everything feels off. My teammates aren't joking like they usually do.

Rolondo is quiet and pacing the sidelines as they prepare to sing the national anthem. The guys have tense faces. Cal Alder is sitting on a bench, his skin pasty and sweaty, though Coach doesn't seem too worried that our starting quarterback looks like death warmed over.

I swear the stink of defeat hangs over us, and we haven't even started the game.

My fingers are ice-cold as the anthem is sung. By the time a few of our defensive linemen trot out to do the coin toss, I'm ready to scream.

From the corner of my eye, I see Alder scramble over the bench. He pukes into a half-filled ice bucket, and a few guys jump back.

Cursing, I jog over to him as he throws up again.

Wiping his mouth with the back of his hand, he glances up at me. "You gonna make it?" I ask.

His expression is blank. "Yup."

"Here." I grab a Gatorade and hand it to him. "Refuel and wash your mouth. I'm not smelling that when you call plays."

He doesn't smile but takes the bottle and drinks deep. On the field, the kickoff is already underway. Our guy Taylor manages to catch the ball and run to the forty. It's almost time to go to work.

"What's the deal?" I ask Cal. "You sick?"

Those frosty eyes of his don't blink. "You my nurse?"

"I'm your fucking teammate and tight end," I snap, annoyed as shit. "So answer the fucking question."

Cal's tight expression eases. He sets his bottle down and stands. "Right as rain, Grayson."

Well, fucking great. Sure, whatever. I'm about to yell at him to give me the truth, when Dex walks up. He's got his helmet in hand and his dark hair is already sticking up with sweat. He takes a long look at Cal then nods. "Stage fright."

Cal's eyes go a little wide, but he nods too. "Every time."

"You get over it?" Dex asks as though this is all just fine and dandy.

"Once I begin to play, yeah."

"Good enough for me." Dex puts on his helmet as Cal heads toward our offensive coach.

I just stare after him as I put my helmet on too. "It's a little freaky how well you read people, Big D."

Dex's eyes crinkle behind his face mask. "It's a gift. And a curse."

I can't respond because the whistle has blown.

"Gentlemen." Coach steps closer, his voice booming yet steady. "I've already said everything there is to say. Let's get 'er done!"

"Red Dogs!" we all shout as one. We always do. But this feels rote.

In the huddle we're subdued. Fucking *subdued*. Intolerable.

"Hey," I shout over the noise of the crowd. "With sufficient thrust, even pigs fly."

They look at me like I've grown another head.

"What the fuck, G?" Diaz shouts back with a confused snort.

"We gonna make those pigs fly." I nod toward the defense taking their positions. "When we knock the shit out of them."

The guys start to smile but our old spirit isn't quite there.

Cal's head snaps up. There's a gleam in his icy eyes that none of us have seen before. It's like he's flicked an internal switch and it's lighting him up from the inside. "We're going to win. Because we fucking own this game."

He isn't Drew. Never will be. He doesn't have a shit-eating grin or a cocky attitude. But he has something else: a quiet authority that demands respect.

We all seem to feel it in our bones. Because suddenly we're all grinning. Energy ripples over the huddle, making us squeeze closer together, rumble with agreement. My old friends, anticipation and adrenaline, return with a vengeance, drawing my balls up tight and lifting the hairs on the back of my neck.

Cal looks over us, his voice stronger than I've ever heard it as he calls the play. He finishes with a sharp "Go Dogs!"

Which we echo. And then break. At the line, a defensive back snarls at me, trying to intimidate, talking shit I don't bother listening to. I just grin. Because I'm about to smoke his ass. Game fucking on.

TWELVE

GRAY

DESPITE THE VICTORY high that still rushes through my veins, I decide to go back to my room and order room service instead of hitting the local clubs to party with the guys. The idea of being out holds little appeal. What would I do? Dance? Hook up with some girl?

I can't dance anymore without thinking about Ivy's horrific moves and wanting to see them again. And the thought of touching someone other than Ivy does absolutely nothing for me. Scratch that, the thought of touching someone else makes my dick want to retreat like a turtle into its shell—an image that creeps the ever-loving hell out of me, but there you go.

When I make my intentions known, Johnson tries to check my brow, convinced that I am coming down with something. I slap his hand away. Dex just turns his attention to picking out a place to go.

Unfortunately Drew and Anna are with us. Their knowing

looks chafe. I'd given Drew hell when he'd started foregoing clubs because he was clearly gone on Anna. So I am not surprised when he leans close to Anna and says in a voice obviously meant to carry, "Fifty bucks says he calls her within the hour."

Anna's green eyes narrow as she slants a look at me. "Gray does like his food, though. I'm thinking he'll eat first, then call."

"And I'm thinking you both can kiss my left—"

Drew's elbow to my gut cuts off my words.

Scowling and rubbing my admittedly empty belly, I leave them to their night, almost making it to the elevator before Anna calls out, "Give Ivy my best!"

I flip Anna the bird as the doors close on their laughter. But I'm not really pissed.

They're right; I am going to call Ivy. I cannot fucking wait to hear her voice. Her absence is an emptiness in my chest.

However, Anna knows me well, because I order room service first. After a hot shower, my food is here. I don't bother dressing but settle down to eat. I could call Ivy now, but I hold off, playing a waiting game with myself. How long can I take it? How much do I need her?

The questions bounce around in my head as I chomp down my steak with record speed.

By the time I lie back on my bed and pick up my phone, my heart quickens in anticipation of hearing her voice. In other words, I'm totally screwed. But I'm willing to dive in anyway.

She answers on the third ring. "Heeee!"

"Jesus, my eardrums, Mac." Despite the fact that my ear is ringing from her squeal, a huge grin pulls at my face.

"I'm sorry," she says. "I'm just so fricking happy for you, Cupcake."

And there it is: the warmth that's been missing in the center of my chest.

Still smiling, I rub the area as if to keep it from going cold again. "You watch the game?"

"You know I did. You rocked it."

"Eh, I wasn't bad."

"Oh, sure, not bad at all. Only eleven pass completions, one hundred twenty-four yards, and two touchdowns." Ivy's tone is dry. "Are you fishing for compliments, Cupcake?"

I love that she knows the game.

"Maybe," I say with a smile. "Would have been better if you were here."

Ivy huffs. "Are you going to guilt me over this for the rest of our lives?"

"I don't know. Are we going to be together for the rest of our lives?" My breath hitches at the thought of forever with her, and I laugh to cover it up.

But she doesn't seem to notice. She's as saucy as ever. "Not if you keep bitching like a cranky old man."

I snort and stroke my chest in an idle rhythm. But it doesn't really settle me. I'm too twitchy, my bent knee rocking as I talk to her.

"We're coming back tomorrow. Want to do something?"

"Sure." There's a noise in the background like she's moving around, fussing with something. Ivy's never still. She's a lot like me in that regard. "So are you going out?"

"No, I'm in for the night."

"What? Why?" She's so freaking cute when she's irate. "You should be out celebrating."

Smiling, I reach over and grab my headphones so I can talk hands-free. "I'm celebrating with you."

Awkward silence follows, and I inwardly curse my big mouth. "Mac?" I ask when the moment stretches too far. "You there?"

"Yeah… I'm here." Her voice is soft, hesitant. "I just… I wish I was there. I should have been there for you."

"You're here." My hand stops over my heart, and I spread my fingers wide, pressing down as if it can ease the ache inside. "Now, I mean. This counts too."

"Gray?"

"Yeah?" I whisper.

"Are we good? I mean, what I said—"

"I told you, Mac. We're good. Can we just move past it?" Fuck if I want this tension between us anymore. It's killing me.

"Okay, okay." More scuffling noise comes from her side of the phone. "Grumpy Gus."

"That's Sir Grumpy Gus to you." I smile a little. "What are you doing? I hear noises."

"What noises?" Mac says in a stage voice that makes me smile full-out. "I'm not hiding a body, I swears!"

"Har."

"I'm getting into bed, if you must know."

Instantly, my body goes tight. It doesn't help that I'm naked and spread out on a bed. It's a strain to sound unaffected. "You want me to let you go?"

"Nope."

Somehow I can hear her slide under the covers. The little hairs on my skin stand on end. My hand edges down to my abdomen, the muscles hard and tense there. I imagine Ivy's hand running along my skin and suppress a groan.

As it is, a small grunt escapes me, and I hurry to speak. "I'm getting into bed too."

"Jesus, you really are acting like an old man. Are you sure you're all right?" The affection in her voice comes through loud and clear. "I feel like I should be pressing a hand to your fevered brow."

"I'm tired, Mac," I tell her lightly. "And if you don't cut it out, I'm going to hang up. Would serve you right if I am sick and end up wasting away from some sort of Victorian disease. Then how will you feel? Knowing you let me go."

"What kind of disease are we talking about? Like consumption? Or cholera?" Mac snickers into the phone. "If it's cholera, you're on your own, Cupcake."

"Cute." I rest my hand behind my head, getting more comfortable. "Mac?"

"Yeah?"

"You said it was bad. The sex, I mean, and—"

"Gray!" Her exasperation is sharp. "Didn't we *just* agree not to talk about that anymore?"

I wince, feeling like an ass and cursing my big mouth.

"Shit, yes. I know. It's... Okay, fine, it's bugging me. Not," I interject before she can speak, because I can hear her taking an indignant breath, "because you aren't having sex. But you said it was bad. And I want to know why."

"Why?" she repeats faintly.

My heart pounds against my ribs. "Did he... Did he hurt you, honey?"

It's inexcusable that I haven't made certain until now. And I will burn the fucking earth down if he did.

Mac's soft voice comes at me through the buzzing in my head. "No, Gray. No, not that."

She goes silent, and I take the moment to draw in a deep, not-so-steady breath, nodding even though she can't see me. Relief makes me sag further into the pillows.

When she speaks again, it's low and tense. "It was just... Gah! The foreplay was awesome. I wanted it, Gray. Badly, you know?"

Again, I nod. My voice seems to have left the building. I don't really want to think about some fuckwit giving Ivy "awesome" foreplay. Why did I have to ask?

"I mean, I planned for it, went to the doctor's and got on the pill and—"

"That's some dedicated planning for your first time."

She makes an annoyed noise. "I know. But that's how I am. I plan. I commit. And I don't trust condoms to—"

"You don't?"

"To protect against diseases, yeah, but you do realize they have about an eighteen percent failure rate for birth control?"

I don't want to even think about failure rates. The idea that little Grays could be out there gives me the willies. But I chuckle instead, wanting to change the subject. "Okay, okay, lesson learned, Doctor Sex Ed."

She snorts. "I was sixteen. I did not want to get pregnant, and I figured if I worried about that, I wouldn't have any fun."

And that strange dichotomy is my Ivy. Super planner mixed with a free spirit who goes with the flow. A surge of affection hits me, and I sink even further into the pillows.

"Anyway," she drawls as if to say I'd taken her off track and not to do it again. "I was all in. But then we got down to it, and he basically…er…"

I can almost hear her embarrassment.

"He didn't get the job done?" I offer wryly.

She huffs out a laugh. "It was just so fast. Jab, jab, jab, strangled cry, done!"

Despite myself, I laugh too. "Pretty sure that's how most high school guys do it, Mac."

"Yeah, well, from what I've heard, most college guys do it that way too. Once they get the green light, it's so long, foreplay, hello, fast fuck. Thanks, but no thanks."

What can I say to that? We can be selfish bastards. I wince inwardly, thinking of the times I took my own pleasure, accepting it as truth when the girl beneath me acted as if I was a god simply because I chose to stick my dick into her. My face burns. Fuck, I'm an asshole.

Closing my eyes, I pinch the bridge of my nose as I talk. "How would you want it to go, Mac? If you could have it your way?"

"What?" There's a protracted half laugh from her. "Sex?"

"Yeah." It's weak, barely audible, but I have to ask her.

The silence on the other end has a weight that I feel in my chest. "Come on, Mac. It's just me."

"Why do you want to know?"

"Maybe because most of us guys need a wake-up call."

Maybe because I want to know how to please you. Or I'm a dirty bastard who needs to hear your honey-smooth voice talk about sex. Take your pick.

Anxious, yet filled with anticipation, I rub the flat of my belly again. "Tell me. Tell me how it would be good for you."

Her breath hitches, and for a moment I think I've gone too far. But when she speaks, it's in a whisper that has an edge to it, one that sends heat straight to my cock. Because she sounds excited, tempted. "Just between us?"

My breath quickens, lighter, faster. God, this is stupid. So fucking stupid, like opening Pandora's box. I'll regret it, I know. And yet…

"Just between us."

She makes a little, strangled noise. "I can't… Okay, okay. Screw it." Another soft breath, and then, "It would start out slow. Just kissing. That lazy sort of kissing that goes on and on, all soft and melting, until you're drugged with it and your lips are all swollen and sensitive. And you're just kind of breathing each other in, you know?"

I swallow reflexively, my voice totally gone. No, I don't know that kind of kissing.

I've never had the desire to go there with any girl. But fuck, I can imagine kissing Mac that way. Learning her mouth, shaping her lips with mine. Mine thrum with the need to feel hers, to sink into her taste.

Her soft voice glides over my skin. "And then he'd touch me."

"Are you standing up or lying down when he touches you?" It's a rasp, and a miracle I got the words out, I'm wound so tight.

She pauses. "I don't know."

"Are you… Are you lying down now?"

"Yeah." It's a gentle whisper.

My breath hitches, and I actually shiver.

"Then you're lying down. On your back." I close my eyes,

images flooding my head. "Your hair spread out on the pillow. Your eyes on him, watching what he does to you."

Her soft breath is in my ear. "He runs his fingers along my neck, his touch barely there. But I feel it. Burning a trail over my skin, down to my collarbone. And it gets me so hot, waiting for him to unbutton my shirt."

"You want him to see you, don't you, honey?" And, oh, fuck, I can imagine it, spreading open Ivy's shirt, exposing her smooth skin.

"Yeah," she says. "My..." A huff of breath. "My nipples are so hard. Aching."

Jesus. "And he slides that shirt apart. Exposes your sweet tits to his gaze."

Ivy makes a sound. A moan. My lower gut clenches like a fist.

I can't breathe. Can't fucking think. Slowly my hand eases down over my stomach, shivers breaking out in its wake. I shouldn't do this. I can't stop.

I'm so hard that my dick has a heft to it, like it's a separate entity, pulsing with the need to fuck, fuck, fuck. I give it a squeeze to alleviate the pressure, and it throbs against my palm. My teeth dig into my lower lip as I hold in a groan. I'm so fucking hot and thick I'm surprised I haven't come already.

"What does he do to you next?" I practically beg as I give myself a small tug.

"He sucks my nipple." Her voice is a stroke along my balls. "Gently, so all I can feel is his warm, wet mouth. And it drives me crazy. I want it harder."

As if obeying her command, I fist myself tighter. "Yeah?"

"Yeah. I arch up into his mouth, seeking it. But he doesn't give it to me. Not yet." Her breath is coming on faster now, her voice light and agitated. "He flicks my nipple with his tongue, plays with it. Giving it little sucks, long, lazy licks."

I shudder, and I swear she does too. My tongue hits the roof of my mouth. If I close my eyes, I can feel the tight bud of her nipple there.

"They throb, Gray."

Oh, Jesus. I squeeze my eyes shut against the sound of her plea, so thick with need that it makes me ache. "Pinch them," I grit out. "Give them a tweak."

And she does. Holy hell, she does. A small, muffled whimper comes through the speakers, and my dick jumps in response. I'm full-out jacking myself now. Every inch of me vibrates.

Ivy. Her soft breaths are driving me crazy. And I know, I fucking *know* she's touching herself too.

"Are you wet, honey? Has he made you wet?"

"So wet. Wet and swollen. It's trickling between my thighs. I hurt. I need…" She makes a little hiccup of sound. "I need…"

"You need him to touch you, baby. Ease that ache. Rub your clit, spread all that slick sweetness around."

"God."

"Would he finger you? Would he fuck you with his fingers? Push them in and out, nice and slow?"

"Yes."

I lick my lips. "I think he'd have to taste you, honey. I think he'd need that so badly. To know how sweet you truly are."

"I want him to. I want his mouth there."

"It is. He's lapping you up. Making you scream his name."

"Gray."

"I know. I know." I'm barely aware of what I'm saying anymore, only that I need more. The bed squeaks beneath me as I jerk myself.

Ivy's breathless voice is disjointed, hitching over the words. "I… You… He needs to fuck me. I can't take it any longer."

"You want him to sink his cock into you?"

"Yes."

"Pump into your tight heat like he'd die if he stopped?"

"Yes."

"Oh, fuck, he wants that too. He wants it so much he can't

think of anything else." I'm so hot, I'm leaking come. It weeps over the swollen head, coats my shaft as my fist moves faster, harder.

"I want him to fuck… Fuck me. Gray…"

And then I hear it. The sweetest fucking sound ever. A low, keening wail, almost pained but so full of pleasure that the hairs on the back of my neck lift.

Everything is muffled, like she's trying to stifle the sounds, but she can't. I'm so attuned to her right now I hear every one of them. I bite my lip and taste blood. *Ivy coming.*

My chest heaves. Heat licks over my balls, down between my thighs. My ass clenches on the next thrust. "Oh, shit. Honey, I'm gonna—"

The orgasm hits at full velocity. I arch up, my hips leaving the bed, my body locked in pleasure. A strangled, broken shout leaves my lips as come lands in hot strips across my abs and chest. My vision goes dark, my hand jerking every last drop of lust and need from my abused cock. Then I fall limp upon the bed.

Jesus.

For a moment I lie there, shaking and damp, fucking weak as a kitten. Licking my dry lips, I try to get my bearings, the room rocking drunkenly around me. And then I remember. Oh, shit. Ivy. I came harder than I ever have in my life on the phone with Ivy.

Panic punches into my chest, and I lurch up, scrambling for the phone lost amidst the rumpled covers. My ears burn hot, as my heart races. What to say? What will she say?

Hands shaking, I yank free the headphones and lift the phone to my ear. "Iv—" My voice cracks, and I clear my throat. "Ivy? You… Are you—"

My mouth snaps shut. Because she's not there. The line is dead.

THIRTEEN

GRAY

I'M HOME. WHICH IS to say, I'm standing in front of Ivy's door. I've been standing here too long. The neighbors are going to start to wonder what the hell I'm doing. Fuck if I know. My balls are in danger of freezing, and I can't make myself knock.

We had phone sex. I'm almost positive of it. And how messed up is it that I'm not sure? Had she realized I'd jacked off to her breathless voice? Had she hung up before or after I came? I'm not certain. And it's doing a number on me.

I'm all twitchy and tense. It's like a false start. Am I going to get called for stepping over the line before the snap? Or is the fact that she enjoyed it permission enough to let this transgression slide?

Because there is one thing I do know: she got off on our conversation too. I heard those little strangled whimpers she'd made. As if she'd tried so hard not to be heard but the orgasm was too strong to fully contain. Oh, sweet hell, just thinking about it has my cold dick heating up.

I know when she opens the door and I see her face, I won't be able to stop myself from touching her. I don't want to resist anymore. I want to sink myself into Ivy, surround myself in her warmth and breathe in her freshness. I want to hear her sounds again and discover new ones, make her lose control, shout my name.

My hand shakes as I lift it to knock. Knuckles rapping against the door, my heart pounds out a rhythm that sounds like *Ivy, Ivy, Ivy* in my head.

I hear her approaching. Mouth dry, I wait. My dick is so hard now, it's pushing against my jeans with an eagerness that's staggering. I have never *wanted* this badly. Never waited this long.

I almost whimper when the door swings open. But then I see her and promptly wilt.

"Mac," I get out. "Honey, you look…"

"Awful," she finishes for me with a voice that sounds like a dying frog's. Pale and pasty, her eyes are swollen and red, her nose running. She makes a pitiful face and then sobs. "I feel like ass."

I hate sickness. Being around ill people freaks me out now. I don't hesitate. I step into the house and pull her close.

IVY

My face hurts, literally hurts, like someone has used it as a punching bag and stomped on it for good measure. Add the fact that my head feels like a bowling ball teetering on the top of my neck, and I'd wanted to weep when I'd trudged toward my door. I'd known who was banging on it, and I hadn't felt like facing him while I looked like the walking dead. To be honest, I hadn't felt like facing him at all. Not after the things we'd last said to each other.

Gray's affable expression had faded the moment he'd seen me. But he hadn't turned and run off to get an axe, so there was that to be thankful for.

Now that he is here, his big, strong body offering me support—literally, because I can only lean against him and pray that the pounding in my head will soon end—I sigh with relief. He is here. I don't care about the phone sex. Or anything other than his presence making me feel better.

His chest rumbles when he speaks. "You really do look awful."

"Thanks," I mutter, too achy to put any emphasis behind it. "I feel *bad*." Now *that* came out like a pitiful pout.

"Yeah, I'd say that you do." Looking fresh and way too healthy for my taste, he rests his cool hand on my forehead. "Jesus, baby, you're burning up."

"That's because I have a fever. And I'll try to ignore that you called me baby. Do I look like I need diapers?"

"I see we're a grumpy patient as well."

At the very least, sickness is an excellent defense against any post-phone-sex awkwardness.

Gray tries to take my hand and lead me toward my room, when the haze fully lifts from my brain. Instantly, I lurch back so he can't touch me.

"What the hell are you doing?" I shout, and wince at my aching head.

"What the hell does it look like I'm doing? I'm getting you into bed."

"Oh no, you aren't." My hands cover my mouth, which is probably ineffectual, but I don't know what else to do. This also muffles my words when I continue to yell at him. "Get out, Gray. You cannot be here."

He actually looks hurt, his open expression twisting into a wince, and I soldier on, because he's obviously being thick.

"Gray, you cannot get sick! You need to stay healthy to play, you big oaf. Now, go!" I wave one hand in the direction of the door, while still covering my mouth. "Out with you."

Does he listen? No. He laughs as though I'm the oaf. "Oh, please, I never get sick. I've had my flu shot."

I roll my eyes and snort, which really isn't advisable with a stuffed nose.

"And have the immune system of a god," he adds.

"Fuck! Don't say that! Quick, knock on wood." I flail my arms. "Knock on your big, block head."

In my outrage, I start to cough and almost lose a lung.

His brows draw together in a frown. "Let it go, Mac. There is no way in hell I'm leaving you like this."

"I'll be fine. Really."

A world of skepticism lives in his eyes. "Yeah, not buying that. Now, quit arguing. I'll be careful with your germ-ridden ass, okay?"

"I so want to blow a raspberry at you right now. You're just lucky I care about your football career too much to risk spraying germs."

"I'm touched." He purses his lips when I sway on my feet. "Hell, you shouldn't even be walking around."

His arm wraps around my waist, his other arm snakes under my thighs, and then I'm airborne, all six feet of me. As simple as that, as if I'm no heavier than his gym bag.

Arguing has left me weak and whiny. I rest my head against his shoulder and enjoy the novelty of being carried.

"Don't scold," I say as he puts me down in my bedroom. "I was getting the door."

I give him a pointed look, which he ignores in favor of pulling back my sheets. The bed swims before my eyes, glimmering like an oasis in a sea of misery. But I'm so hot; the flannel PJs I'd thrown on to answer the door suffocate me. Hesitating, I glance at Gray. "I can take it from here."

The floor tilts.

Gray's arm slips around my shoulder. "Sure you can, Special Sauce." Cool blue eyes study me for a moment, and then he starts to ease my pajama pants down my hips.

"Gray!" I make a furtive attempt to hold on to them.

He pauses, looking up at me with brows lifted in confusion. "What? You're burning up. And you have underwear on, right?"

"Yeah. But—"

"It's not any different than seeing you in a bathing suit." He gives me another look, grinning now. "Unless you're wearing naughty panties?"

"You sound way too hopeful there, bud."

"I always hold out hope for sexy underwear. Step."

I do as told, way too aware of my bare legs and the fact that I'm sweating like a farmer. But he's right. I'm wearing basic boy briefs that cover me more than a bikini would, and frankly, I'm too sick to put up a fuss any longer.

Gray turns into Mr. Brisk Efficiency, neatly pulling off my shirt and not even looking at my bra as he handles me into bed and covers me with cool sheets. With a sigh, I sink into the bed, and Gray closes the curtains against the harsh daylight.

I drift in and out as he leaves the room then comes back to give me painkillers and a glass of orange juice. His care has my heart clenching within the walls of my aching chest.

"Thank you," I rasp past the needles in my throat. "You don't have to—"

"Yeah, I do. I would never leave you like this."

Gray takes my glass, then rounds the bed to the other side. Without pause, he unbuttons his jeans, and I try not to gape as they slither down his long legs and expose thighs that are truly magnificent. No, I will *not* check out his package, nicely held by a pair of blue boxer briefs. Before I can utter a word, he's sliding in and gathering me up.

I'm not prepared for it, or the feel of his hands against my bare back. The touch sends little shivers over my skin but I snuggle in closer, wrapping my arm around his torso and resting my head on his shoulder with a whimper.

The only man who's ever given me comfort is my dad, and that was in the form of awkward pats and general fussing with thermometers and medicines. Nothing like this. This is Gray. Strong, solid Gray, who smells like happy dreams. It feels good. So good that tears threaten.

"I hate being sick," I grump against his chest to hide my fit of emotion. "It sucks."

His big body shifts, and he makes a sound that I know means he's smiling. "Sucks big." His long fingers trace idle patterns along my back. "Poor, non-baby Mac."

Closing my eyes, I let my hand wander. Despite my fever, my fingers are cold. I find a swath of Gray's warm skin, exposed where his shirt rides up on his side.

Gray lets out a small yelp, his flesh jumping away from my touch. "Hell, Mac. Your hand is ice!"

"I know." It sounds like a whine. "It needs warmth. Gimme."

His abdomen twitches as I rub it, seeking his heat.

"Stop that!"

"Ticklish?"

He twitches again. "Yes."

Intrigued, I explore the bumps and ridges that define his torso. I've never touched a body like his—a gross injustice that needs to be remedied because I've clearly been missing out.

"Jesus, Gray, I can't get over how cut you are. What do you do? Live at the gym?"

"Daily workouts and five hundred sit-ups a night might have something to do with it." There's a smile in his voice.

"Overachiever."

"More like doing my job." He ducks his chin to look down at me. "Are you complaining?"

Hell no. "Just feeling inadequately squishy."

"I love your softness," he says in a low voice.

Slowly, his hand eases along the dip in my side, up and down, stroking me as if I'm the best thing he's ever touched. It's so lovely that I shiver, and he stops as if he's just realized what he's doing.

I should put space between us, but I can't. Not when his body feels so solid, his skin smoother than silk. God, I could run my hands over his rippled abs all night and not tire of it.

But Gray sets his hand over my roaming one. "Cut it out, Mac." His voice is rough, almost pained. "You're killing me here."

I didn't think I could possibly burn any hotter, but I do. Trying to ignore the rush of embarrassment flowing over me, I duck my chin and burrow into his side—because I couldn't let him go right now, even if my life depended on it. "Sorry."

His hand relaxes, and he gives me a little squeeze. "It's just… You're touching my stomach. I'm gonna react," he adds with emphasis.

His meaning hits me full force and I freeze. Does he mean…? The supreme urge to let my hand drift down and investigate is so strong that my fingers curl into a fist against his skin.

It doesn't matter if he's hard as a post. The fact that he stopped me makes it clear that he doesn't want to be.

I'm being so damn inappropriate, it isn't funny. I'm like some creeper. Gah. It's bad enough that I'd basically talked myself to orgasm on the phone with him. Oh, God, I can't think of that now. I'll curl up and die.

In vain, I search to say something other than *Your body is irresistible to me, and I had to stroke it.* I fall back on, "I'm sorry. I'm…I don't know, twitchy. Did I mention how much I hate being sick?"

His laughter rolls over me. "Once or twice." Almost absently his thumb draws a slow *S* over the back of my hand. "I get it. You want to move, but it hurts. You want to get up, but you're too tired."

A sigh escapes me. "Tell me a story."

"Oh, God, like 'Goldilocks and the Three Bears' or something?" He sounds horrified.

"No. Ass." Smiling, I poke his side, and get a nice yelp out of him. "About you. Something to take my mind off the fact that I hurt everywhere."

"My poor little Special Sauce." His big hand spreads over my hip, a comfort and a brand on my heated skin. "All right." He's silent for a moment. "When I was seventeen, I shit myself."

A shocked laugh breaks free. "Gray! That's disgusting." I laugh again. "What kind of story is that?"

"The kind that will stop you from thinking about being sick, and me from thinking about you stroking my stomach?"

Well, that kills my laughter. Me and my damn roaming hands. "So, you were saying… About your lack of bowel control?"

He snorts, a good-natured sound. "I had the stomach flu. Something fierce. But, back then, I was also a starting offensive lineman—"

"Of course you were. Like I said, overachiever—"

"Hush." He gives my butt a light smack. "Anyway, I had it in my mind that I'd suck it up and play, do it for the good of the team. Man, it was bad. I could barely stand. My guts were cramping up in pain. And then a big fucking defensive end smashed into me." He pauses. "He literally knocked the shit out of me."

I bite my lips. "Oh, Cupcake." I lose the battle and laugh, hard. "Just…no…"

Gray's body shakes as he presses his lips against my forehead, his breath coming out in gusts as he clearly tries to control his laughter, and then it hits me: he's trying not to jostle me. Deep inside my chest, my heart makes a tiny flip.

"Want to know the worst part?" he asks after a moment.

"There's something worse?"

"Our uniform pants were white."

"God." I clutch his lean waist. "Cupcake."

"They called me Stain from then on." He makes a sharp, quick snort. "Some of those fuckers still call me that when I go back home."

"Fuckers," I agree vehemently.

He glances down and his eyes crinkle at the corners. "I would think you'd have been one of the first in line to call me that."

I press my grin against his pecs. "Can I?"

"Not if you want to live," he says darkly.

"With the way I'm feeling now, chances of living are touch and go."

Instantly, his body stills, and his hold on me grows more secure. "Don't say that, Mac. Not even as a joke."

Then I remember his mother. Horror has my heart skipping a beat, and I cling to him. "You're right, it was a thoughtless joke."

His lips brush the top of my head. Not quite a kiss but as if he's drawing in my scent. "It was a bad story. I should have said something else. Something nice to put you to sleep."

Tenderness swamps my chest, and I swallow with difficulty. "It was perfect."

He is perfect. And I am so grateful he's here with me that I nestle down, wanting to sink into him and never let go. "I love you, Gray."

It slips out without warning, the words hanging in an awkward silence. Gray's chest lifts on a sharp breath, and my skin prickles with mortification. I force myself not to tense, not to make my gaffe any worse.

But he simply sighs and rests his chin on the crown of my head. "I love you too, Ivy."

The lightness of his tone and the gentle way in which he says it makes it clear that we're talking about the love of friends.

In silence, his hand glides down my thigh, a slow stroke designed to comfort.

Suddenly I am too tired to keep my eyes open. As I drift off to sleep, I count myself lucky that he didn't take my words the wrong way. I ignore the small part of me that kind of wishes he had.

FOURTEEN

IVY

I AM SICK for days. Fi and Dad stay away. Fi because she just had a flu, and I don't want to give her my cold, and Dad because he's become an extreme hypochondriac in recent years. Just the mere mention of illness has him running for the hills.

But I have Gray, who only leaves me to finish up his finals and attend practice. Then he's back. He's made me meals, fluffed my pillow, nagged me to drink my juice like a good little Mac, and given me antibiotics when I needed it for my bronchitis.

Every night, he sleeps by my side, spooning me for comfort, and rubbing my back when my hideous, hacking cough gets the better of me. As if by silent consensus, neither of us mention that having phone sex or that sleeping together every night might be crossing the line of friendship. It feels too good to have him there, and he doesn't appear to want to leave.

But now, lying in bed with the morning light stretching across my pillow, I know I'm well. Nothing hurts. No more cough from hell. I glance at the closed bedroom door. From the other side of it come the sounds of Gray in the kitchen. He's been feeding me copious amounts of steel-cut oats topped with blueberries in an effort to "promote healing."

Oatmeal and I have a tempestuous relationship. Somehow, every time I attempt to make it, the fucker revolts and turns to glop. Not Gray's oatmeal. It's like the pinnacle of oatmeal, what all little oats hope to one day become: fucking delicious and nutritious—Gray's words, not mine.

Truth is, I knew I was better last night. I think Gray knew, as well. We'd both ignored it. He'd fussed over me, carrying me to the couch and wrapping me up in a blanket. And when we'd settled into bed, there had been a moment of awkward silence, our bodies going tense in the cool darkness, before he pulled me close in that way of his—possessive yet tender.

"Try to get some sleep," he'd murmured gruffly. I hadn't been sure if he'd been talking to me or to himself.

I'd pretended to still be that sick, fitful woman who needed comfort, not the one who relished the feel of his hard body pressed against mine, the needy girl who wanted to turn in his arms and explore those fine, firm muscles. At length.

I never pegged Gray as the nurturing type. Which isn't fair. Gray is a kind man. And the more I know of him, the more I understand that he goes out of his way to make others happy. But, in my admittedly limited experience, most men don't do well with illness. It makes my chest hurt to imagine a younger Gray caring for his dying mother.

With a sigh, I sit up, and my head doesn't spin. Yep. Better. All of Gray's attentive care will end today. I can't hide my good health any longer. It would be wrong and weird.

Reluctantly, I head to the bathroom. His toothbrush sits next to mine, the sum total of the personal effects he's brought with him. Not enough to signify. I try to ignore that as I brush my teeth.

With slow movements, I take a shower and scrub myself clean. The hot water is bliss, highlighting my new and improved state. Which is depressing. It had been a mistake to let Gray stay so close. I'm used to him now.

When I finally leave my bedroom, dressed and bright-eyed, my heart is a lead weight in my chest.

Gray is setting down bowls of oatmeal, but he stills when I walk in. We stare at each other for a long moment, neither of us moving.

"All better now," I tell him.

He nods, his gaze slipping away to focus on setting down a pair of spoons. "I figured."

It's as if he is drifting away, like a boat that's had its line cut. His gaze turns inward as he scratches the back of his head, the action bunching his biceps.

"I'm glad you're well again."

"Yeah." I'm not glad at all.

GRAY

I miss Ivy. I started missing her before I'd even left her house. My time being her protector was up. I'd known the night before that she was better, and that she'd no longer need me to take care of her. I'd stayed over anyway because it had been my last chance to hold her as she slept. Fuck, it wasn't smart to stay with her every night. She is under my skin now. Well, more so than before.

I refuse to rub the ache in my chest as I cross the small quad, heading for the gym. Taking care of Ivy was eye-opening. Sure, I'd gotten flashbacks of looking after my mom, memories that made my throat tight and my stomach hurt. But my focus soon zeroed in on Ivy.

That was all I needed. Making Ivy feel better satisfied me in a strangely quiet way, as if I'd finally found the place where I needed to be. I can see myself watching over her for a lifetime. And it had felt nice. Homey.

Only, sometimes my gaze had wandered down to those endless legs of hers, and I'd found myself wondering what it would feel like to run a pattern along them with my tongue.

Fuck.

I'd planned to make a move on Ivy. But she'd given me a hardy "You're the best friend a girl could have" as we'd parted this morning. Right. Because we're buds. Best buds. Which is both a gift and a curse.

We're getting too close. The danger of my heart being annihilated is real. Ivy plans to live in another country. How am I supposed to give her up? I think of how I'd held her when she was hurting. I'd been content with that. Until she pulled the rug out from under me.

I love you, Gray. Sweet words, spoken out of friendly gratitude, I know. And yet they'd crashed into me like a blindside hit, knocking the air from my lungs and making my chest squeeze tight.

I don't know what to do with this feeling. It's equal parts longing—yes, fucking *longing*—and outrage. I want to hear those words again. It's a kick in the pants to realize that I want to be loved, like I'm worth something to someone. Not for what I can do for them, but just for me. And outrage, because how dare Ivy say those words to me? Three little words, and she's made me all sorts of needy. My anger is plain ridiculous and irrational.

But there you go. I'm now Irrational Gray. Confused and Grumpy Gray. Horny as All Fuck Gray. Nice to meet you.

Eventually I lose myself to the day, working out, practice, lunch, more working out, until my body is battered and sore and just maybe I will get so tired that I can simply crash without thought.

But all routes lead to Ivy. And no matter how hard I try, I find myself running that pattern over again, heading to her house as if it's the end zone.

FIFTEEN

IVY

FI TEXTS TO say she's staying over at her boyfriend's house. When I get home in the evening, my little house is quiet and dark. Empty. During high school, I loved having the house to myself, pretending that I was on my own, living life on my terms. I'd light a few candles, get in my jammies, and curl up with a book, dreading the moment when someone else would come home and fill the house with noise.

Now? I'm moving around the living room, clicking on lights. My chest feels hollow, and I don't like the sensation. Or the fact that silence no longer satisfies.

I'm used to Gray's noise. His constant laughter and the way he fills up the house with his vitality. I've never met a person who occupies a space as wholly as Gray does. It has nothing to do with what he says or does; it's simply his energy, his joy. Everyone instinctively knows he loves life, and they want to soak up that joy.

Me? I want Gray. Here, now, a gorgeous distraction that makes me love life as well. But I can't call him. He's been here every night for nearly a week. And I refuse to turn into *that* needy friend.

A shiver runs over me, and I realize I'm still standing before the open fridge. I wrinkle my nose at my choices for dinner: a slice of old pizza or a sandwich. I have no desire to cook alone anymore.

"Gah." I grab a Sprite and shut the door with a sigh.

The phone rings, and I jump in the silence. But when I see it's Gray, I grin hard enough to make my cheeks ache.

"What up, Killer G?"

His deep voice is a caress against my ear. "Mac, that was literally painful to hear."

"Fine. Hello, Mr. Grayson. How are you on this fine evening?"

"Why, I am very well, Miss Mackenzie," he drawls. "You decent?"

"Is this a trick question?" I grin into the phone. "Why do you want to know?"

"I'm outside. Open the door for me."

Suppressing a squeal that would make me sound pathetic, I hang up and practically skip across the room. I open the door in time to see Gray walking up the front steps, grocery bags in one hand and his gym bag in the other.

I'm in so much trouble because, damn, he does it for me. Instantly, my breath goes light and quick as heat rushes up my thighs. He's giving me that lopsided grin of his. The one that looks a little bit boyish and a little bit naughty, as if to promise that you'll have fun when he does dirty things to you.

The old university sweater he's wearing can't hide the width of his shoulders or the strength in his arms. Worn jeans hang low on his narrow hips, but stretch tight around his massive thighs and lovingly cup the distinct bulge between his legs.

I shouldn't look there, but it's impossible to miss; Gray is built on a grand scale all over.

My fist tightens around the doorknob. Because I have to hold myself back. I know how warm he'll be, how firm that body is, and that he'll smell like home and sex all rolled into one.

But what hits me the most is the way just seeing him makes me feel as though night has turned to day. Everything around me feels brighter, fresher. Gray is my joy. I know this now.

And maybe I'm his, because his eyes are on me and there's a restrained happiness in his expression, as though he's holding back too. Or maybe I'm imagining things I want. I can't tell anymore; this man has turned my world on its head. I can only watch as he bounds up the stairs in that effortless way of his.

"I thought we'd make steaks." He holds up the grocery bag by way of greeting.

"Wow, big spender."

"Okay, don't judge, but the grocer is a fan and gave me a sweet discount." He gives me a guilty little grin.

"Playing the football card? I approve, because steaks!" I lean against the door. "You brought your gym bag too."

Gray's smile turns sheepish. He's so close now, the vanilla-citrus scent of his skin wraps around me like a blanket. "I…uh… well, you might have a relapse."

"I might."

"Don't worry, Special Sauce." He gives my forehead a peck. "I'm here to save the day."

Gray Grayson. My hero.

GRAY

I lean back into the pillows with a sigh. I'm a man well-fed and content. We'd had dinner, the best I'd eaten in ages. I'd made a pan-seared hanger steak with caramelized onion-bacon relish and roasted butternut squash. And now dessert—sweets being Ivy's gig.

She'd gone for simple, making super-creamy vanilla shakes. They're perfect. How she does this, picking the perfect thing for the perfect moment, is beyond me. Like suggesting that we watch TV in bed.

Okay, perfect *torture*. But perfect, nonetheless. We're sitting side by side under the covers like some old married couple. It freaks me out how much I love this. How much I want this to be an option every night.

Of course, we had stalled a bit when getting into bed, me in my T-shirt and boxers, Ivy in her usual tank top and little cotton shorts. When she'd been sick, I'd been able to block the reality of her being barely dressed and concentrate on her illness.

Now? Yeah, endless legs, the rounded swells of her hips, and the skimpy top that clings to her sweet breasts are messing with my mind. Thank God she'd kept her bra on or no way would I be able to hide the effect she has on me.

It was hard enough when we stood on either side of the bed, staring at each other, tension heavy in the air as we slowly peeled back the covers. We were getting into bed with each other with the intention of sleeping together, and there was no excuse of illness to hide behind. We just wanted to. I knew. She knew it.

Ivy's eyes had been huge in the delicate oval of her face, her pink lips parted and soft. She'd looked at me, hesitant, confused. And for a moment, I'd feared that she'd ask what the hell we were playing at, why was I here? So I'd panicked and jumped into bed, announcing that I got remote control privileges.

It cracked the tension. After a brief but torturous wrestle for the remote, all was perfect once again.

Well, except for the fact that Ivy has the remote.

I rub my nipple, which still burns, thanks to Ivy's evil, pinching fingers. "You know, you're lucky I can't retaliate in like manner."

"If you did, you'd be clutching your balls right now. In pain," Ivy clarifies, because she knows me too well.

"At least I'm comfortable. Have I mentioned how much I love your bed?"

Ivy gives me a sidelong glance, her lips twitching. "So what exactly do you love about my bed?"

That you're in it. With me.

"You have a California king," I tell her instead, which is the truth as well. "Fucking gorgeous, this big-ass bed. I can actually fit in it without my feet hanging off. And how is it that women have the ability to find the best sheets, comforters, and pillows, and put them together to create a cloud of comfort?"

"Because we pay attention to detail, like buying more than one pillow and a flimsy blanket to keep warm. As for the mattress, for as long as I can remember, every bed in our house has been a California king. I'm pretty sure my dad buys these babies in bulk."

God bless Ivy's dad.

"I guess when you're nearly seven feet tall, the largest mattress in production just looks normal."

"Yeah. Dad loves his comfort and assumed his daughters would like the same bed." Ivy's expression turns inward, happy. "When we were little, Fi and I used to call them our 'Princess and the Pea' beds."

"The 'Princess and the Pea' chick had a bed of mattresses stacked to the ceiling, not a big-ass mattress."

Ivy's brow quirks. "And how do you know all these fairy tales, Mr. Grayson?"

"My mom read them to me when I was a little guy."

God, I can still remember the sound of her voice as she tucked me up in bed and told me those old stories. My brothers, as usual, had made fun of that nighttime ritual. I hadn't cared. I'd had Mom to myself, and she'd made me feel like the most loved boy in the world.

Throat thick, I run a finger along Ivy's pristine white covers.

She's silent for a beat, then leans into my arm. "Bet you were a cute little boy."

I nudge her back. "I bet you were a cute princess."

I can just imagine little Ivy Mac with her button nose and messy hair.

"As a fucking bug." Ivy picks up the remote. She flicks through the channels, and I yell, "Stop!" just as she squeals, "*Rear Window*! Yes!"

We grin at each other. "Best movie ever," we say as one. Ivy sets down the remote and grabs her shake.

"I love Hitchcock," she says. "I'm pretty sure I'd wet my panties if I got a chance to talk to him."

Since "wet panties" can go two ways, my dirty mind chooses to think of sex. And Mac being wet. Clearing my throat, I discreetly adjust my dick, tucking the eager head back under the band of my boxers.

"Too bad he's long dead."

"One can dream. He was a creative genius, you know?"

"So you like guys with big brains, huh?"

Her lips curl but she keeps her eyes on the screen. "Big brains and big dicks. Yeah."

I nearly choke, but manage to keep a straight face, because Mac, the little stinker, is definitely grinning now.

"Honey," I drawl as if my dick isn't getting bigger by the second, "you've basically described me."

Her mouth twitches, and she finally glances my way. Her eyes are alight with evil Mac mischief. "Oh, right. I forgot about your big...brain."

"Don't forget my big dick."

Please don't forget about him. He's lonely. And needy.

"You're only allowed two dick brags a night, Grayson," she deadpans before wrapping her plump lips around her straw and sucking.

My own lips part as I watch her work that thick vanilla shake up into her mouth. Fuck me standing, she's killing me. I'm so hard now, I throb. I imagine how good it would feel if she'd lean over and take the tip of me into her mouth. Just suck it a little. Her tongue would be cold from the ice cream, soothing my heat. And then…

I clear my throat again, but my voice is rough. "So I'm cut off?"

"Yup." She doesn't even look my way, too entranced by the movie.

I lean back, squeezing my eyes shut. "Cruel, Mac. Just cruel."

"Drama queen." She snorts, not even noticing I'm slowly unraveling next to her, and elbows my side. "Watch the movie, Mr. Big Stuff."

Somehow I manage it. But then the movie is over. Mac turns off the TV, plunging us into darkness. I slam into hyperawareness. My skin hums, tuned to Ivy's every move. The syncopated rhythm of our breathing is overloud in the silence.

Mac shifts. My body tenses, expectation rushing through me. But she doesn't turn my way. She's wriggling around, her elbow hitting me in the chin.

"Sorry," she mutters, and I realize that she's taking off her bra from under her tank.

Hell. Visions of her soft breasts swaying beneath thin cotton fill my head. My palms practically feel their firm weight filling them up.

I lie stiff as a plank and try to regulate my breathing. In. Out. In. Out. *Fuck*.

Ivy settles down into the bed once more and turns away from me. Moonlight ghosts over her slim shoulders, highlighting her skin and turning it silver. I clutch the covers, so I don't reach out and touch her. My entire body throbs with a *please, please, please*.

What the fuck am I doing here? I'm like some masochist, killing myself slowly. I shouldn't be here. But the idea of leaving is as impossible as asking me to catch a pass and just stand still. Not happening.

Sometimes I think she might want me too. When her gaze glazes over and focuses on my lips for a brief, breathless moment. But then she's treating me as old buddy Gray, and I don't know. Maybe I'm just guilty of wishful thinking. But the want isn't going away. It's growing, drowning out reason.

Biting my bottom lip, I stare at her in the darkness, and contemplate the best way to broach the subject of wanting to lick my way down her body and *not* kill our friendship in the process.

"Gray?" Her soft voice wrenches me out of my haze, and my gut tightens.

"Yeah?" I rasp.

"Is it weird that I'm glad you're here?"

My heart slams against my chest like it's trying to break free. *Please, please, please.*

"No. I'm glad I'm here too."

"It kind of reminds me of when I was a kid, and I'd have sleepovers with my best friend. I never wanted it to end because it was so fun. You know?"

Hope crashes in my chest, so potent I almost hear the shards of it clatter against my ribs.

"Yeah." Fun. This is fun. Rolling onto my back, I press my fists against my eyes.

Sleep. Just go to fucking sleep and this torture will end.

Mac rolls onto her back too, her warm, bare shoulder touching my arm. All the nerves in my body engage, focusing on that small stretch of skin-to-skin contact. I breathe slowly in and out through my nose.

Her voice is soft and thoughtful in the dark. "Our family has always been so private. I don't have many true friends. I know a lot of people, and I like talking to them. But none of them really know me."

Swallowing past the lump in my throat, I finally answer her.

"You don't trust easily." I understand this because I don't either. Everyone knows a version of me, but the whole person? Not really.

"I don't."

The sheets rustle and I know Mac has turned toward me. In the dark, her doe-shaped eyes gleam like onyx beneath the line of her bangs. Aside from my mother, no one has ever looked at me that way, like I'm special. It's like a surprise tackle, knocking me off my feet and onto my head. My head spins. But I hold her gaze.

Mac's smile is soft, almost shy. "But I trust you, Gray."

She's giving me a gift, I know this. And it fills me with warmth even as it punches through my heart. Because I'm even more lost now. It takes me a moment to answer, and my voice is as unsteady as my thoughts.

"I trust you too, Ivy."

SIXTEEN

IVY

I DON'T REMEMBER falling asleep. I wake slowly, my senses coming back online in stages. It must be dawn because pale light stretches through the windows, and everything is slightly hazy, as if the world can't decide between night or day. I'm not an early riser, so I don't know why I'm awake now.

Especially since I'm so comfortable and so very warm, tucked into the protective curve of Gray's body, with his arm securely around my waist. We're locked together, his legs curled under mine, his nose burrowed in my hair. I can't help closing my eyes again and letting my weight fall back onto him. The rise and fall of his broad chest lulls me. He feels too good. Perfect.

But a new set of realizations hits me. That my tank top has ridden up in my sleep and is now twisted high on my torso, exposing the underside of my breasts. That Gray's huge hand is on my bare belly, and with every slow breath I take, the tip of his pinkie finger grazes my hip bone.

That slight tickle grabs all my attention and has my body slowly tensing with awareness. I lie as still as I can, staring at the wall, muted gray in the dawn.

Like the uncoiling of a string, my senses move outward to Gray's body against mine and the fact that he too has gone unnaturally still.

Side by side we lie, his soft breaths stirring my hair, his hand resting on my belly. Except it isn't at rest. His fingers shift, a slight caress, as if he can't help but test the texture of my skin. It's the tiniest of movements. Every nerve in my body focuses on that one spot.

When I don't move away, he strokes again, the same hesitant exploration. Heat flares over my skin. My heartbeat is a drum in my ears, and I struggle to keep still. Because I don't want him to stop.

He doesn't. Slowly, his pinkie skims over my skin. His touch is so soft, I might have missed it. Only, all of my awareness is on him and the progress he makes. He keeps going, and when he grazes the edge of my panties, my thighs clench, my clit tightening as if he plucked it.

I wiggle just a little, a silent plea, a breath of *please. Please don't stop*. He's so in tune with me now, he knows it's a sign of permission, even if I can't yet find the courage to vocalize it.

His touch grows bolder. Gently, he draws his fingers over the sensitive skin on my stomach, down, then up. Behind me, his body is rock-solid, his breath stilted as if he's holding it.

And I lie there, as we both pretend this isn't happening. But it is. A slow tremble is working its way through me as heat licks between my thighs. With each delicate pass over my skin, he covers more ground.

I close my eyes, focus on those fingers, how they tickle along my side, trace my panties, then trail upward over my ribs.

I want to arch my back, push against the large swell of his cock that's growing hard against my ass. His fingertips graze the underside of my breast, and I stop breathing. My nipples draw tight. He hovers there, just under my breasts, barely touching them.

My mind races. What are we doing? We're crazy to do this. Everything will change. I should stop this. But I don't want to.

I hear him swallow, feel the rapid thump of his heart against by back. My teeth sink down on my lip. It's torture staying still, not begging him to go higher. Because I want him to. So fucking badly my breasts ache. I want him to go lower as well, stick those long fingers of his under my panties.

Somehow, by silent agreement, we both understand that if we don't talk, don't verbally acknowledge it, we can do this.

And so I lie still, breath short, body aching, waiting.

Then he moves, sliding his fingers over the curve of my breast, up toward my nipple. I bite my lip harder, trying not to moan. God, but my nipple throbs, waiting for that touch. But it doesn't come. The bastard traces under it, slowly stroking my skin, teasing me.

I shiver, my back tensing as I arch just a little bit, silently begging for more with my body. He tenses against me, pressing closer. His breath hitches, and I know he can see over my shoulder. That he's watching.

Blindly, I stare forward, but in my periphery I can see his hand, inching up my shirt, exposing me. A small sound rumbles deep in his chest. I'm so hot now, I can barely breathe. I want to move. I don't. We both freeze, knowing that if he slides any closer, if he touches my nipple, we've fully crossed a line.

My chest rises and falls in a quick, light pant. I can't help myself. His fingers draw closer. Gray's body is so tight, he's shaking. I can't take any more.

And then I don't have to. The blunt tips of his fingers run over my aching nipple. I almost groan, but hold on to it. Gray's touch grows firmer, moving the stiff nub back and forth. And it feels so fucking good I can't stand it. My thighs clench. My clit swells, growing wet and needy. It's almost illicit what he's doing to me, a naughty secret here in the dim quiet of my room.

His hot breath stirs my hair, the muscles along his arm twitching as he moves. My fingers dig into the sheet to keep myself still.

And then his hand is sliding away. I almost protest, but I'm too distracted by the way he's gliding over my skin, heading down. He stops at the top of my panties. We both take a slow breath together. I know he'll go no further. It's my turn.

Closing my eyes, I ease my thighs apart—just slightly—and the action *aches*. His breath hitches, because he knows it's an invitation. His long fingers slip under my panties. The sheets rustle as I edge one leg higher, making room for his hand.

Gray trembles, the wall of his chest flush with my back. His arm runs along my side as he reaches down, and the calloused pads of his fingers graze my clit. A tiny whimper escapes me, just as his breath gusts out in a soundless *unh*.

I'm so slippery wet, he slides right over my swollen flesh. And my entire body responds, coiling with heat that throbs.

I bite my lip so hard it hurts, tiny sounds making their way through my clenched teeth, little whimpers I can't hold back as he works me over in a slow, torturous circle. My ass grinds back against his stiff cock, and he rocks his erection into me.

Silent, barely moving, we lie there, our bodies trembling, Gray fingering me. Lower he goes, sliding over my sex, down to my opening. I'm panting now, my skin covered in a sheen of sweat. I'm so close to coming, my head spins.

As if he can feel the orgasm rising within me, Gray presses his lips to my bare shoulder and holds me tight as his thick finger enters me, deep. I can't help it, I groan, my hips canting into his touch. He fucks me with his finger, and everything goes fuzzy.

There is just him invading me and the undulating rhythm of my hips. I'm panting, my flesh hot and pulsing. I come on a wave of heat and helpless cries, my body twitching, trapped in the clutch of his arm.

"Fuck, honey," he rasps. "Fuck."

And then his hand is sliding away. He's turning me, his fingers threading through my hair.

He looks in pain, his gaze darting over my face as if he wants to say something. But he doesn't. His attention drifts to my mouth, and, God, I feel him there, as if he's already kissing me, already taking my mouth the way I know he wants to.

I lick my lips, tip my chin up so I can get closer. I want a taste of him so badly.

A tortured sound escapes him, his broad chest lifting and falling on a hitched breath. "Ivy."

His mouth finds mine, and I'm lost.

That first touch is a sonic blast, sending a wave of heat through me so hard and fast that I lose my breath. I gain it back on a sigh of sheer pleasure. His lips are softer than I'd imagined, firm yet tender. He skims them over the hypersensitive corner of my mouth, finds the plump swell of my lower lip and nuzzles it.

I feel it in my spine, between my legs. And maybe he feels the same because he makes a low, almost growling sound in his throat and kisses me again, firmer this time, demanding more.

"What are we doing?" I whisper between quick, searching kisses that mold my lips. We're both shaking so hard, it's enough to make us frantic, uncoordinated, noses and chins bumping as we desperately come at each other again and again.

"I don't know... Oh, shit, Mac, you taste so good."

His tongue touches mine, a savoring glide of velvet warmth. "Just one more." He groans, licks into my mouth like he's lapping up honey. "One more taste."

Gray leans into me, his broad chest crushed against my breasts, as he ducks his head and kisses me deep. Opening my mouth wide and taking what he needs.

He's shaking, his voice rough when he speaks. "I've wanted

this… Wanted to taste you for so long. It's all I think about. Fuck, that's good. One more, honey. One more."

My arms wrap around his neck, holding on as he pulls back, comes at me from another angle, over and over. He's making a study of my mouth, discovering every inch of it. And it gets me so hot, I'm panting, my skin drawing tight. "Once isn't going to be enough."

Gray shudders, his grip clenching on my nape. "You're right. Don't stop. Give me your mouth, honey." He suckles my bottom lip, licks along my upper lip. "Let me take care of you for a while."

His kisses turn messy, opening me wide enough that I feel the stretch in my jaw. My mouth is being fucked by his tongue. Raw and raunchy and so good that I moan, close my eyes, and fuck him back like I'll die if we stop. I just might.

Gray's big body shifts as if he can't keep still. With a noise of impatience, he pushes his thick thigh against my sex, nudging the sensitive flesh there. And I groan, my legs clamping down on the muscled length. The hard throb of his erection is at my hip, demanding my attention.

"Gray. What are we doing?" I'm seconds away from begging him to fuck me hard and fast against the mattress.

His hand slides down my back, drawing me closer. "Don't think," he says, not leaving my mouth. "It doesn't matter. It doesn't have to matter."

It takes a second for his words to sink in. And then they do. It surges like an ice-cold wave, stealing my breath and making the walls of my chest clench. We're just fooling around. At least in Gray's eyes. And I thought…

Another wave hits me, this one hot with humiliation. I'm emotionally invested.

Completely.

So stupid. Especially since Gray has flat out told me that sex is just sex to him. I know he cares about me. But what we're doing doesn't matter to him in the same way it does to me.

He doesn't notice I've gone still. Almost roughly, he palms my ass as he kisses a path along my jaw.

"Mmm… So good. Why did we wait so long to do this?"

Yes, why? When we could have been friends with benefits all along, had a quick fuck whenever the mood struck us?

I can't breathe. I need to breathe. His big body pressed against mine is no longer a comfort but a weight I can't bear. My stomach lurches.

"I think I'm going to throw up."

It's enough to make him pause and lift his head in shock.

Wrenching free, I scramble from the bed and sprint to the bathroom just as Gray calls out to me.

Ignoring him, I slam the door behind me and lock myself in the safety of the bathroom a second before Gray catches up to me. A thud vibrates the door as if he's bumped into it, and I hear his muffled curse.

"Ivy." His voice is urgent. Worried. "Ivy, what—"

"I'm okay," I practically shout. I'm not. Nausea has me panting and my face is too hot. I lean against the door, pressing my cheek to the cool wood. I want to sink down and curl up into a ball.

God, I'm so stupid. So weak, letting sex cloud my judgment. I can't do casual. My heart is already invested.

Gray's voice is so close I know he's leaning against the door too. "Talk to me, Mac. Please. You're kind of freaking me out here."

My eyes close. What do I say? I don't even know what to think right now. Only that his words are spinning in my head. *It doesn't matter. It doesn't have to matter.*

The slickness between my legs and the residual tenderness from my orgasm has me shuddering. I press my thighs together as if the action can blot out what he'd done to me and how perfect it had felt.

"Ivy, honey, I know that was unexpected." He gives a wry laugh. "And not exactly within the bounds of friendship, but—"

"Stop," I blurt out, panic and regret rising once more. "Just please stop talking."

I can't stand hearing him say those words again, that the best feeling of my life didn't matter to him the way it mattered to me. I'll scream.

"All right," he says slowly. Another scratch against the door has me wondering if he's put his hand to it. "But can you come out? I need to see that you're okay."

I hate the worry in his voice. Because it means he knows I'm way more affected by this than he is. It grates. And there is no fucking way I'm facing him right now.

"Look," I say to the door. "I just need a moment to myself. Could you…" I lick my dry lips. "Could you just go home?"

Silence is heavy. When Gray finally answers, he sounds pained. "Ivy… Don't send me away. I'm sorry that I—"

"No!" My shout echoes in the bathroom. "No more, Gray. I can't talk about this now. I can't." Tears prickle behind my eyes. I'm so humiliated. I just want the floor to swallow me up. "Not right now. Okay? Just. Go."

He doesn't respond, but I can feel his resistance like a heavy hand against my skin.

"Go," I insist again. "We'll talk tomorrow, I swear. I just need to be alone right now." My voice warbles with the plea.

And I almost cry in relief when he sighs and his low voice grinds out, "Okay, Mac. I'll go. Just… Call me soon. I… Shit, I don't like leaving you this way."

When I don't answer, he sighs again. "All right."

And then there is silence. I press my heels against my hot eyes and realize how very much I've grown to hate silence.

SEVENTEEN

GRAY

IvyMac: Meet me at 8? At Java Cup?

GrayG: Will do.

ONE TEXT. THAT'S ALL I get from Ivy. I've held off from calling her, hunting her down, because I'd promised. But it's been hell. I'm so twitchy, I could burst out of my skin. I can all but feel Ivy thinking things through. And it terrifies me, because I also feel her slipping away.

I hope it's simple paranoia that has me tied up in knots. But Ivy asking me to meet her in a coffee shop instead of at her house or mine isn't a good sign. Like she needs neutral territory. Hell.

I get there early, securing a table in the back corner. Normally not a huge coffee drinker, I'm on my second cup by the time she arrives at eight p.m. on the dot.

The first sight of her steals my breath. It's that instantaneous—I look at Ivy, and I cannot breathe properly. Those dark eyes, that kissable rosebud mouth, those cheeks that I want to cup as I taste her.

God, I slid my fingers over her sweet, slick clit, all plump and sensitive to my touch. I made her come with my hand.

Heat shivers over my skin at the memory. The tips of my fingers throb, and my heartbeat is in my throat as she approaches, her gaze not meeting mine but focused somewhere around my shoulder. It hurts that she won't truly look at me. It hurts that she's so unsure.

I've done this to her.

Dressed in black jeans and a gray turtleneck sweater, she also looks as though she's trying to hide all the skin she can. Fucking hell.

It had hurt more than expected when she'd torn away from me and locked herself in the bathroom. Hope and happiness had crumbled within me. Now there's nothing but a hollow cavern in my chest. I need to fix this.

On shaking legs, I rise to greet her, fumbling the move when I reach out to… What? Kiss her cheek, give her a hug? I don't know. I just want to touch her and reassure her that everything will be okay.

None of that matters, because the moment I lean in, she's ducking into her seat with a quick "Hey."

She makes a pretense of being worried about spilling her coffee, setting it down with undue care as I sit across from her. But her continued focus on the table sends a punch of dull pain through my center.

"You're not going to look at me now?" I ask in a low voice.

At that, her head snaps up, her dark eyes wide and pained. "No. I mean, of course. Sorry. I'm just…" She trails off with a bite to her lower lip.

"I know." Resting my arms on the table, I lean in. "I'm sorry, Ivy. I shouldn't have—"

"Hey, Grayson," a guy at my elbow butts in. I hadn't even noticed him approaching. But he's grinning down at me as his friend hovers at his side. The bright red university sweaters they're wearing are my first tip-off as to why they're here.

The guy slaps my shoulder like he knows me. "Great season, man. You guys are gonna crush it in the playoffs."

"Go Dogs!" the other guy yells.

More than anything, I want to tell these two to fuck off. Can't they see I'm talking about something important? But I don't. Fans are fans and they have my gratitude.

I give them a brief nod. "Thanks. Thanks a lot."

I try to make it clear that I'm in the middle of something, but one of them wants me to autograph his baseball cap. Quickly I sign it and turn my attention back to Ivy.

Thankfully they amble away.

Ivy watches them go before acknowledging me.

"No, don't apologize," she pleads, glancing up at me and then back to her cup. "I shouldn't have freaked out like that. It was totally immature."

My hand covers hers, and she flinches. But I don't let go because I need to touch her. My voice is as soft and comforting as I can make it. "It's okay, Mac."

Her shoulders lift on a breath and then she sits back in her chair, sliding her hand from mine as she goes. Her lashes conceal her eyes as she slowly turns her cup in her hands.

For lack of anything better to do, I clutch my cup as well. The heat of the coffee seeps through the cardboard and warms my icy fingers.

I don't know what to say or how to start the conversation. I open my mouth to try.

"Hey." A girl is now standing next to me. "You're Gray Grayson."

She's looking at me like I'm a latte she'd like to drink down. Irritation spikes. This is why I didn't want to meet Mac in public. Not when football fever has hit an all-time high on the campus.

I'm about to give this chick the brush-off when Mac slaps her free hand on the table.

"Oh, for fuck's sake, Gray," she says to me in exasperation. "Irritable bowel syndrome is treatable. There's no need to fear. It's the rampant gas that you really should worry about, because, dude, it's bad."

Her words hang in the air, and I gape at her, shock and horror tingling through my skin. The girl beside us pretty much does the same before her face goes beet red and she backs away from me.

"I...uh... I'll leave you to your conversation," she gets out.

I don't answer. I can only stare at Mac. Part of me wants to strangle her. I can just imagine how fast this little nugget of gossip will spread. I can hear my new nickname: Gaseous Gray.

"So...social annihilation is on the menu today, huh?"

Flushing, she shrugs. "Got rid of her, didn't it?"

The little shit. I bark out a laugh. Whatever has happened between us, she's still my best friend. The one person I want to be with most in the world. And I adore her. I'm so gone on her, I don't know my left from my right anymore. She's my center line. All thoughts run through Ivy Mackenzie.

I reach out for her, ready to tell her just that. Tell her that I want everything with her. That she is my everything.

But she speaks first, her words coming out fast and tight.

"Things got out of hand. It happens. We've been in each other's pockets, seeing each other all the time. And if we just stepped back and took a break from that, not hang out so much..." She spreads her hands as if to say, problem solved, no big deal.

Take a break. Not be together so much.

Hurt slams through me so hard that my knee jerks, hitting the underside of the table and almost knocking it over.

"Sorry," I mutter, as she scrambles to keep her cup from falling.

I want to shout at her that this is the worst fucking idea she's ever come up with. That taking a break sounds like torture. But she's not finished ripping my heart out.

"And if you're not always with me, you can…you know…go out. With girls. Hook up or whatever."

I'd like to think her expression conveys the same misery as I feel. But I can't be sure. I can no longer think straight.

"Kind of hard to do that," I snap. "When the entire campus will soon think I have a flatulence problem."

She cringes. "Right. Sorry. But I doubt anyone will believe it. Or even care. Most women obviously would overlook anything to get to you."

Oh. Joy.

I don't give a ripe fuck what other women believe. I don't want to be with anyone other than Ivy. Her helpful comment makes me want to scream. And then another horrible thought hits me.

"Wait, why are we talking about hookups?" My voice is rising, along with my panic.

Her gaze slides away from mine. "Well… We're both clearly in need of some sexual relief. Why shouldn't we find it—"

"Am I cramping your style? Blocking you from all these potential dates you have lined up?" I don't even know what I'm saying. Panic has me by the balls. She's slipping away from me, and I can't seem to hold on.

Her eyes narrow. "You think I can't get a date?"

"Hey, I did *not* say that."

The tension leaves her with a sad sigh, and she slumps a little. "This is getting off track, and we're sniping at each other, which is not what I wanted."

I rake a hand through my hair and blow out a long breath through my nose.

"Are you…" I take another breath. "Do you want to go out on random dates?"

I'm going to be sick. I'm going to fucking throw up. All over fucking Java Cup.

"I don't know. Maybe it's time that I do."

Mac. On a date.

The cup in my hand crumples, sending hot coffee splattering every which way.

"Shit." I jump up, shaking coffee off my hand.

Mac jumps up as well, grabbing napkins to mop the mess, until she sees my hand. "Did you burn yourself?"

She touches my reddened hand, but I snatch it away.

"I'm good." My throat is closing in on me. I can't be here. I back away, tripping over the leg of a chair before righting myself.

"Gray," she says in a soft plea. "I'm just trying to fix things."

"Use me," I blurt out.

Ivy stills, the space between her brows furrowing. "What?"

"You want to fuck someone. Fuck me."

She rears as though I've spit on her face. "Are you kidding me?"

"No," I say, a little desperate now. "You want to have sex. Have sex with me."

"We. Are. Friends." She enunciates every word through her clenched teeth as color rises over her face.

"Oh, please, Ivy. You came on my fingers. I think we're way past just friends."

Bad route to go. Bad fucking route.

Her face flames red, her nostrils flaring. "You asshole. You think because you got an orgasm out of me that I'm now some sort of easy lay—"

"No, Ivy. *No.*" Fisting my hands at my sides, I lean in. "That is not what I meant, okay? Just that we're obviously attracted to each other. And there's this tension. So why not alleviate it by—"

"No," she hisses. "Screwing around will ruin everything. Not to mention that you're one of my dad's potential clients."

A sharp breath shoots through my lungs, as if she sucker punched the air out of me.

"Your dad? You're worried about my relationship with your dad?" I let out a strangled curse, and rake my hand through my hair, the urge to rip it out making my hand clench.

The guys had warned me about this, but I never imagined she'd think the same.

Gaze sliding away, her chin firms. "It would make things awkward, complicated between you two."

"Then let's make this simple. I won't pick him as my agent."

Ivy's hair swings over her shoulders as she whips around. "No. You can't do that. I won't be responsible for him losing you as a client. Do you have any idea how shitty that would make me feel?"

"And what about us? Am I that expendable to you?" Fuck if my voice doesn't crack.

"Of course not." She wraps her arms around her middle, taking a step back. "But it's foolish to enter into a relationship with you if he's going to be your agent."

"We're already in a relationship, Ivy." My voice bounces over the walls, turning heads, drawing stares. I put my back between the room and her. "And it's the most important one of my life."

The words barely leave my mouth when it hits me just how much I want a relationship with her. Ivy has been my girl all along, the One. I've just been too scared, too cautious to fully admit it to myself.

She blinks, her face pale, a bead of sweat breaking out on her upper lip. "I meant a sexual relationship."

"Sex doesn't have to mean the end of—"

"But it does! It always fucks things up." Her wide brown eyes stare up at me. "Please. I don't want to ruin everything with sex. We just need to cool things down. And it will be the same again. We've been in each other's pockets…"

"Yeah. You've said that already."

Problem is, that's the only place I want to be. But Mac obviously wants something else. Jesus, but that makes my insides constrict.

I swallow convulsively. Holy hell, but there's a hot prickle behind my eyes. "Right. Well, I'm going now."

Before I totally lose my shit.

She doesn't stop me. I walk out of the coffee shop, each step leaving me colder and colder, until the dark night swallows me up.

EIGHTEEN

GRAY

IvyMac: I created a new donut. It's called the Bad Sack: salted caramel with a chocolate ganache center that gushes when you bite into it. Personally, I refer to it as Sacked Gray. But I won't tell anyone but you its true name. ☺

GrayG: Sounds delicious. I'll have to try it sometime. Got practice all day. See you later.

IvyMac: Okay. See you.

IvyMac: Haven't seen you in a while.

GrayG: Haven't been able to do anything but train. I can't feel my legs anymore.

IvyMac: I'm sorry.

IvyMac: I don't like thinking of you in pain.

GrayG: Don't worry, Mac. All pain eventually goes away.

IvyMac: You going out to Palmers tonight? Fi and I are going to dance. You should come with us.

GrayG: Can't. Booster party in honor of the playoffs at some fancy country club. Whole team has to go. Suits required. Cue my ass being pinched by cougars.

IvyMac: So not all bad then? ☺

GrayG: Yeah, there's that.

GrayG: Night, Mac. And be careful out there.

IvyMac: Night, Gray.

I HATE BOOSTER PARTIES. Hot, stuffy, with too many people watching your every move. Too many fake smiles, fake laughs, slaps on the shoulders by rich dudes who call you "son." Too many rich women pressing their gym-toned bodies up against you, while you try not to react because they're old enough to legitimately call you "son." Mind your p's and q's because you can't embarrass Coach, the athletic director, the dean, and the dozens of other campus bigwigs circling the room, pressing palms.

A fucking circus.

I tug at my collar, sweat damping my shirt that's buried beneath layers of suit jacket and vest. Around me guys are doing the same, or trying not to. Most freshmen and sophomores are stuck in ill-fitting suits bought off the rack at some big-and-tall store.

Their biceps stretch their coat sleeves, the overlarge size sagging at the shoulders.

At the very least, I can say I look all right in comparison. Last year's championship swag featured vouchers for free tailored suits at a national luxury retailer. I'd taken them up on the offer, standing stock-still, side by side with Drew, making immature jokes about which side we dressed on, as two annoyed-looking tailors measured us up.

So yeah, I look sharp as new cleats standing here and sweating my balls off. Awesome.

A waiter passes, and I nab a glass of champagne from his tray. It's lukewarm, because really champagne shouldn't be slowly passed around a hot room, but I take a long sip anyway.

Inside my pants pocket, my phone vibrates with a text. Instantly, my pulse kicks up. I want it to be Mac. I don't want it to be Mac. My chest literally hurts every time I get a text from her. Every time I have to play it cool, like some distant, half-assed friend.

Gripping my glass too hard, I weave through the room, stopping every few feet to accept congratulations or someone wanting to talk.

"Excuse me," I tell each person. "Nature calls."

Best excuse I got, but it still doesn't prevent people from trying to chat me up. By the time I make it to the terrace doors, I'm ready to lose it. God, this PR bullshit is only going to get worse in the NFL.

Frowning, I slip out into the cool night air and take a deep breath to clear my head.

But my pulse doesn't slow as I pull out my phone. I sag against the wall. The text isn't from Mac. Disappointment and relief churn around in my gut as I peer at the unknown number, ready to delete the text.

Unknown: Hey there, sexy mountain of man-flesh. Having fun at your suit parade?

Sexy mountain of man-flesh? Why does that ridiculous name sound familiar? I rub a hand over my face and then it hits me. Fiona calls me that. What the hell is Fiona doing texting me?

GrayG: Yeah, it's awesome. What's up, Fi?

As I wait for her to answer, I stare out across the dark sweep of trimmed lawn. Everything is blue and gray, the moon hanging low along the horizon as wispy clouds drift past. The scent of snow is in the air. My hand vibrates.

LittleFi: Just wanted to let you know that I'm watching out for our girl tonight. Don't worry, she's having fun. Catch ya later, sexy.

A picture pops up, and it's a fucking punch to the throat. Mac's on the dance floor, her long arms waving awkwardly in the air and gleaming with sweat, her dark hair plastered to her face as she smiles—fucking glows—with happiness. And some fucko frat boy has his hands all over her.

I zero in on his big, fucking-fuck palm pressing against her belly, his hips grinding into her ass as he clutches her thigh, holding her against his—

My shout echoes over the terrace, followed by the sharp crack of glass impacting against stone.

Panting, I glance down at my empty hand and then at the carnage that used to be my phone, lying some twenty feet away. I hadn't even known I'd thrown it.

I don't care. Every inch of me hurts, a dull, pulling pain, as if I'm slowly being torn apart from the inside out. My throat seems to swell, closing down, convulsing. I blink down at my shiny wingtips as if trying to make sense of how they got on my feet.

But all I can see is that picture. I hear Ivy's voice in my head, telling me that she needs space, that she doesn't want me.

The muffled sound of laughter from inside grows loud and

clear, and a blast of warmth hits the side of my face. I turn. A girl stands framed in the doorway, her body slim and tight, her smile welcoming.

"Hey," she says, strolling over, each step sending her hips swaying. "What are you doing out here all alone?"

Everything in me recoils at the thought of talking to this girl. I want to go home and crawl into bed. Maybe sleep for a week. But I push deep down inside myself, remember the Gray I used to be. The one who had fun and never thought about anything real. The Gray who never felt pain.

I pull out a smile. "Doesn't look like I'm alone anymore." That's all she needs to hear.

NINETEEN

IVY

MAKING *PAIN AUX RAISINS* is soothing. The steps I have to go through, the yeasty scent of dough, and the warm fragrance of almond cream. I push myself, creating dozens of delicate, buttery layers. Rolling and folding, rolling and folding.

A fine ache spreads along my neck and shoulders. It feels good, this movement. Proactive in the face of my inner silence.

Music plays and I sing along. Rolling and folding. Layer after layer. The dough is like cool satin against my palms.

The phone rings, and I rub my hands on a rag before answering. It's Fi.

"Hey there, mama bear."

"Hey." I try to insert some enthusiasm into my reply. I really do. But it's an epic fail.

Unfortunately, Fi notices. "What's up with you?"

"Nothing." Which is true. Life has basically become a void. I'd tried to go out, have fun. Dance with guys and pretend I loved it. But I've never been very good at pretending.

We're both quiet for a minute. Me not being able to respond without sobbing to Fi, and she's playing detective.

This becomes obvious when she says with suspicion, "Are you listening to 'Shadowboxer'?"

Sometimes it sucks to have a sister who knows me inside and out. "No."

I flick off my speakers.

"Why are you listening to my moody namesake?"

Fi knows perfectly well that I listen to Fiona Apple when I'm in a funk.

"What are you, the DJ police?"

"Yes, and you're in violation of drowning in sad-sack music for the emotionally imbalanced."

Giving up the ghost, I confess. "I miss Gray." I draw in a deep, shaking breath. "I miss him like a loose tooth."

"What?" She laughs, clearly confused.

"You know, it's like a constant ache, and even though I should ignore it, I can't help but prod." Provoke that itchy, dull pain that digs deeper the more I touch on it.

"Ah, a vicious circle of self-torture," Fi says.

I can picture her nodding now. I don't say anything, but pluck at a spot of dried flour on my apron.

Fi's gentle voice drifts through the phone. "Do you want me to come home tonight?"

She's been spending more time at her boyfriend's house. I'm almost envious, but I'm not going to drag her over here. "No. I'm okay."

"Call Gray, Ivy."

"I've texted him." A stab of pain hits my heart. "He's been distant. Doing his own thing."

He's doing what I asked him to do. And it sucks. All I can think of is Gray out, meeting girls, moving on.

Fi sighs. "Yeah, not the same. Call and tell him that you've been a fool. A big ol' flaming fool—"

"Hey!"

"And that you want him bad."

My pulse spikes. "I don't—"

"You *do*. Lie to me if you want, but don't lie to yourself, Iv."

Grimacing, I press my cold fingers to my eyes. They feel too hot. Prickles are forming behind my lids.

"It's for the best. Us cooling things down. I'm leaving for London anyway."

"And yet you told me you don't want to work with Mom. So why go away? Stay here for a while, Ivy. I know I'd love it. Dad would too."

"Which bring us to the fact that he's going to work with Dad," I say weakly. "He wasn't happy about the idea of me being with Gray."

"So the fuck what? Have you ever considered that Dad might be more worried about you getting with that hot-ass mountain of man sex than the possibility of losing Gray as a client?"

"What? No."

"Oh, please. He's still our dad. And he's never liked us going out with anyone. You just made it easy for him because you never really cared before."

I clench the back of my aching neck. "Look, it doesn't matter what Dad thinks. Or where I live. Not really. Gray… Shit, Fi. He's my best friend. What if I tell him I want to take it further, be exclusive, and he doesn't? Or if we do get together and it ends? I can't lose him."

But I already am, and it's killing me.

Fiona's silence is like a condemnation.

"Why do you think it will end?" she finally asks.

"Oh, come on," I whisper brokenly. "He's a football star and will soon be an even bigger one. The odds are stacked against us."

"Not all men cheat."

I flinch, her words like a slap. I'd meant that our lives were on divergent paths, and Gray doesn't even believe in relationships.

"I don't think he'll do that," I say.

"But you fear it."

Suddenly I don't have the strength to stand. My ass hits the stool hard, and I stare off, not seeing my kitchen but the past.

Fi and I witnessed the fights. Heard the phone calls when Mom tried to find out where he was. The hideous sound of Mom crying behind her bedroom door when Dad didn't come home. I was ten when they divorced. Even then, I'd vowed never to let a man do that to me.

Did I really think Gray would be like Dad? Did I put that on him?

"Shit." The sides of my throat hurt, as if a hard hand is squeezing it. I lick my dry lips, wanting Gray more than I've ever wanted anything. Everything is clear and pure when he's with me. Without him, it's all static.

"Call him, Ivy," Fi whispers into the phone. "Let him in."

My voice sounds like a frog's when I can speak. "I've got to go."

By the time I hang up with Fi and dial Gray's number, my fingers are shaking. I don't know what I'm going to say to him. *Come back to me. I need you* might scare him. *I was a chicken. A big ol' special sauce–covered chicken* is probably better.

The call goes straight to voicemail. And when I text, telling him that I need to talk to him, he doesn't respond.

GRAY

"He's not eating, Drew. It's beginning to freak me out."

Anna's stage voice drifts through my fog, but I don't respond to it. I can't. I'm a goddamn mess.

I tried being the old me. Crashed and burned. Couldn't even

keep up the pretense of Happy-Go-Lucky Gray for more than five minutes with that chick at the party before I fled. Can't get my mind focused on football. Can't do anything but inwardly bleed.

I keep replaying every word Ivy uttered when she demolished my heart, keep visualizing that evil-as-fuck picture of her dancing with another guy.

"Maybe he's coming down with something," Drew answers before giving my foot a kick under the table. "You feeling all right, Gray-Gray?"

"Yeah," I get out, because he won't stop if I don't respond. "Great."

It was a mistake coming to Drew and Anna's house for dinner. It is freezing cold and raining out, not the best night for driving. But I needed the distraction their happy chatter could bring. Now I just want to leave without any more questions being thrown my way.

"Well, it can't be the food," Anna says, getting up to clear her and Drew's empty plates before taking my full one. "My lasagna is killer."

She's not lying. Anna doesn't make the heavy American version of lasagna, but a masterpiece of thin, delicate noodles between layers of béchamel and Italian sausage. She gave me the recipe, and I'm never going back to the old way. It's a shame I can't stomach one bite tonight.

"So I'm guessing no humble pie for dessert, huh, babe?" Drew gives Anna's ass a playful swat.

"If you ever want pie again," Anna warns, "you'll eat those words, bud."

Drew hauls her onto his lap, where she happily settles in. "Now, Jones, you and I both know that prohibiting me from eating pie hurts you more—"

Anna slaps a hand over his mouth before he can finish. But they're both grinning at each other.

Fuck me. Did I really think it would be a good idea to hang

out with Mr. and Mrs. Perpetually in Love? Worse, they both notice my scowl.

Drew's brow lifts, and Anna simply peers at me before reaching across the table to rest her small hand on my arm. "What's going on, Gray?"

It's her touch, feminine and light and caring, so similar to Ivy's, that does me in.

I exhale with a shaking breath. "Ivy dumped me."

"Dumped you?" Anna frowns. "Were you two going out?"

"No," I mutter. "As a friend. She thinks we've been spending too much time together. She wants to date…people."

The words feel like broken glass against my throat. I tell them the rest of my disastrous argument with Ivy in short, terse sentences.

When I'm finished, my friends are silent. Probably pitying me. Then Anna gets up and starts messing with her beloved espresso machine—the very one I'd taken care of when she and Drew were on the outs. I still kind of mourn giving it back to her.

Deftly she makes an espresso, adding a spoonful of sugar, then handing me the cup. "Drink it down like a good boy, and you'll feel better."

Doubtful, but I take a sip anyway. Dark, sweet coffee hits my system like a welcome slap. Weirdly, it does make me feel better. Not by much, but enough. And I realize that this is why I'm here. Being in Drew's familiar kitchen, talking to him and Anna, helps.

Drew braces his arms on the table. "I think we're going to need a bit more explanation. You're both obviously into each other—"

"Oh, obviously," I sneer. "Seeing how she kicked me to the curb."

"Please." Drew waves a hand. "I've seen you two together. You're like…"

"Drew and I are," Anna supplies with a grin.

"What? Going at it like horny bunnies? I wish." I truly do. Fuck, how I do.

"Baby steps, Gray-Gray." Drew starts tapping his thumb against the table—thinking. I hate when he does that. "So you kissed Ivy, and she freaked. Did it happen right after you kissed her? Must have been some shitty kiss."

"Fuck you," I say without heat, because I know Drew is messing with me. I'd have said the same to him.

I haven't told them about the things we did before I kissed her. It's too personal.

But I think about it now. The sounds she made, how she came against my fingers. My head hurts and is too heavy to hold up.

I push away my cup and rest my face on the table. It's cool against my cheek. "She seemed into it but then she wasn't."

"You must have said something boneheaded, then."

"You don't know that, Drew." Anna gets up and makes herself a cup of espresso. The machine whistles and grumbles.

"Oh, no? Because I'm betting he did. Gray often speaks before he thinks. Kind of like someone else I know." Drew ducks the towel Anna throws at him, then he gives me an expectant look. "Well? Think, bonehead."

I lift my head to glare. "I did everything I could not to freak her out. She asked me what we were doing, and I told her that… Oh, shit." On a groan, I slam my head back down on the table. "Shit, shit, shit."

"Told you," Drew says to Anna.

"Zip it, Baylor," Anna says. "What did you say to her, Gray?"

Don't think. It doesn't matter. It doesn't have to matter. Because that's what I thought she wanted to hear. Because I was afraid to tell her the truth.

"All the wrong things." I shove back from the table. "I've got to go."

TWENTY

IVY

I'M DEPRESSED. GRAY IS ignoring me, and I'm avoiding Fi. I don't want a pep talk. I don't want to go out. I don't want to bake. I just want to sit in my house and ignore the world. Thankfully, Fi gives me space and heads out to her boyfriend's house.

It's been raining all day. A miserable, cold downpour that beats against my roof.

I've got the heat turned up and am curled under a thick blanket, while watching *North by Northwest*. If anything can take my mind off Gray, it has to be Hitchcock.

I tell myself this again as I sip my cocoa and stare blankly at the TV. My eyes are dry and hot. I should go to bed. But I know it won't help. Sleep has eluded me for days.

My fingers curl tight around the mug as a surge of anger rushes through me. I'm mad at myself. I'm not being proactive. I should hunt Gray down, force him to talk to me. Apologize for being a jerk. Tell him he's the most important thing in my life.

I'm setting down my cocoa when someone pounds on the door. Do I want it to be Gray? With my whole being. But he hasn't called or texted. And he never shows up without warning.

Wary, I make my way to the door. "Yeah?" I call, visions of psychos dancing in my head.

"Ivy." Gray's voice is muffled by rain and the door. "Let me in."

Two seconds later, it's open and I'm facing him. He's soaked, his big body hunched against the rain that bounces off him.

"Ivy."

"Gray. What the hell?" The rain has mixed with icy sleet and hard pings of hail. It's freaking twenty degrees out, and he's only wearing a wet long-sleeve shirt. "Where's your truck?"

"Broke down a mile back. Think it's the fuel pump." He sounds like a zombie. His skin is too pale, his lips blue.

I grab hold of his arm and tug him inside, slamming the door shut against the icy wind that gusts into the house. "Why didn't you call so I could get you?"

"Broke my phone last Saturday."

"Oh." Well, at least I know why he hasn't answered my calls.

He doesn't move, but stands there dripping onto the floor. Straggling strands of his hair fall into his eyes. Eyes that are haunted, gazing at me with pain and desperation.

"Ivy… I ache. For you."

My breath hitches.

His fists clench. "I can't do this. Staying away. I can't…" A full-body shiver wracks him. "I n-need you… I'm through being… considerate…"

He's shivering so badly, his teeth clatter.

"Shhh. Gray. You're freezing. Come here."

Worried, I take his hand and lead him into the bedroom. He lets me tug him along, his steps wooden.

"Take off your shoes and socks," I tell him once we're in my room. And he does, never moving his pained gaze off me.

"Ivy…"

I pull his sodden shirt free. In the soft light of the table lamp, his torso is pale and prickled with cold.

"Let's get these things off first," I murmur.

Together we tackle his jeans, our fingers tangling. Gray pushes everything off, down to the buff. I don't look. I can't right now. My eyes stay on his shoulders as I lead him to my bed, lifting the down comforter up so he can slide in.

Fully dressed, I follow and pull him close. Instantly, he wraps an arm around my waist and burrows his face into the crook of my neck. I get cold just holding him, and I tuck the covers tighter around us.

"Of all the irresponsible…" I murmur, my hand rubbing soothing circles over his broad back and down his arms to get his blood flowing. "You're half frozen."

Gray grunts, his grip on me tight. The cold wet of his hair seeps through my shirt. But he's getting warmer.

It feels so good to hold him. The low place in my belly that has been hard and pained eases. Then awareness sets in, of the heavy weight of his arm along my waist, of how he's completely naked, wrapped around me, his thick thigh pushed between mine.

I touch a damp strand of his hair. "I should have gotten you a towel."

Slowly he stirs, and then his breath gusts against the sensitive skin at my neck. "I should move. But I don't want to."

He sounds so petulant, like a boy in threat of losing his favorite toy, that my lips tremble on a smile. "Oh sure, get me all wet. I don't mind."

Gray makes a strangled noise, and a weak laugh escapes him. "Oh, Mac, so many things I could do with that. It's almost too easy."

A furious blush hits my cheeks as I realize what I've said. But I find myself snickering against his temple. The urge to kiss his forehead makes me bite my lip.

"I've missed you, Gray."

He lifts his head. His thick lashes are clumped together with damp. "You told me to stay away."

"I didn't mean all the time," I say, still stung.

"Truth, Ivy? I can't be around you and not think of what we did together. Not want to talk about it."

That quickly, all the confusion and fear I've been feeling surges like an incoming tide. The need for escape has me breaking free from his hold and jumping out of bed.

From the corner of my eye, I see Gray lurch up. His hard, irate voice follows. "Don't you dare run again, Ivy."

"I'm not running…" My words die on my tongue because Gray is out of bed and stalking toward me and, sweet mother…

Wide shoulders, flat-packed muscles leading down to a narrow waist—he's so gorgeous my knees go weak. His massive thighs bunch and shift with each hard step, his cock hanging thick and heavy between them.

Out of breath, I lean against the wall to keep from toppling. But he doesn't notice. His gaze burns bright and angry. He walks right up to me, not stopping until he's caged me in, bracing his arms on either side of my head. And then I see it isn't anger in his eyes, but desperation.

His voice comes out soft but insistent. "Looks like running away to me."

God, he's too close. I can't think. My breath comes out choppy, my breasts nearly brushing the taut wall of his chest. "Gray, get back in bed—"

"Only if you come with me," he rasps, his gaze roaming my face. But the bluish tinge of his lips worries me.

When he shivers again, I duck under his arm, earning a sound of protest, and head to the bathroom with Gray hot on my heels.

"Ivy—"

"Hold on," I tell him when we enter the bathroom.

Because it's my dad's guesthouse, the shower stall is massive, with white marble slab tiles and a glass partition wall to keep the water from splashing everywhere. I turn the shower on full heat. "Get in. I can't talk to you when I know you're half frozen."

I cross my arms over my chest and wait, not looking at him. Naked Gray is not something I can handle without dissolving on the spot. But I feel him brush past me, muttering under his breath about stubborn women.

"I'm in." His deep voice echoes throughout the room as steam begins to rise. "You happy now? Can we talk?"

"So talk."

He doesn't answer. The steady beat of the shower fills the silence. And the air grows humid.

"Ivy. Look at me."

"Um. You're naked."

"You just saw me naked." There's a smile in his voice.

"Yeah, I think we need to have that boundaries talk again."

A drop of water hits my neck, and it sends a bolt of feeling to my toes.

His voice is close now, and I know he's leaning past the glass. "Ivy Mac, I want you to see me. Nothing between us. Please, honey. Look at me."

The request wraps around my heart, has me turning. And, holy hell. My mouth goes dry, and I have to brace myself.

Standing half behind the water-streaked glass, nothing is hidden. Wet is a good look for Gray. Droplets of water bead silver on golden skin, trickle in paths over valleys and hills of muscle.

My fingers itch to slide along that slick skin, to run along his dripping hair, now bronze with wet. But it's the way he's looking at me, his blue eyes pleading to let me in, that has tenderness fluttering in my chest.

Smooth glass meets my palm. Gray's hand lifts, presses against the other side, his fingers so much longer than mine. "Ivy, I kissed you and—"

"You told me it didn't matter. You acted as though it was all just a spur-of-the-moment thing, a fucking impulse, and I just happened to be convenient." The painful truth pours out. It hurts to hear it again, like a burn that's been prodded.

Gray grimaces as if it hurts him too. "I lied."

It punches the breath out of me. "Lied?"

The corners of his eyes crinkle in pained expression. "Yes."

"Why?"

"Because I'm a dumbass. Okay?" Gray takes a breath and leans his head against the edge of the shower glass. "I thought if I told you it wasn't a big deal you wouldn't freak out. And it was the worst thing I could have said."

"Yeah, it was."

With a solemn expression, Gray reaches past the glass partition. His big hand cups the base of my neck and draws me close.

"Ivy, I can't lie to you anymore. Nothing about you is convenient. And you are the only one who has ever mattered. I look at you and I want to kiss you. Touch you."

His lids lower, his gaze hot and needy on my mouth. "I want to learn your body, find all those secret places that make you go crazy."

A puff of air leaves my lips, and he gives me a half-pained smile. "God, I want those things, honey. I want them so badly—"

"Gray—"

"No. Let me finish." He takes a breath, his shoulders tensing. His thumb ghosts over my chin. "I don't want this to be some half-assed friends-with-benefits thing. I want you to be mine. My girl. I want to be your guy. The thought of you with someone else… Shit. It rips my heart out."

"Gray."

He closes his eyes, giving his head a sharp shake. "I keep seeing that picture of you with that guy. It guts me, Ivy."

"What picture? What guy?" Of all the things to focus on. But my thoughts have gone haywire. He isn't making any sense.

Gray's eyes fill with hurt as he looks at me. "Fiona sent me a picture of you dancing with some…"

His head drops forward as he glares at the floor.

Fi, that little shit. Carefully, I touch Gray's jaw. "It was just one dance. I can't even remember the guy. That was me trying to have fun without you. And failing."

His breath hitches then shudders. Relief, pain, anxiety. I've caused this in him. And it tears at my heart.

"I don't want another guy, Gray."

It seems as though his entire body stills at my words, and his gaze grows searching and vulnerable. "But do you want me?"

I wrap my arms around his damp neck. Holding on. "I'm scared," I blurt out. "You're my best friend. I can't stand it when we're apart. And if it goes bad… I don't want to lose you."

The tips of his fingers press into the curve of my jaw. "You will never lose me, Ivy. Never. I will always be your friend." His wet palm cups my cheek. "I know you're worried about how it will be with your dad—"

"No," I cut in. "That was wrong. I should never have said that. He has nothing to do with us."

"No, he doesn't." Gray's thumb glides over my chin. "And I know you're leaving for London. I don't care. Not enough to turn my back on this. We'll work it out."

"I'm not going back to London."

Gray stills, his gaze snapping to mine. "Don't mess with me, honey, not about this."

I give his neck a gentle squeeze. "I'm going to talk to my parents. I want to try to be an agent." Just saying it sends a little burst of nervous excitement through me. It feels right.

Gray slowly smiles. "You'll kick ass, Ivy Mac."

I lean into his hold, letting him support me. "I don't know where I'll live, but I'm not leaving the States."

"You don't know how happy I am to hear that," he whispers. "Because I'm not quitting on you."

He no longer looks scared or hurt, but confident. "It will be so good, Mac. So fucking good between us. We just have to try. Tell me you want to try."

My heart beats so hard, he has to hear it. Gently, I reach up and wipe a drop of water from the corner of his mouth, my touch lingering. "I don't think we've ever been just friends, Gray. I think I've wanted you from the beginning."

His eyes close tight, a sigh leaving him, and he bites his lower lip. When he opens his eyes again, they shine sapphire blue. "You've owned me from 'shenanigans,' Ivy Mac."

For a moment, we simply smile at each other, the reality of us as a couple, as something serious, vibrating in the air, tickling my skin, making my heart beat fast and strong.

Then he's pulling me into the shower, warm water soaking my clothes, my skin, the air humid on my face. And we're kissing, melting explorations of lips and tongue and teeth. My hand grips his hair, holding him closer.

Gray groans, angles his head to penetrate me deep. His tongue slides against mine, honey-sweet to my starved senses. All I can think is that I'm kissing Gray without worrying about why. *Gray* is kissing me.

We both seem to revel in this new freedom. Each press of lips, each nibble and soft suck, saying, *Finally*, and *This, this is what I've wanted*, and *More, give me more. Yes. Like that. More of that. Don't stop.*

"Gray." I suckle his plump lower lip. "I need you."

He shudders, his hands in my hair, on my cheeks. "You have me," he says against my lips. "I don't think you understand how much you have me."

He kisses his way down my neck, pressing his hard body against mine, grinding that thick, long cock of his between my legs.

"I'm crazy about you, Ivy. You have to know that. I'm so lost in you, I don't ever want to find my way back."

One tug of his hands, and my soaked shirt is off, hitting the shower floor with a slap. Skin slides against skin, wet, firm. His mouth on mine, our fingers tangling as we push down my pants. I kick them free.

I move to him, but Gray holds me still with one hand on my shoulder. His lips part, his breath fast and agitated.

"Let me look at you," he says. "I need to look at you."

I've never been fully naked in front of anyone before. That I am now has my stomach clenching, the urge to cover myself tensing along my arms. But this is Gray, asking with his heart in his voice.

So I don't hide. My back rests against the cool, wet tiles, and I let my arms fall to my sides.

A strangled sound leaves him, his grip on my shoulder tightening as he looks his fill.

I know I'm not perfect. My legs are long, but not muscular because I don't work out. My hips are wider than I'd like, my butt a handful, even for him. I like myself just fine, but I'm not perfect. I—

"God." He swallows, the muscles along his throat moving. "You're… I kept trying to picture you. So many times, I thought about you."

Gray rakes a hand through his dripping hair, sending droplets over me. "Now? *Beautiful* seems too small a word. I could look at you forever, Mac."

His gaze travels up, taking in my stomach, which isn't a board, but smooth enough, and lingers on my boobs, average size with pale pink nipples that point upward. The heat in his eyes has my breasts growing heavy, aching at the tips, and I arch my back a little, lifting them closer to him.

He grunts, a sort of "unh" breath of sound, and his broad chest hitches. Slowly, like it has a mind of its own, his hand lifts. The blunt tip of his finger touches my nipple, catching up a bead of water, and I feel it to my toes. I almost sink to the floor when he puts that long finger in his mouth and slowly sucks it.

Gray makes a little hum of pleasure and smiles. His large hand, so perfect for clutching a football and protecting it until he enters the end zone, engulfs my breast, swallows it whole. Warm, calloused palms and strong fingers. The way he gently kneads my breast feels so good I feel like I'm floating. His gaze is slumberous and hot on what he's doing to me.

And God, he's beautiful, his body so tight. Perfection. How am I supposed to keep from devouring every substantial inch of him? And then I realize I don't have to refrain. He's mine now.

My hands are on him before I can think, running along his broad chest, over the small nubs of his nipples, and down the hard planes of his abs. Jesus, he feels good.

Gray shudders, his head falling to my shoulder so he can nuzzle my neck. "More. Touch me, Mac. Please."

The blunt length of his erection brushes my belly. It's like a brand, catching all my attention. And I haven't even had my hands on it.

Without another thought, I sink to my knees and my mouth catches the tip of his cock, drawing it in before he can utter a word. The large head is smooth and hot, swollen so tight that it throbs against the roof of my mouth. I give it a slow suck, and a helpless gurgle leaves Gray's lips. His palms slap against the tiles as he braces himself, that long, lean body of his bunching with tension.

"Ivy… Sweet Jesus."

My thoughts exactly. He's big, and there's no way I'm getting all of him in my mouth. God, but I'm tempted. He's beautiful, substantial, and so hard there's no give to him. My fingers wrap around his base, squeezing, testing his strength. Gray whimpers, his hips shifting a bit as if he's trying to hold still.

I glance up at him. His muscled torso curves over me, a shelter from the water raining down on his back. Our eyes meet and his expression slays me—pleasure, tenderness, hesitation, as if he isn't sure how far to take things.

Give me all of you, I tell him with my eyes. *Don't hold back. I want everything.*

His throat works on a swallow. He sinks his teeth into his lower lip as he begins to move. In and out, a slow, long glide.

"You want a taste of me, huh?" The whisper echoes through the shower. "Open that mouth wider and let me in so you can get it good."

My jaw aches as I do as he says, taking him deep.

Gray grunts, his cock twitching in my mouth. "Yeah. Yeah, like that. Oh, fuck, like that. You like me filling up your mouth?"

I hum, jerk his cock with my hand as I suck him. And he shudders, his voice growing raspy.

"You know how many times I stood in a shower, fucking my hand while pretending it was your hot little mouth, Ivy?"

He pauses as if remembering, a look of raw pleasure parting his lips. Then his hips jerk. "Fuck, honey. Don't. Don't stop."

I couldn't if I tried. I have a vivid imagination, and I've thought of doing this to Gray. A lot. I let myself play, do all the things I've wanted for far too long.

All the while, Gray makes gasping, almost pained sounds as he pumps between my lips, the movement restrained, shaking in its intensity. He's drawing this out, letting me torture him.

It makes me so hot that I close my eyes, pull him in, run my tongue over every inch that I can, show him how much I love this. I've done this before, but not like this. Not with Gray, not holding back, savoring every gorgeous inch. And I've underestimated how good it would feel to give him pleasure.

Gray. Delicious Gray, whose hard body and hot skin drive me wild. I run my hands up his thighs to cup the taut swells of his ass. God, his ass. It flexes tight with each thrust. I suck harder, faster, and he moans, his body shivering.

Somehow I know he's close. I can feel all that restrained energy rising up in him, ready to break free. But then he's out of my mouth, the sound a smacking pop, and he's hauling me up, pushing me against the wall as his mouth takes mine.

It's almost frightening the way I lose all sense of myself. There's only him, his mouth, his warmth. He kisses me there against the tiles, my butt cupped in his big hands. My legs wrap around his waist, and he lifts me as if I weigh nothing. I can't get over his immense strength and how he never uses it against me but only in service of me. I don't want to leave this spot. Ever.

Then my attention shifts. To the heat of his cock, and the fact that it's between my spread legs, the rounded crown at my opening. Gray notices too, and he trembles, shifting his grip a bit.

My breath hitches as just the tip of him sinks in, spreading me. I thought he was big in my mouth. He's enormous now. All I can think about.

Gray stills, his muscles bunching with effort. "We… Hell… We should stop."

My eyes snap open. "We should?"

The corner of his mouth curls in a weak smile at the sound of my protest. But he can't hold that smile.

"Okay, not stop. Move locations. This means something to me. And I want—I should do right by you. Take you to bed."

I cup his cheek, press the corner of my mouth against his, just breathe the same air as him. "It's you, Gray. That's all I need to make it special."

His skin pebbles, and he nods once. "Get a condom, then?" And then his expression falls. "Fuck. Fuck. I don't have…" He expels a breath. "I didn't plan on tonight."

Half of my attention is on his cock, still there, teasing me, making me feel empty and wanting. "We're both healthy. I'm on the pill." I hold his gaze. "Unless there have been others since—"

"No." It's almost a shout. He rests his forehead against mine. "Only you. It's only ever you now, Ivy."

"Then—" I wiggle, moving against him, making him pant. "Can we..."

He gives me a soft kiss. "Tell me you're my girl."

I kiss him back. Soft. Light. "I'm yours. And you're mine."

"Fuck yeah, I am." He smiles as he nuzzles my nose with his. And though I'm so hot, so ready for him, tenderness has my chest aching.

His breath gusts over my lips. "I know you wanted it slow, soft. But...shit, honey, I don't... I don't think I can the first time. I'll try—"

I kiss his lips, quiet him, my thighs gripping tighter, drawing him closer. He shudders around me. I shudder too. It's been a long time, and he's big. But the stretch of him feels so good, it highlights that aching emptiness inside of me.

My voice is breathy, impatient. "I don't need it slow. I just need you. Now."

He nods, kissing me almost absently. "Okay. Okay. Just... fuck." He groans, moving in a bit deeper. "Tell me to stop. Any time you want me to stop. I will."

"Now, Gray."

"Bossy." He's grinning.

"Cupcake."

"Fucking love when you call me that." He thrusts upward, and I groan, pushing my body down onto his cock, needing more.

His gaze locks with mine, our lips brushing, tickling with each breath. As if he can't help himself, he licks into my mouth, tastes me as he pushes again.

"You're perfect," he says. "Perfect."

And then he's fully in, so deep and solid it throbs. The crinkly hairs at his base rub my clit with each hard pump of his hips. And I've died. Because it's too much. Too good.

"Perfect," I whisper, holding on tight.

GRAY

I think I'm going to die. My chest feels like it's about to crack open, expose my bleeding heart, and leave me wasted on the floor. I've never had sex with someone who mattered to me. It's almost too much to handle. Because this is Ivy.

I'm inside Ivy. Finally inside Ivy. No barriers. Her tight, wet heat clasping my dick so good I have to grit my teeth to keep from shouting.

My fingers sink into her plump, sweet ass, spreading her wider as I thrust. Hard.

Deep. Steady. No more talk. Just Ivy. *Having Ivy.* Her long legs are wrapped around me, holding on tight. Water rains down on my back, slides over us, makes Ivy's smooth skin slick, wet. It's heaven.

Ivy utters a little whimper, like she's as impatient and needy as I am. She cups my cheeks, finds my mouth. Wet lips, soft tongue. She kisses me as if I'm the best thing she's ever tasted. And, fuck, it screws with my head. I want to cry, or laugh, or both. I don't understand it, but I don't want this to end. It's agony and perfection all at once.

I angle my head, opening my mouth wider for her, thrust my tongue into her warm mouth. I kiss her until I can't breathe, until I'm fucking dizzy on her taste.

Ivy makes that hot, feminine whimper again.

It's too much. I'm losing my mind.

I pump into Ivy. Harder. Harder. I should be gentle. Slow. I can't. I want to pound myself into her until I'm a part of her. Our lips slide apart, our movements too frantic now for kissing. My face burrows into the crook of her neck, my mouth open on her soft skin.

"Ivy." I'm saying it over and over, with each thrust.

Ivy, Ivy, Ivy.

I don't even know why. I want to tell her better things. That she's everything to me. The best part of me. That I'll take care of her, protect her—from what, I don't know. But I will. I'll keep her safe and happy. Because it's my job. The most important job I'll ever have.

But all I can say is her name, fuck her like I'm about to die.

She's panting now, her slim arms sliding over the wet tiles, as if she's trying to get away from the pleasure and reach for it all at once. Her thighs clamp down on my waist as she arches her hips into mine. And those sweet-as-fuck tits lift high. I haven't even gotten a taste of them.

I duck my head, capture a pink nipple, and suck it in deep, lick the stiff little nub, flick it with my tongue. She loves it, her pussy milking my dick as she cups my head and writhes.

Fuck yeah. Heat washes down my back, up my thighs. My balls draw tight, my dick pulsing.

I grind against her, feel her clench as she comes, her cries echoing throughout the shower. And then I'm the one crying out. I don't even recognize the sounds I make. They're desperate, loud, and disjointed. I lose sight of Ivy, of myself. It feels so fucking good that, for a moment, I truly wonder if I am going to die. But I won't, because nothing, *nothing*, is going to keep me from doing this again. And again.

Because I'm Ivy's. Forever.

TWENTY-ONE

GRAY

THERE IS SOMETHING utterly satisfying about taking Mac out as her guy. This time when she dances in her wacky way, I can hold her close, run my hands over her curves, duck my head, and draw in her luscious scent. And when we sit with the guys, I can pull her onto my lap and kiss my way across her neck, taste her smiling mouth.

She cuddles me back, pets my hair, touches me as though I'm her own personal plaything. Which I am. In short: Best. Night. Out. Ever.

Mac is happy-buzzing by the time we leave Palmers and is singing Prince's "Raspberry Beret." Only it comes out as a throaty but off-key, "Raspberry bidet. I'm trying to find the helping hands floor."

I don't even bother to hide my laugh as she side-dances toward my truck. Alcohol does not improve her technique. If anything, her long limbs are even more uncoordinated, moving to a rhythm apparently only she hears. I can't help but drink her in as she flails about, until she bangs into an unsuspecting trash can, nearly knocking it, and herself, over.

"Who put that there?" she says in outrage before leaning against it and snickering in little bursts of sloppy glee. In the yellow brightness of the streetlight, her eyes shine like onyx as she looks at me. "Get over here, Cupcake."

My back hurts from purposely dancing badly to help her again, and I've got an early wake-up, but I don't want the night to end.

"So now I'm your beck-and-call boy?" I ask, as I head over to her.

Mac snickers again. "Call boy. Get it?"

Rolling my eyes, I stop in front of her, close enough to catch her should she fall. "Yeah, I get it, Mac. You're hilarious."

She's so damn cute. I tuck a lock of her hair behind her ear and run my thumb along the edge of her jaw.

"Mmmm…" It's a near-purr of sound, way too throaty. Her warm hands clasp my waist, holding me steady as if I'm the one who's about to fall. Dark eyes peer up at me. "I totally am."

"Am what?" I'm drawing a blank, distracted by the sweet curve of her lower lip and the way it's jutting out in a little pout.

I lean down to claim a soft kiss. God, she is delicious—the sweet tartness of margaritas mixed with pure Ivy Mac.

"Hilarious," she says with exasperation against my mouth. But then she's kissing me back, exploring a little deeper each time.

Her warm tongue licks a path along the sensitive edge of my inner lip—exactly one second before the tip of her left index finger steals under my shirt and runs lightly along the edge of my jeans. I feel the action like a stroke behind my balls. My breath hitches, and my gut clenches. It takes everything in me not to cant my hips and beg for her to explore lower.

If I start fooling around with her, I'm not going to want to stop. The things I want to do to her require space and privacy.

I draw in another deep breath of cold air, then gently take hold of her wrists and place her hands in front of us where I can see them. Mac simply gives me a goofy smile and leans in until her chin rests on my ribs. Her head moves with the cadence of my breath, lifting and lowering. The motion and her proximity to my increasingly interested dick are weakening my resolve.

It begins to crumble when her gaze turns sleepy, her lids lowering as she peers up at me, her hands stroking my thighs. God, she's pretty, all flushed, her silky hair mussed and her lips softly parted. My cock pulses in protest. He wants in. My mouth just wants to claim hers again.

"My hands are cold," she says.

I cover them with my own, my hands so large that they completely engulf her fists. "Let's get you home, honey." My voice sounds rough and too thick.

"Okay. But I'm tired," she says. "Carry me."

At this point, I'm willing to carry her across the state if it means I get to fuck her. I scoop her up without another word.

She gives a little happy squeal, and her long legs kick the air as her arms strangle my neck.

"Easy," I choke out as I carry her to my truck.

We're halfway there when I see him. I freeze, my entire body seizing up. My knee-jerk reaction is one of fear, cold and tense. Rage follows on its heels. I've reacted in fear and from simply laying eyes upon him.

Ivy lets out a sound of protest, and I realize that I'm holding her too tightly.

Ivy. Fucking. Hell.

My fear returns. I don't want her anywhere near Jonas. I'm barely aware of setting Ivy down.

She stands close to me as if she knows I need the support. I don't, and yet my arm snakes around her waist and holds on.

Jonas leans against my truck, hands tucked in his pockets, his legs crossed at the ankle. Somehow, he still manages to make the pose look threatening. Maybe it's because I know he won't hesitate to damage my truck if he thinks it will upset me. The fucker.

He's enormous, the small gut he'd been sporting four years ago now a full barrel. His arms are still built for brutality. Then again, every inch of Jonas has been crafted and forged for aggression.

The bottom drops out of my stomach as our gazes clash. It's been four years since I've seen my brother and still I feel sick just looking at him.

"About time you showed," he says by way of greeting. "Fucking sick of hunting you down, Gravy."

Asshole. "I wasn't aware we had a date."

He sneers at the word *date*, but his eyes ooze over Ivy. My grip on her tightens. She hasn't said a word, but she's clearly lost her buzz. Tense and alert next to me, her fingers slide along my back and then curl around the belt loop of my jeans. I want her away from here like I need my next breath, but her simple hold grounds me in a way I haven't felt in years, if ever.

"I'm not discussing shit in front of your piece of ass," Jonas says.

My breath comes out in a rush. But I stay still. I'm good at locking it down in front of Jonas.

"*Ivy* isn't going anywhere. So I guess you're shit out of luck."

Jonas smiles. I used to see that smile a lot. Right before he struck. And while every old fear in me is shouting to lower my eyes—or better yet, get the fuck out of here—I'm not that little boy anymore.

"You're getting mouthy with freedom," he says with a frown. When I don't answer, he goes on. "You haven't returned my texts."

I don't bother to tell him that I've blocked him. If he didn't look like a burly version of my dad, I'd think Jonas was adopted because he got neither of our parents' intelligence.

"What do you want, Jonas?" I ask in a bland voice.

At my side, Ivy is quiet but close, her hand yet to leave my back.

"You're two games away from being draft eligible. It's time to make plans."

"As touching as that sounds, I've got it covered." Not that I think my brother has any interest in looking out for me.

His look of disdain tells me as much. "Yeah, well, my agent says you haven't returned his calls either."

Which is because I have no interest in signing with Jonas's soulless bloodsucker.

Not that he's actually Jonas's agent anymore. They parted ways when Jonas fucked up his career. But I'm guessing this is a way to get in good with his old cronies.

"Didn't want to return them," I say.

"You're an embarrassment to this family. You will call him."

Suddenly, I'm just worn out. I hate this. Hate that my remaining blood relatives are nothing to me.

"No, Jonas," I say in a low voice. "I won't. I'm signing with Mackenzie."

"That weak-ass fucker?" Jonas barks out a laugh. "He doesn't have the balls to get shit done."

"Hey!" Mac snaps, stepping forward. "That's my father you're talking about, so shut your mouth."

Inside I groan, cursing this whole situation. But my awareness goes on high alert as I sling an arm around Mac's waist and haul her back against me. Every inch of her vibrates like she's about to throw a punch, and she doesn't know who she's dealing with.

"Ignore him," I murmur. Not because I disagree. But I know Jonas.

Jonas leers as expected. "I can't believe this. He has his daughter riding cock to get clients? I underestimated the guy."

Mac lurches in my arms, unable to get free but doing a good job trying. "You disgusting fucker, you don't know dick."

That shuts him up. He pushes off my truck, rage in his eyes. "Watch your mouth, girlie."

Blood races through my veins, and it feels ice-cold. Not taking my eyes from him, I firmly set Mac behind me, telling her, "Don't move."

Something in my voice must convey the seriousness of the situation, because she does what I say.

Jonas, on the other hand, takes a step toward her. "I should shut that mouth for you."

"You need to get the fuck out of here," I tell him, standing in front of Mac. "Now."

"You don't tell me what to do, Gravy. You fucking obey. As always."

It burns that Mac hears my shame. That I ever obeyed this asshole. But no more.

"You're making a fool out of yourself," I tell him. "Go on. We're done here."

Jonas's nostrils flare. Instinct has me transferring my weight onto the balls of my feet, my thighs clenching, prepping for a tackle. Jonas is a big motherfucker, but he's been out of the game for years, and I'm stronger, faster, with better balance. He'll go down and stay down.

Because he is, at heart, still a lineman, he reads my intent with perfect clarity. It's in the eyes. We've been trained to broadcast *I'm gonna fuck your shit up* with one look.

"You think you can take me, little bro?" Jonas smirks like there's no chance.

"I can bench four-thirty, so that just might be enough to toss you." I shouldn't taunt Jonas but he brings out the worst in me.

He bares his teeth at me. "I shit bigger than you."

"I believe it."

When he makes a noise as if he'll soon charge, I clench my fists. But Ivy's cool hand lands on my stomach. "He isn't worth it, Gray."

Her dark eyes are wide and worried, gleaming up at me with a silent plea. And I soften. I don't want her to see this ugliness. But my distraction is a mistake. I hear Jonas snarl.

"Thought I told you to mind your fucking business, girlie."

He lunges, and I can only think of Ivy, threatened. My vision goes white and a roar tears from my throat. I slam into Jonas with enough force to rattle my bones. Fisting his shirt, I propel him upward, my thighs bunching with effort until he goes airborne.

His massive shape is a silhouette in the streetlight, and then he's crashing down onto the pavement with a loud thud. I stand over him, my teeth grinding. A slow shake works deep through my guts.

"Get the fuck out of here, or I will end you."

He stares at me, all wide-eyed with his mouth hanging open. Blood dribbles from his lip, and my knuckles throb. Had I hit him? I don't even remember doing it.

He spits a glob of red from his mouth as he rolls over, so I must have. Slowly, he stands.

We stare at each other for a long moment. When I speak, the finality feels like shards going down my throat. "Don't ever talk to me again."

He just shakes his head. "Mom wasted her time on the wrong kid." And then he leaves me there, gutted and filled with useless rage.

IVY

Rain has started to fall. It taps against the roof of Gray's truck with a metallic rattle and runs in rivulets down the fogged-up windows. Inside, it's warm, the old heater blowing steadily as we sit, not speaking.

We're parked in front of my house, listening to Nine Inch Nails's "Right Where It Belongs" play softly on the radio, the sound haunting in the relative silence.

Gray hasn't moved, and I'm hesitant about saying a word. He's clearly in his own world right now, his strong profile as hard as carved stone as he stares blindly forward.

Every line of his body is tense, as if he might shatter if he moves, and I hate it. I saw the rage and the fear cloud his eyes when his brother taunted him. I saw the hurt and shame. Gray is in pain, and that is unacceptable.

Slowly, my hand slides across the truck's leather bench seat. His fingers are curled into a fist, but the moment I touch him, he opens his hand, turning his palm upward to clasp my own. Until I feel the warmth of his touch, I don't realize how much I'd needed it.

We don't speak. Gray's hand engulfs mine. For a moment, I simply sit and soak in the small connection between us. It's strange how good it feels just to do this. Almost absently, he traces the back of my hand, down the sensitive edges of my fingers and over my knuckles. Pleasure hums along my skin.

I explore as well, sliding a finger along the length of his, as the tip of my thumb strokes his palm. I love Gray's hands. Warm, rough skin. Long fingers and broad palms, and strength. He could crush my hand without effort yet he holds on to me as though I'm made of spun sugar. Tenderness washes over me.

"Hey," I whisper. "What kind of shoes do spies wear?"

At first I don't think he's heard me, then Gray's lips twitch. "Don't know."

"Sneakers."

"Har." The corners of his eyes crinkle as his smile grows. Still he stares out the window.

I give his hand a small squeeze. "What do you get when you cross a vampire with a snowman?"

"What?"

"Frostbite."

Gray snorts. And then his eyes find mine. They glint with humor in the dim interior. "What's green and smells like pork?"

Relieved that he's engaging, I have to bite my lip to keep from grinning. "What?"

"Kermit's finger."

"Eew." I laugh as I bat his arm. "That is vile."

His broad shoulders shake as his laugh rolls out. He has a gorgeous laugh, booming and infectious. And right now, it's the best sound in the world.

I'm still laughing when I give him another one. "What did the duck say to the hunter?"

Gray chokes down a laugh before asking, "What?"

"I don't know." I shrug. "I wasn't there for that conversation."

And he laughs again, his expression open and happy. "That is the goofiest one ever, Mac."

"I know. Hey." When he looks at me expectantly, I give his hand a tug. "What's up with you and your brother?"

Gray's expression falls as abruptly as a lid being slammed shut, and a twinge of guilt hits me. It's a sneak attack and shitty of me. But there's a difference between slapping a bandage over a wound and trying to help heal it. I can't heal all of Gray's hurts, but I want to try.

"You don't have to tell me," I say when he doesn't say anything.

Gray leans back against the seat and runs a hand over his face before looking off. "I don't want to."

It shouldn't hurt. He has a right to his privacy. But a lump rises in my throat anyway. And it takes effort to nod. Not that he's looking my way to see it.

A gust of wind hits the truck and it shudders. I should take him inside, comfort him with my body, and forget trying to make him talk.

He sighs and turns to me. His eyes are haunted.

"Gray…"

"It's okay, Ivy." He seeks out my hand and holds it again. His fingers have gone cold. With his free hand, he rubs his eyes as if his head hurts.

As if in a fog, Gray stares at his hand, his fingers spread wide. Red abrasions mar his knuckles. He makes a fist and lowers it.

"I hate violence. Believe me, I get the irony of being a football player. But it isn't the same. On the field, it's controlled. Well, mostly. And we're fairly matched up. But off the field?" He shakes his head. "Only a coward uses his fists when he can easily walk away."

"I'm sorry I egged your brother on and made you fight."

Gray's brows lift in surprise before snapping together in a frown. "Don't ever be sorry for being yourself. I will always defend you, Ivy, and I won't lose a wink of sleep over it." He looks down at his hand again. "I wanted to beat the shit out of him for even talking to you like that. It…unsettles me. I don't want to be like them."

"Like them?" I ask.

"I have three brothers. Jonas is the oldest. Twelve years older than myself. Then there's Leif, who is ten years older, Axel is three years older, and I'm the youngest. Axel is all right but we're not close. Jonas and Leif are total assholes."

He glances at me, his brows pulling together in a bemused frown. "You really didn't google me at all, did you?" There's no accusation in his voice, only a soft wonder.

"No," I confess quietly. "Truth? I wanted our friendship to be about Ivy and Gray. Not what the rest of the world thought about you."

For a long moment he just looks at me, his expression giving nothing away. Then, with his free hand, he reaches out, and the tips of his fingers graze along my cheek.

"Same here, Ivy Mac." His touch drifts away. "So I'm assuming you didn't recognize Jonas, did you?"

"Was I supposed to?"

He laughs without humor. "I guess not. Though it'd probably

piss him off to hear that." Gray rolls his shoulders. "Jonas Grayson, superstar offensive lineman, two-time Super Bowl winner—"

"Holy shit," I interrupt as understanding dawns. "Jonas and Leif Grayson. Leif is a fullback. And Jonas..." I try to think of what I know and horror dawns. "Four years ago his wife pressed charges, saying he beat her. There was a big trial."

"Yep." Disgust rides Gray's expression. "Apparently he beat the shit out of her for years, and she finally had enough. He found himself a slick lawyer and got off with probation."

My stomach turns. Jonas had abused a woman. And I'd taunted him. If Gray hadn't stepped between us... A shiver passes over me.

"Unfortunately for him," Gray says, "his contract was up for renegotiation at the time, and his team didn't renew. No one wanted him. Didn't help that he'd been playing like shit for two seasons prior."

"That'll do it," I murmur.

"And Leif," Gray adds, his disgust clearly mounting, "just got off a two-game suspension for a DUI. Though I can tell you from personal experience that he does more than drink and drive."

"Your father is Jim Grayson." One of the best and most beloved coaches in the whole damn NFL. "You're part of a football dynasty. How did I never make this connection?"

Gray shrugs. "You didn't look me up. I don't talk about it to anyone. My guys know I don't like to discuss it. Though sports commentators *love* to mention it every game I play."

He runs a fist along his thigh, digging in. "My dad... He believes in physical strength. For as long as I can remember, he'd take me out to the yard for practice and have my brothers 'toughen me up.' No holds barred."

I don't like the sound of that. At all. "But your bothers are over ten years older than you. They could have killed you."

Gray's words become stilted like he's forcing them out. "Endless drills. Hard tackles. All acceptable. They got off on it. Axel didn't really, but he was small too. What could he do?"

I stay silent and let him talk.

"I don't think Dad really knew though. That Jonas and Leif liked to pummel me off the field too. Or maybe he did." He shakes his head. "Who the fuck knows? When I complained, I was lectured. 'Football isn't for whiners or quitters. Buckle up, buttercup. Back to work.' And so on."

"How can you love the game?" I whisper.

His hand clasps mine. "I don't know. But I do. Because when I'm out there doing my thing, I forget all about them. It's my game, and I own it. I don't know… It's the control amidst the chaos. Same with math. There are rules, boundaries, numbers. Patterns run. Victories won by inches. It gives me joy. That's fucked-up, isn't it?" He looks at me then, his eyes haunted.

"No. I get it. I should resent sports like Fi does. It took our dad from us. Ruined my parents' marriage. But I love sports anyway."

He nods but lets my hand go to grip the steering wheel. "I hate my brothers. Always have. Hate my father too for letting them do that to me, either by direction or ignoring it."

"And your mom?" I shouldn't ask but can't help it. "Did she know?"

His face goes utterly blank, his knuckles white on the steering wheel. "I never told her." A ragged breath leaves him. "Because what if I did, and she…"

He glares out the window.

"What if she didn't stop them?"

A bare nod is his answer. God, I want to hug him. But I don't move, not knowing if he can handle it right now.

"I feel like shit for thinking that. Because my mom was awesome to me. Kind, caring, patient." He huffs. "I have no fucking clue what she saw in my dad. They met at some college staff mixer. He was a visiting head coach, and she was a Norwegian exchange student finishing up her postgraduate degree. Mom always claimed that Dad charmed her into following him anywhere."

Gray shakes his head as if disgusted.

"When she got sick, though, it was my job to look after her. Dad couldn't handle it. My brothers didn't want to. My brothers hated me for Mom too," he whispers. "I was her favorite. Her baby."

I think of a teenage Gray forced to watch his mom slowly die and not have any help from the rest of his family.

"I bet you were an awesome caregiver," I tell him softly.

He leans back against the seat and blinks up at the ceiling. "I left her alone to die."

The rain patters against the hood of the truck, and the radio softly plays on.

"What do you mean?" I finally ask.

"She died alone." He closes his eyes. "I left her."

"You mean she died when you weren't there? Gray, that happens sometimes—"

"No, I did it on purpose." His eyes squeeze tight. "My mom… We both knew it was coming. That she was near the end. The state championship game was that Saturday. I wasn't going, no way. But she took my hand and said I had to go. For her. The thing is…"

He swallows hard, his throat visibly convulsing. "I knew what she was saying. I knew she didn't want me to see her die. That it would be too hard for her if I was watching. And I…"

He presses a hand over his eyes.

"I couldn't do it, Mac. I ran from that room like a coward. Went to that game like a coward. Because I couldn't watch her go."

I can't hold back anymore. I slide over and put my arms around him, drawing his big body close.

Woodenly, he leans into me, trembling. His face burrows

against my hair, and he takes shaking breaths. "My dad fucking hated me for that. I was supposed to watch over her."

"*He* should have been there," I say fiercely. "She was his wife."

Gray shakes his head. "I was supposed to be stronger than them."

"You are the strongest man I know." I kiss the top of his head, his cheeks, anywhere I can reach without letting him go. "And you did what she wanted. Don't you ever think less of yourself for that."

Gray trembles like he can't get past his regret. I move back to my side of the truck, pulling him down, so that he's lying across the bench.

He's too large to be doing this. But he settles his head in my lap with a sigh as if it's the most comfortable thing in the world. Smiling slightly, I run my fingers through his hair. It's surprisingly thick, the strands like silk.

"God, that feels good." Gray settles down with a sigh. On the next breath, his arm steals beneath my knees, wrapping around my legs and hugging tight. "Ivy, I'm sorry to dump on you like this."

"Stop." I cup his cheek, letting my palm warm him. "I asked you to tell me. I'm your girl, right?"

"Fuck yeah, you are." His hold grows more secure, as if I might pull away. "And don't you forget it."

"Never. This is what girlfriends do, you know."

Beneath my hand, his cheek rises as he smiles softly, and little crinkles form at the corners of his denim blue eyes. His lashes are unfairly long and lush, coming in gold then darkening toward the tips.

"I'm not letting you go, Ivy Mac. In case I wasn't clear before."

Warmth blooms inside my chest.

When he closes his eyes with a contented-yet-still-sad sigh, I reach up and turn off the overhead light. The interior of his truck turns shady, and Gray relaxes a bit more. I go back to stroking his hair.

He grows heavier, warmer. "My mom used to do that. Run her fingers through my hair when I was upset." He shudders, takes an unsteady breath. "I miss her, Mac." His voice is broken, and it breaks a little of me as well.

Lightly, I run my thumb along his temple. "I know, Cupcake. I'm sorry."

He doesn't say anything, just keeps his eyes closed and holds on to me. I stroke his hair as my free hand rests on the hard swell of his biceps.

"Mac?"

"Yeah?" The sound of the rain and the press of Gray's body has lulled me into a state of warm relaxation, and my head rests heavily against the window. My fingers don't stop running through his hair.

"I'm so fucking glad I borrowed your car." He grips my calf. "The thought of you not being in my life tears me up. I… You… You are the happiness I never realized I needed."

His words fill me with light. I know exactly what he means, because it is the same for me. I've made plenty of friends throughout my life, but no relationship has happened so swiftly or meant as much to me as what I have with Gray. My attachment to him almost frightens me, the emotion threatening to overwhelm.

I find myself blinking rapidly, my vision as blurry as the windshield before me.

Feeling far too tender, I curl over him and place a kiss at the crest of his cheek. He smells so good, like citrus and baking bread and pure Gray.

I pepper his face with soft kisses. He turns slightly, slings his heavy arm over my neck to hold me close as his mouth finds mine.

Emotion inside me bubbles over and rushes through my veins with absolute surety. I love him. I love Gray Grayson more than I ever thought possible.

GRAY

Some people grow up gradually, the foundations of their childhood steadily sinking into the earth so slowly they barely notice the change. Until one day they're simply standing on their own two feet with little idea how they got there.

Then there are people whose childhoods are smashed to bits in one blow. They topple into adulthood, flailing about for something to hold on to, and the terror of falling leaves a permanent scar on their psyche. Do those people ever end up feeling safe?

I wonder about that, because I fell hard. For so long there were days when it seemed as though I was still falling, when I couldn't find a single good thing to hold on to, when nothing felt safe or secure.

Then I met Ivy. Somehow, she caught me. Ivy is peace and warmth and hope, and I find myself holding on tight, afraid that if she lets me go I'll be in a free fall once again.

The fact that one person has so much power over my happiness scares the shit out of me. I know how fragile life is. Here today, dust tomorrow. But only a fool cuts his one lifeline.

I'm no fool, even if I act as though I am to the outside world. So I'll do whatever it takes to keep Ivy.

TWENTY-TWO

GRAY

GrayG: I think we need to put a sexting rule into our playbook.

IvyMac: There's a playbook? When did we get a playbook?

GrayG: We've always had one. The Book of Ivy and Gray. It's epic. I've added a large addendum to cover sex. Play Pattern 1 (Shenanigans): fuck as often as my dick and your pussy hold out.

IvyMac: Lovely. You are truly gifted with words. Is there a reason you're texting me when we're in the same bed?

GrayG: To test out my new phone. And so I can see that little smile you make when you read them. Have you always smiled like that over my texts?

IvyMac: Always, Cupcake.

GrayG: Lie back now, honey. I'm going to lick that sweet pussy and see you smile some more.

"GRAY!" IVY TURNS to glare at me from over her bare shoulder. Her cheeks are pink. "Do you have to use *pussy*? It's so crude."

She sounds annoyed, but those gorgeous dark eyes of hers glaze over with want. It makes my hard dick throb.

"Vagina then?" I give her a leer. Her nose wrinkles.

"Er...no."

"Lady lips?"

She's laughing now. "I'll never live that down."

Grinning, I toss my phone aside and reach for her. She's all warmth and long limbs and smooth skin.

"Love pot?" I murmur, skimming my lips down her long torso. "Honey muff? Secret garden of delight?"

"Nut bag," she calls me.

"Now, Mac, we're going to have problems if you can't tell the difference between a nut and a pussy. Here..." I ease her thighs apart. "Let me educate you."

Her phone falls from her hand. The sound of her squawking protests and laughter drift into a gurgle as I bury my head between her legs and kiss her softly. Again. And again. Until I finally take a long, savoring lick and lose myself, drunk off the honey-sweet slickness that is Ivy.

IVY

Gray decides to convert my bed into a tent, hanging all my available sheets over the canopy until not a bit of the room peeks through. That he's naked as he does this serves as my entertainment. I bite the edge of my lower lip as his pale, taut butt flexes and the muscles along his back and shoulders ripple. Gray completely owns his body and always moves with assured grace. Though I suppose if I were as fit and firm as he is, I'd flaunt myself that way too.

Right now, I can't think about moving. I'm sore all over, a delicious kind of ache achieved by a night of marathon sex. I smile into my pillow. Last night, we'd gone at it with single-minded devotion, stopping only to doze or talk. In the middle of telling a joke or simply talking, we'd remember that, yes, we can touch. And that would be it, mouths caressing, hands touching, Gray moving inside me.

When the sun came up, Gray hunted down the leftover *pain aux raisins*, which he declared the best thing he'd ever had in his mouth. Well, aside from my "sweet-as-fuck pussy."

I had to give him points for being both complimentary and crude.

Standing above me now, Gray catches my smile and grins back. Everything we've done—every dirty, sweet, raunchy thing—passes between us like a shared secret. Heat swells within me, but I don't move.

Finished with his task, he scrambles under the covers and pulls me close. His skin is cool, and I wrap myself around his big body to warm him.

Gray exhales on a sigh before slowly peppering my face with soft kisses. "Ever since I was a kid and saw *A Christmas Carol*, I've wanted to sleep in an enclosed canopy."

I run my hands over his shoulder. Warm satin and carved granite. I love touching him. "Hmmm. This feels more like we're in one of those old-fashioned canvas tents."

He glances at the white sheets surrounding us. With the sunlight filling the room, the enclosed little space glows golden. But it is cozy and quiet, and ours. I burrow closer to Gray, touch his jaw, the plump curve of his lower lip.

He nips my fingers. "Yeah, it really needs dark sheets for the full Victorian effect."

"That's okay, I've always had an *Out of Africa* safari fantasy." Smiling, I run my fingers along his temple. "You can be my Robert Redford and wash my hair later."

"Isn't he a little old for you, Mac?" He wrinkles his nose in mock horror.

"Sexy doesn't have an expiration date, Cupcake."

"Well, at least I know you're into blond dudes." Gray hunkers down further into the pillows. Against our nest of white sheets, his skin is like amber honey, his eyes lapis blue. He's so freaking gorgeous, he takes my breath.

"I'm into you," I say.

As if he's equally mesmerized, he traces along my face, his long fingers deft and gentle. "I meant what I said before, Ivy. I'm so fucking crazy about you. I've never felt like this. I don't want to fuck it up."

Worry and possessiveness darken his gaze, as if he wants to grab tight to this moment so it won't slip away. Tenderness swells in my throat. I lick my lip, now sensitive from his kisses.

"I know," I whisper. "This is big, Gray. But if we're honest and talk to each other when we're freaking out, it will be okay."

"Then that's what we'll do." The blunt tip of his finger runs along my brow and down to my cheek. "Mac?"

"Yeah?" I can't stop touching him either. His neck. The hard curve of his shoulder.

The vein that runs along his inner arm.

"What's your fantasy?"

I pause my exploration. "What, you mean as in sexual?"

"Yeah."

Heat washes over my cheeks. "I'm not… No. I can't tell you that."

"Why not? You told me in explicit detail how you wanted to be fucked." He grins wide. "Which was incredibly hot, by the way."

I duck my head, pressing it to his shoulder. "That was different. We were on the phone."

"I wanted to be in that bed with you so damn badly, Mac. I think I bruised my dick jacking off to your voice."

A shocked laugh escapes me, and I give his chest a kiss. "I wanted you there too."

Gray hums again, his big hand smoothing over my head before he eases away to catch my gaze. "So what is it, then? What's your deep, dark, naughty fantasy?"

"Why do you want to know so badly?"

A little furrow grows between Gray's brows as he studies me. "I want to give you everything. Every experience you ever dreamed of. And things you never knew you wanted."

Oh, my.

"Come on." He nuzzles my nose with his. "Tell me, honey."

I close my eyes. "Okay. It's nothing dramatic or even very creative. I'm seduced by a stranger."

"'Seduced'?" Gray kisses me as if he needs a quick taste. "How so?"

God. So embarrassing.

I huff out a breath. "I'm reluctant, you know? But he cajoles, talks me into it. Makes me undress when I don't want to. And… you know," I trail off with strangled sound. "Fucks me."

"Kind of kinky in a subtle way." There's a smile in Gray's voice. "I'm impressed, Mac."

I open my eyes to glare. "It's *not* a rape fantasy. I'm not into violence. I don't get off on stranger danger. In real life, I'd punch a guy in his throat if he—"

"It's okay, honey." He cups my cheeks, his expression open, earnest. "I get it. They're called fantasies for a reason." The corners of his mouth curl as heat enters his eyes. "I like yours."

My response is a grumpy grunt. He chuckles, giving me another light kiss.

My embarrassment fades in the face of his care. "What about you? What's your deep, dark fantasy?"

Gray starts as though I've surprised him. "Me?"

"Yeah, you." I frown. It's as if he never expected me to bother with his needs. "Why shouldn't we try yours too?"

His touch slides away as his lids lower, hiding his eyes from me. "Nah. I don't really have one."

"Bullshit. Everyone has a fantasy."

The broad line of his shoulders tenses. "Not me."

I rise to my elbow, leaning my weight on it as I scowl down at him. "You won't tell me. Unbelievable." I poke his pecs. It's like poking a rock. "You don't trust me."

At that, Gray's eyes narrow. "I trust you more than anyone in the world."

He looks so stubborn—his jaw set as if bracing for a fight—that I clamp down on my frustration. I won't force him. Even if it hurts that I confided to him when he refuses to do the same.

Taking a breath, I rest my hand on his arm. "I know it's hard, but I won't laugh. I promise."

Gray refuses to meet my eyes, biting his lip instead as his cheeks pink. "I don't think you'll laugh. I just… This particular fantasy, if you can call it that, doesn't work if I have to ask for it. It's stupid. I know that. But it's the truth." There's a plea in his eyes.

He knows he's being unfair, yet he's asking me to understand.

With a sigh, I rest my head on my pillow. "Fine. If you can't ask for it, then I'll have to figure it out on my own."

Though his shoulders are still tense, a teasing light comes into his eyes. "Give it your best shot, Special Sauce."

"Let's see."

Something that embarrasses Gray… My options are limited. Gray isn't shy about sex. I run my finger down the little valley along the center of his chest. His nipples tighten in response.

I test the waters. "Is it you with another man?"

Gray chuffs out a laugh, but he's relaxing. "No. Although I can see that interests you."

"Well..." My finger circles the tiny nub of his nipple. "It would be kind of hot to see."

His breath hitches, and he cants his hips. His cock, now hard and seeking, presses against my side. "That sounds more like your fantasy than mine, Mac." A small smile pulls at his mouth as he rests his head on his hand and leans in. "I feel so cheap and used."

"Mmm...poor baby." Softly I press a kiss to the crook of his neck where his pulse beats. I love the way his body reacts with a shiver of pleasure and the feel of his big hand smoothing along my hip, as though touching me gives him pleasure as well.

Everything is warm and lazy, and that low, sweet ache for him builds. I let it grow slowly, just touching him for now, enjoying the anticipation of having him again.

My voice is husky when I whisper, "Don't worry, Cupcake, I'd be there to hold your hand."

Gray's chuckle is a rumble in his broad chest. His hand slips back up my hip and around to my butt. He rests it there as his head lowers so that we're nose to nose. "Nice try, Mac. But no chance. I don't want to share you."

"Even if it's with another girl?" I tease.

His nostrils flare on an indrawn breath, his gorgeous lips curving upward just a bit. "That image has definite possibilities. But, no, I don't want another girl in our bed either."

I love that he says *our bed* and that his fingers twine with mine. His other hand slowly slides down my ass to my thigh, lifting it with languid slowness and resting it on his hip. Spreading me. The tips of his fingers skim along the opening of my sex, such a light, fleeting touch that I might have imagined it. I clench in response.

Slightly distracted, my voice goes breathy. "So having a bunch of girls in your bed at once isn't your secret fantasy?"

His smile remains but his eyes dim with wariness.

"Right," I say with false levity. "You've already done that." Of course he has. He's told me how wild a sex life he's had.

I want to turn away, close my eyes and not think about Gray and all the women he's been with.

But he knows me too well. He cups my face with gentle care. "Hey. I don't like that expression. Makes me worry that you're thinking the wrong things."

I try to smile but fail. "It's ridiculous. I shouldn't be jealous—"

"No, you shouldn't," he agrees softly, his thumb caressing my cheek.

"I can't help it. I think of all the things you've done and..." I bite my lip to stem the flow of anxiety leaving my mouth. But I've gone this far. Hot-faced, I tell him the rest. "What if being just with me gets boring to you?"

"Boring?" Gray rasps. I hazard a glance and find him staring at me, his eyes wide and shocked. "You think I'd rather have a bed full of chicks?"

God. I sound so insecure when he voices my fears. "I don't want to think that way," I murmur.

He rests his forehead against mine, his breath a warm caress against my lips. "Ah, Mac. You have it so wrong."

I resist the urge to squirm. Almost absently, his hand drifts over my sex again. Nothing more, not seeking, but as if he can't help exploring. But his focus is on my face. "You want to know what it was like?" he asks. "All those things that I did?"

"Not really," I mumble.

"Well, I'm telling you. I promised never to lie to you, so you know what I say is true." His expression turns earnest. "It was a novelty act. Half the time I was outside of myself, snickering at the fact that I was doing those things. The other half was awkward, elbows going where they shouldn't, impersonal desperation, weird shit like girls obviously faking that they're into each other because they think that's what I wanted to see."

He clears his throat. "Yeah. Not hot. Not like it is with you."

"Gray..."

"No, Ivy. Don't blow this off. You gotta know, I get hotter from just kissing you than any sex I've had before."

As if to prove this, his lips find mine. His kiss is a slow, seeking exploration that has my insides melting and his breath quickening.

Our lips meld and part, and he gives my lower lip a sexy little lick. "So hot. So perfect."

In one smooth roll, he moves over me, his arms bracketing my shoulders, and then he's entering me, all hard, heavy cock and steady intent. The action is so unexpected, so good, that I gasp, my legs spreading wider to take more of him.

"Yeah," he says. "Like that."

He grunts when he pushes, as if he has to work hard at fitting his thick cock in. My body tightens at that delicious feeling of him stretching me, filling me. Going just a bit deeper each time.

In the diffused light, he is golden, his blue eyes burning bright.

Gray's lips coast over mine. "This, Mac. Doing this with you is the hottest thing I've ever fucking done. Because it's you. You get me so worked up I want to pump my dick into you. Over and over."

A shudder runs through his body, his skin prickling. "It's the best feeling in the world. I don't want it to end. I don't want to go back there, to that cold-ass place where nothing really matters."

On a sob, I wrap my arms around his shoulders and draw him close until his sweat-slick chest rubs against mine. Gray burrows his face into the curve of my neck and groans as he fucks me.

God, the way he moves, using his whole body to thrust, an undulating, hard rhythm that's just a bit dirty, as if my body is his to use. And yet tender, as if he's worshipping me.

He's right; it is the best feeling in the world. My hips rise to meet his, my hands sliding to the hard swells of his ass that flex with every thrust.

"That's it, honey." He groans. "That's it. Move that sweet little ass and fuck me back. God, that's good." He's panting now, sweat making his skin glisten. "Don't stop. Don't ever stop."

He goes deeper, hitting a spot that makes me lose my mind. I lose track of how long he fucks me. There's only pleasure and Gray and yearning for more. Always more. And when I come, he lets go, his pace hard and desperate. He follows me with a long, low groan that vibrates his chest.

I hold him, my lips pressed against his sweaty brow. He thinks he's distracted me from learning what he secretly yearns for. But I know what it is now, and I'm going to give it to him. As much as I can.

TWENTY-THREE

IVY

GRAY AND I spend every moment we can together. Which isn't really any different than our normal routine, only now our moments involve bouts of hot, sweaty sex. And it isn't nearly enough for either of us. Gray's classes are done for the semester, but intense workouts and training regimens to prepare for the playoffs take up most of his time.

"I swear to God, my quads and hamstrings feel like they've been torn from my bones," Gray tells me over the phone as I make chicken salad.

I stare down at the chicken breast I've been pulling meat from and, with a grimace, toss it aside.

"Maybe we shouldn't be partaking in any shenanigans until you can catch a break," I say—reluctantly, because I pretty much want Gray all the time.

He makes a rude noise that nearly vibrates my phone. "I'm

going to pretend you didn't say that, Mac," he drawls. "Otherwise my fragile feelings might get hurt."

I scoff at that. "Don't worry, Cupcake, I'm basically thinking about your cock in my mouth right now."

Gray makes a strangled sound. "Jesus, Ivy. You can't be saying that when you know I'm stuck watching footage and studying plays for the rest of the day. Are you trying to kill me? You're lucky I'm soaking in an ice bath right now."

"Gray! You shouldn't be on the phone while in a bath. I'm hanging up right now."

He laughs. "Okay, okay. Geesh. I'll hang up, but tell me one thing first."

"I'm not having phone sex with you. Again."

"You loved it. But not the question. Have you talked to your parents about not wanting to return to London?"

I frown down at the counter. Gray is right to bug me. I've been avoiding telling them. Mainly because I'm a total coward, but the guilt is getting to me. Hell, I need to tell them about Gray as well. One thing at a time, though, and letting them know about Gray isn't the news I dread.

"Fuck it," I say to Gray. "I'll tell them today. After I hang up with you."

"Honey," Gray murmurs. "It will be all right."

A breath gusts out of me. "I just don't want to disappoint them."

The sound of water sloshing fills my ear, then Gray's voice, low and soothing. "Ivy Mac, you couldn't be a disappointment if you tried."

"Gray..." My hand slides along the cool counter, and I wish it was his skin I was stroking. "You're really sweet sometimes, you know?"

"That's just my thick and creamy frosting. Tell them. And call me afterward, okay?"

★★★

Fi is home, an increasingly rare occurrence. But I take advantage of the occasion and track her down in her room. Where mine is an oasis of whites, hers is a dark nest of plums and pinks. It's disturbingly womblike and features an excess of satin fabric hanging from windows, her wrought-iron canopy—because we both have a thing for canopies—and even skirting her chairs.

Curled up like a little Thumbelina on one pink satin chair, Fi is reading a textbook and making notes on her iPad.

"What's up?" she asks, not taking her eyes from her work.

"I invited Dad over. He'll be here in five."

Her brow furrows as she finally looks at me. "Yeah. So?"

I set my hand against my fluttering stomach. "I'm going to Skype Mom. You know…tell them about not wanting to work with her."

Fi sets aside her things. "You need a little moral support?"

"Yes." It's a burst of breath.

From the living room Dad's voice booms out. "Anybody here?"

"We're coming," I shout back as Fi glares at the door.

"We need to get that key back from him," she says.

"He never comes when he isn't invited." Well, almost never. I think about Gray pressed on top of me, his gaze on my lips, and Dad finding us. "Yeah," I say a little raggedly. "I guess we should ask for it back."

"Well." Fi stands. "He's here now. No use stalling."

Right. Only I drag my feet as I follow her out.

I don't tell Dad why he's here before Mom is on the computer screen. I set the laptop up on the counter, facing it out toward us, which makes it seem as though her head is a hovering specter in the room.

Although my mother is blonde and green-eyed, I look the most like her. Fi has Mom's coloring, but Dad's features.

"Hello, my darlings," she says to Fi and me as we sit on the couch. "While I'm happy to see you both, is everything all right?"

"You've got me, Helena," Dad tells her. His attitude with her is, as always, slightly stiff but cordial.

I take a deep breath. "It's me. I'm just going to say it. Mom, I've been thinking about this for a while, and I'm sorry, but I don't want to manage the store."

"What?" Dad snaps.

"Darling, why?" Mom says in a shocked voice.

It's hard to explain to them my reasons, but I do, with Fi holding my hand the entire time. It's funny, usually I'm the one holding her hand while she disappoints our parents.

And disappoint them I have.

"Oh, Ivy," Mom says with a sigh. "I don't understand this. You've spent so much time learning the business. And you love baking. Are you quite certain this is what you want to do?"

"I do love baking. But, Mom, baking and running a bakery aren't the same things, are they?"

Her mouth presses flat in the same way mine does when I'm annoyed. "No," she says. "They aren't. But you cannot run a successful bakery without loving baking."

"And there's the fact that I didn't have a social life when I worked with you," I say softly. "I'm sorry, but it's true. Early to bed, early to rise. Everything becomes about the bakery."

I glance to Dad and back to Mom. "My whole life, I've focused on school or working. I want more. I want to love what I do and have time to enjoy the rest as well."

"All right," Mom says slowly. "I do understand, Ivy."

"Well, I don't." Dad lowers his dark brows at me. "For years this has been your focus. I expect this of Fiona—"

"Leave Fi out of this." I squeeze my sister's hand before she can shout at him. "This is about me and what I want."

"If this is about wanting to spend more time with Grayson…" he begins.

"Finish that thought," I say softly, "and I'm walking out of here."

Silence greets me.

"Sean," Mom finally says. "Ivy's twenty-two years old. She's an adult now, so let's treat her as one, shall we?"

That earns Mom a mulish look, but he relents. "I'm just a little shocked. But all right, Ivy. You don't want to work with your mother. That's your call. What do you want to do?"

A small laugh leaves me. And I bite down on my lips to prevent any more. Because I feel slightly unhinged for what I'm about to tell them. I *know* they're going to think I am.

"I…" God, getting the words out is harder than I thought it'd be. "I think I want to look into sports agenting."

Fi's mouth falls open as she stares at me. "You're shitting me, right?"

Mom and Dad are no better.

"Pardon?"

"Are you out of your mind?"

The last one from my outraged father.

I take a deep breath. "I'm perfectly serious. I've been talking to Gray and his friends, and I realized that it makes me happy to give advice. I love sports. I love interacting with athletes. It excites me."

"Yeah, but…" Fi makes a helpless gesture. "That world, all the sleaze…"

Dad glares at her as Mom mutters something censorious.

Then Dad focuses on me. "Fi's vivid imagery aside, she isn't entirely incorrect. It's a hard life, Ivy, and not something I want for you."

"The thing is, at some point I have to do what I want for my life. Not what I think the two of you want for me."

Mom's lips press together. "Is that what you've been doing? Appeasing us?"

"Not entirely. I thought I wanted the bakery too. But I won't say your feelings didn't factor into it."

Dad shakes his head, as if this confession is neither here nor there. "You've always hated my job. Do not lie to me, young lady. You have."

"I know. Hell." I stand and pace. "I don't know, maybe I can make it something more."

"Sweet Jesus," Dad snaps. "Don't you dare go Jerry Maguire on me."

I almost laugh. Sports agents hate that movie, calling it a fantasy.

"I'm not naive," I say quietly as I sit back down. "Though, really, Daddy? You do care about your clients' lives. Don't deny it."

"Of course I care. I'm not going to work my ass off for a job I don't care about. And don't you use 'Daddy' to soften me up," he counters with a pointed look.

"Fine. And maybe I'm not entirely clear on what I want. Perhaps I can go into life coaching and planning for athletes. That's the part that inspires me, not the deals."

Fi nods slowly. "I can see that."

Sighing, I run a finger along the edge of the sofa. "I know it sounds weird, and it's true I've resisted having anything to do with Dad's business for so long. But when I think of doing this, it feels good. Right." I can't explain it any other way.

Everyone grows quiet.

Then my mom speaks up. "Darling, I want you to be happy in your life. If you believe this is the way, then I support you."

My throat goes tight. "Thanks, Mom."

Dad just sighs and plops his butt on the arm of the sofa. "You want to work with me." He sounds so shocked that I do laugh.

"I can go it on my own, Dad. I don't mind the challenge. I'll apply for an internship at an agency."

"No. You want to learn this business, you're going to learn it right." His stern expression eases to wariness. "Or I can set you up with one of my colleagues if you want your independence."

"If you think you can treat me like any other intern, I'm happy to work with you."

"Oh, well, thank you for that," he says dryly. Then he laughs. "Get ready for hell."

I find myself smiling. "Yes, sir."

It feels strange, this new course I'm plotting, and my insides are still shaking from excess nerves. But for the first time, the future excites me. For the first time, everything feels just as it should.

IvyMac: It is done. Parents are okay with my change of plans. I'm going to try to work with my dad. Tell me I'm not crazy.

GrayG: Not crazy. You're my girl. So proud of you, Special Sauce.

IvyMac: Come over?

GrayG: Better idea. Go to Red Room Lounge at 8 p.m. Wear a skirt (panties optional but greatly discouraged). Head for the bar. Hot blond dude will be there. Let him say hello first.

IvyMac: ?? And what's with the cryptic text? Are you on something?

GrayG: No more questions. You'll like what I have planned. Trust me.

IvyMac: Ok. But only because it's you.

GrayG: Don't forget: No questions. Wear a skirt. And a hot top too.

IvyMac: *grumble*

TWENTY-FOUR

IVY

THE RED ROOM LOUNGE isn't the kind of place I'd usually frequent—at least, not on my own. The decor is tasteful, moody, the walls a deep, lush red. Low-slung leather couches are arranged in intimate seating groups. Votive candles flicker on glossy wood tables. For all the style, it's clearly a meat market. Not in the lively college-age way of Palmers, but for serious businessmen on the prowl.

Eyes follow me as soon as I give the hostess my coat and walk in. I'm aware of every step I take, the way the black-and-white-striped A-line skirt I'm wearing slides over my bare legs. On an average-height girl, it would probably rest a few inches above the knee. On me, it's midthigh, and I'm far too aware of my panty-less state.

The thought of flashing the bar with a flick of my skirt fills me with horror. It's also oddly arousing. I feel naughty, sexy. A rarity for me—I usually either feel a bit like a giraffe or act like one of the guys.

If I wasn't looking for Gray, I might have missed him at first glance. He's standing at the bar, his back to me. I know it's him because I know every line of his body, from the way he likes to plant his feet slightly apart, as if he's waiting for his next play, and how he always sets his broad shoulders ruler-straight.

But he isn't dressed like the Gray I know. He's wearing dark dress slacks that cup his fine ass and a soft, gray knit sweater that hugs his muscled torso.

As if sensing my gaze, he turns. Holy hell. His hair is combed back from his brow, highlighting the strong bones of his face, making him appear older, sharper. But it's how he looks at me that sears my skin and has my heart kicking against my ribs. He knows the effect he has on me. It's there in his eyes and the way the corner of his luscious mouth slowly kicks up.

He's smiled at me dozens of times, but never like this. It's pure sex, no tenderness, no familiarity. I should be offended. I'm hot instead, slippery between my legs as I walk toward him.

That assessing stare travels over my body, and the tip of his tongue flicks out to swipe his lower lip.

"Hey," he says when I stop at the bar. "I've never seen you around here before."

He's not even looking at my face but leers at my chest. My nipples stiffen, and he sucks in a sharp breath, a little grunt rumbling deep in his throat.

My lips part, but no words come out. He's treating me like a stranger. Like he's Gray but Not Gray. And I remember the text. *Head for the bar. Hot blond dude will be there. Let him say hello first.* Not "let *me* say hello," but *him*.

Flutters fill my belly. I think about the sexual fantasy I told him that lazy morning in bed.

His eyes meet mine, and a look flickers there: Is this all right? Do you want to play?

It's a struggle not to grin, not to fling myself on him and kiss the hell out of him. I lower my lids and turn my attention to the bartender instead, pretending that my insides aren't a mass of nerves and anticipation.

"I'm waiting for my friends," I tell Not Gray, which is how I choose to think of him now, my tone standoffish.

"Sure you are," he murmurs.

Mellow music softly plays, highlighting the quiet between us. His tanned forearm rests against the bar. A thick steel sports watch is on his wrist. I've never seen it before. Or seen him drink Scotch. That strong arm lifts as he takes a drink. The peaty scent of whiskey fills the air between us.

I order a citrus martini and try to ignore Not Gray, because he's doing his best to unnerve me, standing close enough that the light hairs on his sun-kissed forearm tickle my arm. Close enough that I feel his stare.

It's strange, knowing that this is Gray eyeing me like I'm some cheap conquest. I should be appalled. But no one on earth turns me on the way he does. That he's acting this out for me has me growing wet and breathless already. And he hasn't even touched me.

Vodka sloshes over the sides of my glass and slides cold over my fingers as I take a sip. I lick my wet lips, tasting the tart sweetness, and Gray grunts deep within his chest.

"I'd like to do that," he says to me in a low voice.

My throat goes dry. I keep my gaze on the bar. "Do what?"

He's closer, his shoulder pressing mine. "Lick those lips."

Playing the shy girl, I look the other way as if I'm shocked. It doesn't deter him.

My skin shivers at the soft brush of his lips against the shell of my ear.

"When I'm done with your lips, I'll lick the tips of those sweet little nipples perking up beneath your top. They're begging for it, aren't they, sweetness?" Warm breath gusts down my neck as he exhales. "To be licked and licked."

Heat snakes down my body, clenches in my belly.

He keeps talking in that low, rumbly way. "I'll get you nice and wet playing with those little buds. So fucking wet that when I finally lick your plump pussy, you'll come on my tongue at the first taste."

A strangled sound leaves me, and I have to lean against the bar, my knees have gone so weak. My heart pounds against my chest, so hard I wonder if he can see it.

The tips of his fingers take my elbow, a light but steady grip. "Come with me."

I'm breathless, my voice faint. "No. I… My friends…"

"We won't be long," he says against my neck before taking a taste with a flick of his tongue. "Come on, sweetness. No one will know. It will be our little secret."

Oh, God, I know it's an act, but my body shakes with illicit lust. I can barely nod. But he sees it, makes a sound of satisfaction. Then I'm being led to the back of the club, the sound of my blood whooshing through my ears. No one stops him or even looks our way. Not even when he opens the door to a small supply room and closes us inside.

Not Gray leans against the door and simply watches me. Bathed in the light of one dingy bulb that hangs overhead, his big body seems larger, looming and taut with tension. It's so strange seeing him this way, dressed like a stranger, acting like one, that it's easy to slip into the role, lose myself to it.

"What do you want?" I ask him, plucking at the folds of my skirt as my heart races.

A small, calculating smile. "Oh, I think you know, sweetness."

Sweetness. Gray never calls me that. Never uses that slightly smarmy tone. It only serves to make him more foreign, more dangerous.

It's almost too easy, the way he backs me up, guiding me to

a low counter that runs along one wall. His hands settle on my hips and he lifts me onto its cool surface. It brings us eye to eye. Grasping the edges of the counter, he crowds me, his gaze hot and roaming.

"There," he murmurs. "That's better."

"I should get back to the bar." A weak protest.

The backs of his fingers skim up my arm, raising goose bumps on my skin. "Nice top."

Even though it's thirty degrees out, I chose a black silk tank that hugs my waist but gathers loosely over my breasts. A tie around my neck holds the top secure. That I am braless is not lost on him. He stares at my stiff nipples as his fingers drift to the bow at the back of my neck and give it a little flick.

"Take it off."

"Wh-what?"

"Let me see those sweet tits you've been teasing me with since you walked in the bar."

"I—" My breath catches. "No. I'm not taking my clothes off for a stranger."

"But you want to, don't you? You want me to look at you." He bends his head until his lips are at my ear. "You're dying to expose yourself, to let me see those pretty pink nipples."

My skin draws tight. I struggle not to sway into him.

He leans back, his attention on my top again. "Untie the bow."

"Someone might come in." Despite our play, my fear of getting caught is real, though not completely unwelcome.

"They won't. I took care of it."

I believe that. Gray would cover all the bases. In his own way, he's as much of a planner as I am. But I can't think of him as Gray now, not when he's doing this for me.

His fingers are back, skimming over my inner arm, teasing the edges of my top. "Just a little peek."

My breasts ache so badly—they're hot, heavy, the silk covering them an irritant. With shaking hands, I reach up. The fabric tugs against my neck then comes free. It slithers over my skin like a caress.

He sucks in an audible breath as my breasts are exposed. I see myself through his eyes, sitting half-naked in this dim back room, my nipples puckered, my breasts quivering with each shallow breath I take. The vulnerability of it feels naughty, forbidden, and I nearly whimper.

A noise of pure satisfaction leaves him. Not bothering to lift his gaze from my breasts, he reaches out, runs the tips of his fingers over my nipple. I'm so sensitized now, the touch sends a bolt of pure, searing lust straight through me. I flinch, clench my teeth to keep still.

He hums, strokes me back and forth as if he owns me. "So pretty. You like that, sweetheart?"

Eyes closed, I bite my lower lip and nod.

I feel him move. The wet flat of his tongue drags over my nipple. My eyes fly open on a strangled cry.

He grins up at me, his mouth hovering at my breast. It isn't his usual cheeky grin but something more wicked. "Mmm. Delicious."

He takes a step closer, and I swallow convulsively. Gray's voice lowers. "I wonder where else you taste good. You want to show me, sweets?"

I'm practically panting now. My hair swings as I give my head a hard shake. He leans in, trailing the blunt tip of his finger up the curve of my breast. I nearly yelp when he gives the stiff peak a quick, crude pinch.

His smile is pure male smugness. "Lift up your skirt and show me where you're wet."

God. My thighs shake. I want to resist him. I want to do exactly what he says. As if against my will, my hands lower to the hem of my skirt.

Up, up, up. Every inch that slides over my thighs pushes my agitation higher. I can't take it. I gather up the skirt until it's around my waist. Cool air caresses my wet skin.

The silence is deafening. There is only the roar of my blood beating and the quiver of my sex, now fully on display. He just stands there, his eyes narrow, his expression almost fierce. I don't miss the way his broad chest moves with agitated breaths.

I expect him to touch me. He doesn't. He stares, his gaze fixated on my sex. And it drives all my awareness to my exposed state, to the fact that the small bud of my clit is throbbing.

He licks his bottom lip as if he's imagining my taste. When he speaks, it's a raw demand. "Spread wider."

I do, wide enough that I feel the strain in the tendons between my thighs.

Still he doesn't touch me, which drives up my need. I want him to so badly now that I bite the inside of my lip, arch my back just a bit to entice him with my breasts.

That bastard simply gives me an evil look. "You're dying for it, aren't you?"

"No," I whisper. A lie.

He knows it. The corner of his mouth curls as his hand drifts to his belt.

Short of breath and aching, I watch him slowly unfasten his belt, the metal buckle clinking in the silence. He doesn't unzip immediately but runs the heel of his hand down the significant bulge of his erection.

I have to clench my fists so I don't reach out and cup him.

The hiss of his zipper lowering buzzes in my ears. I only have eyes for his hand, reaching in to pull out that beautiful cock. Long, hard, thick, a bead of precome glistening on the wide head. I know how smooth his skin is. I know his taste. How well he'll fill me.

"Do you want this?" he asks.

"I'm a good girl," I whisper.

He wraps his fingers around his wide base, his eyes on me. "Let me put it in you. See how it feels."

"I don't know…" I trail off, biting my lip, pretending that I don't want it.

He steps between my legs, and gives his cock a stroke as if he needs that small relief. The sight has my sex clenching. Licking his lower lip, he guides himself to my opening.

"Just the tip, sweets." He nudges against me, slipping along my wetness, as I whimper. His voice goes dark. "Just for a second."

That thick crown pushes inside. I'm so worked up with lust, I begin to moan and wiggle, ripples of heat running along my body.

He shudders, his cock sinking further, stretching me, invading as he groans out, "Oh, fuck, I'm gonna need more."

Like that, I'm coming around his hard cock, even as he glides in, deeper, deeper, until fully seated. The orgasm quakes through me so hard and fast that I arch back, my inner walls squeezing him tight.

"Jesus," he says, holding on to my neck. "Jesus."

Somehow, I manage to lift my head, catch his eye. He's no longer Not Gray, but *my* Gray, looking at me as if I'm beautiful, as if I'm his world. I don't want to pretend anymore. Maybe he sees the knowledge in my eyes, because he gives me a look that's part pain, part helpless want. Deep inside me, his cock pulses.

I draw in a breath, touch his cheek. "Gray."

That's all he needs. With an impatient sound, he hauls me close, bringing us chest-to-chest, mouth-to-mouth. He kisses me, no longer detached but pure Gray, sweet and seductive and just a little dirty.

"Ivy. Honey." He fucks like he's savoring me, holding my upper body against his so that the only movement is his cock pushing in and out. A steady pounding, so good and raw that I shiver.

"More," I whisper before finding his mouth again.

Without pause, he grabs my ass and backs us up until he's leaning against the wall. My legs wrap around his waist, and he lifts me with ease, steadily works me up and down his swollen cock. I can only hold on, feel his muscles shift and the stretch of him inside me.

"Ivy." He kisses me quick, needy. "I'm close."

He thrusts up, moving his hips in a little circle, the pressure hitting my swollen clit just right, and my sex clenches, pleasure licking up my thighs, over my skin.

I suck in a breath, my lips coasting over his. "Finish it."

My ass hits the counter. I'm pinned, spread wide for him as he takes what he needs.

He's beautiful to me like this, his brows drawn tight, his lips parted as if he can't get enough air.

Our eyes meet, and I'm the one who can't breathe. Everything seems to pause. There is only Gray, his gaze wide and clear, his cock lodged deep as though it's found home.

My body tightens like a fist, my heart so tender it hurts. I feel him everywhere, draw in his scent and heat. But it's that look, as though there will never, ever be anything more important to him than me, that does me in.

This time my orgasm is an almost painful roll of pleasure. Crushing my lips to his shoulder to keep quiet, I cling to him and let go. And he follows me, his mouth on my neck, his fingers digging into my thighs.

He comes with a quiet shudder that wracks his whole body. All the tension leaves him on a sigh.

We're still for several breaths, then he pulls out and sets me on my feet before tucking himself back into his pants and doing them up. My skirt flutters down as I reach for him. I hold him close, stroke his hair, my face pressed into the warm hollow of his neck. He smells of sex and sweat and whiskey.

I can't stop kissing his silky skin. "Thank you."

Gray runs his hands down my back. "For what?"

"You gave me my fantasy."

"Not a hardship, honey." Slowly, he kisses his way up my neck, scattering fine shivers in his wake. "In fact, that now rates as one of my top fantasies too."

I tilt my head to the side to give him better access. "You were good. Maybe you should consider acting."

His laugh is a huff against my neck. "It wasn't an act. I meant every word I said."

I hadn't meant a single one of my protests. But my body's response had been real and so intense, I still feel pleasurable little aftershocks. I adore Gray for that, for making me feel safe to play. For wanting to do that with me in the first place.

"I haven't forgotten about yours, you know," I say against his temple.

Gray lifts his head. "My fantasy?" He looks blank, but he doesn't fool me.

"I know what it is."

"Oh, you do?" Gray smiles yet his tone holds a note of caution, as if he doesn't want to believe me.

"Yeah, Cupcake, I do." I kiss the tip of his nose. "You take care of everybody. But who takes care of you? That's what you want, isn't it? To be cared for."

My palm smooths down his cheek, as he stares at me with wide eyes. "That's my job now, Gray. I'm always going to be the one there for you."

His throat works on a swallow, and when he speaks, his voice is husky. "How did you know?"

I rub my cheek against his, drawing in his familiar scent. "Because I know you."

Gray is very still for a breath. Then he eases back. His hands settle on either side of my neck, his fingers so long they bracket my jaw. Gently, as though I'm suddenly breakable, he presses a kiss to my forehead, my cheeks, my closed eyes, the tip of my nose, and finally my lips.

"Every inch, Ivy," he whispers against them.

I open my eyes and smile. My arms wind around his neck, holding him close. "You said that once, before your last game. But you never really told me what it means."

Gray's hands move to my waist. "Before you, it meant I'll fight for every inch of yardage, never give up until I'm in the end zone. But now?" His blue eyes meet mine. "It means I'll fight for every inch of you. That I love every inch of you."

For a second, the air between us goes heavy and still. His words settle on me like a warm blanket. It sinks beneath my skin when he slowly smiles, as if he's realized what he's said and likes it.

"I love you, Ivy Mac." His smile grows and he cups my cheek. "I really do. So much." A husky laugh leaves him. "It feels good saying that."

He loves me. No man has ever said those words to me. I've never wanted to hear them from anyone else but Gray.

I draw in a tremulous breath, my heart swelling within my chest. "I love you too."

The corners of his eyes crinkle. "Yeah?"

Standing on my toes, I kiss his forehead, his cheeks, his smiling mouth. "Every inch, Cupcake."

Gray sighs and hugs me close. "I've never been in love before."

I smile in contentment and wonder. "Neither have I."

Gray breathes in deep. "Drew was right. It's better than football."

A shocked laugh bursts out of me. "Oh, wow. That's huge."

He pulls back to look down at me. The love in his eyes comes through crystal clear. "Huge as in, 'Oh, Gray, let me give you a celebratory blow job' huge?"

I give him a look. "You're killing the moment, Cupcake."

Gray grins, his hand caressing my side. "It's turning you on. Just admit it."

"Yeah, okay," I whisper. "A little." Sexy stranger Gray was exciting, but this is the Gray I love with all I am.

He chuckles low, contented, and gently cups my breast. "I knew it." He palms me, moving in a slow circle. "Let's go home, and we can celebrate properly."

I'm about to agree when he hits a spot that is tender. "Ow, careful."

Gray frowns. "That hurt you?"

"Yeah, it's a little sore."

His face grows eerily blank as he gently touches the spot, then draws a sharp breath. "What the fuck?"

"What?" I ask, alarmed.

"This," Gray hisses, wrenching my shirt further down. With a grim look, he bends close and prods at my breast. "This...*lump*." The word comes out like a curse.

Frowning, I bat his hand away and feel for myself. Okay, there's a small lump on the fleshy side of my breast. "Huh. I've never noticed that."

"Never noticed?" he cries in outrage. "Jesus, Ivy. Don't you check your breasts?"

Normally I'd laugh, never expecting a guy to even know about that. But this is Gray. He's seen his mom die from breast cancer. So I keep my voice low, calm. "Of course I do. This is new."

"New?" He presses his fingers to his eyes. "Fuck. Fuck." His hand falls, and he levels me with a wild-eyed glare. "You have to get it checked. Now."

"I can't go now. It's late at night—"

"We'll go to a clinic." He paws at my breast again, moving it this way and that, angrily prodding it as if he can scare the lump away.

"Gray," I snap, pushing at his hand and trying to pull up my shirt. "Would you stop?"

"No." He's beside himself, his voice almost shrill. "Are you even listening to me? You need to get this checked."

My temper breaks. "Calm the fuck down. Someone is going to come in here any second."

As if timed, there's a knock on the door and a tentative "Uh, is everything okay in there?"

"Fine," I shout, just as Gray yells, "Go away."

"Not helping," I snarl at Gray. But the distraction lets me get my top up and my breasts covered.

"I don't give a fuck what that guy out there thinks," Gray snaps back. "You're not taking this seriously. You have a lump." He's shouting now. "A goddamn lump. Do you even care?"

I've never seen him like this. His skin is ashy, his eyes wide and wild. He's shaking so hard now, I'm afraid for his health.

"Gray, baby, you need to calm down. It's okay—"

"It's not okay," he bellows. "You have a lump. Fuck."

Gray stumbles back, his hip hitting a shelf and sending brooms clattering to the floor like matchsticks. "Fuck! I can't..." He grabs the ends of his hair and clutches them as he stumbles backward to the door. "Can't breathe."

"Gray!"

But he's wrenching the door open. "I can't do this again."

Before I can say another word, he flees. Gone so fast, I swear I feel the air stir. And I'm left alone, wondering what the hell just happened.

TWENTY-FIVE

IVY

IT'S SCARY HOW quickly life can turn to shit. One second, you're the happiest you've ever been. The next, your head is spinning and your heart is a bleeding wound within your chest. Thirteen hours after Gray's complete meltdown, I'm still reeling. And I can't find him. He's just gone.

Though hurt at Gray's abandonment, I did as he asked. I'd swallowed back the urge to cry or rant and went to see the on-call doctor. One exam and a few tests later, I have my answers and am free to walk out of the clinic on legs that feel wooden and uncoordinated.

Standing on the sidewalk, I stare blankly at the parking lot. My brain has gone on vacation or something, because I can't seem to process what I've been told. The results were not what I'd expected, not at all. In the distance, my little pink Fiat shines like a beacon. I focus on it, trying to bring my thoughts to order. Gray. I need to find him. I *need* him.

Hot rage surges up my throat, and I grind my teeth against the urge to scream. He left me. Ran away. I know why. Of course I do. It doesn't stop the anger. Especially now.

I look down at the papers I'm clutching. My hand shakes a little, and I draw in a deep breath of cold December air.

Jamming the papers into my purse, I fish out my phone. The shaking has stopped, replaced by steely determination. Dialing, I start striding to my car.

Drew answers on the third ring.

"It's Ivy." My throat feels like raw meat. "I can't find Gray."

It's hard telling Drew the whole, shitty story. But he needs to know why Gray took off so he can help me track him down.

"Hell," Drew says when I finish. "I think I know where he might have gone. Let me talk to him, okay?"

"You do that." It amazes me how calm I sound—when inside, I'm falling apart.

"Ivy." Drew hesitates. "You have to understand—"

"I do," I cut in. "Doesn't make it right."

"No," he agrees slowly.

I sigh, wrenching open my car door. "Just let me know when you find him. I..." My voice almost breaks. I keep it together with sheer force of will. "I need to talk to him."

"Will do," Drew says quietly. Then hangs up.

Sitting in the little car that still carries Gray's scent, I wrap my fingers around the steering wheel. My nails dig into the puffy pink grips. I won't cry. I won't. But a sob breaks free.

I cry myself dry in the car where it all began.

GRAY

I've got to go back. I need Ivy, and Ivy needs me. But I can't seem to make myself move. I worked out for hours, until my body gave out on me. Sitting on the floor of the team-gym showers isn't productive, but the scent of bleach and deodorant is familiar. Safe.

It's quiet now, the gym long since closed. I slump in a corner, asking myself what the fuck I'm doing. No answers come. Only this sick, fucked-up fear and the need to curl in on myself and shut everything out.

Some distant voice in my head tells me I'm losing my shit in a big, bad way. On the field, I'm a fighter. I never give up. I have got to get my head in this. But everything is silent, numb.

"Thought I'd find you here."

I jump at the voice. My head is heavy as a rock when I lift it to find Drew in the doorway. His cast thuds on the floor as he walks over. Slowly, he lowers himself next to me, his broken leg stretched out in front of him.

He doesn't say anything, just sits close enough to press his shoulder against mine.

And then I remember. The night his parents died, I hunted him down, found him in the locker room of his school gym. I sat with him as he quietly lost it on my shoulder.

The memory works like a ball snap. All the terror and panic I'd been holding down rushes up.

"Fuck," I choke out, pressing my fists against my forehead as I bring my knees to my chest. "Fuck."

Drew's shoulder pushes harder against mine. "What's going on, Gray?"

There's a clump of pain inside my throat the size of a baseball. I push past it.

"Ivy. She had a lump..." I take a harsh breath. "On her... And I remembered Mom. When she told me about the lump and how she—Fuck."

I choke on fear and shudder. I don't know when Drew put his arm around my shoulders. But he's hugging me to his side. And it all pours out of me in the form of tears and snot. Not my best moment.

But Drew doesn't care. He remains silent and lets me do what I need to.

"I can't do this with Ivy," I rasp. "I can't see her…" Shit, I'm going to lose it again.

Drew's grip goes hard. "You don't know what's going on with Ivy."

I don't, because I can't handle knowing. But I can't seem to handle not knowing, either. I have never run from adversity, and yet I just walked out on the most important person in my life. The thought makes me sick.

"I've screwed this up badly."

"We all screw up. Kind of think it's a requirement of being human."

I snort, but I'm too weak and sorry to really make a sound. "I've got to make this right."

"Yeah." Drew gives my head a tap. "But get yourself together first. 'Cause you look like shit."

Wiping a hand over my face, I glance at him. He smiles, but his expression is too serious to carry it off.

Lightly, I elbow his side. "Thanks. For being here."

"Man, you know you don't have to say that."

I do know that. He's the brother I wish I had instead of the fucknozzles I've been stuck with.

Just like that, all things circle back to the family I have left and what I've lost.

Blinking rapidly, I grind my fists against my lips. Because I need to find the one person I want to be my family. Ivy.

And I realize that she is here. She's found me instead.

TWENTY-SIX

GRAY

I FEEL HER before I see her. It's a struggle to lift my head, face her. But I do it. She deserves that and more.

Ivy stands in the doorway, her expression blank, the harsh overhead lighting a haze around her long frame. Her face is so pale, it looks bleached out. Red blotches around her eyes and nose. She's been crying. Something inside of me seizes. Need, fear, guilt, desire, self-loathing. I can't move. I want to tell her I'm sorry, but I'm frozen.

Her dark gaze flicks to Drew, who is rising to his feet. He gives her a nod, and I know he told her where to find me. With a final squeeze to my shoulder, Drew walks out, leaving me alone with Ivy.

"Ivy, I..." Words fail me.

She steps forward, extending her arm. "Come here."

I take her hand and stand. She doesn't let me go, doesn't say a word. Like a zombie, I follow her lead, tethered by her hand in mine. She ignores me, clicking away at her phone, sending texts to God only knows who. I don't ask because I should be apologizing now, not questioning her. I know this, but shame holds me silent.

We don't speak as she drives, me crammed for once in the passenger side of her pink car.

Inside her house, it's cool and dark. But when Ivy leads me toward Fi's bedroom, I halt, confused.

"Fi isn't here," Ivy says, tugging me along. "And she has a bathtub."

The room is dim. A single lamp glows, casting the room into shadows. We walk into the bathroom. Someone's drawn a bath and left the lights on low.

"I asked Fi to help me out before she left." Ivy's voice is subdued. I expected anger, or at least an accusation. But she simply turns and pulls my sweaty shirt over my head.

I stand there, letting her undress me, watching her. She's so fucking beautiful. I know every line and curve of her face better than my own, and yet each time I look at her, it's like she's brand-new.

"Get in," she says, not looking at me but at the tub.

And because I'll do anything for her, I obey. The water is hot, soothing. I don't want to be soothed; her kindness is killing me. I lean forward and press the heels of my hands to my eyes.

She steps in behind me, and my eyes snap open. I hadn't even noticed her undressing, but now her silky legs slide along mine, wrapping me up in her embrace. Water sluices over my back as she begins to wash me.

Such a simple thing, but strangely effective. With each stroke of her hand, a bit more of the ugly, clenching, sick feeling leaves me, and I'm so grateful for her that my vision blurs.

"Say something," I whisper past the lump in my throat.

"Something," she repeats, equally quiet. Her strong fingers massage my scalp, and a heated prickle forms behind my eyes.

I blink rapidly, willing myself to calm down. "Why aren't you yelling at me?"

Her movements still, and she rests her forearms against my back. "That would be easier for you, wouldn't it? If I yelled and relieved your conscience."

I wince, because she's right.

Ivy sighs and starts washing me again, briskly now, picking up a bar of soap and scrubbing beneath my arms.

"I wanted to scream my throat raw at you. When I couldn't find you, I wanted that." She slows, her lips just brushing between my shoulder blades as she takes a deep breath. "But you looked… You're in pain, Gray. And it hurts me when you hurt. So, no, I'm not going to scream at you now. I never want to be the one to kick you when you're down."

This girl. A breath tears out of me, and I capture her slim hand, bring it to my mouth to hold it there. "I'm so sorry, Ivy. So fucking sorry that I ran out on you." Because she's right—it hurts worse knowing that I'm the cause of her pain.

Ivy doesn't say anything, just pulls her hand from mine and turns on the shower attachment. That efficient manner returns as she rinses me clean. A flick of her wrist and the water is off again. Before I can say another word, she launches from the tub, all long limbs and slick skin.

"Ivy—"

"I'm pissed." She grabs a robe and wrenches it on before facing me. "Okay? I don't want to yell but…" Her eyes go glassy, and she makes a face of self-disgust. "You hurt me, Gray."

God, the disappointment in her voice, it rips through my chest. Water sloshes over the edges of the tub as I rise. "I know, honey, and I'm—"

She strides out of the room. I hop out of the bath, pulling a towel around me as I go. "Ivy."

She faces me in the bedroom, her eyes flashing. "I get why you freaked. Breast cancer, your mom. I understand, Gray. I do. But you just ran out on me like I had the plague. I needed you…" She takes a shaky breath. "More than you know. I needed you to talk to me. You promised—"

Two steps and she's in my arms. Without pause, I pick her up and carry her out of Fi's room and into hers, stopping only when we reach the bed. She's stiff as I sit with her in my lap. But it doesn't stop me from kissing her lips, her cheeks, any spot I can get.

"I'm sorry, Ivy. I panicked. If I could go back and change that, I would."

She's shaking, her body stiff against mine, leaning a little but not yielding. "You ran away from me."

My fingers thread into her hair, and I hold her steady as I meet her eyes. "I ran away from myself. Shit. Ivy, you're right. I freaked out. Since my mom… I haven't wanted to care about anything. Live day-to-day, enjoy the moment, nothing deep. The funny thing is, Ivy, falling in love with you was as easy as breathing. The best time of my life."

"Then why—"

"It's easy to love you, but it scares the shit out of me." Our foreheads touch, and I close my eyes. "I felt that lump, and it was my mom dying all over again. It hit me. I can't lose you. Not you. So, yeah, I panicked. Because I… If you…"

Terror tries to rush over me again. I don't know what to do with it. Nothing scares me on the field. Not a three-hundred-pound lineman, not the possibility of getting hit so hard that my neck might break. But this? I struggle to breathe.

Until she touches my cheek. Her dark eyes meet mine, and all I can think is *home.*

"Hey," she says softly. "I can see you're freaking out again, but it's okay."

"It's not." I shake my head. "I hurt you."

And then she smiles. Nothing in the world affects me like her smile. I can only stare, speechless.

"I'm not hurting anymore, Cupcake."

I kiss her. Soft. Reverent. She's everything. My world. My happiness. My hand slides beneath her gaping robe to cup her warm breast. The tips of my fingers glide over her skin, careful not to hurt her.

"And you're…?" I can't finish.

Ivy cups my hand, pressing it to her flesh. "It's fine. Not cancer, I swear."

But her expression suddenly twists, and she moves off me. With agitated breaths, she paces in front of the bed, her hands shaking.

"What's wrong?" My heart skips a beat, but I'm not running this time. "Tell me."

"The thing is, Gray…" She takes a deep breath. "It's not cancer, but—Fuck."

"Mac!"

She stops in front of me and grips her hands until her knuckles turn white, and I'm rooted to the spot.

"You're scaring the hell out of me, honey." My voice is a rasp in the tense quiet. "Whatever it is I'm—"

"It was hormones. The lump." She waves a hand, kind of flailing around. "I have fibrous breasts, which really just means that hormones can cause noncancerous lumps. Such as excess hormones due to…shit. Shit."

I find my feet and stand, reaching for her.

Mac's eyes fill. "I'm pregnant."

A whoosh of sound fills my ears and everything goes still, tight. Numb.

Mac curses, takes a step, then stops and steps the other way, as if she doesn't know where to go but just wants to escape. I have to move. To talk. But I'm frozen and the ringing in my ears grows.

From a distance, I hear myself speak. "Pregnant?"

"Yes." She clears her throat. "It's early. So early, I wouldn't have noticed yet, except they took some tests. I... It's all my fault." Blinking fiercely, she looks down at her toes.

I find myself smiling, though it feels wobbly and uncomfortable. "Pretty sure this is a fifty-fifty kind of culpability deal here, honey."

Her head snaps up and she looks lost, her eyes round and scared. "Yeah, but I didn't... I was so stupid. I forgot about the whole antibiotics-weakens-the-effectiveness-of-the-pill thing. Talk about hubris. My sixteen-year-old self was more informed. But no, I take one look at your dick and become a ditz."

If it were any other time, I'd laugh at that. I'm certainly just as susceptible to her charms. But I need to calm her down now. "Well, I didn't even know that was an issue." I make another attempt at a smile. "Condom man, here."

She snorts and then bursts into tears.

"Hey," I whisper, pulling her close. "Hey, now. Don't cry."

Mac just sobs harder as I lead her to the bed. I curl up with her at the head of it and hug her close. Christ, I left her to deal with this alone. I can barely think right now, and she's been carrying this knowledge around. Alone.

Wincing, I burrow my face into her fragrant hair, not knowing how to apologize enough. But somehow she's the one apologizing.

"I'm sorry, Gray. You trusted me and—"

"Ivy Mac, if you say another word of apology, I'm going to be pissed."

Her hand clutches my neck as she half laughs, half sobs.

I kiss her temple, rub her shaking back. "Now, calm down. Breathe. Again. You can do better than that, Special Sauce. Deep breaths."

"Okay." It's a pathetic whimper of a response, but she's calming. Her wet cheeks press against my heart, and I close my eyes and keep stroking her.

I hold her until she settles and becomes soft and relaxed against me, and I realize that, despite all the thoughts racing through my mind, the one thing I'm not doing is freaking out.

IVY

"What are we going to do?" My voice is a raw whisper in the silence.

The room is dark. Every inch of me feels battered and heavy with fatigue. But I'm in Gray's arms, and he's idly running his long fingers through my hair, making it a struggle to keep my eyes open. Beneath my cheek, his chest rises on a breath and his heartbeat increases.

"I don't know," he says quietly. "I guess that's up to you."

I stiffen and lift my head to look at him. "Why me?"

Gray's blue eyes are solemn. "It's your body. Your choice. Isn't it?"

He says it so matter-of-factly, so sincerely, that I kiss his chest before answering. "I don't want to be the only one with any say. Your opinion matters."

The corner of Gray's mouth curls as he traces a line down my cheek. "Okay. But, Mac, I feel like I'm walking through a minefield here."

"Coward," I tease, giving his side a nudge.

"Yep," he says, unapologetic. His grin sparks then fades. "Honey, just tell me how you feel, and I'll listen."

Sighing, I rest my chin on his chest and wrap an arm around his waist as if holding on to his body can anchor me and stop the fluttery feelings of panic that keep coming and going. "I don't know. We're so young. We have barely begun to live our lives. The idea of having a baby..." I press my lips against his firm skin. "It just seems like we're setting ourselves up for disaster."

Gray is silent for a second then his big hand engulfs the back of my head. His touch is warm, secure. "Okay, true. But we're also way ahead of most people our age. Barring unforeseen calamities—and I really want to knock on wood—I'm going to be making a ridiculous amount of money in less than a year. And even if something did happen, we both have excellent educations and our massively impressive brains..."

I grin at him, and he wags his brows. "So we're not going to be hurting for money. Not to mention that your parents are loaded—"

"Gray!"

He holds up a hand, but a smile lingers in his eyes. "I'm just saying that we wouldn't be suffering for funds."

"Fine." I rest my head on him again. "You're right. But a baby? I don't know." I pause and peer up at him. "You're not freaking out. Why are you not freaking out?"

He sputters a laugh, and suddenly I'm on my back and Gray's big body hovers over me. "You thought I'd lose it, didn't you?"

"Well, I..." Hell, I almost lost it, why wouldn't he?

Gray shakes his head slowly, a smile creeping over his face. "Mac, you're the love of my life. I'm all in, come what may. This? Yeah, it's a shock, nothing I expected. But this is you and me we're talking about. Please don't hold what I did today against me. I can adapt to a change in play."

"I know," I tell him. "And I won't."

He nods as though relieved then his lips brush mine. "Maybe I should be panicking. But I'm not. If you want this baby, then we'll learn as we go. If you don't—" He kisses me again. "Then I'll hold your hand every step of the way."

TWENTY-SEVEN

GRAY

"SO," I SAY to Drew. We're sitting at the bar, ginger ales in hand—Coach has set down a no-beers-from-this-point-on rule, and Drew's trying to be supportive. Good man.

"So," Drew says back then takes a drink.

"Ivy's pregnant."

It's almost worth my current anxiety to watch him choke and spew ginger ale all over the bar. The bartender gives him an annoyed look then walks over to wipe up the splatter with a rag.

"Baby steps, hon," she mutters before leaving us.

I laugh into my glass.

Drew glares, but then his expression grows serious. "Shit, Gray-Gray. You're not joking, are you?"

"Nope." I take another drink and concentrate on the feel of cold bubbles sliding down my throat.

"Holy hell." Drew braces his hands on the bar. "What are you two going to do?"

"Don't know yet. Ivy's thinking things over." I pick at the damp edge of my cocktail napkin, ignoring Drew's stare. I don't want to see pity.

"You okay with… I mean, if she decides to keep…" He trails off.

I finally look at him. "If it were Anna? How would you feel?"

At this, Drew straightens. "Scared, sure. But it's Anna. She's it for me, so I guess I'd be starting a family early."

"Exactly. Ivy's my girl. She always will be."

Drew really looks at me now. "You're not freaking out."

"Why does everyone assume I'd freak out?" I grumble. "It's insulting."

"Because I'd freak out." He shrugs. "And, well, you're…"

"What?" I'm quickly moving from insulted to pissed.

"Come on, Gray. You've been Mr. Party, give-me-a-new-girl-a-night since I've met you. It's just a little shocking to see you not get spooked over something as big as this."

Okay, he has me there. I take another sip of my soda.

"I'm a little unsettled, sure. What the hell do I know about babies? I'm afraid I'd accidentally crush it in my big-ass hands. But then I think of me and Ivy together, watching the little guy grow and…"

I trail off and clear my throat. I've said too much anyway.

A slow, incredulous smile spreads over Drew's face. "You want this baby, don't you?"

I shift in my seat, resisting the urge to hunch. My cheeks are uncomfortably warm.

And yet. "Yeah, I think I do."

Nothing is settled, but suddenly all I can think about is the future, wanting a family, a life with Ivy. It's all dancing in front of me, as solid as smoke.

IVY

"I'm beginning to think that life will never be one hundred percent perfect." My head is in Fi's lap, and she's giving me random braids.

"Is this because you're gonna be Man Mountain's baby mama?"

"Jerk," I mutter then glance up at her. "But, yes. I mean, here I was, life plan finally making sense. I'm in love with the best guy in the world, and now...*boom*! Guess what, genius, you're knocked up!"

Fi pulls up another section of hair to braid. "Not to mention Dad is going to shit puppies when he finds out. Mom will probably bake a ten-tiered stress cake, then kick it."

"Has anyone ever told you that you suck at commiserating?"

"You. Like, tons of times. Which makes me wonder why you keep talking to me."

I cuddle closer into her lap. "Seriously, Fi, what am I going to do? It's all fun and games to call me a baby mama, but isn't that what I am? God, how many prenup contracts have we seen Dad draw up for this shit?" I laugh without humor before pressing my hand to my hot eyes. "I'm a fucking cliché."

"You are not! Gray loves you. Do not put yourself in that category of sad female who tries to trap an athlete through pregnancy."

"But people will think—"

"Whatever the fuck they want to think. Their opinions mean dick-all."

We're both quiet. Despite my inner turmoil, I feel better. Fi is the comfort of my childhood and the one person, aside from Gray, I can say anything to.

"Do you want this baby, Ivy?" Fi's voice is soft, almost hesitant.

"I think Gray does."

"Really?" Fi makes a surprised chuckle. "Huh."

"He gets this look in his eyes. Like he's excited. Happy." That look makes my insides melt and my hormones kick into high gear, and I have to fight not to cry. Even now my smile is wobbly. "It's kind of cute."

"And you?"

I sigh and turn my head to give her access to the rest of my hair. "Fuck if I know. I don't feel ready. But then it's Gray and me, and I can't..." I swallow hard. Twice. "I just don't know, Fi."

Her hand comes to rest on my cheek. "Talk to Gray about it."

My vision blurs hot and wet. "That's the problem, Fi. I'm afraid that if we disagree on the decision, I'll lose him."

I turn and press my face into her belly, hiding in the dark. I think of my life, how it began. Fi doesn't know everything. I can't even *say* everything. "I don't want Gray to be with me based on obligation."

The real fear is that I'll lose him regardless. Nothing good ever came from being forced into life-altering decisions.

TWENTY-EIGHT

IVY

GRAY WON'T BE spending Christmas with me. His team has to leave for New Orleans the Monday before to get ready for their bowl game. Two weeks he'll be gone. And because I know I'll be a distraction to him, I'm waiting until New Year's Eve to join him there.

So Gray and I make our own Christmas early with Fi, whose boyfriend has gone home for the holiday.

Fi has decorated our small house with such enthusiasm it looks like Santa's elves have invaded us during the night. Every doorway is fringed with lighted garland. Tiny novelty houses grace the sideboards. A big—pink—Christmas tree, hung with little glittering footballs and helmets and miniature pink Fiats, sits in the corner.

Gray has a good laugh over that. "Awesome tree."

"It's deranged," I say in an undertone.

"It's kitsch," Fi stresses. "And it's fabulous."

"Where in the hell did you get these little Fiat ornaments?" I ask, truly impressed.

Fi grins wide. "The internet is a wild and wonderful place, my friends."

"It needs one thing," Gray says before bounding into my bedroom. His grin is devious as he jogs back.

Fi shrieks when she sees that he's holding the tiny Tinker Bell doll I had sitting on my dresser, but I laugh. I'd told Gray once that it reminded me of Fi.

He doesn't even have to stretch to reach the top of the tree. "There." He nestles the little Tinker Bell on the upmost branch. "A teeny Fiona to watch over us."

"Asshole," my sister mutters, then laughs.

We exchange gifts first, and I love Gray even more for giving one to Fi too. His gift to her is a pair of novelty Fiona the Ogre slippers. Which Fi uses to bat his head with. But I can tell she loves them. It's not like Fi is any better, giving Gray a T-shirt that says *Man Meat* across the chest.

Gray grows flustered when he hands me my gift. "It's not much. I'll do extravagant next year."

Clutching the thin package to my chest, I give him a swift kiss. "Quiet, Cupcake. Let me enjoy my present."

"All right," he says, flushing. "I'll shut up."

I tear open the wrapping and find a tiny silver four-leaf-clover pendant lies in a long black box.

"For luck in your new career," he says quietly as he puts it on me.

"It's perfect," I tell him with a kiss.

Gray fairly tackles me when he opens my gift to him, a blue enamel Le Creuset Dutch oven, which is extravagant but something I've wanted to give him for a while.

"I'm gonna cook you short ribs and brisket," he promises between kisses. "And stew, and pot roast, and goulash..."

"We get it," Fi cuts in, annoyed. "Now stop mauling my sister before I vomit."

For dinner, Drew, Anna, and Gray's closest teammates come over. Gray cooks us meatballs—Norwegian, not Swedish—and potatoes, which he says is a Grayson Christmas tradition. Dex acts as his sous chef, and they spend the time bickering over Dex's knife skills, while the rest of us snicker in the living room.

The guys treat me as if I'm one of them now, joking and randomly tousling my hair like I'm their kid sister. Gray has told Drew I'm pregnant, which means Anna knows by extension. They don't mention it, but they're careful to offer me apple cider when one of them grabs a beer. And I keep getting goofy grins from each of them at random points during dinner.

I don't really mind; after all, I told Fi about it, but it drives home the fact that I have a decision to make, and I need to do it sooner rather than later. Just thinking about it has me wanting to run to my mother and hide away under her arm, which feels vaguely ironic, given that I'm considering motherhood.

As if he can hear me mentally worrying, Gray turns his head and catches my eye. A soft smile curls his lips, and he kisses my forehead. "No worries tonight, Ivy Mac."

I rest my head on his shoulder for a moment. "Okay."

"So," Fi says, as I serve sticky-toffee pudding for dessert. "Is there some standard thing to say to wish you guys luck on your game?"

"What, like a superstition?" Drew asks.

Fi nods.

"'Good luck' works for me." Dex's tone is uncharacteristically gruff, but I don't miss the way his gaze keeps sliding toward Fi when she's not looking. He sees me watching and promptly tucks into his pudding.

I don't know much about the big center, other than he's quiet, the team's captain, and likes to paint. Bearded and tatted along his muscled arms, with a shock of wild brown hair that grows thick on his head, he's hot in a broody, lumbersexual kind of way.

Because, yeah, I can totally see him rocking a plaid shirt and chopping some wood. Not wanting to make him uncomfortable, I turn my attention elsewhere.

For the rest of the dinner, I have fun. Only Gray seems off, his voice louder than usual when he tells a joke, his muscles tight, even when I put a hand on his neck and rub it.

But he leans in close and whispers in my ear, "After these guys leave, I'm taking you out for a ride. I have a surprise."

I waggle my brows. "Color me intrigued."

"You'll see soon enough." Gray flashes a quick smile, but it doesn't reach his eyes.

And I wonder if we're both trying too hard to be brave.

Gray refuses to tell me where we're going or why. Not even give me a hint, which leaves me with all sorts of possibilities, none of which are realistic. I'm up to guessing it's a ride in the Goodyear blimp when we enter the campus.

He parks in front of the stadium, and my excitement turns to confusion. "Why are we here? If you think I'm playing some random game of midnight touch football on a full stomach, you've got another think coming."

"No football, I promise." He's grinning like a kid on a snow day. "You'll see. Come on."

Taking my hand, he leads me to one of the stadium's side entrances.

"Are we allowed to be here?"

Gray's texting something on his phone, but gives me a quick look. "Now, Mac, you know me better than that. Of course not."

I huff, but then the door opens and a security guard waves us in. "Thanks, Rufus," Gray says.

Rufus, a portly older gentleman, gives a gruff nod. "Just remember our deal and clean up after yourselves."

"What was the deal?" I ask as we walk farther into the stadium and Rufus ambles off, his large frame waddling slightly.

"Tickets to the bowl game and that I don't trash the place."

"Ah." I trot alongside Gray, whose hand has become slightly damp. He glances down at me a few times, his smile tight, but his eyes shining as though excited.

All questions stop when I see the soft glow in the center of the field. A nest of blankets has been laid out, along with a basket, a camp lantern, and, a little ways away, a small heater.

Gray leads me to the spot. "I wanted to give you your last present here."

"I get another present?" I sit on the blankets, curling my legs under me so that he has room. "Gimme."

Gray laughs but pulls a carafe out of the basket. "Cocoa first."

The little heater provides warmth, but not as much as Gray's big body. I snuggle against him and drink cocoa. The dark stadium is still and quiet, the high, slanting sides looming up around us. Only a few lights by each end zone are on, shining a harsh bluish-white.

"It kind of feels like we're in the bowels of a spaceship," I say.

Gray shifts closer, and his chin rests against my shoulder. "I guess it kind of does now. I've never been here when it's dark like this."

I feel his head turn and know he's looking around. His voice lowers to reverence. "To me, it's a cathedral. I sit here and I feel calm, centered. And yet it's also as though all the energy of games past remains, coursing through my veins, and I can't wait for the next game."

My hand finds his, and I hold it as he continues. "I don't even think it matters what stadium I'm in. It just feels right." Soft lips brush along my neck. "The same way you feel right."

This man. He does it for me in every way. I turn and kiss him, loving that I can. That he's mine. Gray's fingers thread through my hair to cup the back of my head as he deepens the kiss, tasting me like it's the first time. Heat flares over my skin, but he pulls back, his breath coming a little faster.

He gives me one more soft peck. "Love you, Ivy Mac."

"Love you, Cupcake."

Gray takes a deep breath, his nose against my hair as if he's taking in my scent. Then he gives himself a little shake. "Okay. Present."

He fumbles around in the basket, his shoulders inching up, and it hits me that he's nervous. Really nervous.

Which makes me nervous. When he turns, he's so tight the muscles along his thighs bulge against his jeans. "Ivy..."

My attention drifts to the little black box he holds. Shit. I can't move. My heart slams against my ribs.

Gray sits back on his heels, facing me. With shaking hands, he opens the box. The ring is gorgeous, an elegant design of three flat, emerald-cut diamonds on a platinum band.

I stare at it, numb inside, then look back at Gray. His whole heart is in his eyes. The corner of his mouth quirks, trembling a little. I want to hug him close, only I'm frozen.

"This was my mom's," he says. "The only tangible thing I have left of her. Seeing it on your finger would give me joy."

"Gray..." I swallow hard. "What—"

He quiets me with a touch. "Ivy Jane Mackenzie, I want to marry you. I want you to be my family. And I'll be yours." Hope and longing fill his gaze. "Say yes?"

Shock has punched the breath out of me. I'd feared this. Yet his words, the look in his eyes, makes me want to hug him close. Which makes it harder to answer.

"I can't."

He winces but doesn't take his eyes off me. "Why?"

He says it so reasonably, as if I'd refused another cup of cocoa.

A choked laugh escapes. "Ah. Because we're twenty-two, for one thing."

"Pretty sure lots of twenty-two-year-olds get married, Mac."

Yeah, and I'm pretty sure I know why he wants to marry me. I love him for it. And I hate him for it.

Grinding my teeth, I struggle to think of something to say to make him understand. "You're the best college tight end I've ever seen."

Gray cocks his head to the side. "Okay, not what I was expecting. Is there a point to this?"

"You could go number one."

"I hope so." His bronze brows lift as if to say I'm off my nut. "Again, your point?"

"That's a lot to take in. Worrying about a wife shouldn't be part of it."

With a curse, Gray looks off, his glare focused on the yellow uprights down the field. When his gaze returns to me, his focus is so intense, I feel it in my belly. "Were you planning to dump me, Ivy? When I'm thrust into this so-called awesome life?"

His anger vibrates through me. "No. Of course not."

"Then why bring this up? And what about your wants and needs?"

"I am thinking about that." I don't want to be proposed to for the wrong reasons.

"So you don't want me in your life come Draft Day?" he shoots back, his eyes wide and hurt.

"That's not what I meant."

"Then tell me what you do mean, Ivy."

"I was a mistake," I blurt out.

Gray blinks. "A mistake? What? You think I view you as a mistake?"

"No." I take a breath. "I was an accidental pregnancy. My parents were only dating when Mom became pregnant. She was supposed to go back to England, not stay here. They got married because of me." The irony is a twist in my guts.

For a second, Gray just stares. Then he reaches for me, and I'm cuddled tight against his chest.

"Honey, no. No."

Burrowing closer, I clutch his waist. "How can you say no when you don't even understand what I mean?"

"Because I know you." He leans back a little to look me in the eye. "You think we're like them? That I'm asking you because I feel obligated? Fuck no."

His fingers trace my jaw. "We're nothing like them. First off, we're not *dating*." His mouth twists like it's an ugly word. "We're together, as in I wake up every morning and think, 'Thank fuck, Ivy wants me. How can I persuade her to keep me forever?'"

I snort and lean my head against his chest. "I do want you," I whisper. "But that doesn't mean we have to get married. Don't ask me because of this pregnancy. That would be the very worst way to start a marriage. You'll regret it, Gray. Trust me."

Gray blows out a frustrated breath. "Did your dad ever say why he cheated?"

Caught off guard, the answer tumbles out of me. "He said he felt like it was his due. Women and fame."

"Well, that's not me. I've had that already and just..." He shakes his head. "No. I'm twenty-two and I feel like an old man with that shit. The thought of fooling around like that again exhausts me, makes me ill. I haven't even looked at another woman since we started texting. Because I only want you. With or without a baby, I want you, Mac. Just you."

"But you're asking me to marry you, Gray."

"Uh, yeah, and you keep rejecting me, damn it." He laughs, but the vulnerability in his voice guts me.

My palm spreads over his heart. "Are you going to tell me that you'd have asked if I wasn't pregnant?"

His chest lifts on a sigh, and he peers down at me. "Ivy, you woke me up. I thought I was living each day to the fullest, but it was bullshit. I was playing a part, being a joker. And I didn't know it."

"That's not an answer."

He frowns. "You think I'd planned to let you go? That was never going to happen. Yeah, I'm asking sooner because of this. Because it gives me an excuse to do it. Fuck, Ivy, deep down I knew you were it for me from the beginning. Only it would have looked weird if I said it so soon."

My smile is wobbly. "Not weird."

Gray cups my cheeks and presses his forehead against mine. "So say yes."

"Gray… The first year of marriage is supposed to be the hardest. And that's without the pressure of caring for a baby. It's a recipe for disaster."

"I like a challenge." Gray gives my shoulders a squeeze. "If anything, I should be worried. You've only had one crap experience and then me. Who's to say you aren't the one who gets bored?"

"I find that idea laughable. I'm never bored when I'm with you."

His smile is crooked. "Yeah, well, same here. I told you we'd be so fucking good together. And I'm never wrong about these things."

I can't help nipping the clean curve of his jaw. "Know-it-all."

"You know it," he murmurs as his mouth chases mine. His kiss is tender.

When he pulls back, we grin at each other. But the shaky, nervous feeling returns, and I take a breath.

"But, Gray, marriage? I can barely get past this whole being-knocked-up thing and, hell, I don't know…"

Gray runs his fingers along the fringe of my bangs, calming me. "Look, I know it feels like everything is happening too fast. I probably just made it worse. Damn it. We don't have to get married. It's just I wanted to give this ring to you. To show you what you mean to me. That I have your back. Always."

Sitting in its little black box, the ring shines, the diamonds clean as ice and winking. Gray glances at it then back to me.

"It doesn't have to be an engagement ring if that scares you. Wear it because we're together. Wear it because I love you." He rubs the back of his neck. "That is, if you want to. Hell, I've fumbled this whole thing—"

I cup his warm cheeks and kiss him. His lips part on a surprised breath, then he's kissing me back, deep and needy, his arm wrapping around my waist to haul me close. We're a bit sloppy, taking and receiving kisses as though we've been apart for years.

By the time we calm down, I'm a little dizzy and a lot giddy. My nose touches his, nuzzling. "Maybe we can be engaged to be engaged?"

"As long as we're together, it can be anything you want."

"Put it on me."

Our hands shake only a little as Gray slides the ring on my finger. It's beautiful. So beautiful my vision blurs, and I blink to clear it.

Gray rests his forehead against mine. "So I didn't completely fuck it up?"

Gently, I stroke his cheek, and the diamonds glint in the low light. "No, Cupcake. You're perfect. This ring is perfect. I love you so much."

"That's my line," he whispers, and then he kisses me again.

We tumble back onto the grass, laughing softly. Gray maps the contours of my face with his lips, all the while telling me the same thing. *I love you. I love you. I love you.*

TWENTY-NINE

GRAY

FOR ALMOST TWO WEEKS, my home has been a hotel in New Orleans. I live and breathe football now. Practice, study, drills, sleep. Press junkets and mindless interviews. That's my life. The playoff game is tomorrow, and everyone is so keyed up we just want it to be game day already. No more wading through a sea of agents and scouts and sponsors. No more smiling for the camera as we eat our free gumbo dinner. No more reading playbooks and watching footage until it runs through our heads in our sleep. Just let us play football.

This is the worst it's been for me. Ivy thought that by staying away she'd help me keep focused. Not really. I've discovered that I need her with me or I feel unbalanced. I miss her so much my chest feels hollow, yet tight.

But finally she's on her way and is due to arrive in a few hours. I'm antsy as all hell to see her. So much so that I physically have to keep moving to distract myself. One brutal workout later and I get a text from Sean Mackenzie asking me to meet him in the hotel bar.

I've been avoiding him for a while. Mainly because Ivy and I haven't decided what to do with the pregnancy. I know what I want, but I'm not going to push Ivy. I'll state my case, but I won't push. Stepping out of the shower, I towel off and text Mackenzie to set up a time.

Because there is one thing I'm not okay with hiding from him any longer.

Mackenzie is waiting for me at the bar. He's already halfway through a tumbler of whiskey. I take the seat next to him and order an ice water.

"You ready for the game?" Mackenzie says by way of greeting.

"What's that line?" I quip. "I was born ready."

"John Wayne." Mackenzie nods. "Cute."

"John Wayne, really?" I take a sip of water. "I thought it was from *Big Trouble in Little China*."

Mackenzie rolls his eyes. "Stop trying to make me feel old. *Big Trouble* was my generation's movie. Used to watch that movie on the couch with Ivy's mom."

The thought of Mackenzie with Ivy's mom brings everything back into focus. I take a breath and brace my palms on the bar. "Listen, there's something I need to tell you."

"Ivy already told me." His mouth twists. "Via text."

At my incredulous face, he hands over his phone. I read the text out loud. "'Gray and I are together now. Don't be pissy with him. It's serious. And I'm happy.'"

Laughing low, I rub a hand over my face and give him back his phone.

"Little wuss," I mutter under my breath.

But apparently not low enough, because Mackenzie gives me

a look. "Here's a tip. My daughter likes to cut and run when she's overwhelmed."

"Already figured that one out." Ivy and I are similar that way.

Mackenzie grunts. "You shouldn't have touched her, Grayson. You know better."

So, Ivy gets her directness from her dad. Good to know. I straighten my shoulders and turn to fully face him. "Well, this is awkward."

Mackenzie snorts as if to say, *No shit, kid.*

I take a quick drink of my ice water before forging on. "The part of me that's talking to Ivy's dad says I respectfully understand your fears, sir, but I assure you hurting Ivy is the very last thing I'd ever do." My grip on my glass tightens. "The part of me that sees you as a potential agent wants to tell you to fuck off."

He laughs outright. "Then we're of a like mind, kid. Because part of me wants to kick your ass for even looking at my daughter. And the other part wants to warn you to keep away from distractions. Namely of the female variety."

Female variety. I want to roll my eyes. But he's not saying anything new.

"I love her."

He snorts again, and I give him a hard look.

"You might as well hear it from me. I put a ring on her finger. We're engaged to be engaged."

Slowly Mackenzie lowers his glass and looks at me. His rough features are worn, pale. "Engaged to be engaged? What the hell does that mean?"

"Ivy's words. The point is, I want to marry Ivy. She's the best thing that's ever happened to me."

He pinches the bridge of his nose. "Are you fucking with me? Kid, marriage is the last thing you need at this point in your career."

I figure now is not the time to tell him Ivy's pregnant. Plus, if we end up giving that news, it will be together. No way is Ivy wriggling out of it with a text.

"I know you think I'm like you," I say in a low voice. "But I'm not."

And I really don't give a shit that he's now glaring murder at me. I continue without blinking. "Nothing on earth makes me happier than Ivy. And that includes football. So you can be pissed if you want, but I'm never going to be the one to walk out on Ivy."

We sit locked in silence, the noise of the bar humming around us.

Then Mackenzie sighs. "Well, then, if I was your agent, I'd advise that you keep your fiancée out of the spotlight as much as possible. I'd also advise that you play up your image as a family man, which will be difficult given your outer persona."

"Outer persona?" I ask with a laugh.

"Shit." He grimaces. "Don't make me say it. Your looks, kid. Women go crazy over guys like you. They'll view you as a sex symbol."

His mouth puckers like he's sucked a lemon, and I laugh again.

"Fair enough," I say. "And as my father-in-law?"

I'm playing with fire, but I can't help needling him.

His black brows pull together. "Ah, fuck, I'm stuck with you regardless, aren't I?"

"'Fraid so, Big Mac."

Grumbling, he throws back the rest of his whiskey. "Well, then, welcome to the family, kid."

In an unexpected move, he grabs hold of the back of my neck and gives it a friendly squeeze. At least, I hope it's friendly.

THIRTY

GRAY

SHORTLY AFTER I leave Mackenzie at the bar, Ivy texts me.

IvyMac: I'm here. Dex already sent your stuff up to my room, btw.

GrayG: Wait, DEX got to see you before I did? Foul! Personal foul!

IvyMac: *eye roll* That just means we don't have to leave the room when you get here, Cupcake.

GrayG: Keep talking…

IvyMac: I splurged on a suite.

GrayG: A suite? Babe, that's too much.

IvyMac: It's a treat.

GrayG: An expensive treat.

IvyMac: I collected wages when I worked with Mom. Now I want to spend them pampering my man.

GrayG: Pampering, eh? You're forgiven for Dex. Now, where you at, Ivy Mac?

IvyMac: SO glad I'm forgiven. 😛 12th floor. Rm. 1210

GrayG: Spooky. My room number is 1184.

IvyMac: Erm...why is that spooky?

GrayG: 1184 and 1210 are amicable numbers ☺

IvyMac: I love it when you talk nerd. So sexy.

Hitting the elevator button, I grin wide and tap out my next message.

GrayG: Almost there. Be naked.

IvyMac: Bossy.

GrayG: If you could start playing with yourself, get nice and wet for me, that'd be good too. ☺

Snickering, I tuck my phone into my pocket without waiting for her reply. By the time the elevator coasts to the twelfth floor, my dick is already throbbing.

The door to suite 1210 is open a crack, and I smile, knowing Ivy left it that way for me. Unrelenting need has my skin too tight for my body. I'm practically panting as I walk in, my heart thudding in time to my hard, quick steps.

Standing in the middle of the small living room is Ivy, wearing an oversize red T-shirt—and nothing else. I pause, take in the sight of her long, smooth legs, the way the shirt falls off one toned shoulder. White lettering across her breasts states, *If you can't handle my Tight End, you need a stronger D.*

A coy little smile plays on her pretty pink lips, and her dark eyes shine beneath the heavy line of her glossy brown bangs.

She's five feet from me, but I swear I can smell her scent, sugar and spice and everything nice. Lust hits me so hard, I actually shiver, my skin prickling, my knees going weak. Something that sounds like a growl rumbles in my chest, and her eyes go wide, her lips parting.

"Hey there, Cupcake—"

My mouth is on hers, my hand cupping her neck, before she can finish. I kiss her like she's my only sustenance, going deep, licking into her mouth for that first taste.

Heaven. Home. Delicious. And she's kissing me back as if she can't get enough either. It makes me lose my mind.

My hands find her ass, and I haul her up, take two stumbling steps to the couch. Knees hitting the cushions, I maul her mouth as I fall on top of her, wrenching her shirt up to get at her sweet tits. She arches up, a little whimper escaping, as I suck at one perfect nipple.

Mac fists my shirt, pulling me up so she can attack my mouth again. I groan, my kiss so frantic our teeth clash. Her thighs spread wide as I tear at my jeans, my hands shaking so badly it takes two tries to get the button open.

My cock springs out, slaps against my belly. Fumbling, I cant my hips, find her slick heat, and thrust. Mindless, pushing into that hot, tight clasp. This time we both groan, our breath mingling. And then I'm pumping hard and deep. There's just the sound of our flesh slapping together, the greedy, animalistic grunts I'm making, and the need for more and more. Fucking her is a heady mix of relief and agony. I'm frantic with wanting Ivy, and I know it will always be like this.

Long legs lock around my waist, her nails digging into my shoulders. When she sinks her teeth into the soft flesh at the crook of my neck, my body seizes, and I'm coming on a strangled cry. Ivy strains against my hips, gasping, her pussy milking me with rhythmic pulses that have me pushing as deep into her as I can get.

I collapse against her, jelly-kneed and head spinning. Her arms come around my shoulders, limply holding on. We're both panting hard, my open mouth pressed in the folds of her shirt that's gathered high on her neck.

Taking a breath, I manage a casual, "Like your shirt."

Ivy's laugh is weak. "Thanks. I was totally going for a 'gimme a hot and dirty quickie' look."

"Glad to oblige." I smile, kiss the edge of her jaw.

Gently I detangle her from the shirt, pulling it free and throwing it aside. Ivy takes my shirt off as well, and I settle back, loving the feel of her skin against mine. A few more awkward wiggles and I'm out of my sneakers and jeans. But my softening cock stays deep inside her. I don't want to leave her heat. Ever.

Somehow we've ended up on the floor. I frown, not even remembering tumbling.

"Are you okay?" I ask, touching her cheek. The fact that she's pregnant comes back to me in a rush, and I go cold. "Shit. I wasn't too rough, was I?"

"No. You were perfect." Her fingers thread through my sweaty hair. "You always are."

"You sure? I had this whole slow-seduction thing planned, but you looked so hot, and I've been dying for you, and—"

"Kiss me, Cupcake," she says, tugging on my hair.

So I do. I kiss her softly, stroking the edge of her jaw with my fingertips. I kiss her as I carry her to the bedroom. I kiss her as I lie beside her, gathering her close, until we're skin-to-skin. This is what I needed, the scent and feel and taste of Ivy all around me. The tightness in my chest eases.

Never am I more aware of my size than when I'm touching Ivy, of how my hands span the sides of her head, of how fragile yet necessary she feels to me.

"Ivy Mac," I whisper, brushing my lips over hers. I hold her in my grasp as I come at her mouth again, sipping at her lips, tilting my head to experience her from a new angle.

Her hands slide over my back, stroking, urging me closer. We kiss with lazy slowness, learning each other's mouths over and over, until our lips are swollen, and my jaw is sore. But I don't stop. My head is spinning, my cock a hot slab between our pressed bellies. It would be so easy to spread her legs wide and sink in deep, fuck her again. But I hold back, enjoy this simple act. It sharpens everything, sends my body into hyperawareness.

Our breaths mingle, the edges of our lips just touching. My tongue flicks over hers, a tease that I feel in my balls. Sweat covers my skin and hers, makes me shiver. Yet I'm so hot, so drugged on her mouth, I can barely breathe.

Ivy moans a little, her hips rocking slightly. I know she wants to be filled, but she doesn't push it either, just holds on to my neck like it's her anchor and suckles my lip, slides her warm, slick tongue over mine.

My breath hitches. It's a struggle not to roll her over, not to go wild and thrust my tongue as deep as it can get into her mouth. I want those things. Yet this self-inflicted torture feels so good, I'm close to coming. Just from kissing Ivy.

And it does something to me, makes my gut clench and my heart pound. I reach up, find her hand that's burrowed beneath my pillow. Our fingers twine and my thumb presses against cool metal. Ivy's wearing my ring.

Mine. She. Is. *Mine.*

"Ivy." My thigh slides between hers, intent on parting them.

But her hand grasps my shoulder, and she gives me a nudge. I let her ease me onto my back.

"What are you up to?" I murmur as she crawls over me, nuzzling her way down my neck.

Her voice is warm honey over my skin. "Let me take care of you for a while."

I've had sex more times than I want to think about. Girls have gone down on me, done all they can to impress me. But take care of me? Kiss their way around my body like it's some divine experience? Never. Not like Ivy.

My hands shake a little as I touch Ivy's hair, pushing it back so I can see her face.

"Hey," I whisper. "Turn around, so I can take care of you too." This I know. I want to taste her, lose myself in making her feel good.

But she shakes her head, her hands gliding down my sides. "Not now. This is for you."

Glossy brown hair slides over my skin, leaving goose bumps in its wake. Throat tight, I glance down, take in the sheen of her skin, those long, lean thighs, the way her tits sway as she moves. So damn beautiful. The tightness in my throat becomes a lump, and I swallow hard, draw in an unsteady breath. "Mac."

At the sound of my voice, she lifts her head, her eyes meeting mine. I blink rapidly, my heart pushing against my ribs. She smiles, a soft curving of rosy lips, then presses a light kiss to my side. I feel it in my toes.

Ivy is clearly trying to torture me. Her sly tongue follows the line of my hip, runs along my abs, goes everywhere but where I want her to be. My cock lifts as if trying to flag her down. Finally, she gives the head a lazy little lick, and I practically swallow my tongue.

She's done this before, but now, after kissing her for so long, I'm strung tight as a wire, sensitive to every touch. When she sucks me in, I moan so loud it sounds almost pained. My eyes squeeze shut, heat rippling over my skin.

My hand falls to the crown of her head. I hold her there, slowly pump my dick in and out of her willing mouth. She hums, the vibration going straight to my balls. My grip tightens. "So fucking good, honey. Like that. God, like that."

Ivy grips my length as she sucks, then goes so deep, her mouth sliding over her fingers too. When she draws back, her wet fingers trail between my thighs, parting them. I let her do it, my muscles twitching under her hands. She caresses my balls, my ass, all the while sucking and licking my cock in a slow, steady attack.

"I love your mouth." Watching her pink lips stretch around my dick is the hottest thing I've ever seen. I almost miss it when her fingers slip down past my balls.

Almost. Only her fingertip circles a place no one has ever touched.

My ass clenches, but I don't move. I can't. Her boldness has me off-kilter. Blood rushes through my ears. Half of my focus is on her warm, wet mouth, the other half on that finger. It's kind of kinky, and fuck if that doesn't make my dick go even harder.

She strokes me, the lightest of touches. And it feels good. Too good. With a little groan, she sucks me deep and then pushes that finger against me, seeking entry. I shouldn't let her do this. It's too much.

"Mac? I don't know about… Never mind… Oh, fucking hell, yes." Her finger slides in, a strange invasion that sets my body on fire. "Jesus, fuck…"

Chest heaving, I fight to stay still. God, but I want to rock my hips, push against that finger. Because it's so indecent, so fucking erotic and good I grit my teeth, so close to coming that I can feel it rising up my balls. And then she hits a spot that stops my breath, maybe my heart.

"Oh, fuck, Mac." I thrust into her mouth, writhe against her hand. Which makes me feel it more. She's taking me. *Me,* the one always in control. She is making love to me with her mouth and fucking me with her finger. It's so intense, I don't think, only pant and move with her as if my life depends on it.

My hand slides from her hair, slams to the bed to grasp the covers as I arch up into her mouth, my entire body drawing tight. Pleasure punches through me. I come so hard, the room turns hazy.

And she just takes it, drinking me down, sucking my cock with sharp tugs that have me babbling demands. "God, honey, promise you'll marry me one day. I have to have this for the rest of our lives. Forever. Always. *Fuck.*"

She releases me with a long pull, her finger sliding away.

My skin prickles. I feel vaguely empty, my body sore in places I don't want to think about. And as she slowly kisses her way up my stomach, I'm still babbling. "Give it to me on Christmas. Birthdays." Her tongue flicks in my belly button. I grunt, my hips twitching. "My days off. Major holidays. Midnight surprises…" Mac licks my nipple, and I shiver, my voice going raspy. "Twice on Tuesdays."

Her dark eyes gleam brightly. "Just Tuesdays?"

"*Twice* on Tuesdays. Maybe once every day?" I crane my head, give her a hopeful look, and she utters a husky laugh that is so fucking sexy my thighs clench and my words come out strangled. "Just, you know, let's keep this particular fun on the down-low…"

A flush of heat washes over my cheeks. Jesus, I can't believe she did that. And how fucking good it felt. I've underestimated my girl.

Mac's lips twitch but her expression is solemn as she rises over me and bends to kiss me softly. "Your secret's safe with me, big guy."

She tastes like me, her mouth all swollen and red and plush. I want more. My hand slides over her neck, holding her there so

I can kiss her deeper, a languid glide of tongue and lips. Little pulses of heat ripple through my dick like aftershocks. Holy hell.

"Definitely twice on Tuesdays, Mac."

IVY

Gray flops on the bed with me, making the massive mattress bounce. He's wearing a pair of sweats that ride low on his lean hips and nothing else. "Checking out the swag?"

Swag being the large duffel bag I'm picking through filled with goodies that various sponsors have gifted Gray and his teammates.

"Dad used to bring home travel soaps and T-shirts." I pull out an elegant plastic box that holds a certain watch people have been dying to get their hands on. "Nothing like this haul."

Gray waggles his brows. "Pretty sweet, huh? I think there's a voucher for a year's worth of steaks."

"I'm surprised you didn't cry."

"I might have shed a tear or two." Gray pushes up the hem of the T-shirt I'm wearing and rests his head on my bare thigh. With a little hum of pleasure, he strokes my leg, his expression content, his body loose-limbed and lazy. Give the man a blow job and a little unexpected ass play and he's practically purring. There's probably a lesson in that, only I'm equally susceptible. Gray merely has to look at me a certain way, and I'm ready to offer him anything.

"Ivy?"

"Yeah? Ooh, look, soundproof headphones. I've been wanting a pair of these."

"They're yours." His hand moves along my calf, the touch soft, steady. "When I told Drew about you being pregnant, I realized that I wasn't afraid. That the idea of having a baby with you was kind of great."

My heart seizes.

Clearly he feels me stiffen because his grip tightens on my shin. "I'm not trying to push you," he says. "But you asked me once what I wanted." The bed creaks as he rises up on his elbow. Gray's expression is earnest yet almost shy. "I want it all with you."

Warmth flutters through my chest as I look down at him. Gently, I brush back a lock of his hair. "I thought you might."

His gaze moves over my face as though he's trying to read my mind. "But do you?"

Running my fingers through his hair, I stare off. "When I think of this baby as you and me, I want to protect it with all that I am."

Gray gives my leg a gentle squeeze, but I keep talking.

"But when I think of trying to be a mother right now..." I trail off with a strangled breath. "I mean, a baby—a child—needs constant care. I can't do that on my own. I don't *want* to do that."

Gray's brows snap together. "Who said anything about being on your own? We're in this together. One hundred percent."

"Gray, you're going to be starting the NFL. July through January, they'll basically own your ass."

"Okay, yeah, that will suck." Gray sighs and rests his forehead on my thigh again. "But we can work it out. And never think for a second that I won't be all in when I am there." His big body flops back onto the bed, and he blinks up at the ceiling. "Shit, I don't know. Maybe we should wait."

I lie back too, my head next to his. "Only I'm pregnant now. When I think of ending it, I just can't." With a muttered curse, I press my forearm over my eyes. "Why is it so hard, Gray?"

Gray rolls to his side and lifts my arm off my face. "I wish I had the right answer," he says slowly. "All I can say is that the hardest decisions in life are often over the things that mean the most. So what means the most to you, Ivy?"

"You. Being together."

His expression turns tender. "And what do you fear the most?"

"Making the wrong choice."

"Then make the choice that scares you the most."

Cupping his strong cheek, I peer up at him. "You never let anything stop you, do you, Cupcake?"

"Not for long, Ivy Mac." His large frame moves over me until I'm surrounded by him. "It's my nature to work past obstacles." His lips skim up my neck, nipping and tasting as they go. "And look what I have to show for it. Top of my sport and, in my bed, the woman I love more than anything."

"Our bed," I correct, pulling him down to me.

His hard body presses against mine, and everything kind of short-circuits. He feels so good, all satin-smooth skin and hot, hard muscle. I need him again. Now. Thick and slow within me. In a haze, I think about luck and how mine had always seemed slightly off. I think about how happy I am in this moment with Gray, knowing that he's mine. That we could actually be a little family.

I'm afraid. But maybe a little fear is a good thing.

THIRTY-ONE

IVY

GAME DAY. GRAY COMES out of the bedroom, and it's all I can do not to swallow my tongue. All the guys wear suits to the stadium, but I wasn't expecting Gray to look so hot in one. Dressed in a charcoal pinstripe three-piece suit with a crisp white shirt and an ice-blue tie, he's long and lean and gorgeous. Like my own extra-tall James Bond.

I resist the urge to strip him. There isn't time; he's expected downstairs in about five minutes.

He gives me a searching look and an uncomfortable laugh. "Why are you staring at me like that? Shit..." He shifts his feet. "I look like an asshole, don't I?"

Shaking my head, I walk over to him. Or rather, I stalk him, because I still want a bite. His smile is lopsided when I stop before him.

"Damn," I say on a sigh. "You are fine in this suit."

I smooth my hand down one silky lapel and press into the solid wall of muscle hiding beneath it.

Gray grunts as if I'm talking nonsense, but he blushes as his hands settle on my hips. "Want to play dress-up later?"

"Yeah." Gently, I run my knuckle down his stomach, stopping at his belt buckle, loving the way he sucks in a breath and nudges forward with his hips as if to urge me lower. I glide my knuckle back and forth along his waistband. "We can play Interrogate the Spy."

Gray lowers his head and nips my earlobe. "You gonna be a spy, Mac?"

"No. You are. I'll tie you to a chair and do dirty things to make you talk."

A full-body shudder wracks Gray, and his fingers tighten on my hips. But he takes a breath and steps back. "Damn it, Mac," he says with a husky laugh, "I can't be boarding the team bus with a massive hard-on."

"I kind of like the image, but okay." Putting some needed distance between us, I lean against the arm of the couch. "I hear your dad is going to be at the game."

His nose wrinkles on a scowl. "Way to go with the bone kill. Yeah, I suppose he is." Gray fidgets with the white cuffs peeking out from his coat sleeves. "And how the hell did you know that, anyway?"

"Pfft. I've got connections you can only dream of." My teasing fades. "Are you going to talk to him?"

Not looking at me, Gray shrugs. "Maybe. I guess after the game."

"Just get it over with, Gray. Like ripping off a bandage."

He makes a rude noise, then eyes me. "And then we celebrate with a little bondage and light sexual torture?"

I laugh. "Not my choice of words, but yeah, that's what we'll do."

His smile is devious. In two steps he has me. Soft lips kiss my forehead, eyes, nose, chin, mouth. "Every inch, Mac."

I press a kiss to his lips. "Every inch, Gray. Now go kick some ass."

THIRTY-TWO

GRAY

"SO ARE YOU engaged now?" Dex asks me as he squints into his locker mirror and begins to smear on eye black.

Smiling, I continue wrapping my wrists. "More like engaged to be engaged."

Which I'm totally cool with. Ivy's wearing my ring, and that brings out the caveman in me. Better yet, she wants me as much as I want her. It's all I need.

"And the dreams of horny chicks all over the sporting world are dashed," Johnson pipes in from the other side of me.

"Guess they'll just have to settle for you, big guy." I give his belly a light slap and it jiggles, earning me an irate look from Johnson as he covers his gut with one hand.

"Married?" Marshall parrots from behind us. "Man, I can't believe it. You're the last dude I'd expect to fall for that trap, Grayson." He shakes his big head. "Next thing you know, one of you will confess to being gay."

I don't even have to be looking Rolondo's way to know he's gone stiff. I worry for him, wondering just how much shit he'll get if he ever comes out, and how hard it is for him to keep his life secret. But for now, I keep my eyes on Marshall. "Careful, man, your asshole is showing."

"What?" Marshall whips around, craning his neck to look at his ass. And the guys laugh.

"He was being figurative," Diaz deadpans. "As in you're being an asshole."

Marshall's beefy face turns red. "You know what you can kiss, D?"

Diaz just grins and continues tying up his cleats.

We finish dressing, and Coach walks in with the staff. "Take a knee, gentlemen."

It's time for the pregame talk. Now, some coaches shout and yell to rev up their team. Not our coach. He's always calm, almost meditative. He likes philosophy, visualizing a victory, thinking in terms of mental toughness. And not one of us has ever complained. Because his methods work. He speaks, and we listen to every word.

We all drop to one knee, forming a circle around him. Coach stands in the middle, his body loose and relaxed, his voice steady and low. "So, here we are. The playoffs. It's what we've worked for. What we knew we could achieve."

He looks around.

"I know each and every one of you. I know your strengths. I know your weaknesses. And if those boys have done their homework, they'll know them too. Strengths and weaknesses. Everyone's afraid of weakness. Don't be. Use it to your advantage. They think you've got an ego to exploit? Let them think it. Twitchy on the snap if taunted? Make them believe it. Turn that weakness into your strength. Confuse them. Do the unexpected." Coach points to his temple. "This game is as much up here as it is on that field."

We're silent, watching as he strolls before us.

"Lot of knuckleheads in this game. Guys who think they'll play the hero and do it all alone. But on that field..." He points toward the doors. "We play as a team, and we win as a team. Teamwork. We're the team they all want to beat. They want our blood." His gaze wanders over us. "Because we're the best damn team in the nation."

"Red Dogs!" we all shout as one.

"'Victorious warriors win first and then go to war, while defeated warriors go to war first and then seek to win.' Sun Tzu." Coach's voice rises. "Men, we've already won. Now go out there and get the job done."

"Yes, Coach!" It's a roar.

Coach's eyes flick to mine, and he gives a small nod. Every team has their traditions, little rituals that they do before games. Ours is no different. The university tradition is to get into a mass huddle and bump our helmets together before running out on the field. Here, in the locker room, we have another one for just after Coach's speech.

It started when I was a redshirt freshman, and I'd plugged my phone into a set of speakers, making the guys listen to music before a game. We'd crushed it that day, and, being superstitious bastards, we'd decided that we had to listen to the same song before each game.

I complete the ritual now, pulling up "Radioactive" by Imagine Dragons and hitting Play.

Some guys close their eyes, let the pulsing music roll over them. Others kind of sway, start getting worked up, their blood pumping.

"Visualize," Coach says over the music. "See the win. It's there. Yours. Already."

It happens slowly, heads bobbing to the heavy beat. It draws us together, makes us form a huddle. Then we're jumping, one mass of bodies feeling the same rhythm, same beat, same mind.

We are one. When the refrain hits, a bunch of them shout it out: "Woahoh."

Energy flows through us, vibrating with the bass. The power of eighty guys jumping in unison shakes the floor. The music fades, and it's just us, revving up. My heart pounds, my body pulled tight with anticipation. That tension within us reaches its peak, and as if we'd planned it, we roar as one,

"Go Red Dogs!"

IVY

"God, I'm nervous," Anna says at my side. "And Drew isn't even playing. I don't know how you deal with this."

Third quarter and the score is 35-30, and our team is the one down.

Fi shrugs. "I deal by people watching and hitting the buffet." She nods toward the impressive buffet spread at the back of the luxury box we're sitting in.

Anna laughs. "I used to cater that buffet spread. Well, not *that* one, but you know what I mean."

I'm trying not to notice the buffet because my stomach is roiling. Is it nerves or morning sickness? I don't know. Aside from slight fatigue and breast tenderness, I haven't had any pregnancy symptoms. It's early, so I'm guessing they'll develop. My fingers are cold too, so maybe it is nerves.

I take a bracing breath. "They'll win."

"Of course they will." Anna nods then glances at me. "You're looking a little peaked. You want me to get you a ginger ale?"

"Yeah, that would be great, thanks."

From the corner of my eye, I see my dad chatting with the university's athletic director, and a tinge of guilt hits me that my friends know about the pregnancy but my parents don't.

One thing at a time. Bowl game, then confess to the parents. Yay.

Leaning back in my chair, I wave the big foam finger Fi gave me back and forth to get some air movement. It's freaking hot in here and too confining. I cast a longing glance at the stadium seats below. I want to be out there where it's nice and open. But Anna, Fi, and I are all up here with my dad, the university staff, and a couple of wealthy boosters.

I watch Gray take the field again. He's not hard to miss, towering above most of his teammates, the number eighty-eight clear on his wide back. Football uniforms aren't exactly sexy. Pads and helmets obscure a lot. But the pants? Shining red Lycra lovingly covers Gray's tight ass, which is now currently displayed on the multiple flat-screens along the suite wall as the cameras zoom in on his team's huddle. I have to smile; if Gray were here, he'd be making tight end jokes.

He looks focused now. They have plenty of time, but I know Gray won't be complacent. He'll push and fight for every inch gained. Always will. His confidence on the field borders on cocky. Only he never shows off—he simply plays with his whole heart.

Anna comes back with my soda, and I take a grateful sip. The ginger ale is ice-cold and fizzy. But it doesn't shake off the growing nausea. If this keeps up, I'm going to give up a good chunk of this game to the porcelain goddess. Grimacing, I run a hand along my aching neck.

Oppressive heat swarms up my body. Saliva coats my mouth and sends my stomach churning. Setting aside my soda, I stand up. My lower belly feels heavy, as if a bowling ball is rolling around in the small space between my hips. Queasiness rises within. The heaviness turns into clenching, and I rest a hand on my middle.

Faintly, I hear people talking. Someone is calling my name. But my innards are writhing too much to pay attention. The room swims in and out of focus, and my heart begins to pound. I need to get to the bathroom. The thought barely passes my mind when a violent cramp wrenches through me, knocking the air from my lungs. I double over, and a gush of slick, hot wetness flows between my legs.

"Ivy?" Anna's voice comes at a distance, buzzing and indistinct.

Tears blur my eyes. Something is running down my legs. I lift my head, find Fi reaching for me.

"It's bad," I say through cold lips.

The room is spinning.

Dad is suddenly at my side. "What the hell is wrong with her?"

Fi is whispering in his ear. He turns pale and glances down at my lap. He winces. They're moving me back, making a circle around me. The room fills with murmurs, gawking faces.

"Daddy. I'm sorry." I want to tell him I'm pregnant, but I don't think I am anymore. Someone calls for a doctor, and all I can say is, "Don't tell Gray. Not now. Promise not to tell him yet."

Fi's hand is strong and warm on my icy one. "It's okay, Ivy. It will all be okay."

But I know it's a lie.

THIRTY-THREE

GRAY

FOURTH QUARTER, THIRD-AND-TEN with a minute on the clock, and my blood is pumping.

There is a sharp, metallic scent in my nose. The crowded stadium buzzes around me, a dull hum at this point compared to the ringing in my ears. Every inch of me hurts. My bones ache, my joints throb. I have a gash on my knee that stings. Sweat runs into my eyes. And I wouldn't change a thing. My entire body is alive and working to accomplish one thing: winning this fucking game. One touchdown and we have it.

I head back to the huddle, and a defensive lineman shoulder-checks me as he passes, taking the moment to taunt, "Gonna bring you down, pussy boy."

"I do love pussy." I face him while walking backward, my arms wide. "But yours smells a little off. Better get that checked."

Mr. No Humor points at me. "You're going down."

"Gotta catch me first. So far you've been tasting my cleats." At that I jog off and join my guys, ignoring whatever else the dumbass has to say.

"Please tell me I get to smoke Ninety-Two's ass," I say to Cal as we gather at the forty.

Behind the grill of his face mask, Cal grins wide. "Funny you should say that, Grayson. Time to become the Gray Ghost."

Gray Ghost. Because stopping me is as impossible as catching a ghost. Which is both apt and awesome.

"Gray Ghost it is then, Frost," I tell Cal, giving him a nickname as well. Because damn if he didn't earn one today.

He nods. "Let's put this game to bed, boys."

Cal gives us the play, and I smile with teeth. For me, it's a simple hook play, with a lot of intricate subterfuge on my teammates' part to throw the defense off the scent. My body hums with anticipation.

At the line Mr. No Humor is glaring. "You ready for me, Blondie?"

I put my toe on the line, hunkering down low enough to let him think that I'll charge him at the snap.

"Now, I'm gonna block your ass," I tell him nice and conversational-like. "But that don't mean I want your pussy, 'kay?"

The dumb ones fall the hardest. It's almost too easy. He practically vibrates with fury. "Gonna run right over your pretty face."

I blow him a kiss, pretending I'm paying attention to him, when really I'm breathing hard and deep, drawing in more oxygen to enrich my blood, moving my weight to the balls of my feet so I can take off. My body draws tight, like a crossbow about to be launched.

Cal's voice rings out. "Hut!"

The world explodes into motion. Thinking I'm going to block, the lineman steps left, roaring with aggression. I step right. He blows right past me as I sprint down the open lane my guys have made for me. Blood rushes through my veins; everything is muffled grunts, bodies smashing into each other, and my pounding feet.

Ten yards out, I cut right, pivot, body angled toward Cal, and the ball sails into my waiting hands.

That's all I need. Another burst of energy surges. Spinning, I sprint down the field, a lineman on my ass. In my periphery, a safety is barreling toward me. They don't know what I know. Now it's all about physics. Velocity, mass, momentum.

The lineman hooks his arms around me, intent on dragging me to the ground. But I'm bigger, stronger. Holding the ball low and tight, I hunker down, dropping my center of gravity. I drag him with me, the bulk of his body colliding into mine actually increasing my momentum. And when the safety hits us, he's useless because he's coming at the combined weight of me and the lineman. It's too much mass for a guy his size to handle.

Their dead weight works against them, dragging them down my moving body. I break free. One, two, three tiptoe steps along the edge of the sideline, then I'm off again, maximum velocity toward the end zone. Footsteps pound behind me. Hot breath on my neck.

Fuck that noise. I run full-out. My lungs burn, my muscles scream, but I don't stop.

Another safety comes at me from the left.

Still running, I reach back and strong-arm him, my hand at his collar. We're barreling down the field, almost at the end zone. He falls in front of me, and I leap, my foot clipping his helmet.

Ball clenched tight, I flip head over ass. Don't lose sight of that little orange cone, though. It's right there. Just get the ball over.

With a grunt, I twist, fall toward it, body extended and arm outstretched, my hand holding on tight to the ball. Bodies slam into mine with explosions of pain and deep grunts.

We crash into the turf with bone-shaking force. I see stars. But I've done it.

Touchdown. Whistles blow, refs' arms in the air. And the roar of the crowd rushes over the field.

Winning a huge game is like nothing on earth. The noise of the crowd is deafening.

A roar that vibrates my bones and rings in my ears. Confetti flies, and the energy of eighty thousand shouting spectators surges across the field on a wave that gives me a hard-on. I'm so high on it that I'm literally bouncing, screaming and whooping as I go.

My team is bouncing with me. Hard slaps of victory hit my back, my pads, my head. I thrust my fist toward the sky. We fucking did it. We fucking won. We're going to the National Championship. My skin prickles with pride.

Pandemonium is the name of the game now. I barely remember giving interviews. I know I said the standard lines, of being grateful for my team, of being happy to win, and the need to buckle down for the championship game. It's all true, but my attention is diverted.

Around me, my teammates, coaches, and staff are celebrating. Confetti sticks to my hair, a big chunk of it tickling my neck where it's stuck under my collar. I move past friends and well-wishers. Ivy. Where is Ivy? I need to see her like I need my next breath.

Through the sea of faces, I spy Drew making his way toward me. I let out another whoop and run to him.

"Fucking hell, man," I shout happily when I reach him. "We did it! Can you believe it?" I give him a bear hug, hauling him off his feet.

Drew chokes out a laugh, and I let him go so he can breathe. His smile is wide, but oddly forced. "You guys rocked, Gray-Gray."

He sounds off. Shit, is he upset he didn't get to play? I feel like an ass. Running my hand through my damp hair, I try to think of something to say, that he'll soon be playing again. His leg will heal.

But Drew steps in close, his expression suddenly tense. "Gray… Shit. Ivy's been taken back to the hotel."

Sharp pricks of dread stab my face as my body goes rock-hard. "What? Taken? What does that mean?"

People bump into us. The dark shape of a TV camera is in my periphery. But I focus on Drew.

He leans close. "Ivy had a miscarriage. I'm so sorry, man."

It comes at me like a hard hit, shattering something deep in my chest. I can't make myself move. A metallic taste fills my mouth, the ground beneath me tilting.

"Is she okay?" *Please, God.* All the blood seems to be draining from my head down to my toes.

"Rakin is with her."

Rakin is one of our team physicians. I expel a breath, feeling a little better, then pin Drew with a look. "When?"

Drew just shakes his head. "Sometime during the game."

I explode. "Why didn't you fucking tell me sooner?"

"You were playing—" His fist pushes against my chest when I charge him. "And I didn't know until five minutes ago. Anna just texted me."

"Aw, yeah," shouts a voice behind me. A second later, Rolondo slams into us, sending my shoulder pads into my jaw. "That's what I'm talking about! Whoo!"

His grin fades as he looks at me and Drew. "What's going on?"

Drew gives a tight shake of his head. "Ivy."

That's all he says, but it's enough. Fear surges once more. I sway, dizzy and sick to my stomach. We're surrounded now, reporters moving in. Maybe they smell blood in the water, or maybe they just want a sound bite.

Rolondo puts his hand on my shoulder. "Go to your girl. We got this." He turns, cutting the crowd off from me. "Who's got a question?"

I take off running, cutting through the crowd like a hot blade. My head is pounding by the time I reach the locker room. My gear falls where I toss it. I'm hauling up my jeans when my dad walks in. I've managed to avoid him all day, and *now* he shows.

Time and hard living have left my dad wrinkled and paunchy. I don't really look anything like him. He's wiry and dark-haired, his frame a good four inches shorter than mine. I look a lot like my mom—something that I know pisses him off. The only feature we share is the color of our eyes. Doesn't matter that he's responsible for giving me life; every time we're in the same room, I instantly want out.

"Gray—"

"I don't have time for this," I grind out, jamming on my sneakers. My fingers shake as I try to tie them.

Dad takes a hard step forward, his face red. "You're going to talk to me, goddammit."

"No. I'm really not."

"Listen up, young man—"

"My girl needs me." I head past him.

He grabs my arm. "You're walking out to see a piece of—"

I wrench free. "She is the woman I love. So show her some respect. She's pregnant." An ugly, raw sound breaks free. "Or was. She lost it. While I was on that field—"

Cursing, I turn away, head for the door. It takes me a second to see that my dad is following me.

"I'll drive you," he says grimly.

"I don't need you to drive." But it hits me that I don't have a ride.

Something my dad knows as well. Even so, he can't help but get a dig in. "Don't give a shit what you think you need, son. I'm doing it." He sighs as he holds the exit door open. "I'll see that you get to your girl safely. Now let's go."

THIRTY-FOUR

GRAY

STUCK IN THE passenger seat of Dad's cushy rental sedan, I can barely sit still. My knee bounces, and I'm rocking back and forth as if the motion can somehow make the damn car go faster. This traffic to get clear of the Superdome is killing me. Not being with Ivy is killing me. Is she okay?

In my haste, I'd left my phone behind. I'm cursing myself now.

Pressing my fingers against my aching eyes, I try to focus on deep breathing. I need to calm down before I totally lose it and end up kicking a hole through the floorboards.

"So it's true?" My father's gravelly voice cuts through the silence. "You're with Sean Mackenzie's oldest?"

"Ivy," I croak out. "Yeah." I don't ask how he knows. Gossip is a disease in football.

"Nice kid."

I glance at him, incredulous. But then shake my head. Of

course Dad has met Ivy. She apparently knows everyone in professional sports.

He catches my look and shrugs. "Haven't seen her since she was a teenager. But she seemed to have a good head on her shoulders. Pretty too, in a subtle way."

I snort and grind my clenched fist against my mouth.

"And you love her?" he presses.

"I want to marry her." Not that he needs to know. But it feels good to say. As if, every time I do, it becomes more real.

Finally, traffic breaks, and my dad turns the car onto the main road. For some reason, I find myself looking at his hands. Those big hands that always felt like a hammer crashing into my skull when he'd cuff my head for some minor infraction. They look old now, the knuckles swollen, the skin spotted with age.

A sick lurch goes through me. I lean back, stare out the windows.

"It's been a long time since you've been home," Dad says in a low voice.

"I am home," I say. When he doesn't answer me, I glare at him. "Did you really think I'd ever come back?"

His profile is like granite. "Why wouldn't you?"

My laugh is bitter and short. "Here's a tip. You want your child to visit? You don't fucking beat his ass when he's a defenseless kid. You don't let his older fuck-head brothers beat his ass." I'm yelling now, my voice ringing in the space between us. "And you don't fucking leave him alone to take care of his dying mother."

Dad had been stoic until the mention of my mom. His gaze slices to mine. Red flushes over his weathered cheeks. "First off, I never beat you. I pushed you to excel."

At my ripe curse, he talks over me. "And look at you now. The best in your position. Hell if you won't be the number one pick. That discipline helped forge you into a champion."

"I *excelled* due to innate talent and hard work. Not because you and Jonas and Leif whaled on me when I did something wrong."

His lips press together. For a long moment, he doesn't say a word. Which is fine by me.

"I didn't know how bad they'd gotten," he says finally, quietly. "I was just trying to do right by you. Make you tough."

"Well, brilliant. Only don't expect me to care." I lean my head against the window. Will this ride ever end? My chest is so tight it hurts to breathe. I refuse to think about Ivy right now. Not in this car.

Again, my dad speaks. "I shouldn't have left you to deal with Liv."

Grinding my teeth to keep from shouting, I force a detached tone. "I didn't 'deal' with Mom. I was there for her. I wanted to be. I just didn't want to be the only one to do it." Something sticks in my throat, and I struggle to clear it. "I needed help. *She* needed her whole family, Dad."

"I know. I was wrong." His knuckles turn white. "I couldn't… I wasn't strong enough. But you were. You're the best of us, Gray."

His words sit like a stone on my chest. I say nothing.

"I'm proud of you, son."

"Because I win games." It's not even a question.

"No. I'm proud of my son. Of the man you've become." He turns a corner and we're pulling into the hotel's drive. Dad eases the car into a spot before looking at me. "And I'm sorry to hear about your loss."

My throat convulses, and I can barely nod. Ivy is in a room upstairs. Likely devastated. I am too, yet my legs are like lead. I take a deep breath and reach for the door handle.

"Gray," Dad says as I move to get out. His blue eyes, the exact color of mine, are rimmed in red. "I'll try to do better."

I don't really know what to say. That he cares should make me feel better. But I'm numb now. So I answer the only way I can. "Okay. Bye."

And then my thoughts turn to the person I love more than anything on earth.

★★★

My fingers are ice as I let myself into Ivy's room. I just want to get to her, but I'm a wreck, shaking and nauseous. My heart is thumping so hard, my breath so short, I'm afraid I might topple.

As soon as I enter, Mackenzie and Dr. Rakin stand and face me.

"Where is she?" I get out.

"Resting in the bedroom," Dr. Rakin says in a low voice. "I gave her some acetaminophen for the pain."

"How is she?" God, just let her be okay.

"As well as can be expected, Grayson," Dr. Rakin says. "Sporadic miscarriages during early pregnancy are not uncommon, and Ivy is young and healthy."

Words I want to hear, but I know there's a huge difference between physically fine and mentally okay.

"Shouldn't she be in the hospital?" I press.

He doesn't meet my eyes. "There really isn't anything they can do for her." It's a punch to my heart to hear that. "Just keep a lookout for a fever or undue bleeding. I've said this to Miss Mackenzie as well."

"Right." Stuffing my shaking hands as hard down into my jeans pockets as they'll go, I make myself ask the question I fear most. "Is it… Was it because—?"

My throat closes in on me as my vision blurs. I blink rapidly. "We had sex. Today. And—"

Shit. I'm going to lose it. Ivy's dad is right here. He must fucking hate me. *I* hate me.

But Rakin shakes his head, his expression almost pitying. "No, son. Put that out of your mind. When a pregnancy aborts like this it's usually due to a chromosomal abnormality in the fetus."

Logically I know this. But I can't stop myself from thinking of how I slammed into Ivy. Taking her hard and fast, like a rutting bastard.

My eyes burn hot, prickling. I draw in a shaking breath.

"Okay. Right." I don't know where to look. "Thanks. For being there for her."

"Not a problem," Dr. Rakin answers. "I heard about the win. Excellent job, Gray."

I could give a shit about the win right now. Ivy is in the other room. Waiting. I'm fucking wobble-kneed and ready to bawl. The sense of loss guts me. I don't know what to do with that emotion now, or how to even handle it. Rakin is saying something about Ivy seeing her OB when she gets home. I nod, but my gaze turns to Mackenzie. He's been silent this whole time.

He's looking at me now, those thick black brows of his slanting over his eyes. I want to apologize to him.

But he speaks first. "I'm sorry, son." He comes closer to me, and I suck in a sharp breath through my nostrils. His big hand lands on my shoulder. "I really am."

"Yeah," I croak. "Me too." I turn my attention to the closed bedroom door and move toward it, but stop and look at Mackenzie. "I know you're Ivy's father, but don't ever keep something like this from me again."

He knows I mean it. I let him see the rage and fear I'd felt when I learned Ivy was hurting and I wasn't there for her.

Mackenzie gives me a tight nod. "Never again."

THIRTY-FIVE

GRAY

OPENING THE DOOR is hard. I don't want her to see me cry. I need to be strong for her.

Yet my throat is working like a bellows, opening and closing. I take another breath and go inside.

She's in the center of the bed, curled up against the pillows, and wearing one of my team shirts. She looks fragile, defeated, her brown eyes huge in the oval of her pale face. My heart bleeds for her, a physical ache that has me leaning against the door frame.

She meets my eyes, and her lower lip wobbles. I think mine does too.

"Hey," I whisper.

"Hey," she gets out. And then bursts into choking tears.

Instantly, I go to her, toeing off my shoes as I move. My jeans come off next. Only then do I notice Fi sitting next to Ivy. She rises, leaving us, as I make it to Ivy's side.

Without pause, I push aside the pillows and slide in behind

Ivy. I'll be her pillow now. My legs ease around hers. As gently as I can, I scoop Ivy up and settle her in my lap, drawing the covers up high over us.

I rock her as she cries, my face burrowed into the crook of her neck so she can't see my tears. It takes me a moment to realize she's saying "I'm sorry" over and over. My hands shake as I stroke her back, trying to calm her.

When she relaxes a little, I lean us back against the headboard. "Why are you sorry?"

Ivy's huge eyes find mine. "It's my fault."

I smooth her bangs back from her forehead. "How?"

"Gray…" Her fist clenches my shirt. "I…" She starts to cry again, a quiet roll of tears. "When I found out I was pregnant, I didn't want it. I was afraid, angry. What if…? I thought those horrible things…"

A sob leaves her.

I hug her close. "You're fucking human. That's all. You didn't make this happen. It just wasn't the right time, honey."

But she isn't listening. "And then I lost—And I feel so guilty. So…sad. It hurts, Gray."

"I know." I cup her head to my chest. "I know it does."

"I didn't want this to happen. No matter what I thought, I didn't want this." She sounds so broken, it kills me.

"I'm sorry," I say. "I should have been here. I should have been here."

"You were playing your game." Her voice is small against my skin. Guilty. "I told them not to get you."

"Yeah." I'm trying not to sound pissed, because if I think about it, I will be. "We're going to have words about that later."

Ivy's head nods, but she grips me tighter. I reach past her and grab the tissue box someone left on the side of the bed. Ivy blows her nose, then settles back onto me.

We're quiet for a long time. My left hip is numb and my shirt is damp with her tears. But I don't move.

"I've been thinking," I say. "About things. My mom died a slow, painful death." I breathe past the tightness in my chest. "Drew lost his parents overnight… Truth is, life ebbs and flows no matter what we do. All these years, I've been trying to get some control over that by not giving a shit about anything. What kind of life is that?"

Ivy's fingers play with mine as she leans more of her weight on me, sinking into my strength for support. I'm glad I'm strong, that my body can be used for more than sex or football. That it can be used in service of her, to protect, comfort.

"Bad things happen, Mac," I whisper thickly. "And this? It tears my heart apart."

Ivy shudders, a little sniffle coming out. I hold her as close as I can without squeezing her too hard, and then press my lips to her head. "I hurt for you. For me. For… Shit."

A choked sound comes out of me. And then it's Ivy holding me tight, her face pressed against the crook of my shoulder. "Gray…"

"I know, honey. I know. Hell, I'm not saying this right." Gently I cup her cheek, tilting her head back so she meets my gaze. Her dark eyes swim with tears, and it guts me all over again. My thumb glides over her damp skin. "We can't control the bad things, Ivy. But we can be there for each other when they happen. And the good stuff? It's worth everything and anything if I can share the good stuff with you."

Tears spill over Ivy's cheeks as she reaches for me. "Cupcake." Her lips find mine.

And I don't want to talk anymore, or to think. I just want to kiss her and hold on. Forever.

IVY

We go home the next morning. Gray doesn't leave my side. Not for three days. He holds me when I cry; he holds me when I don't. He takes me to the doctor to get a checkup, then takes me home and makes me cream of tomato soup with grilled cheese sandwiches, because I'd once told him that it was a childhood favorite. And when I want to watch a movie, he drags the TV into our bedroom and creates a makeshift theater.

This morning I assure him it's fine to leave me alone for a while. He's got more practice and a meeting with his team to start prepping for the National Championship.

It's evening when he comes home, catching me in the act of dancing around the living room to "Why Can't I Be You?" A tilted smile graces his face as I stumble to a stop, my breath light and panting. Flushed, I push a hand through my sweaty hair. "Hey. Gotta love The Cure, eh?"

"I've never heard them before." Gray sets his duffel bag down. "Sounds like something Anna would listen to. She has a thing for Siouxsie and the Banshees."

"Oh, they're great too. I used to find a lot of vintage records of theirs in London. Mom has a player…" I pick at the hem of my shirt. "I was restless. Felt like dancing."

I don't know why I'm explaining. I wasn't doing anything wrong, but I'm weirdly guilt-ridden.

Only that smile of his is still there. "I can see that. Feel free to carry on." He leans a shoulder against the wall and waggles his brows as if encouraging me.

With a huff of laughter, I turn off the speakers. "Why do I have the feeling you like watching me dance? And not because I'm great at it?"

Truth is, I *know* I'm not great at dancing. But I like doing it, so I don't really care.

His smile grows. "Because you're cute as a bug."

Slowly he strolls over to me. His body is warm and smells of soap. I hum in pleasure as he hugs me close and peppers soft kisses over my face. "I'm glad you felt like dancing, Ivy Mac."

With his arm wrapped around my waist, he guides me over

to the couch, his nose nuzzling my hair. "It's okay to let yourself be happy again, honey."

I know he's right. Somehow, his words make me feel free to let myself relax.

We settle down, Gray propping his big feet on the coffee table, and me leaning on his chest. His hand rests on my thigh, and I notice that all his fingers are wrapped in bandages. On both hands.

"What happened?" Alarmed, I pick up one of his hands. "Did you get in a fight?"

"Nah," he says easily. "Nothing like that." Gray shifts around a bit and starts pulling the bandages off his left hand. "Got this done earlier."

Past the slightly puffy redness of his skin, I see that he now has a black number tattooed on each of his four fingers. "One-one-eight-four," I read out loud.

"Yep." Gray unravels the rest of the bandages. He holds his other hand out in front of us, his fingers spread wide and displaying the numbers one-two-one-zero, before letting it rest on my leg once more. "I've been wanting another tattoo. I've thought about using an amicable number pair for a while. But after New Orleans, I knew."

"I have no idea what an amicable number is," I tell him.

"It's like this. The sum of all the natural divisors of 1,184 is 1,210, and vice versa. It's almost as if the number is the other's soulmate." His gaze connects with mine. "Like you and me."

I start to smile, then sit up. "Wait, are you trying to say this tattoo is about us?"

"Of course. You probably don't remember, but my room number in New Orleans was 1184. And yours was 1210."

A little jolt of surprise hits me. "You texted about that."

"Yeah," he says gently, because he clearly realizes I've had other things on my mind. "But that's not why I got these tattoos. That was just a sign."

Gray's thumb strokes along my knuckles. "When I first met you that day at the airport, you seemed so familiar to me, so right, that I thought we were like a pair of amicable numbers."

Warmth floods my chest. "Gray. That is..." I lean over and kiss his soft lips. "Perfect."

His fingers briefly touch my cheek as he kisses me back. "The fact is, Ivy, for me, there is one absolute truth. The sum of my existence equals you."

Suddenly I want those numbers tattooed on my skin too. My vision blurs as I grab hold of him, claim his mouth with mine, whisper his name against his lips.

Love. I've been surrounded by it my whole life. I know how lucky I am to have that. And yet it's always been a comfortable kind of love, expected in the way of family. What I feel for Gray? It isn't comfortable. It's so intense and so enormous, sometimes I fear my soul can't contain it.

I kiss him deeper, my arms twined around his neck, holding him close. Every time I kiss him, I want more and more. I want to draw him inside of me and keep him there.

Safe. Protected. Part of me.

Gray's hand spans my jaw, fingers curled around my head. His size makes me feel small and delicate, and yet his words, his actions make me feel strong and invincible, even when my heart has been sliced in two by our loss.

He kisses me back. Not frantic, but slow, steady, melting. As if we have all the time in the world to explore each other. As if he could live right here, wrapped around me, lips seeking and tasting.

"I love you," I say into his mouth. Because he should hear that. Every day.

Gray grunts, skims a path along my cheek with his lips. He kisses my closed lids.

Light. Tender. "Love you more, Ivy Mac."

"Not possible." I ease back to look at him.

Gray's eyes are a little bloodshot and puffy. He hasn't been sleeping well, all his efforts focused on me. I think of the times he cried with me, trying to hide the fact by pressing his face into my hair. I'd noticed, but had been too soul-sick to do much about it.

Tenderness swells in my chest as I trace one bronze brow. "Hey," I whisper. "We're going to be okay."

Because I know this now. In truth, I knew the second he walked into that hotel room after the miscarriage, his focus entirely on me. It had felt like a missing piece of me—one I'd never really realized was gone until then—had clicked back into place. No matter how badly I hurt, or how lost I feel, Gray's presence makes everything bearable.

Gray's lids lower a little as he leans into my touch. "Of course we are." Not even a shadow of doubt in his voice.

I give him a soft kiss. I love his mouth. Love the way it feels against mine.

And Gray sighs. He's warm and relaxed and holding me as if he'll never let go.

Love. It's this fierce thing rushing through my veins, making my heart pump harder. I'm twenty-two years old, and I know with every insistent beat of my heart that I love this man. My rock. My lover. My best friend.

"Gray?"

"Hmmm?" Eyes closed, he's running his fingers slowly up and down my back.

"I wanted to ask you something." Despite the light tone I use, butterflies war in my belly.

"Lay it on me, honey."

"Will you marry me?"

Gray's eyes snap open, his big body going utterly still. Beneath golden lashes, his deep blue gaze narrows as if he's misheard. "What?" It comes out like a croak.

My heart still hurts from sorrow. But I reach for what happiness I can. Because marriage to Gray no longer sounds foolish. It sounds exactly right.

So I smile and ask again, using his words. "Gray Grayson, I want to marry you. I want you to be my family. And I'll be yours." I look up at him with all the hope and fear and longing he'd once shown me. "Say yes?"

A slow, wide smile breaks over his face. "Holy shit, you're serious."

"Of course I am—ack!"

Gray has me on my back in an instant. Leaning over me, he grins, looking so happy that I'm in danger of tearing up. "You gonna put a ring on me, Mac?"

"Let me guess, you want a big, gaudy knuckle-buster covered with diamonds."

His chest rumbles on a chuckle. "Oh, I'll be getting one of those soon enough, honey."

I don't doubt it. "You'll look good wearing a Super Bowl ring."

"Mmm," he agrees, dipping down to nuzzle my ear. "Don't distract me, Ivy Mac. I want a ring. Platinum. Wide band. Engraving optional, but preferred."

I laugh. "Bossy much?"

"Just know what I want." He lifts his head to gaze down at me. His smile is lopsided, bittersweet, but growing. "That would be you, if I wasn't clear."

I thread my fingers through his thick hair. "Me and a ring. Crystal."

"Then, yes, Ivy Jane Mackenzie," he says in a hoarse voice, "I will marry you."

Grinning like loons, we stare at each other for one long moment, then he's kissing the hell out of me. And I don't mind a bit.

Lounging on the couch, we kiss and talk and pet each other, eventually falling into a lazy, comfortable silence. I'm hungry, and I'm sure Gray is too. We probably should have something to eat. But he doesn't leave my side, and I don't want to move.

"You won," I say, thinking about his playoff game. "I never got to congratulate you."

Spooning me from behind, his hand slides up my waist to cup my breast. Not sexual but comforting. "I did. And thank you."

He doesn't sound like he's talking about the game. I smile a little and rest my hand on his forearm, stroking the silky skin along the edge of it. "I'm proud of you, Cupcake."

Gray snuggles closer, and his lips press against the crown of my head. When he speaks, his voice is low and soft. "And that's what makes it all worth it."

EPILOGUE

IVY
TWO YEARS LATER...

GrayG: Big Daddy has landed. Are shenanigans in play tonight?

LOOKING DOWN AT the text I snort but can't hold back a smile. My thumb taps away at my phone as a woman's voice buzzes over the speakers to announce the arrival of Gray's flight from New York City.

IvyMac: There will be no shenanigans if the use of "Big Daddy" comes into said play. That's a personal foul. 15 yard penalty. Do not pass Go to collect your prize.

GrayG: Aw, but, baby...

IvyMac: NOPE.

GrayG: Just to clarify, putting the perfectly reasonable and technically correct name aside, shenanigans are a go?

Laughing now, I lean back more comfortably in the ugly plastic airport seat and answer.

IvyMac: All night, Cupcake. I can't wait to taste your frosting.

A couple seconds pass and then:

GrayG: Mac, you sent a dirty text. I just shed a tear of pride. I also have a hard-on. I think the little old lady sitting next to me is checking it out.

IvyMac: *snicker*

GrayG: Revenge will be mine.

Putting my phone away, I haul myself to my feet. Around me, an endless stream of people flow past, all of them either headed somewhere else or coming home. For most of my life, I was the one coming or going, drifting without realizing it. Now I'm in California, holding down the home fort. Gray and I have lived here ever since he was drafted to play with the 49ers.

I love the Northern California coast. Wild and rugged, with chilly weather and fog that reminds me of England. Gray isn't so fond of the damp, but he loves soup and deems this the perfect place to make it constantly. Who am I to argue when he's the one cooking it?

And I love having a home with Gray. While it isn't exactly close to the stadium, we settled on a renovated Victorian town house in the Pacific Heights section of San Francisco. We love the place. To my surprise, it was Gray who had the most fun combing through flea markets and antique shops to find vintage furniture for our home. Fi helped decorate, and after listening to the two of them squabble over Eames versus Knoll, I bowed out of the project and kept my sanity.

I turn my attention back to the domestic arrivals gate. In the distance, one golden head bobs over all others. My cheeks pull tight with a grin. Slowly, Gray comes into view. His gaze meets mine. As always, I'm suddenly breathless, joy and anticipation fizzing like champagne through my veins.

I'm practically dancing in place, watching him walk to me, his smile as big as mine. He quickens his pace until he's almost jogging. Those long legs of his eat up the distance between us.

Then his hand is wrapping around my neck, drawing me as close as I can get—which isn't very.

"Ivy Mac," he whispers a second before he kisses me. And I'm lost.

Desire surges along my skin and my heart races with glee. I sink into his kiss then take over, tasting him, sucking his plump lower lip. His scent, his heat, the strength of his big body, all of him, flips a switch within me, like I'm not fully living unless he's near.

"Cupcake," I say when we part, "I've missed you."

We've only been apart for a long weekend, but I always miss Gray when he isn't near. I would have gone with him, but I'm not up for flying right now.

The corners of his eyes crinkle as he looks down at me. "Missed you too, Mrs. Grayson."

"How are Anna and Drew?" I ask between the little kisses he keeps giving me.

Last night, Gray called to talk about the fact that Drew had just played the best game of his career. Since I'm his co-agent, I'd been on a conference call with Drew's GM before the game had even ended. The media was going crazy over his performance, dubbing him the Comeback Kid. Now that his leg had fully healed, he was once again in top form.

"So fucking proud of him," Gray says into the crook of my neck. He breathes in deep. "Mmm, you smell fantastic, Mac. You been baking?"

"A tray full of warm Sacked Gray donuts are waiting for you at home."

"Love when you talk dirty to me." He gives me a leering grin before turning more serious. "How'd it go with Mitchell?"

Brian Mitchell is a hot, young quarterback out of Stanford who's going pro this year. I'd met with him to discuss his future in the NFL. And while it wasn't the easiest thing being a female sports agent, I've been making headway, learning from my dad and forging contacts as I go. I love the hell out of my job.

"He seemed interested," I say. "Well, he liked the plans I mapped out, anyway."

"As he should," Gray says with his unfailing confidence in me.

"I assured him that Dad was on board." When Gray frowns, I give him a look. "Dad and I are partners, after all."

Surprisingly, we're a pretty awesome team. Dad does the majority of recruitment and contract negotiation, while I mostly deal with career planning and player maintenance—which really means I soothe ruffled feathers and try to keep athletes' heads on straight.

"Still," Gray mutters. "You shouldn't have to assure the little shit. You're the bomb, Mrs. Grayson."

Smiling, I shake my head. "You can't blame him for worrying right now. And it was my concession. One I'm happy to make."

Gray's scowl fades as he glances down. Oblivious to the people walking past, he drops to his knees before me to cup my belly. Though I vaguely resemble a wind-filled sail, his big hands make me look small. A gentle smile graces his face as he leans forward to kiss my stomach.

"And how's my Baby G? You being good for Mommy?" A dull thud vibrates my insides as Baby G kicks. Gray chuckles and gives the spot another kiss. "Yep, Daddy's home. All is right with the world once more."

I run a soothing hand over my side. At eight and a half months pregnant, I'm ready for the little guy to come out. Fi called us crazy when we decided to have a baby so soon. But something had happened to us after the miscarriage. A seed of want had been planted.

So, yes, we're both just starting out in our careers, but we also want to start a family. And because we've decided to live life how we want, when we want it, we decided not to wait any longer.

It might be difficult. But we'll manage.

"You don't find it ominous that Little Dude here kicks your face every time you put it near me?" I ask, smiling down at Gray, who continues to baby talk against my belly.

"You're just jealous that he responds to my voice," Gray says happily.

"He responds because your voice is so loud," I retort, teasing him.

"I'm not the one who's loud. Have you heard yourself when you—"

I end that line of conversation with a hand to his mouth. Grinning like a fiend, Gray jumps to his feet. People are starting to notice him, or rather who he is. I'm pretty sure a few camera phones went off when he was kissing The Belly. It's the price of fame. But Gray doesn't let it bother him. He simply grabs his duffel and takes my hand in his.

"Uncle Drew gave us a little hat for Baby G." Gray directs this toward my belly as we walk along. "I told him we'd use it for target practice come toilet training."

"You do realize that I practically grew up in New York, and that's like my home team?"

He halts and gives me an outraged look. "Hush your mouth, Mac. Little Dude might hear you."

I roll my eyes. "Won't matter if he did. Because our favorite team will always be the one you're on."

Gray's eyes light up, but his smile is soft. His bag lands on the linoleum floor with a thud. A little shiver goes through me as he cups my cheeks. His mouth meets mine, the kiss so tender it makes my chest clench, but there's heat behind it. A promise for later.

When he draws away, his voice is husky. "Take me home, Mac. We've got shenanigans to get to."

★★★★★

AUTHOR NOTE

DEVOTION TO A team can be absolute. To that end, I deliberately did not name a college or a team, preferring to leave it to the reader's imagination.

In 2021, the NCAA allowed for college athletes to financially benefit from their name, image, and likeness. This book was written before the rule changes. Regardless, I am aware that Gray borrowing an agent's car—even one belonging to said agent's daughter—falls under a gray area of the time. Please excuse this liberty as I couldn't resist telling a love story that started with a little pink car…

EXCLUSIVE NEW BONUS SCENE

TYPICALLY, I DON'T end books with "and baby makes three" themes. But Gray and Ivy both suffered from the loss of theirs, not really realizing it was something they wanted until it was gone. As their creator, I figured why not give them that gift? I also happen to think they'd be awesome parents and have great fun with it.

This scene is what I'd call "and later on..." as it takes place just after the epilogue when Ivy and Gray come home. You'll see a lot more of them in *The Game Plan*, so this is more a little sweet bonus of their happiness—you know, like putting extra frosting on a cupcake! ☺

—Kristen Callihan

GrayG: You know what seems odd to me?

IvyMac: What?

GrayG: Numbers that can't be divided by two

IvyMac: Hur!

GrayG: I know, I know. Terrible. But it was better than starting the conversation with pi.

IvyMac: *raised eyebrow* Okay, I'll bite. Why not?

GrayG: Because it will go on forever

IvyMac: *eye roll*

GrayG: No smile? Not even for that?!? Ok ok the pressure…

GrayG: Hey, Mac.

IvyMac: Yes, Cupcake.

GrayG: How do you make seven even?

IvyMac: NO! I'm not listening!

GrayG: Subtract the "s"

GrayG: Hello? Hello! Ivy? IVY???

GrayG: Oh, come on. That was classic!

IvyMac: Knock, knock…

GrayG: ☺ Who's there???

IvyMac: Deez

GrayG: Deez who?

IvyMac: Deez terrible math jokes R drivin' me nuts

...

...

GrayG: Speaking of Deez. Why don't you come over here and give deez nuts a little love?

"GRAY!" IVY SITS up at her end of the couch with an outraged laugh.

I give her my most innocent face, which I know she's a sucker for. "What?"

Her eyes narrow. "Pervert."

"Pervert? I resent that. I happen to know you're always trying to get your hands on deez nut—ack!"

With surprising speed and agility, my girl is up from under the blankets and launching herself dead center at my chest. Luckily, I have quick hands—the best in the business—and catch her before she lands. I settle her securely on top of me, which was the plan all along.

This is more like it. I'd been away from her for far too long. And while I love my job, I loathe being away from Ivy. I used to roll my eyes when people in love spoke of missing a piece of themselves when they were parted. But it's true; I don't feel whole when she's not around.

Sure we talk, text, and FaceTime. But it isn't the same. Nothing compares to physically being together. The strangest thing? Even though I know every inch of her by heart, every time I get her back in my arms, it's as though she's brand-new, and I find myself studying her as though I've discovered some rare and fine treasure.

Her hair is a wild nimbus around her smiling face, and I smooth a strand back from her forehead, so it won't fall into her eyes. "Well, hello, Ms. Ivy Mac. Fancy meeting you here."

She snorts in that happy-but-pretending-to-be-disdainful way I love. "This was your plan all along, wasn't it? Annoying me into jumping you."

God, she knows me too well.

"Annoy? I resent that." I grab hold of her butt and settle her more firmly—and more conveniently—on top of me. "Seduce, entice, charm, maybe. But annoy? Never!"

She squirms, clearly feeling my growing interest. And being the little fiend she is, she rotates her hips just enough to make me sweat. Gently, she kisses the tip of my nose, the sensitive corner by my eye. "Oh, you're charming, all right."

"Glad you noticed." I affect a little sniff of affront. But the effort fails. I can never hide my smile from her.

Ivy chuckles warmly, the vibration blooming over my chest and seeping into my bones. "Poor baby. You need some love and attention?"

Always. I don't even care what that says about me. Ivy is in this world, and I need her. It doesn't matter that we've been curled up on the couch together all night, our legs intertwined, watching our favorite shows. Eventually, we'd grown quiet. I'd looked down the couch and seen her face, pale in the glow of the TV, the corners of her eyes crinkled with laughter, and I'd needed to play.

"Now that you mention it—" My breath catches as her hand drifts down my side, sneaking under my shirt to bare skin. "I wouldn't object."

My words become muffled as our lips brush, catch, linger.

She hums again. Nips my bottom lip. Heat rises, languid and lush. I cup the back of her head and delve into her sweet mouth.

"Maybe..." She kisses me again. "Maybe, I should..."

Her teeth nip my bottom lip. I groan, seek out her lips again. Ivy Mackenzie Grayson: my absolute favorite flavor.

She takes a shuddering breath. "I should..." Her hand creeps beneath the waistband of my shorts. Soft kisses pepper my cheek, heading toward my ear. I'm so hot now, I can't think. Her voice is a rasp. "I should..."

"Should what?" I murmur, distracted and trying to ease her shirt up.

She slides a hand down low to cup me gently. Oh, so gently. "Give deez nuts a squeeze."

I freeze. Shock courses through me like a bolt. I give a cry of utter outrage. "Why, you little..."

In a blink, she's on her back, me looming over her, holding my weight on my forearms as she laughs and laughs. She's the most beautiful thing I've ever seen. My chuckle turns into a full-on laugh, and I dip my head into the crook of her neck.

"You're going to pay for that, Special Sauce."

She's still snickering, even as her hands go back to roaming over me. "Sure, Cupcake—ack!"

Her clothes are off before she can say another word, and I slide down to make myself at home between her legs. "Hush now. All this talk of nuts has made me hungry." I spread her legs a little wider, and my voice lowers. "Let me feast, woman."

She touches my head, her voice dreamy. "If you insist..."

I do.

I do a lot. Until we're both boneless and satiated.

"I'm glad you're home," she says when we've calmed down enough to talk without panting. It's a quiet confession, the fan of her lashes hiding her eyes from me.

We're on our bed now; it's all well and good to make out on the couch, but my pregnant wife needs the supportive comfort of a mattress for me to properly tend to her. So, after making a meal of her, I'd carried Ivy to our room, despite her protests that I'd "throw my back out." Ha! As if that would happen.

I turn more fully onto my side to cuddle her close. Ivy sighs and rests her head on my shoulder. I capture her hand and set it on my heart. My lips brush over her sweaty temple. "I was thinking earlier about how much I miss you."

She smiles at that. "Good." And then, "I miss you too. So much sometimes it feels like a wound."

My eyes squeeze shut as I hug her. "I know, Mac. I *know*."

We're silent, breathing each other in. The room is shadowed and cool. I think about reaching down for the comforter, but lately, Ivy's been a furnace and will only kick off the covers if I do.

"The reunions are the best, though," she says with clear satisfaction in her voice.

My lips curl upward—smugly, if I'm honest. "The reunions are fucking awesome."

When she happily hums, I rest an arm behind my head and look around. Aside from our massive bed and a dresser, there's not much else. We'd finally bought a town house in the city. Ivy loves it because of the bay views and the hardwood floors. I love it because the entire structure is built on a grand scale. With towering ceilings, windows, doorways, there is no chance of me or my friends hitting our heads on anything.

However, it is pretty much just as we'd bought it months earlier. "We really need to decorate this place." I pause and wince. "I can't believe I just said that."

Ivy snickers. "Look at you, all domesticated."

I woof, and she pokes my side.

"I didn't want to do anything without you," she says.

"Babe, I am as clueless as you about decorating. More so. At least you know how to fix up a bed."

"Which is why I asked Fi to come and save us."

I perk up. Fiona is studying interior design. And although I'd prefer to have Ivy to myself, I love Fi as if she were my own sister. Besides, we need to make this place more comfortable.

"Tell her she has carte blanche. As long as she does it quickly, I don't care how much it costs."

"I said the same thing."

"Which is why we're perfect together."

Tenderly, I kiss her. She's cooled off enough that I can finally cover us. Contentment and homecoming steal over me, better than any blanket. It's her, all her: my best friend, my greatest love.

As we're drifting off, curled up together, I whisper, "Hey, Ivy?"

"Mmm?"

"Why can't a nose be twelve inches long?"

I feel her smile against my neck. "Why?"

"Because then it would be a foot."

She laughs, a whisper of sound. And I think she's fallen asleep. But then her voice drifts out. "Hey, Cupcake. You know there is a fine line between a numerator and a denominator..."

My entire soul lights up. "Oh, yeah?" I admit I'm a little giddy with lust as I wait for the punch line.

"But only a fraction would understand."

God, this girl. It will always be This Girl.

The next day, I send her a text.

GrayG: Roses are red, violets are blue, your husband, Gray, is completely in love with you.

PLAYLIST FOR THE FRIEND ZONE

A selection of songs that appear in and inspired Kristen Callihan while writing this book.

"American Girl," Tom Petty
"SexyBack," Justin Timberlake
"Material Girl," Madonna
"Raspberry Beret," Prince
"Right Where It Belongs," Nine Inch Nails
"Radioactive," Imagine Dragons
"Why Can't I Be You?" The Cure

Not named in the book, but I listened to a lot of late '80s and '90s music because it fit the vibe of *The Friend Zone*'s bouncing, goofy happiness mixed with confused growing pains. ☺

"Steady, As She Goes," The Raconteurs
"Bitter Sweet Symphony," The Verve

Pills 'n' Thrills and Bellyaches (full album), Happy Mondays
"Fools Gold," The Stone Roses

Theme song for the book:

"Love Rears Its Ugly Head," Living Colour—because it absolutely fits Gray's confused anguish when he finally falls in love.